About th

Scarlet Wilson wrote he
has never stopped. Her fa
Shirley and the Magic P
all with names beginning
reader, Scarlet started with every Enid Blyton
moved on to the *Chalet School* series and many years
later found Mills & Boon. She trained and worked
as a nurse and health visitor, and currently works in
public health. For her, finding Mills & Boon Medical
Romances was a match made in heaven. She is
delighted to find herself among the authors she has
read for many years. Scarlet lives on the West Coast of
Scotland with her fiancé and their two sons.

A three-time Golden Heart® finalist, **Tina Beckett**
is the product of a Navy upbringing. Fortunately she
found someone who enjoys travelling just as much as
she does and married him! Having lived in Brazil for
many years, Tina is fluent in Portuguese and loves
to use that beautiful country as a backdrop for many
of her stories. When not writing or visiting far-flung
places Tina enjoys riding horses, hiking with her
family and hanging out on Facebook and Twitter.

Having tried a variety of careers in retail, marketing
and nursing **Louisa George** is thrilled that her dream
job of writing for Mills and Boon means she gets to
go to work in her pyjamas. Louisa lives in Auckland,
New Zealand, with her husband, two sons and two
male cats. When not writing or reading Louisa loves
to spend time with her family, enjoys travelling, and
adores eating great food.

Midwives' Christmas Miracles

SCARLET WILSON

TINA BECKETT

LOUISA GEORGE

MILLS & BOON

First Published in Great Britain 2018
By Mills & Boon, an imprint of HarperCollins *Publishers*
1 London Bridge Street, London, SE1 9GF

MIDWIVES CHRISTMAS MIRACLES© 2018 Harlequin Books S.A.

A Touch of Christmas Magic © Harlequin Books S.A 2015
Playboy Doc's Mistletoe Kiss © Harlequin Books S.A 2015
Her Doctor's Christmas Proposal © Harlequin Books S.A. 2015

Special thanks and acknowledgement are given to Scarlet Wilson, Tina Beckett and Louisa George for their contribution to the Midwives On-Call at Christmas series

ISBN: 978-0-263-26851-5

9-1118

MIX
Paper from
responsible sources
FSC™ C007454
www.fsc.org

This book is produced from independently certified FSC™ paper to ensure responsible forest management.

For more information visit: www.harpercollins.co.uk/green

Printed and bound in Spain
by CPI, Barcelona

A TOUCH OF CHRISTMAS MAGIC

SCARLET WILSON

This book is dedicated to my fabulous fellow authors Louisa George, Tina Beckett and Robin Gianna. It's been a pleasure working with you ladies!

CHAPTER ONE

THE LITTLE FACE stared back out of the window as Freya gave her a nervous wave from the new school. Bonnie sucked in a breath and kept the smile plastered to her face, waving back as merrily as she could. *Please be okay.*

Her thick winter coat was stifling her already. Even at this time of year, Cambridge was unexpectedly warmer than Scotland. She could feel an uncomfortable trickle of sweat run down her spine. The teacher came to the window and, glancing at Bonnie, ushered Freya away. Freya's red curls had already started to escape from the carefully styled pleat. By the time she came home later her hair would be back to its usual fluffy head style. She could almost hear the teacher's thoughts in her head: *over-anxious parent.*

She wasn't. Not really. But travelling down from Scotland yesterday with their worldly goods stuffed into four suitcases was hardly ideal. The motel they'd ended up staying in was even less pleasant. The smell of damp and mildew in the room had set off alarm bells that it might cause a flare-up of Freya's asthma. With Christmas not too far away, she desperately needed to sort out somewhere more suitable to stay. And the combination of everything, plus dropping Freya at a brand-new school this morning, had left her feeling rattled.

The director of midwifery at Cambridge Royal Maternity Unit had been quite insistent on her start date. No compromise. The ward sister had just taken early maternity leave due to some unexpected problems. They needed an experienced member of staff as soon as possible. And she hadn't felt in a position to argue—despite the fact they'd had nowhere to stay. The job in Cambridge was her way out of Scotland. And, boy, did she need out.

Working at such a prestigious hospital was appealing. Everyone knew about the two-hundred-year-old hospital and one night, midway between tears and frustration, she'd applied. When they'd emailed back the next day to arrange a telephone interview she'd been surprised. And when they'd told her the next day she had the job she'd been stunned. Things had moved at a rapid pace ever since. References, occupational health forms and a formal offer telling her they wanted her to start straight away.

Thankfully, she'd had a sympathetic community manager in Scotland who knew about her circumstances and had done a little jigging to allow her to take annual leave and special leave to let her only work two weeks' notice. The last two weeks had passed in a complete blur.

This morning had been hard. There had been tears and sniffles from Freya, a normally placid child. Bonnie held her breath. The school window remained empty; it was clear the teacher had successfully distracted her.

With a sigh of relief she glanced at her watch. Yikes. First day and she was going to be late. She hurried back to the bus stop. Getting a car was next on the 'to do' list. She phoned and left a message on the director of midwifery's answerphone—hardly a good start for her first day on the job. But it couldn't be helped. The woman knew she wasn't arriving until last night and that her daughter was starting a new school today. She still had to hand some paperwork into HR and pick up her uniforms before she could start on the labour ward.

For once, she was in luck. The bus appeared almost immediately. Now it was daylight and she could actually see a bit of the beautiful city she'd decided to live in on almost a whim.

Well, a whim that was a result of catching her husband in bed with her best friend. She should still feel angry and hurt. But all she really felt was relief. As soon as the ink was dry on the divorce papers she'd started job hunting. She needed a fresh start and there was something so exciting about coming to a historic city like Cambridge. She watched as the Victorian-style shops and Grade II listed buildings whizzed past and allowed herself to smile a little. Cambridge was truly an atmospheric city; seeing it in daylight made her all the more excited to get a chance to see round about.

The hospital came into a view. A large, imposing building based in the heart of the bustling city. A little tremor of anticipation went down her spine. This was it. This was where she worked. As the bus drew to a halt, climbing down, she took a final glance around the city of Cambridge. *Her city.* Full of possibilities.

This was now home.

Jacob Layton was more than mildly irritated. He was mad—but, these days, that was nothing unusual for him.

He hated disorganisation. Hated chaos. He prided himself on the fact that his unit ran like clockwork. Any midwife or medic not up to the job at this hospital was quickly rooted out and dealt with.

It might sound harsh. But in Cambridge Royal Maternity Unit the lives of women and babies were on the line every day. He was a firm believer that all expectant mothers deserved the best possible care and it was his job to ensure they got it.

This morning, he stood at the nurses' station with his hands on his hips as his temper bubbled just beneath the surface. There was no sign of any member of staff. None of the whiteboards were up to date—he didn't even know which patient was in which room. Case notes were spread all over the desk with a whole variety of scribbled multicoloured sticky notes littering the normally immaculate desk.

'Where is everyone?' he yelled.

The frightened faces of a midwife and junior doctor appeared simultaneously from separate rooms. The midwife hurried towards him, her eyes fixed on her shoes. The junior doctor walked slowly, obviously hoping the midwife would get the brunt of Jacob's rage this morning. He should be so lucky.

The midwife handed over a set of notes with slightly shaking hands. 'I think this is the set of notes you wanted. I was just doing Mrs Clark's observations. Everything seems fine.'

He snatched them from her hands and reviewed them quickly. Relief. Things were looking better for Mrs Clark. He raised his head, keeping his voice in check. 'Good. Tell Mrs Clark I'll be in to see her shortly.'

The midwife disappeared in a flash. The junior doctor's legs practically did a U-turn in the corridor. He didn't want to be left with Jacob.

'Dr Jenkins.'

The young guy's legs froze midstride. Jacob flung case notes onto the desk one after another. 'Ms Bates needs her bloods done, Mrs Kelly needs her bloods repeated, where is the cardiac consult for Lucy Evans—she's been here more than six hours—and how long ago did I ask you to arrange another ultrasound for Ms Shaw? Get it done, now!' His voice rose as the anger he was trying to contain started to erupt. He hated incompetence. These patients were in the best maternity unit for miles. They should be receiving top-quality care.

The doctor's face paled and he gathered up the notes in his arms. 'Right away, Dr Layton,' he said, practically scampering down the corridor to the nearest office.

He sighed. This place—normally his pride and joy—was becoming a disaster zone.

Ever since he'd diagnosed the ward manager with pre-eclampsia and sent her home with the instructions not to come back until she had her baby, this place had gone to pot. There were four other senior midwives. All of them excellent at clinical care—and none with an organisational bone in their body.

The director of midwifery had promised him that their new employee would be able to help with all this. But he'd just read her CV, and was struggling to see why a Scottish community midwife would be able to do anything to help a busy city labour ward.

But the thing that was really making him mad was the fact that she wasn't here. He glanced at his watch again. First day on a new job—after nine-thirty—and the new start wasn't here.

The doors at the bottom of the corridor swung open right on cue. Bonnie Reid. It had to be. Jacob knew everyone who worked here and he didn't recognise her at all. Dressed in the blue scrubs that the labour ward midwives wore and bright pink trainers, she had her red hair coiled up on top of her head in a strange kind of knot. How on earth did she do that? That, coupled with the curves not hidden by the shapeless scrubs, reminded him of a poster he'd had on his wall as a teenager. He felt a smile form on his lips.

Was she nervous? Her hands fidgeted with her security pass and she seemed to make a conscious effort to slow her steps. What irritated him most of all was the fact she didn't seem to notice him standing, waiting for her. Instead, she stopped at every room on the way along the corridor, nodding and introducing herself to the members of staff. She even disappeared for a second to obviously help with a patient.

Then, she appeared with a load of laundry, which she put into the laundry bags, reorganised two of the hand scrubs outside the doors and tidied the top of the cardiac-arrest trolley on her way past.

He waited until she'd almost reached him. 'Bonnie Reid?' His voice dripped with sarcasm. 'Nice of you to finally join us.'

Something flickered across her face. Her skin was pale under the bright hospital lights and he could see a few tiny freckles under her make-up. She'd looked good from a distance. Up close, she was much more interesting.

She had real knockout eyes. Dark, dark blue. Not the pale blue normally associated with a redhead. But then her hair wasn't the average red either. It was a dark deep auburn. The kind of colour normally associated with Hollywood actresses who probably had a whole team of people to get it that colour. Almost instantly he knew that

Bonnie Reid's was entirely natural. She gave him the slightest glance from those eyes. And for the first time, in a long time, he took a deep breath.

It had been a long time since a woman had ignited something in his system. Maybe it was her dark blue eyes against her pale skin? Or the look of disdain she gave him as she walked past into the treatment room and started washing her hands.

Had he just imagined it? No. Something in her eyes told him this was a woman who had lived—had experienced life. She must be in her early thirties. As she finished washing her hands he glanced at her finger—no ring. It had been a long time since he'd done that too.

She turned to face him. 'Bonnie Reid, new midwife at Cambridge Royal Maternity Unit.' Her eyebrows rose. 'And you are?'

It was her tone. It rankled him right away. He'd never been a person to pull rank. 'Jacob Layton, Head Obstetrician, CRMU.'

It was almost as if a box of chocolates or tray of cakes had appeared out of thin air at the nurses' station. Just about every door in the corridor opened and a whole host of previously hidden staff appeared. Did they avoid him every morning?

Bonnie didn't appear to notice. She blinked and pointed towards his scrubs. 'You should wear an ID badge, Dr Layton. You could be absolutely anyone. I expect all staff members I work with to be clearly identified.'

She was just here. His skin prickled. Patience was not his friend. In any other set of circumstances he might have said their new staff member had an attitude problem. But he got the distinct impression that Bonnie Reid was only reacting to his initial barb.

He didn't know whether to give her a dressing-down or to smile. 'It's Jacob,' he said quietly. 'Everyone calls me Jacob.' Not true. Only the few people not terrified by him called him Jacob. For a second their gazes meshed. It startled him, sending a little jolt around his system.

More than a year. That was how long it had been since he'd felt a spark with someone.

She gave the slightest nod of her head and extended her hand towards his. 'Bonnie. Everyone calls me Bonnie.'

As soon as he connected with her skin he knew he'd made a mistake. The warm feeling of her palm against his. Touch. That was what he'd missed most of all in the last year. The warmness of someone's touch. He pulled his hand back sharply as her eyes widened at his reaction.

'You're late.' It came out much snappier than he intended. Her hand was still in mid-air, suspended from their shake. She drew it back slowly and her gaze narrowed as she took a deep breath and her shoulders went back.

She met his gaze full on. 'Yes, I'm late.' It was clear she had no intention of giving anything else away. He couldn't believe how much one meeting with one woman could irk him.

She was new. She was working in his unit. And, after talks with the director of midwifery, this was the person he was supposed to offer a promoted post to. *If* he deemed her suitable. Tardiness was not an option.

He felt his normal persona resume. The one that had held most of the staff at arm's length for the last year. 'Staff and patients rely on us. Lateness is not acceptable at CRMU. I expected you here at nine a.m.'

It was the first time she looked a little worried. 'I had to take my daughter to school. We arrived late last night from Scotland. She was upset. I had to make sure she was okay.' She glanced over her shoulder as if she expected someone else to be there. 'I left a message for the director of midwifery—she knew my circumstances.'

Those words annoyed him. He'd seen her CV, but the director hadn't told him anything about their new employee's 'circumstances'. He hated it when staff used excuses for not being able to do a shift, or being late for work.

'We all have circumstances. We all still have to be at work for nine. Work is our priority. Patients are our priority.'

Her face flamed and her eyes sparked. 'Patients are always my priority and I've already dealt with two on my way along the ward. Exactly how many have you dealt with while you've been standing there waiting for me to arrive? Hardly a good use of consultant time.'

She was questioning him. She was challenging him and she'd only been here five minutes. He'd love to sack her on the spot. But they desperately needed the staff right now, and if she was as competent as she was mouthy he'd be in serious trouble with the director of midwives. She was almost questioning his competence. Let them see how she was when someone questioned hers.

'I saw from your CV that you were a community midwife in Scotland. It's a bit of a leap coming to work in an inner city labour ward. Don't you think that might stretch your current capabilities? Are you going to have to refresh your skills?'

It was a reasonable question. At least he felt it was. He still wasn't entirely sure why the director thought a community midwife was a suitable replacement for their ward sister.

It took about a millisecond to realise he'd said exactly the wrong thing.

Bonnie glared at him and put her hands on her hips. 'Please do not question my capabilities or qualifications. In the last year, I've dealt with a shoulder dystocia, umbilical cord prolapse, two women who failed to progress, a footling breech, a cervical lip and an intrapartum haemorrhage. Is that enough for you?' She turned to walk away, then obviously decided she wasn't finished. 'And just so we're clear—' she held out her hands '—I didn't have a fancy unit, staffed with lots of other people to help me. These were home deliveries. I was on my own, with no assistance. Still think I need to *refresh my skills*?'

Her pretty brow was marred by a frown and he could practically feel the heat sparking from her eyes. It was an impressive list—even for a midwife based in a busy labour ward. For a community midwife, some of those situations must have been terrifying. He had a whole new respect for his new midwife.

But Bonnie wasn't finished. It was obvious he'd lit a fire within her and probably touched a nerve. Maybe she was nervous about starting work in a new hospital? Worse, he'd just called her qualifications into question in front of the rest of the staff. He hadn't even considered that might not be entirely appropriate—especially when these could be the people she would be in charge of. Mentally, he was kicking himself.

'My experience with women isn't just in the labour suite, *Dr* Layton.' Oh, boy, she was mad. It was clear, if he was patronising her, they weren't on first-name terms. 'I've spent the last ten years looking after women from the moment they're pregnant until long after the baby is delivered. I've picked up on lots of factors that affect their pregnancy, both clinical and social. And as a community midwife I've dealt with lots of post-delivery problems for both mother and child. Looking after patients at home is a whole lot different from looking after them in a clinical setting. Isolation, post-op complications, neonatal problems, postpartum psychosis, depression, domestic abuse...' She fixed him with her gaze. 'The list goes on and on.'

He didn't want to smile. He should be annoyed. This woman was practically putting him in his place. But he couldn't help but feel he might have deserved it.

He wondered how on earth she'd ended up here. She'd already mentioned a daughter. And she clearly wasn't wearing a wedding ring. It was absolutely none of his business. But Jacob Layton's curiosity was definitely sparked. He liked this feisty midwife.

He spoke steadily. 'That certainly seems like enough experience. So what made you come down to Cambridge? It's a long way from Scotland.'

She didn't even stop to think. Her eyes were still flashing. Bonnie Reid was on a roll. 'That's the thing about finding your husband in bed with your best friend—it makes you want to get as far away as possible.'

Silence.

You could have heard a proverbial pin drop. Bonnie felt the colour rush to her cheeks and she lifted her hand to her mouth. Oh, no. Why on earth would she say something like that out loud?

It was that darn man. Jacob Layton. It wasn't bad enough that the handsomest man on the planet had watched her walking down the corridor as if he were undressing her with his eyes. Then he'd started talking to her and everything he'd said had put her back up. Now she'd lost her rag with him. Hardly the best start in a new job.

But Bonnie Reid didn't take any prisoners. In this life, she meant to start the way she was going to continue. The part of her life where she put up with bad behaviour, indifference and rudeness was over.

Maybe it was the fact he was so good-looking that was unnerving her. If she got any closer she was sure she'd see gold flecks in those intense green eyes. Or maybe it was the fact that no man had even flickered on her radar since she'd walked away from her ex. Certainly not a brown-haired, green-eyed Hollywood-style hunk.

Her insides were cringing. She couldn't believe what she'd just said. And it was clear from the faces around her that no one else could either.

But what made it all the more excruciating was the fact that the edges of Jacob Layton's mouth seemed to be turning upwards.

He was laughing at her.

'Please come with me,' he said sharply and walked over, ushering her towards an office door with Head Obstetrician emblazoned across it, and away from the gaping mouths.

He closed the door firmly behind them and walked around his desk. 'Take a seat.' His voice was firm and she felt a wave of panic sweep over her.

She hadn't even officially started—was she about to be fired? 'I'm sorry. I've no idea where that came from.'

Her stomach did a little flip-flop. It didn't matter. It really didn't matter but she'd just made a fool of herself in front of the resident hunk and her new boss. She'd just told him that her husband had cheated on her. It was hardly a placard that she wanted to wave above her head. She might as well be holding a sign saying 'I'm plain and boring in bed'.

The humiliation burned her cheeks. Right now she wanted to crawl into a hole.

He fixed on her with those green eyes and she felt her skin prickle under her thin scrubs. At times like this she longed for her thicker white tunic and navy trousers. But scrubs were the order of the day in most labour wards.

He pointed to the chair again. 'Sit down.'

Her feet were shuffling nervously on the carpet and she couldn't stop wringing her hands together. Sitting down seemed quite claustrophobic. Particularly with Jacob sitting at the other side of the desk and the door closed behind them.

'Don't ever speak to me like that again in front of my colleagues.' The words were out before she could stop them. And she wasn't finished. 'It was unprofessional. If you want to question my clinical capabilities take it up with me privately, or take it up with the director of midwives who employed me.' She waved her hand. 'On second thoughts, why don't you actually wait until you've worked with me, *before* you question my clinical capabilities?' She stuck her hands on her hips. 'And maybe I'll wait until then to question yours.'

Too much. It was too much. Even she knew that. The shocked expression on his face almost made her want to open the door and run back down the corridor.

Definitely not her best start.

She took a deep breath and sat down. 'Look—' she started but Jacob lifted his hand.

She froze mid-sentence. This was the way she always got when she was nervous. Her mouth started running away with her, a prime example being what had happened outside.

Jacob ran his hand through his hair. It struck her as an odd act. Usually a sign of someone being tired or frustrated. Jacob Layton didn't strike her as any of those things.

He lifted his eyes to meet hers. 'You're right. I shouldn't have questioned your capabilities. But let's start with the basics. Bonnie, I would have preferred it if you could have been here at nine this morning. It would have made our meeting a little easier. Is timing going to be an issue for you?'

She shook her head quickly, wondering if she should be offended by the question. 'No. Not at all. This morning was a one-off.'

He gave the tiniest nod. 'I appreciate you just arrived last night, and that you were asked to start at short notice.' His brow furrowed a little. 'Do you have adequate arrangements in place for your daughter?'

She straightened her shoulders. He was putting her on edge again. Dr Handsome just seemed to rub her up the wrong way. 'I hope so. I have a friend who is a registered childminder. She's agreed to take Freya in the mornings and after school.'

'What about weekends and night shifts?'

Bonnie felt herself pull back a little. 'I was told there was no requirement for night shifts—that you had permanent night shift staff here?' The statement had turned into a question. She had the mildest feeling of panic.

A wave of recognition flickered across his face. 'What about shift work? Will that cause you a problem?

Now he was really getting her back up. She couldn't fathom this guy out at all. One minute he was fiercely professional, the next he looked amused by her. As for the sparks that had shot up her arm when they'd touched…

She'd already snapped at this guy once. She didn't want to do it again. It wasn't his fault she was tired. It wasn't his fault that the journey from Scotland had taken much more out of her and Freya than she'd really expected. It wasn't his fault Freya had been upset this morning, or that the motel room was totally inappropriate for them both. None of this was his fault.

She wanted to respect her boss and get on well with him. He was a bit grumpy, but she'd met worse, and she was sure she could knock it out of him. She'd already embarrassed herself once in front of her boss. It was time for a new tack.

She met his gaze straight on. 'Jacob, I don't think you're actually allowed to ask me questions like that.'

'Aren't I?' He sat back quickly and frowned.

She held up her hands. 'Would you ask a guy these questions?' She was so aware it was all about the tone here. It was a serious subject, but she was quite sure he wasn't even aware of what he was doing. 'What if I asked you, right now, about childcare arrangements for any kids you might have? Would that seem appropriate to you?'

The recognition dawned quickly on his face. 'Well… no.' He put his head in his hands for a second and shook it. When he pulled his head back up he had a sorry smile on his face and shrugged his shoulders. 'Sorry.'

She gave a little nod of her head. 'No problem.'

She heard him suck in a breath and his shoulders relaxed a little. 'I do have a good reason for asking you.'

She raised her eyebrows. 'You do?'

He nodded slowly. 'I do.' He was being serious now.

'Valerie Glencross, the director of midwifery, suggested we should offer you a promoted post.'

Bonnie sat bolt upright in her chair. It was the last thing she'd expected to hear. 'She did?'

His gaze connected with hers. 'She did.' For a second it felt as if time had frozen. She was looking into the brightest pair of green eyes she'd ever seen. She'd been right. He had little gold flecks in his irises. It made them sparkle. It was making her hold her breath as she realised exactly what kind of an effect they were having on her.

'She did,' he reiterated. 'It seems your CV had already impressed her. I'm guessing that your telephone interview with her went well. She wanted me to meet you and ask if you'd consider being Ward Sister on a temporary basis.'

'Me?' Bonnie was more than a little surprised. 'But you must have senior staff working here already. Wouldn't it make more sense to have someone take charge who is familiar with the set-up?'

He gave a little laugh. 'You would think so. Our senior staff are excellent. But none of them have the talent of organisation. Valerie said that before you were a community midwife you were a ward sister. I think she thought it would be good to have a new broom, so to speak. Someone who didn't have any preconceived ideas about CRMU and could bring some fresh ideas about how things should run.' He gave a little sigh. 'Our ward sister Abby has been gone less than two weeks and it's chaos out there. She left sooner than expected and we obviously didn't appreciate just how much she kept on top of things.' He gave his head a little shake. 'I'm feeling bad. I'm wondering if the stress of the ward was a factor in her pre-eclampsia.'

'Is she okay?' It was the first thing that sprang to mind.

He gave a quick nod and Bonnie shot him a smile. 'In that case, you're not making it sound like my dream job. Shouldn't you be giving me the hard sell? And after our first meeting—do you really want to offer it to me at all?' Jacob Layton wasn't good at this. He was being too honest.

He groaned again and sat straighter, giving her a grin that sent tingles to her toes. 'Let me start again. Bonnie Reid—from your extensive experience on your CV we've decided you would be a great addition to our team. You'll know the reputation of Cambridge Royal Maternity Unit. We employ the best obstetricians and midwives and are known as a centre of medical excellence. We have links with Cambridge University and are pioneers in the development and research of many groundbreaking medical techniques. We have a great bunch of staff working in the labour delivery suite. We just need someone who can bring some new organisational skills to the ward.' He leaned across the table towards her. 'How's that for the hard sell?'

She couldn't pull her eyes away from his. He was closer to her than ever before. She could see every strand of his dark brown hair. See the tiny lines around his eyes. And exactly just how straight and white his teeth were.

He nodded towards her. 'And yes, I do want to offer it to you. You're the first person to answer back in about five years.'

Boy, he was handsome. But there was something else. Something so much more than just good looks. Beneath the flecks of gold in his eyes she could see another part of Jacob Layton. There was so much more there than a handsome but grumpy obstetrician. He seemed the single-minded, career-driven type. But what lay beneath the driven exterior?

She returned his smile. 'That was much better.'

He relaxed back in his chair and she was almost sorry she'd replied. 'Thank goodness.' He was so much nicer like this. Why did he act so grumpy around the staff?

She took a deep breath. 'I want this to work. I want this to work for me and for Freya—my little girl. This is a fresh start. I want to leave everything else behind us.' She rolled her eyes and gave her head a little shake. 'And I definitely want to leave men behind. I just want to focus on my new job and getting me and my daughter settled.'

Jacob gave a little nod of acknowledgement as he tapped his fingers on the desk. 'The reason I asked about your childcare arrangements—if you're working as ward sister we'd generally expect you to work nine to five. You'd only occasionally be expected to work late shifts if there were staffing issues, and join part of the hospital on-call rota to do weekends.'

Bonnie frowned. 'How does that work?'

'All of our ward sisters take turns in covering weekends. You're not actually there as a member of the team that weekend. You're covering the management for the whole hospital. Sorting out staffing problems, dealing with any difficult cases or issues across the whole of maternity. It usually works out once every nine weeks.'

Bonnie nodded. 'That's understandable. This would make things much easier with my childcare arrangements. Freya will be much happier if I'm working more or less regular hours. I'll get to put her to bed most nights. And, as I've mentioned, Lynn will happily take Freya every weekday before and after school, and for the occasional late night or weekend.' She gave a visible sigh of relief. 'I'm happy to do the job—in fact, I'm really excited to be asked.'

He seemed relieved. 'So you'll take the job?' His voice went up a little, as if he was still a bit anxious she might turn down this fabulous opportunity.

She stood up and held out her hand towards him. 'Of course I will. I'm a little nervous but am sure in a few days it will feel like I've been here for weeks. That's always the way of it, isn't it?'

He smiled again; this time the relief was definitely reaching right up into his eyes. His hand grasped hers. There it was again.

She hadn't been mistaken first time around. Coming into contact with Jacob Layton's hand was doing strange things to her skin receptors—currently it was the dance of a thousand butterflies. Just as well she'd made it clear she was a man-free zone.

'Perfect. I'll let Valerie know you've accepted. She'll arrange for a new contract.' He held open the door for her. 'Now, let's go and tell the staff.'

Her stomach did another little flip-flop as she walked through, but she couldn't work out if that was the thought of telling her new peers about her role, or from the burn coming from Jacob's hand at the small of her back.

One thing was for sure—CRMU was going to be interesting.

CHAPTER TWO

JACOB HADN'T BEEN WRONG. The labour suite was in chaos.
And it was all basics.

Bonnie grabbed a ward clerk and made some immediate requests about sorting out case notes, filing things
appropriately and keeping the boards up to date. Then
she asked for new lists of contact numbers. The one she
found on the wall was obviously out of date and, with
doctors changing every six months, she didn't want any
problems with pagers in case of emergency.

She spent the next two hours working with various
members of staff and patients. After a few hours she was
confident in the clinical capabilities of the staff that were
on duty. They all wanted to do their jobs and work with
patients. They just didn't want to bother with 'ward' stuff.
Ordering, stocking, rotas, outpatient appointments, phar-
macy prescriptions. It quickly became apparent that her
predecessor had dealt with all these things and her quick
departure meant there had been no handover.

Bonnie gave a sigh. She'd like to spend all day working with patients too—but that wasn't the way a ward
was run. She started making a 'to do' list that she'd have
to work her way through.

The other issue was the phones. They rang constantly—

often with no one answering. First thing tomorrow she was going to ask about a regular ward clerk for the unit. Just as she finished making a few notes about the off-duty rota the phone rang again.

'CRMU, Bonnie Reid, can I help you?'

'Ambulance Control. We need a team on-site at a crash on one of the motorway slip roads. We have a trapped, unconscious pregnant woman. She's reported to be thirty-four weeks. Ambulance is on its way to pick you up.'

Bonnie put down the phone. First day on the job. You had to be joking. She automatically dialled the page for the on-call obstetrician. Most big maternity units had supplies for emergencies like these. It was just a pity she hadn't had a chance to find out where they were.

A few seconds later Jacob appeared from his office just as Bonnie was relaying the message to one of the senior midwives. He was holding his page. 'What have we got?'

She handed over the piece of paper she'd scribbled on. Jacob gestured towards her. 'Follow me. Equipment is in here. Grab a jacket and a bag.' He turned to face her. 'You are coming, aren't you?'

She hesitated for only the briefest of seconds. 'If you want me to.'

No. I'm terrified. This sounds like an initiation of fire. It's my first day, I've just agreed to act as temporary sister in one of the most prestigious maternity units in the country and now you want me to be part of the emergency response team.

He acted as if he did this every day, grabbing a jacket with 'Doctor' emblazoned across the back and handing her the one with 'Midwife'. He shot her a smile as he helped her lift the emergency pack onto her shoulders.

'Let's go. Leave instructions with Miriam, the senior midwife. She'll deal with the calls until we get back.' He walked away, his long strides crossing the corridor quickly, only stopping to wheel a portable incubator to the door.

She could feel the wave of panic lapping around her ankles. There was no way she could let it go any further. She started repeating in her head the list of emergencies that she'd dealt with on her own as a community midwife. She could do this. She could.

Miriam gave her a sympathetic nod as she handed over a few instructions. 'I'm so glad it's you and not me,' she murmured under her breath.

'What do you mean?'

Miriam rolled her eyes. 'If you think Dan Daring is harsh on the ward, you should see him at a roadside emergency. The patients love him. The rest of the staff need counselling by the time he's done.'

'Let's go, Bonnie!' The shout made her jump and she hurried to the exit and into the back of the waiting ambulance. As soon as the doors closed and the sirens switched on they were on their way.

Sitting in the back of the ambulance was more than a little bumpy. She only just managed to avoid practically bouncing onto Jacob's lap. But he barely noticed. He was holding on to the strap in the back with his eyes fixed on the road ahead.

'Any more news?'

One of the paramedics turned around. 'All bad. We've just had a report that they think her membranes might have ruptured. She's still unconscious and trapped. They're panicking. They think she's gone into labour.' He glanced at the clock. 'We'll be there in five minutes.'

Bonnie sucked in a breath. A thousand different potential diagnoses were flying through her head. From Jacob's serious expression he was thinking the same.

When they screeched to a halt Jacob didn't wait, he just flung open the doors, grabbed the bag and started running.

The first thing that struck her was the smell. Fire, burning metal, petrol and a whole lot more. There were four ambulances already on-site. A few casualties were sitting on the edge of the road. Two children with blood on their faces, a man cradling his arm and an older woman who looked completely shell-shocked. Police had cordoned off part of the motorway but the speed and noise of the cars still passing by was unnerving. Rubbernecking. That was what most of the passing cars were doing. Any minute now there would be another accident on the other side of the motorway. She shuddered and jumped out of the back of the ambulance, trying to spot Jacob's bright green jacket in amongst the melee of emergency people.

'Over here.' A policeman gestured her towards an upended car. She stepped around the pieces of car debris that littered the road. Somewhere, she could hear someone crying. The wails cutting through the rest of the sounds. It was horrible. It was unnerving.

She landed on her knees next to the upturned car. The only thing she could currently see of Jacob was the soles of his feet. His whole body was inside the car, his feet sticking out through the broken passenger-side window. 'Do you need anything?' she shouted through the gap.

She adjusted her position to get a better view. Inside the car a pregnant woman was trapped upside down, held precariously in position by her seat belt. It was obvious she was still unconscious, an oxygen mask to her face and a collar around her neck. Jacob was pushing back her coat and gently easing her stretched top over her abdomen. Bonnie didn't wait for instructions. She fished out a stethoscope and a foetal monitor and stuck her hand through a gap in the broken window where Jacob could grab them.

Even from here she could see the damp patch between the woman's trousers. It could be two things. It could be urine or it could be amniotic fluid. She was just praying it wasn't blood. She didn't even want to consider that— not under these conditions.

After a few minutes of wrestling around Jacob finally spoke. 'I've got a heartbeat—albeit a little quick. But I've just felt her contracting and there's absolutely no way to do any kind of examination.'

He shook his head as Bonnie tried to hand him the nitrazine strips. The best they could do in this situation was rub one against her damp clothes. 'There's no point checking. I'm fairly sure her membranes have ruptured. We need to get her out of here now. She's at risk of uterine or placental rupture. There's no way I'm delivering this baby upside down.'

Bonnie stood up and shouted over to the fire and rescue colleagues. 'We need to get this woman out. She's about to deliver. Can we have some assistance?'

One of them ran over. 'Sorry, got tied up trying to lift a car off someone's chest.'

Bonnie gulped. It was chaos all around them and even though the road seemed full of emergency staff, there probably still wasn't enough.

The fire-and-rescue guy pointed at the collar. 'She was conscious for only a few seconds after we arrived and had no feeling in her legs. That's why the collar's in place. The trauma doc said not to move her. He was waiting for you to arrive.'

She nodded. 'Well, tell the trauma doc we're here and she's in labour. We need assistance to move her as safely as possible now. Can you get us a backboard?'

She pushed her way around the other side of the car. The driver's door was wedged up against a van that was on its side. It was a struggle to push her arms through and try and wind a blood-pressure cuff around the lady's arm. 'Do we have a name?' she shouted to Jacob.

'Holly Burns.'

She pressed the button on the machine. Now she'd squeezed around the other side she could see him a little easier. There were deep furrows along his brow; he was clearly worried about this patient and so was she.

'BP's low,' she said quickly as the result displayed.

A number of the fire-and-rescue crew had collected around them, all talking in low voices. 'Doc, we're going to have to move the car. We need to cut the patient free and we can't do it while the van's in place. You'll need to come out.'

Jacob didn't hesitate. 'I'm going nowhere. This mother and her baby need monitoring every second. Move the car with me in it.'

One of them stepped forwards as Bonnie wriggled out from the other side. She could see clearly why they would need to separate the vehicles. There was no way they could get Holly out on a backboard otherwise. If she had spinal damage they had to do everything possible to try to minimise the movement.

She shook her head and touched the fire-and-rescue chief's arm. 'Don't waste your time arguing with him.

He won't change his mind and it'll just get ugly. This woman could deliver very soon and her position makes it dangerous for her life and her baby's.'

She was quite sure this went against every health and safety check imaginable. But she'd seen fire and rescue, paramedic and police services do similar things before. They all made the patient their priority.

She stood back as equipment was positioned and blankets shoved inside the car as Jacob was told to brace himself and his patient.

The car and van were wedged tightly together. The sound of metal ripping apart made her wince. Nothing about this was delicate. Both the car and van were juddering, wheels spinning in the air. It seemed to take for ever before they were finally yanked apart and the fire-and-rescue crew moved in with their cutting equipment.

It only took seconds for them to cut the side from the car. One of the other trauma doctors appeared with the backboard and had a quick confab with Jacob inside about the best way to cut Holly free from her seat belt and support her spine. It was a delicate operation. Twelve pairs of hands ended up all around her, ready to ease her gently onto the spinal board as the seat belt was cut. 'Hold it,' said Jacob abruptly. 'She's having another contraction. We'll have to wait a few seconds for it to pass.'

Bonnie swallowed anxiously. Jacob still had the foetal monitor on Holly's swollen abdomen. She could see the contraction clearly. As an experienced midwife she knew Holly wasn't in the early stages of labour, even though she was upside down. A thought flicked through her mind— had Holly already been in labour and on her way to the hospital before the crash? Or was this a trauma-induced labour brought on by the crash? One thing was for sure:

as soon as they got Holly into the ambulance, they'd better be prepared for a delivery.

As the seat belt was cut and Holly slid onto the backboard Bonnie glanced around. 'Does anyone know about next of kin?' she shouted. They were just about to take Holly away from the accident site. There hadn't been a chance to get all the information they needed.

One of the policemen appeared at her elbow. 'We've sent someone to contact her husband. Are you taking her to CRMU?'

Bonnie nodded. 'Can you give me her husband's name and contact details?'

He nodded and scribbled in his notebook, ripping out the page and handing it to her. By the time she turned around Holly was already being loaded onto the ambulance.

Jacob was ruthlessly efficient. The other trauma doctor secured Holly's head and neck, checking her airway before he left. He was part of the general team from Cambridge Royal. 'I have to accompany another patient back with a flail chest. I'll send an orthopod around to the maternity unit.' Jacob gave him the briefest nod as he attached the monitoring equipment. Bonnie barely got inside as the doors slammed shut and the ambulance started off at breakneck speed.

'There's another contraction coming,' she said as she finished attaching the BP cuff and heart monitor. She helped him slide off Holly's underwear and covered her abdomen with a blanket.

Jacob's frown deepened. 'She's crowning. This baby is coming out any minute.'

Bonnie turned towards the portable incubator, struggling to stay on her feet as the ambulance rocked from side to side. There had to be rules about this. She was sure they were supposed to be strapped in. But this baby wasn't waiting for anyone, and what use would two health professionals be at her head or at her side, while a baby slipped out?

She was doing rapid calculations in her head. 'She's thirty-four weeks. That's not too early. Hopefully the baby won't have any breathing difficulties.' She switched on the monitoring equipment in the incubator, ensuring it was warm and the oxygen was ready.

It was difficult to take up position in the swaying ambulance. She could only try and lift Holly's nearest leg, holding it in position to allow Jacob easier access to the presenting head.

She gulped. 'She's missing out on the birth of her baby.' She blinked back tears. 'I hope she doesn't miss out on anything else.'

This was awful. Her first delivery for CRMU with a mother that she didn't even know would wake up. Why was she still unconscious? The trauma doctor had only given her a quick once-over. There hadn't been time for anything else. A Glasgow Coma Scale chart dangled from a clipboard. As each contraction gripped there were facial twinges—as if she were reacting to some element of the labour pain. Reaction to pain was a crucial part of the head injury assessment. And she was breathing spontaneously. Bonnie tried to focus on the positives. She would hate to think this mother would never get to hold her new baby.

As another contraction gripped Holly's stomach the head delivered. Jacob had a quick check around the baby's neck for any sign of a cord. He glanced quickly in Bonnie's direction. 'No cord. Presentation is good.' He gave an audible sigh of relief. 'Thank goodness.'

One minute later the baby slid into his hands and he quickly handed it over to Bonnie.

A little girl. Just like Freya. A fist squeezed around her heart. She'd heard Freya's first cries, felt her first little breaths against her chest. Holly was missing all of this.

She quickly gave the pale little baby a rub, stimulating her first noisy breath, followed by some sharp cries. She gave Jacob a quick smile before wrapping the baby in the warming blanket and doing a quick assessment. 'APGAR six,' she said as she finished.

It was a little low, but would likely come up before the second check in five minutes. It was certainly better than she'd initially hoped for.

She looked up; they were pulling up in front of the emergency entrance at the maternity unit. Three other staff were waiting for them.

Jacob moved into position as the doors opened and helped lift the incubator down. 'Take her to the nursery and get a paed doc to check her over.'

Bonnie gave a brief nod and headed down the corridor with one of the nursery midwives by her side. The handover was quick. The little girl was pinking up now and was letting everyone know she wasn't entirely happy with her entrance to the world.

By the time Bonnie got back to the labour suite, Jacob was consulting with the orthopaedic doctor who'd come over from the main hospital. Holly's notes had appeared at the desk. Thankfully, she had no significant medical history and her pregnancy seemed to have gone well. Bonnie could see from the whiteboard that Miriam, the senior midwife, was with her.

'Has she woken up yet?' She was having trouble getting her head around the fact that Holly had delivered a baby without being conscious. 'In ten years of midwifery I've never seen a woman labour while unconscious.' She blinked back the tears that threatened to spill over. 'Does she have some kind of head injury?'

The orthopaedic doctor glanced at Jacob, then leaned over and touched Bonnie's arm. 'It actually might not be as bad as first thought. She almost certainly has a head injury but her Glasgow Coma Scale responses are improving. I suspect Holly's in spinal shock from injuries sustained in the crash. She wouldn't have felt the intensity of the labour pains even though her body naturally delivered. Jacob and I were just discussing the fact that we think she might actually have been in labour prior to the accident. We've checked the ward call log. She hadn't called into the labour suite and she didn't have any bags in her car. We're wondering if she was going home to collect her things.'

Bonnie nodded. She could only remember a few things about spinal shock from her general nurse training. It was usually temporary but could cause loss of sensation and feeling. It certainly sounded better than some of the things she'd been imagining.

Jacob's voice cut across her thoughts. 'I take it the little girl is okay?' He was glaring and it took her a couple of seconds to realise it wasn't at her—well, not entirely. His eyes were fixed on the orthopaedic doctor's hand, which was still on Bonnie's arm.

Was Jacob this territorial around all his staff?

She gave a nod to the orthopod and walked behind the desk to pick up some paper notes. 'Baby Burns is doing fine. APGAR was eight at five minutes. The paediatrician was checking her as I left.' She waved the notes at Jacob. 'I'm just going to write up some midwifery notes for what happened out there. I'll get the clerk to put Holly and baby Burns into the hospital admission system.'

There was a bang at the bottom of the corridor as the doors were flung open. Both Bonnie and Jacob jumped to their feet. It wasn't entirely unusual for people to enter the labour suite in a rush. This time, though, there was no pregnant woman—just an extremely anxious man.

'My wife, Holly, is she here? They said there was a car accident. What happened? Is she okay? Is the baby okay?'

Jacob and the orthopaedic doctor exchanged glances. Jacob gestured towards his office. 'Mr Burns, why don't you come into my office and I'll let you know what has happened?'

The man's face paled even more and he wobbled. 'Are they dead?'

Jacob quickly reassured him. 'No, no, they're not dead. And you can see them both. Let's just have a chat first.' He turned to the orthopaedic doctor. 'Dr Connelly, will you join us, please?'

But the man's feet were welded to the floor. His eyes widened. 'Both? The baby is here?'

Bonnie walked over, putting her hand on his arm. 'You have a lovely daughter. I'll take you to see her once you've spoken to the doctors.' She helped usher him into the office and, once he was inside, closed the door behind him and left them to it.

'Debbie' The labour suite domestic was working in the kitchen. 'Would you mind taking a pot of tea into Dr Layton's office? I think the man he's talking to will need some.'

Debbie gave a little laugh. 'Tea, for Jacob? You've got to be joking. The guy drinks his coffee with three spoonfuls.' She shook her head. 'You'll soon learn he usually has a cup from the café across the street welded to his hand. Don't worry. I'll sort it out.'

For the rest of the day Bonnie's feet barely touched the ground. She finished her notes, took over from Miriam for a while, then took Mr Burns along to see his new daughter.

Holly had gradually started to come round. Things were complicated. Midwives really shouldn't be dealing with a patient with a head injury. But Holly had a few other complications with the delivery of her placenta. She really wasn't suitable to be on a general ward either. After some careful calls and juggling, Bonnie finally managed to make sure that either a midwife who was also trained as a general nurse was looking after her, or that an extra nurse be called over from the brief intervention unit. After the first twenty-four hours she'd need to be reassessed and other arrangements made.

By the time Jacob came to find her she'd no idea where the time had gone. Opening one store cupboard to have most of its contents fall on her head, followed by finding some out-of-date drugs in one of the cupboards was making her organisational skills go into overload. She wouldn't be able to sleep tonight with the 'to do' lists she currently had stored in her head.

'Just thought I should check how you are.'

She picked her way back through the untidy contents of the store cupboard. 'I'm fine, thanks.' She glanced at her watch. 'Is that the time already? The childminder will wonder where I am.'

She let out a groan. 'Darn it. I haven't found us some-where else to stay.'

'What do you mean? You don't know where you are staying?'

Bonnie sucked in a deep breath. 'That's the thing about agreeing to start at short notice. I haven't man-aged to find somewhere to rent. I haven't even had a chance to view anywhere. The motel I booked is awful. We got in last night and it's damp and I'm pretty sure there are signs of mildew. It's going to play havoc with Freya's asthma. I need to find somewhere else as soon as I can. I had a quick look online last night and most places aren't available for rent until after Christmas. I've obvi-ously come at the wrong time of year.' She kept shaking her head. She sighed and leaned against the doorjamb. 'I need to find somewhere quick. I just assumed that I'd be able to find somewhere without any problem. It is a city, after all.'

Accommodation wasn't something Jacob had even considered for their new start. As a mother she wouldn't have the option of staying in the hospital flats. They were only designed for singles.

He shook his head. 'Cambridge isn't like most cities. We don't have a huge turnover except when the univer-sity year starts. Most students find accommodation and stay in it for four full years.'

She shrugged. 'I'll just need to try a bit harder, I guess. More importantly I'll need to get a car. Relying on public transport is a bit of a nightmare. The sooner I get home to Freya, the better.'

He spoke before he thought. 'I'll give you a lift home.'

She blinked. The shock on her face was apparent. Had he really been that unfriendly to her earlier?

'You don't have to do that.'

'I know. But I will. You've had a bit of a baptism of fire today. I know you want to get home to Freya and the buses will be busy this time of day.' He shrugged. 'It's only five minutes out of my way. We'll go in ten minutes.'

The phone rang further along the ward and Hope Sanders, one of the other midwives, stuck her head out of one of the rooms. 'Jacob? Can you come and take this call?'

He didn't even give her a chance to respond before he walked swiftly along the corridor. He was impressed. Bonnie was doing a good job. He hadn't even given a thought to where she might be staying. If she was worried about that—would she be able to focus on her work?

Hope handed him the phone. 'It's Sean Anderson. He wants to know if you can help in Theatre tomorrow.'

The call only took a few minutes. Jacob liked Sean, the new Australian obstetrician, and he was happy to scrub in on a complicated case. Hope waited for him to finish the call, her arms folded across her chest, leaning on the door.

'What?' he asked as he replaced the receiver.

'How are you?' she asked steadily.

He felt himself flinch. Hope was one of the few people he classed as a friend. She knew exactly what kind of year he'd had. 'I'm fine.'

She nodded slowly. There was no way he'd get away with that kind of answer with Hope. 'When do you get your test results?'

He shifted uncomfortably on his feet. He hated being put on the spot. 'A few weeks.'

'And you're feeling well? Anything I can do?'

He shook his head and picked up some paperwork from his desk. 'I'm fine, Hope. There's no need to fuss.'

She gave him a tight smile. Hope was never bothered by his short answers or occasionally sharp tongue. She just ignored it and asked the questions she wanted to ask.

'Did you reconsider my suggestion?'

'What one?' Hope made lots of suggestions. He should socialise more. He should do less hours at work. He should eat better. He should be more pleasant at work.

She raised her eyebrows. 'About renting out one of your rooms?' Oh. That one. Her latest suggestion was a bid to encapsulate all her suggestions: it would force him to socialise, he might work less if he had someone to go home to, someone who could cook, maybe.

'Haven't had a chance.' He walked from behind the desk and gave her a cheeky wink. 'Been too busy at work.'

'Jacob…' Her voice tailed after him but he was already halfway down the corridor. Hope was about to go into interrogator mode. He could sense it. It was time to make a sharp exit.

Bonnie was just finishing at the desk and he welcomed the distraction. If Hope saw him talking to another woman she was bound to leave him alone.

'Good first day?' he asked.

Bonnie blinked. 'It's not over yet. Come with me a second.'

She took another quick glance over her shoulder at the bustling labour suite. *Her* bustling labour suite. She hadn't even started to make her mark here. They walked down the corridor together.

So many things needed organising to make the place

run more efficiently. Once she had things running the way she liked and she knew the staff a little better she'd start to delegate some tasks. All of the staff she'd met today seemed fine. No one had even mentioned what they'd overheard this morning, but she was sure—by the time she came on shift tomorrow—all members of staff would know about it. That was the thing about hospitals. Nothing was kept secret for long.

She'd met seven midwives, two doctors and one other consultant who all seemed good at their jobs. The ancillary staff seemed great too. CRMU's reputation appeared to be well founded. All the labour suite needed was its wheels oiled a little to help it run more smoothly.

She smiled. First day. After a bumpy start with Freya, and with Jacob, things appeared to be looking up. Good staff. A temporary promotion. Three healthy babies delivered while she was on shift. And another delivered in the back of an ambulance with a mother who appeared to be on the road to recovery.

Jacob had surprised her most with his offer of a ride home. At their first meeting he'd appeared a little detached. But at times today his mouth had betrayed him by turning up at the edges. There was a sense of humour in there somewhere. She'd just have to find a big spade to dig it out.

She pushed open the doors at the end of the ward and walked along to one of the side rooms between her ward and the special-care nursery. Both of them looked through the window. Holly had opened her eyes and was talking to one of the specialist midwives assigned to her. Her husband sat by her side holding the baby in his arms. Another midwife from the special-care nursery was there with the incubator. It was obvious this was the first time she'd got to see her baby.

The whole scene sent a warm glow around Bonnie's body. Coming here was the best decision she'd ever made.

She met Jacob's emerald gaze. There was a gleam in his eye. He knew exactly what kind of day she'd had. She kept her face straight. 'No. It's not been a good day.'

He raised his eyebrows and she broke into a beaming smile. 'It was a *great* day. I think I'm going to like Cambridge Maternity.'

CHAPTER THREE

JACOB TAPPED HIS fingers on the wheel of the car while he waited for Bonnie. He'd already had a few curious stares from members of staff who obviously wondered who he was waiting on. Bonnie appeared two minutes later and jumped in the car next to him. 'Sorry, just getting changed and sorting out a locker before we left.' She gave him directions to the childminder's house and looked around with a smile on her face.

'I didn't take you for a four-by-four guy. I thought you'd have something sleeker, more sporty.'

He raised his eyebrows. 'Really? Why on earth did you think that?'

She laughed. 'You've got that "I drive a flash car" look about you. Wouldn't have thought there'd be much call for a four-by-four in the city. I've been surprised by how many I've seen.'

'Haven't you heard? It's the latest fashion craze and I'm just following the crowd.'

She shook her head. 'Yeah, yeah. Somehow I get the distinct impression you've never been a crowd follower.'

He tried to hide his smile. 'I'm shocked. We've only just met and you're trying to tell me I'm not a people pleaser.'

She started laughing again. 'Seriously? You were a bit

grumpy this morning. The staff seem quite intimidated by you. Are you always like that?'

'You were late. That's why I was grumpy.' It was the best excuse he could give. The truth was he'd spent the last fourteen months being grumpy—and only a few select people knew why. Jacob had always been a completely hands-on kind of doctor. Some physicians who were Head of Department reduced their clinical time by a large amount. He'd never been that kind of doctor but had been grateful to use his position as an excuse for his lack of patient contact at times over the past fourteen months. That was the thing about some types of chemotherapy—at certain times in the cycle, patient contact just wasn't appropriate. Particularly when you had to deal with pregnant women and neonates—two of the most vulnerable groups around. Grumpy probably didn't even come close to covering his temperament and frustration these last fourteen months.

She shook her head as they turned into the childminder's street. 'I think you were grumpy long before I was late. I need to know these things. I need to know if staff won't want to approach you about things. I need to know the dynamics of the labour suite.'

He liked her already. She was astute. It wouldn't be easy to pull the wool over her eyes—exactly what he should want from the sister of his labour suite. He just wished she weren't using her astuteness on him.

'You haven't mentioned what happens with the special clients. Do I get involved with those?'

He raised his eyebrows. 'The special clients?'

She smiled. 'Cambridge Royal is known for attracting the rich and famous. I haven't had a chance to look over the plans for the general hospital. What happens if we get someone who wants a private delivery? It wouldn't seem safe to have them in another area.'

He was impressed. She'd obviously done a lot of background reading. 'You're right. It wouldn't be safe. It isn't public knowledge but there are six private rooms just outside the doors to the labour suite, only a few minutes from Theatre. We don't want anyone to know where our private patients are.'

She gave a little nod of her head. 'Makes sense. Privacy, that's what people want. Isn't it? I guess we'll need to talk about the midwifery staffing for those rooms.'

There was something so strange about all this. Everything about being around Bonnie made him feel out of sorts. He had looked at her CV and hadn't understood at all why Valerie Glencross had thought she would be a suitable replacement for their ward sister. Then she'd been late.

But from the second her eyes had sparked and she'd given him a dressing-down in front of the staff he'd liked her. She was different. She'd proved more than competent at the roadside delivery. She was asking all the right questions about the ward and she was making all the right observations. Bonnie Reid was proving to be the most interesting woman he'd come across in a while.

She opened the car door as they pulled up outside the childminder's. 'I'll only be two minutes, I promise, and Lynn will be able to give me a car seat for Freya. That's the beauty of having a friend who is a childminder. She has a garage full of these things.'

Car seat. It hadn't even crossed his mind. That was how far out of the loop he was when it came to children. He tried not to focus on her well-fitting jeans as she ran up the path towards the door with her auburn hair bouncing behind her.

What kind of crazy fool cheated on a woman like Bonnie? The guy must have rocks in his head. Jacob had never realised quite how much he liked that colour of hair.

He watched as she ran back down the path holding the hand of a little girl. She was like an identikit of her mother. Same colour hair and pale skin. It only took Bonnie a minute to arrange the car seat and strap her little girl into place. She was obviously a dab hand at these things.

'Who are you?' The voice came from the back seat.

The little pair of curious blue eyes was fixed on his in the mirror. She had a little furrow across her brow. It was like a staring contest. A Mexican stand-off. And Jacob had a feeling he was going to lose.

Bonnie answered as she climbed back in the car. 'This is Mummy's friend from work. His name is Jacob. He's going to give us a lift back to the motel.'

He glanced in the rear-view mirror in time to see her shrink back into her seat a little. Was he really that scary? Bonnie had already mentioned the staff might find him unapproachable. He'd never really given it much thought.

'Hmm…' came the voice from the back of the car. She really didn't seem too sure about it. Bonnie gave him directions to the motel and he flinched when it came into view. If this was the outside—what was the inside like?

'Do you need a hand?'

'No,' she said too quickly, then her voice wavered. 'Actually, could you give me a hand carrying the car seat in?' She jumped out and unstrapped Freya, leading the way inside.

He followed them in, waiting patiently while she unlocked the door of her room. The first thing that hit him was the smell of damp. The really obvious smell of damp. He winced. How on earth did the motel owner think this was acceptable?

He looked around. 'This will play havoc with Freya's asthma.' The words came out before he really thought about it.

Bonnie sucked in a deep breath and licked her lips. There was a sheen across her eyes, as if she was holding back tears.

She'd already told him how much this bothered her. But now, seeing it with his own eyes, he understood.

Bonnie's pretty face was marred by a frown. He liked her. He hardly knew her but he liked her already. What was more she obviously had the skills that the labour suite badly needed right now.

And after what he'd seen today? He didn't want to lose her from CRMU.

His brain was in overdrive. There was no way he could leave them here. Not now he'd seen it. Not now he'd smelled it.

This was about work. He was prioritising the needs of the labour suite above all others. That was what he was telling himself right now, but that was the only way he could make sense of the possibility that had just flown into his head.

'You have to get her out of here. A child with asthma can't possibly stay in an environment like this.'

This time she was blinking back tears. 'What choice do I have?' She sounded exasperated, her hand curled protectively around her daughter.

'You can stay with me.' The words were out before he even had a chance to think properly.

It made no sense. It made no sense whatsoever. He

was a bachelor. After the last fourteen months he liked his solitude. His home was his salvation.

'What?' Bonnie straightened up. 'What do you mean?'

'I mean, you and your daughter can stay with me—until you find something more suitable, of course. I have space in my house. You can stay with me.'

'No. No, we can't do that.' She was shaking her head. 'We don't even really know you.'

A wave of embarrassment came over him. After his behaviour this morning it was understandable that she was wary.

He took a deep breath. 'Look, Bonnie, I'm sorry about this morning. I know I came across as difficult.' He shook his head. 'But that's just me. It probably wasn't the ideal first meeting.' He held out his hands. 'But there's absolutely no way I'm letting you spend the next few days here with your daughter. Not while her health is at risk.'

It took a few seconds for the initial shocked expression on her face to disappear. Her tense shoulders gradually relaxed and she nodded slowly. Relief. That was what she was feeling now. It was palpable in the air all around them. The frown had disappeared from her brow and her blue eyes were focused clearly on him.

'You really mean it?' She seemed really hesitant.

It was clear she couldn't believe it. 'Freya and I can stay with you for a few days?' She glanced around her. 'We don't need to stay in this mouldy motel room?'

'Just until you find somewhere suitable.' From the expression on her face any minute now she would jump for joy.

'Of course.' Parts of his insides were doing strange twisting things. Making him think the word *no* but not letting it come out. This was work. They'd found a new temporary ward sister who needed a short-term solution for accommodation. It was logical. That was all.

'That's such a weight off my mind. Thank you, Jacob. Will your wife or partner be okay with this? The last thing I want to do is foist myself and a five-year-old on someone unexpectedly.'

Jacob gave the tiniest shake of his head. 'No wife. No partner.' He shrugged his shoulders. 'No time.' He squirmed a little saying those words out loud. Most single guys would probably be delighted to declare their freedom to the world. But for some reason it made him sound so isolated.

'And it won't be too much of an inconvenience to you?' Her voice rose a little at the end of the sentence, as if she were worried at any minute he might change his mind.

'How much trouble can a five-year-old be?' He was giving her a half smile as a whole surge of wariness swept over him. He had absolutely *no* experience with five-year-olds. He didn't even know how to have a conversation with one. He tried to rationalise things out loud. 'It makes sense. We need a ward sister to get on top of things in the labour ward. The last thing you need is for your daughter to be sick and to spend your time at work worrying about where you're staying. It's logical.'

She held out her hands. 'You'll need to give us a few minutes to pack. Thankfully we didn't really have a chance to unpack last night.'

It was almost as if Bonnie went into automatic pilot. She started pushing things haphazardly into a large blue case, then sat on it to close it. Now he'd made the offer it was clear she couldn't wait to get out of here—no matter how temporary the solution. And the truth was, he couldn't wait to get out of here either.

'Here,' he said, gesturing her to move. 'Let me. I'll push down and you can snap it shut.'

It did only take her a few minutes. But by the time she was finished there were four bulging suitcases for the car as well as the car seat. He gave her a wink. 'Just as well I brought my four-by-four and not my sports car. How on earth did you get down from the train with these?'

Something juddered through him. *Had he just winked at her?* What on earth was wrong with him? Since when did he do things like that?

This woman was having a strange effect on him.

But Bonnie didn't seem to notice. She just looked a little sheepish. 'It's a bit hard trying to ram all your worldly goods into some suitcases. Particularly when your five-year-old wants to bring all twenty of her favourite cuddly toys.' She sighed. 'I've got some stuff in storage as well at my mum and dad's. Once we find somewhere to stay I'll send for it.'

He picked up the first two cases and carried them out to the car. All of a sudden he felt as if he'd put his foot in his mouth. He wasn't trying to offend her. He'd spent the last year so focused on his treatment and keeping the department running that he hadn't bothered much with social niceties. Maybe it was time to start paying attention again.

Bonnie went to pay her bill as he loaded the last two cases into the car. 'You shouldn't have paid anything. That place is a disgrace.'

She strapped Freya back in and climbed into the passenger seat. 'Don't. He wanted me to pay for the whole week because we've left early.'

'I hope you refused.'

She gave him a wink. 'Of course I did.'

He started the car with a smile. Just as well he hadn't been driving. He'd have probably swerved off the road. She had seen the wink and had taken it as intended— in good humour. Thank goodness. He couldn't afford to tiptoe around someone who would be staying in his house. He must have been crazy inviting her to stay. *She* must have been crazy to accept. Either that, or she was desperate.

And he already knew that she was.

He had to keep remembering that. Otherwise his mind might start to drift in other directions. He'd never shared his house with a woman before. Let alone a woman and child. He was used to his own space. This had disaster written all over it.

His stomach started to churn a little. This was the craziest thing he'd ever done. He knew that his house was tidy—Monday was the day his housekeeper came. He'd texted her earlier and asked her to pick up some food for him. His fridge was currently bare. It was hardly hospitable to invite a mother and child back with not even a drop of milk in the fridge.

There. That was better. A mother and child seemed a much safer thought than anything that involved the name Bonnie.

He pulled up outside his Victorian town house. It had just started to rain and Bonnie pressed her nose up against the glass. 'Please tell me you only own part of that.'

He opened the car door. 'Nope. It's all mine. Including the ancient kennel in the back garden.'

He felt a little surge of pride in his heart that she liked

his house. It was very traditional for Cambridge. Set in a
residential area, in the middle of the city, the three-storey
town house was just moments away from the river and
college boathouses.

'You have a dog?'

Freya. He'd almost forgotten she was there. She had
that expression on her face again. The little frown line
across her forehead. She was standing in the rain staring up at the bay window at the front of the house. He
pulled her hood up over her head. 'No. Sorry, I don't. I
just have a really old kennel.'

He popped the boot and lifted out the first two cases,
then walked up the path and deposited them at the doorway while he fished for his keys. 'Give me a sec,' he said
as he opened the door and turned off the alarm. 'Go inside. I'll get the other cases.'

The rain was getting heavier now and it only took a
few seconds to wrestle the other cases from the back of
the car and get inside. He closed the door behind him and
breathed a sigh of relief.

Home was usually his sanctuary. The place he came
back to after work or treatment, closed the blinds and
ignored the world. Chances were, he wouldn't get to do
that any time soon. Thank goodness his treatment was
over. Now he just had to wait for his results.

Bonnie had picked Freya up and carried her through
the long corridor and turned left into the main lounge.
He heard the little suck in of breath. What did that mean?

He dumped the cases at the door and followed her into
the lounge. She spun around to face him. 'Wow. This
place is just yours? It's gorgeous.' She set Freya down
on the floor and walked over to the fireplace. 'This is
just amazing. Does it work? Do you have a real fire on

a winter's night?' She crouched down and touched the tile work around the fireplace.

He'd always been proud of his home, but for the first time he felt a little regretful. He touched the marble surround. 'No. I've never had the chimney swept. It is apparently in working order. I just never got around to it.' He pointed to the walls. 'I do have the original cast-iron radiators. So don't worry. You won't be cold.'

She shook her head. 'Oh, I'm not worried about being cold.' She looked down. 'The floorboards are gorgeous too. Are they original?' She knelt down and ran her hand along the floor. He was learning quickly that Bonnie was a very tactile person.

'I sanded them down. It took about a year to do the whole house.'

She nodded in approval. 'I noticed the gorgeous geometric floor tiles on the way in too. I always wanted a hallway with those.' She looked a little lost in her own thoughts, then gave a little shrug. 'I'd be happy just to have a hallway right now.'

'Those tiles were hidden under the ugliest shag-pile carpet you've ever seen.'

She gasped. 'Really?' Then shuddered. 'What a crime to cover those up.'

'It probably saved them from being ruined. I've had them all coated now with something that should mean they last the next hundred years.'

She took a look around her. 'I'll never be able to afford a place like this. You're so lucky.'

Lucky. Now there was a word he'd never use to describe himself. Over the course of such an eventful day he'd realised how easy it was to be around Bonnie. Now it struck him how little she actually knew him. How little most of the staff at CRMU actually knew him. He could count on one hand the people he'd actually trusted with his secret. They knew how much he'd struggled this last year. How frustrated he'd been when he couldn't deal with patients because of the type of chemotherapy he was undergoing. How much he wanted just to get back to normal and do his job the way he always had.

Lucky. Maybe he was lucky. His cancer was treatable. Other types weren't. He'd managed to undergo his treatment quietly with only one day off work sick. Good planning had played a huge part in that. Having a cancer treatment team who were willing to allow him to start chemotherapy on a Thursday evening, which meant the after-effects didn't really hit until the Friday night, meant he could still work, then spend most weekends in bed to allow himself to recover.

But he still didn't feel lucky. His mother certainly hadn't been. She'd had the same type of cancer that he had—non-Hodgkin's lymphoma. It was generally thought that it wasn't an inherited disease. But tell that to the families where more than one person had it. There was just so much still to learn about these diseases. So many genes in the body where they still couldn't determine their purpose.

But his last treatment was finished now. In a few weeks' time he'd have his bloods rechecked to see if the treatment had worked and his cancer was finally gone. The whole black cloud that had been hanging over his head for the last fourteen months would finally be gone. Maybe. Hopefully.

Bonnie was still walking around. She had a little look of wonder on her face. As if she really did love the place. She stood with her back to the bay window and looked across the room. A smile lit up her face. She was obviously seeing something that he didn't.

'This place must be so gorgeous at Christmastime. I can just imagine it.' She spun around and held out her hands. 'A huge tree at this window that everyone out on the street can see.' She walked towards the fireplace again. 'One of those green and red garlands for the mantel, with some twinkling lights.' She turned back to the window. 'And some old-fashioned heavy-duty velvet curtains around the window.' She touched the white blinds that were currently in place and gave a little frown. 'Do you change these at Christmas? It's such a gorgeous bay window. You should make the most of it.'

He could almost hear the shutters clanging into place in his brain. He saw it. The pictures in her head that would never be in his. Never. He didn't do Christmas—hadn't since he was a young boy.

She couldn't possibly know. She couldn't possibly understand. He and his father had literally watched the life being sucked out of his mother. She'd died around Christmastime and the season celebrations had been a permanent reminder ever since. He hated Christmas. He'd always offered to work it, and since most of his colleagues had children they'd always been happy to accept his offer. He'd never hung a single decoration in his home. He didn't even own any.

He could see her gaze narrow ever so slightly as she looked more critically now around the whitewashed room with white window blinds. Apart from the wooden floor, the only thing that gave the room some colour was the dark leather suite.

He'd always loved his house. It suited his needs fine.

He didn't want to accommodate anyone else's opinions or tastes.

He walked back out to the hall. Away from the look of expectation on Bonnie's face. Away from her smiling, overactive imagination. 'I don't really have time for Christmas, or to decorate. There's not much point. I'm always on duty at the hospital anyway. Come on, I'll show you both where your rooms are.'

He didn't even wait to see if she was following him. Just picked up the first two cases and headed to the stairs. Bonnie still had that glazed expression on her face. She touched the banister. 'This must be beautiful with tinsel wound around it.'

He swept past her on the staircase. 'Not going to happen. Not in this house.' He was done being subtle. She hadn't picked up on the first clues. He was going to have to hang a sign saying 'No Christmas' above the mantelpiece. What did it matter anyway—by Christmas she wouldn't be here. Not in his house anyway.

He paused at the landing, ignoring her puzzled expression and cutting her off before she had the chance to speak. 'There's three bedrooms on this floor—one of which is mine—and two bedrooms and a bathroom on the floor above. I think you and Bonnie might be better up there. More privacy for you both.'

More privacy for me too. He didn't want to wander along the hall half dressed to find a little red-haired girl with her disapproving glare.

He started up the other flight of stairs before Bonnie really had a chance to reply. The housekeeper had definitely been in today. The doors of both rooms were open and he could smell the freshly laundered linen on the beds. He put the cases in the first room that had a double bed. 'I'm assuming you'll sleep in here and Freya next door. There's a single in there. Bathroom's at the end of the hall.' He walked along the corridor and flicked the light switch in the white-tiled bathroom. He hadn't really thought about it before. Just about everything in this house was white.

He watched as Freya walked suspiciously into the single room, her eyes flitting from side to side. She looked at the single bed covered in a white duvet, the chest of drawers, and then turned around and walked back to Bonnie, wrapping her arms around her waist and cuddling her tight.

Her actions gave Jacob a start. There was nothing wrong with this room. It was fine. Why didn't she like it? He took a few seconds and looked again. Maybe the room was a little stark. Maybe it wasn't exactly welcoming for a little girl. But how on earth would he know what a little girl would like? It wasn't as if he'd had any practice. The kids he was generally around were only a few days or hours old.

'Maybe you'd like to sleep in with your mum?' He had no idea where that had come from. Chances were, he'd just committed some huge parenting faux pas. He was just struggling to understand Freya's reaction to the perfectly acceptable room.

Bonnie looked up and shot him a grateful glance. 'We'll play it by ear. Thank you, Jacob.'

He gave a relieved nod. 'Sorry, I didn't show you the kitchen or the back sitting room. It has a more comfortable sofa—and another TV and DVD player.' A thought darted into his brain. 'The only place I'd prefer Freya stay out of is my office downstairs.' The place was full of research about non-Hodgkin's lymphoma. Statistics for everything, including the most successful forms of treatment. Freya wouldn't be able to read any of that but Bonnie would if she followed Freya in.

'Absolutely no problem.' Bonnie had wound her hand through Freya's hair and was stroking the back of her neck. Did she know she was doing it? Or was it just a subconscious act?

'There's some food in the kitchen. Help yourself to anything that's in the fridge, freezer or cupboards.' He glanced at Freya. 'I'm not quite sure what Freya will like but my housekeeper picked up some groceries for me today. Or you could have some toast if you prefer?'

He had absolutely no idea what he was doing. This had been his craziest idea yet. A woman who was practically a stranger and a child who was clearly uncomfortable around him—and he'd invited them to stay in his home.

For the first time in a long time, Jacob Layton felt well and truly out of his depth.

Jacob was waiting for an answer. He had that anxious look on his face again. The one that kept appearing every few minutes. It was clear he wasn't used to having people in his house and she realised just what an inconvenience this must be to him. Her stomach flip-flopped with guilt. He must have regretted his offer as soon as the words had left his mouth.

But he seemed so anxious to please. It was almost cute. And she could bet that Jacob Layton had never been described as cute before.

She swallowed. She'd kill for a cup of tea right now. But it just didn't seem right to walk into someone else's kitchen and make yourself at home. 'I didn't mean to put you to so much trouble, Jacob. Please apologise to your housekeeper for me. I didn't mean to give her additional work.'

He waved his hand. 'You haven't. She shops for me on occasion anyway. I'm just not sure how much she'll have got as I didn't know I'd have guests. Check the fridge. I'll go and get your other cases.' He disappeared down the stairs as she stared at the bulging cases in the white room. Her blue case looked ready to explode. It was so out of place in here. A huge splash of colour against the stark white room. Thank goodness for the wooden floorboards. They added a little warmth about the place.

She shuffled over to the case, Freya still attached to her waist. It was clear her little girl was feeling overwhelmed by the whole situation. And to be truthful—she was too.

He had no idea what he'd let himself in for. Once she opened those cases his beautiful, pristine house would never look the same again. It wasn't that she was messy—she would never be messy staying as a guest in someone's house. It was just—once she opened the cases—things would start to get everywhere, as if they had self-migrating powers. And she wasn't quite sure how Jacob would feel about that. She let out a sigh and sat down on the bed, pulling Freya along with her. The comfortable mattress almost swallowed them up.

This place was a thousand times better than the motel. Here, she wouldn't be worried about Freya's asthma flaring up. The house was warm without being too hot. It was clean. It was spacious. They had their own rooms—they almost had their own floor.

Money. The thought came out of nowhere and she sat bolt upright. She hadn't offered him any money. There was no way she could stay here rent-free. It was quite obvious that Jacob was putting himself out for them. She would have to find a way to bring it up. But she had a bad feeling about how it would go.

Jacob. It was strange being in his house. *His home.* But that was just it. It didn't really feel like a home.

The white everywhere made it seem almost clinical. She would have imagined him staying in some brand-new luxury penthouse flat—not an old Victorian town house. It was beautiful. There was no doubt about that, and she hadn't even seen the kitchen yet.

But there were no pictures. No family photos. He hadn't even mentioned his family yet. There was no little sign of 'him' anywhere in the house. Who was Jacob Layton?

She ran her fingers across the bedspread. That was what was wrong. This was a beautiful house. But it didn't feel like home. Why?

A house like this should exude warmth, character. And Jacob's house wasn't like that. She had the overwhelming urge to change the curtains in the lounge, to buy some different bedspreads for the white rooms and to add some accessories—some red towels in the white bathrooms, some pictures along the walls in the hall. A splash of colour was just what this place needed. She shook her head. This wasn't her home and she should just be grateful to have somewhere to stay. It was none of her business how Jacob chose to decorate his beautiful home.

'Come on, pumpkin. Let's leave the cases for now and go and find some dinner.' She took Freya's warm hand in hers and led her downstairs, blinking as she entered the kitchen. Just as she expected. White and chrome, all gleaming and sparkling.

But there was one nice little touch. The worktop wasn't

granite like most designer kitchens. The worktop was a thick wooden polished surface that led to a deep white Belfast sink. It offset the rest of the white and chrome, giving the kitchen a little more warmth.

There was no kitchen table, just a central island with high black bar-style stools. She positioned Freya carefully on one and looked in the freezer. No—not a single thing.

She frowned and opened the fridge. Two steaks. One steak pie, some bacon, some eggs and two carefully wrapped bundles from the fishmongers. One labelled as cod in breadcrumbs. Even the fish fingers were posh round here.

Jacob appeared at her back as she was hunting for some oven trays and baking foil. 'Are you getting on okay?'

She nodded and smiled. 'We decided to eat first and unpack later. We both had first days today and we're pretty wiped out.'

He opened a cupboard and took out some wine glasses, then glanced at Freya and swapped one for a tumbler. 'Would you like some wine?'

She shook her head. 'Honestly? I'm just too tired. I'd love a cup of tea though. And I still need to empty our cases. Could you show me where the washing machine is? I'd appreciate it if we could do some laundry.'

He stood up and opened a few cupboards. 'My house-keeper always buys some fruit and some biscuits—they're in here. Tea and coffee is here. If you turn the red button down on the tap you'll get boiling water.'

'From the tap?'

He nodded. 'Saves boiling the kettle—' he glanced sideways '—and it's too high up for Freya to reach. There's a proper cappuccino maker next to the oven if you prefer.' He gave a little smile. 'To be honest there's too many buttons. I've never used it. But the instructions are there—you're welcome to christen it if you wish.'

He pointed behind her as he ducked into a cupboard and pulled out a bottle of diet cola. 'Utility room is through there. There's a washing machine, tumble dryer and dishwasher, as well as another toilet and the door to the back garden. Freya's welcome to play out there if it's warm enough.' He gave a little grimace. 'I think the only thing you'll find out there is an old football.'

'Don't you have a dog kennel?'

They both turned to the unexpected little voice. Freya had been silent since she'd come downstairs. Jacob moved over next to her. 'I told you that in the car, didn't I? There is an old kennel out there. It must have belonged to the people who owned the house before I did. It still has the dog's name above the kennel.'

'What was his name?'

'How did you know it was a boy?' he answered quickly.

She shrugged. 'I guessed.' Bonnie was amazed. Freya had seemed a little overwhelmed earlier. But maybe she was starting to feel a little more comfortable in the house. She was glad that Jacob was making an effort with her daughter. She already felt as if they'd have to tiptoe round about him. Maybe it wouldn't be quite as awkward as she'd thought.

'Well, you were right. It was a boy. His name was Bones.'

Freya wrinkled her nose. 'Bones? That's a rubbish name for a dog.'

Bonnie couldn't help but laugh at her blunt response. Jacob leaned his elbow on the island. 'Really? That's what I thought too. What would you call a dog?'

Freya thought for a few seconds. 'Sandy. I'd like a little dog. One that's white and sandy coloured.' She leaned forwards and whispered conspiratorially. 'That's why I'd call him Sandy.'

Bonnie tapped Jacob on the shoulder as she poured the diet cola into Freya's tumbler. Not the ideal drink for a five-year-old—but she was just thankful that Jacob had anything at all that was suitable. She set about making a cup of tea for herself. 'Don't give her any ideas. One day it's a bichon frise, the next it's a terrier, the next a Havanese. Let's remember that most places we'll be renting won't accept pets. I keep trying to tell her that.'

He smiled conspiratorially at Freya and pretend whispered to her. 'I think you need to tell Mummy to find a house that takes dogs.' She almost fell over. She hadn't thought he had it in him. Jacob was full of surprises.

He walked over to the fridge and pulled out a silver tray. 'Do you want to have fish too? My housekeeper seems to have bought plenty. She seems to have decided to feed me up. It will only take fifteen minutes.' He slid the sea bass into the oven next to Freya's fish fingers, then grabbed an oven tray, covered it in silver foil and tipped something from a plastic tub into it. He gave a shrug, 'Mediterranean crushed potatoes. I'm rubbish at shopping and cooking. My housekeeper always makes a few back-up meals for me. She says it's the only time my kitchen is put to good use.'

She gave an awkward nod and sat up on one of the stools, warming her hands on her teacup. This was all a little strange.

Jacob looked at her as he poured himself some wine. 'You okay?'

She sighed. 'It's been a big day. This morning I dropped my daughter at a brand-new school, took a bus ride through an unfamiliar city, was late for my first day at work. Accepted a temporary promotion, helped at the scene of an accident and moved into my boss's home. All in one day.'

He sipped his wine. 'I think I've got this one covered for you.'

'What do you mean?' She was curious.

He gave a little smile. 'One of my good friends is Scottish. I think this could be the "I'm completely knackered" answer.'

She burst out laughing and Freya's mouth hung open. 'What a terrible accent!' She lifted her cup of tea towards him. 'But the word is perfect, and, yes, it is the one I would have chosen. I'm completely and utterly knackered. I can't wait to climb into bed with Freya and go to sleep. I can guarantee you—we won't wake up until the alarm goes off.'

Something flickered across his face. 'I'm just glad that Freya will sleep safely. You must have had nightmares last night.'

She hesitated and gave a grateful nod. 'Jacob, we can't stay here without giving you some money. Can I give you what we would have paid for the motel?'

'No.' His answer came out a bit sharply and she started.

'It only seems fair,' she said slowly. 'I know we're imposing and you've already gone to too much trouble for us.' She gestured towards the oven. 'The food that you bought. I'll feel really uncomfortable if you don't let me contribute.'

He took a sip of his wine. 'Then feel really uncomfortable—because I won't. It's only temporary. You'll find somewhere to stay soon. It's only a stopgap to give you some breathing space. We both know that. And anyway—you'll buy your own food for yourself and Freya. I just thought you wouldn't have had much opportunity between arriving last night and coming to work today.' He gave a shrug of his shoulders. 'I don't want the new sister of the labour suite passing out from hunger tomorrow.'

He was so matter-of-fact about it. He made it sound so reasonable. Even though she knew it really wasn't.

She held up her cup of tea towards his. 'Thank you. But you need to know—I won't let this go. I'll keep hounding you.'

He clinked his glass against her cup. 'I'll look forward to it.'

His eyes connected with Bonnie's. That was the difference between herself and her daughter. Bonnie's eyes were deep blue—almost hypnotising. Freya's were the more traditional pale blue.

From the second he'd offered her a place to stay he'd wanted to drag the words back. His stomach had churned and he'd conjured up a million different excuses to try to back out. But his integrity wouldn't let him—that, and the relieved expression on Bonnie's face when he'd made the offer. His guts had twisted at the thought of people in his home. His private place. But it wasn't quite as bad as he'd imagined. It was odd. The last person he'd shared a house with had been his father. It was amazing how long two people could live together while barely talking. Particularly when he'd told his father he wasn't the following the military family tradition and was going into medicine instead. His father had barely looked him in the eye after that.

Before dinner he led them through the rest of the house, showing them a dining room, the door to his study, the downstairs cloakroom and the back sitting room and conservatory.

'This house is just amazing, Jacob, and it's so close to the city centre. What do they call this street—millionaire row?' She was joking but he could see the weariness in her eyes. She'd been uprooted from a familiar home and ended up in a bad motel. Now she was going to be spending the next few weeks scouring around for houses to rent or buy, trying to work out if it was in an area she'd want her and Freya to stay in. All in the run-up to Christmas. Her brain must be currently whirring.

He laughed. 'No. Not quite. I bought it around ten years ago before the prices went crazy. It needed a lot of fixing up and I've just done a little bit at a time.'

'Well, I think you've done a good job. I hope I'll get a chance to have a walk around the area in the next few days. It would be good to get a bit more familiar with Cambridge.'

'If I get a chance, I'll show you and Freya around. Point out the places to visit and the places to avoid.' Where had that come from? It was so unlike him. He'd spent the last year living his life in a bubble. Hardly any interaction with friends and colleagues. The few people that he'd confided in about his condition had all offered to help in any way that they could. But offers of help made him feel vulnerable, at risk even.

Jacob had got through this life shutting off his feelings from the world. He hadn't even properly mourned the death of his mother. That wasn't the Layton way. Or so his father had told him. He'd very much instilled the stiff-upper-lip mentality into his son.

And even after all these years it was still there. It was partly the reason he'd never had a lasting relationship. He'd shuttered himself away for so long it felt normal now. And after a while his friends had stopped offering any assistance. Eventually even good friends got tired of being rebuffed.

Bonnie gave him a smile. 'Thanks, Jacob. That's really nice of you to offer.'

The timer on the oven sounded and Bonnie helped him to put the food onto plates. Instead of moving to the dining room, they stayed at the more informal island in the kitchen. By now, Freya was desperate to see the old kennel outside and invented an imaginary dog for her stay. But it was already dark and after she'd finished her fish fingers her little head started to nod.

Bonnie wrapped her arm around Freya's shoulders. 'I think it's time to get a little girl into her bath and into bed. To be honest, I could do with an early night myself. Once I've helped you clear up I think we'll both go to bed.' She stood up and gave him a wink. 'I don't want to be late for work tomorrow.' She gave a fake roll of her eyes. 'You've no idea what the boss is like.'

He let out a laugh and lifted the plates. 'Don't worry. I've heard about him. Forget about clearing up. I'll dump the dishes in the dishwasher and we're done.'

'You're sure?' She'd already picked up Freya and the little girl had snuggled into her shoulder.

'I'm sure. Goodnight, Bonnie. Goodnight, Freya.' It was odd—for the first time in a long time, Jacob actually felt at peace.

Then Bonnie spoiled it. She fixed on him with her unblinking blue eyes. 'Goodnight, Jacob, and thank you,' then turned and walked up the stairs.

There was nothing surer. The sight of Bonnie's backside in those jeans would stay with him well into the early hours of the morning.

CHAPTER FOUR

THERE WAS NO denying it. The labour suite had been in a complete muddle. Her mother would have called it a right guddle—a good Scots word. And she would have been right.

It seemed that in the few weeks since the sister had left, a new ordering system had come into place, and a new electronic system for recording staff working hours. No one on the labour suite had the time or motivation to learn how to use either and things were well behind.

Bonnie was lucky. There were other staff who offered to help. Isabel Delamere, an obstetrician on an exchange from Australia, was quick to give her the low-down on most members of staff. She wasn't a gossip. In fact, Bonnie got the impression that Isabel was quite the opposite. But she'd been new here herself and obviously wanted to help.

Hope Sanders, one of the other midwives, had been great. She'd quickly explained both new systems to Bonnie. It was strange. Bonnie had seen Hope talk to Jacob a few times. It was obvious they were friends. And the tall curly-haired blonde had already told her she was single. But Bonnie could tell there wasn't anything romantic between them.

If anything, Hope just seemed concerned about Jacob. She was always reminding him about the number of hours he worked and telling him to get out a bit more.

Things were a little awkward on the ward. Both of them had decided it wouldn't be wise if the rest of the staff knew Bonnie and her daughter were staying with Jacob. It meant that she tried to jump out of the car before they reached the car park and other members of staff would notice them together. For the last few days things had been fine.

Well. That wasn't entirely true. She'd spent every night poring over the Internet looking at rental properties and houses for sale. Jacob had tried to be helpful. But Jacob's helpful had been telling her that one area where a house was for sale was less than salubrious and three of the rental properties had been similar. There was nothing else suitable in her price range. Trouble was, she'd moved here at the wrong time of year. Cambridge had lots of properties for rent, but most were rented by students and visiting lecturers for a year at a time. If she'd arrived a few months earlier there would probably have been lots of properties to view. Arriving in November? Not a chance.

Kerry, one of the midwives in the unit, leaned over the desk towards her. 'Bonnie, we've just had a call to say that Hayley Dickson is coming in, query spontaneous rupture of membranes. She's twenty-seven, and is thirty-six weeks pregnant with twins. We're expecting her in around an hour and I'll need some assistance. Any chance you can go for your lunch now?'

Bonnie smiled and nodded. 'My first twin delivery at Cambridge? Love to. Have you had lunch?'

Kerry nodded. 'It's only you that's still to go. Better hurry before there's nothing left in the canteen.'

Bonnie stood up. 'No problem. I'll be back in half an hour to help you get set up.'

She washed her hands and grabbed her bag. She was glad that the staff found her approachable and were happy to ask for assistance. It gave a bit of reassurance that they were accepting her as temporary sister around here.

The canteen was quiet. She grabbed a tuna sandwich and walked over to a table to join one of the other midwives that she'd met. Jessica Black worked in the special care baby unit. Her blond straight hair hung in a ponytail but her pretty face was marred by a frown as she stared out of the window.

'Mind if I join you?'

Jess started but gave a smile and waved at the empty seats across from her. 'By all means. Try and cheer me up if you can.'

Bonnie pulled out a chair. 'What's wrong? Man trouble?'

Jess rolled her eyes. 'As if. I wish. That would be easy to sort out.' She picked at her lunch. 'Family troubles. It's my parents' thirtieth wedding anniversary in a few weeks. It's been arranged for near Cambridge so I can't make an excuse not to go and I'm looking forward to it like a hole in the head.'

Bonnie was puzzled. 'Shouldn't that be something to celebrate?'

Jess sighed. 'It should. I love my parents. But it's yet another family event where I'll spend the whole time being compared to my sister. And will, yet again, be found lacking.'

'I can't believe that for a second. You've got a great job

and career ahead of you. You're a gorgeous girl. What on earth does your sister have that you don't?'

Jess paused for a second and let out another big sigh. 'She's not just my sister. She's my twin. Abbie is perfect. She always has been. The sports star, top marks at school, the coolest boyfriend—you name it, Abbie's done it. I've spent most of my life living in her shadow. If Abbie preferred my Christmas presents to hers, she made such a scene she always got them. When I started midwifery training, she decided she wanted to do it too. Then, she decided she wanted the boyfriend I had.' She gave her head a shake. 'So, she got him. Along with the big white wedding and three perfect kids with another on the way.' She held out her hands. 'In fact, here is the only place where I'm known as anything other than "Abbie's sister".'

Bonnie was shocked by Jess's words. She reached over and squeezed her hand. 'Competitive siblings can be a nightmare. My ex-husband was like that with his brother. It made him even harder to live with.' She sucked in a breath. 'And if Cambridge Royal is like every other hospital I've worked in, you'll have heard that I found my ex-husband in bed with my best friend. So, I sympathise. At least I had the option of walking away. I don't need to look at them together.' She leaned back and took a sip of her coffee. 'It sucks that you have to do that.'

Jess burst out laughing and reached over towards Bonnie. 'Yes, the hospital grapevine is in full flow and I love that you just say it like it is.'

Bonnie shrugged. 'After thirty-two years there's not much point in changing the habit of a lifetime.'

Jess gave her a rueful stare. 'I might have heard that about you too. Men suck. Unfortunately, men are my biggest issue. Or namely the fact I don't have one. That's the reason I'm dreading the anniversary party so much. Everyone is just waiting for me to produce who is going to be Mr Jessica Black and create the two-point-four kids we're supposed to have.'

Bonnie took a bite of her tuna sandwich. 'Can't you take a friend?'

'Yeah, but the friend would need to reach my family's exacting standards. They would have to be devastatingly handsome, completely charming and totally unfazed by my sister trying to be the centre of attention.'

Bonnie gave a little smile. 'I have to say, there's more than a few handsome guys around here. Can't you ask one to accompany you?'

Jess frowned. 'Like who?'

Bonnie swallowed and tried to appear casual. 'What about Jacob Layton?'

Jess waved her hand. 'Oh, he's handsome enough but way too grumpy.'

Bonnie tried not to let the wave of relief sweeping over her be obvious. 'Aaron Cartwright, the infertility specialist? An American might go down well.'

She smiled and shook her head. 'He might. But he's not for me. He's too committed to his work. That's the problem with most of the guys around here.'

Bonnie thought again. She was just here. But she'd met most of the consultants in the last few days. 'I've got it. What about an Australian, then, Sean Anderson, the obstetrician that arrived just a few weeks before me?'

'Are you serious?' Jess laughed and wagged her finger. 'I'm going to forgive your observational skills, Nurse, because you've just started. But have you noticed how jumpy Isabel is since he got here?'

Bonnie racked her brains. Isabel was also an Australian obstetrician. Bonnie hadn't connected the two, but maybe there was something… She'd been warm and friendly towards Bonnie since she arrived. She shook her head and shrugged. 'I've never seen them together, so I can't say I've noticed.'

Jess raised her eyebrows. 'She's like a proverbial cat on a hot tin roof. Mark my words, there's some history there. I'm not getting embroiled in that.'

Bonnie took a final bite of her tuna sandwich. When she'd finished chewing she had the perfect answer. 'I've got it. Why didn't I think of him before? You've got the perfect answer right under your nose. Dean Edwards, the SCBU doctor.'

Something flickered across Jess's eyes. Bonnie was on it in an instant.

'What? Has something happened between you two already?'

Jess almost choked. 'No. Absolutely not. But I'll be the only one. He has a different lady for every day of the week. His phone goes off *constantly*.'

Bonnie took a sip of her tea and sat back in her chair. 'Dean's a ladies' man? Who has he dated at work?'

Jess was quick to shake her head. 'Oh, no. He doesn't date anyone at work.' She held out her hands. 'But that leaves the rest of the world wide open for him.'

'And you struck off his list?' Drat. That came out too bluntly. She'd only met Jess on a few occasions.

But it was just the two of them and Jess looked up from her coffee, her light brown eyes rueful. Maybe it was easier to open up to someone who was new?

She blew out a long, slow breath from her lips. 'I guess so. He wouldn't look at me anyway—and even if he did, once he met Wonder Sister he'd be entranced by her. They all are. It wears pretty thin.'

Bonnie reached out towards her again. 'You're a gorgeous girl, Jess. It would be wrong of me to say anything about your sister, but, to be honest, she seems like a piece of work. You've got much more integrity than that, and somewhere—' she held up her hands '—out there, is a man who is just waiting to find a woman like you. You'll probably find him when you least expect to.' She glanced at the clock. 'I'm sorry but I better go. We've got a woman expecting twins due in.' She put her plate and cup on the tray and winked at Jess. 'I gave you the option of three gorgeous men and you said no to all of them. Don't let it be said that you're picky.'

Jess winked back and put her plate on her tray, standing up and walking towards the catering trolleys. 'You gave me the option of *four*, Bonnie. Now I'm wondering if you're keeping one to yourself.'

And she left, before Bonnie could pick her chin off the floor and stop kicking herself.

By the time she reached the ward she could feel herself blushing like crazy. This was ridiculous. No one knew she was staying at Jacob's. Everything at work was entirely professional.

Everything at home was entirely professional too. But Jacob was surprising her. For a guy that acted as though he would run a million miles from kids, he'd been surprisingly good with Freya. Yes, he was still a bit awkward, but he was definitely making an effort. And that mattered. A lot.

It was a dangerous line. If he hadn't been friendly, they could have felt like trespassers in his home. Jacob still didn't give much away. He was obviously a private person. And that was fine. Except five-year-olds weren't always good at knowing when to stop asking questions.

He met her at the doors of the ward. 'You're helping with the twin delivery?'

She grinned. 'I am. Is she your patient? Anything I should know?'

In a labour unit some women would be classed as midwifery care and some as medical care. Any woman with a multiple pregnancy automatically fell under medical care as they were at higher risk of complications. An average woman, with a normal pregnancy, could come into the unit and not come into contact with a medic at all. She would be delivered by the midwives and her follow-up care carried out by them. Babies were different—they were always checked over by a paediatrician.

Bonnie dumped her bag as Jacob kept pace with her. 'Hayley Dickson has had a textbook pregnancy but her blood pressure has gone up a little in the last two weeks. I'm actually glad she's gone into spontaneous labour because I was considering inducing her. She's been scanned for the last few weeks. No problems with the babies. It's non-identical twins and both babies are around six pounds.'

'Does she know what she's having?'

He shook his head. 'She didn't want to know.'

Bonnie smiled. 'Do you?'

'I might do—' he tapped his mouth '—but my lips are sealed. Let's go and introduce Mum to these beautiful babies.' He put his hand on Bonnie's shoulder. 'If it's okay with you, I'd like to let you and Kerry take the lead. I'm only here if there are any issues. I'll set up the epidural I know she wants. But Hayley is keen to have a normal delivery.'

Bonnie gave a nod. 'No problem. I'll go and pick up the cots, be back with you in a minute.'

She was glad that Jacob didn't want to try and take over and respected the birthing plan his patient had decided on. Sometimes medics could be a bit overzealous. She hated when that happened.

She collected the cots and baby warmers and headed back into the room. Kerry gave her a nod as she entered. 'Hayley, this is Bonnie, our new ward sister. She'll be helping with the delivery. Bonnie, this is Hayley and her husband, Jordan.'

Bonnie walked straight to the sink to wash her hands. 'Pleasure to meet you, Hayley. I'm really looking forward to meeting these two new babies.' She nodded towards the cots. 'As soon as the babies are out we'll have one of our paediatricians check them over. After you've had a cuddle, of course.'

Hayley gave a nervous smile, then grimaced as another contraction hit. 'I didn't expect these to be coming so quickly.'

Kerry had already completed all the paperwork and hooked Hayley up to the monitors. One was monitoring her babies, the other checking her blood pressure.

Jacob appeared at Bonnie's back, pushing a trolley with the equipment for the epidural. He gave a nod to Kerry. 'Have you done a check yet?'

Kerry nodded. 'Yes, we're good to go. Hayley is five centimetres dilated and the first baby is head down and in a good position.'

Jacob smiled. 'Perfect.' He sat next to Hayley to explain the procedure. It only took him a few minutes. 'Once the catheter is in place it will only take twenty minutes for the full effect. We'll keep an eye to make sure it doesn't slow your labour, but I suspect everything will be fine.' He gave Bonnie a little nod to help position Hayley on her side.

He was an expert. He had the catheter safely slid into place easily and the medication started. Bonnie stayed in the room with Kerry and they monitored Hayley's contractions.

Things went smoothly. Around two hours later the first little baby delivered easily. Bonnie quickly checked over the baby's mouth and breathing before setting the naked little baby on his mother's chest. 'You have a beautiful boy. Do you have a name yet?'

Hayley's husband couldn't wipe the dopey new-dad smile from his face. 'Dillon. We're going to call him Dillon.'

Sean came into the room with a smile. 'Perfect. I'm just in time. I'm Dr Anderson. I'll check your little man over in a few seconds, folks.'

He spoke with Jacob for a few minutes, checked Dillon over and declared him well with perfect APGARs. He gave them a little nod. 'I'll be back again when your next baby arrives. Good luck, guys.'

Kerry stayed with the new baby for another few minutes while Bonnie checked over Hayley again. The labour progressed quickly with the next baby's head being delivered; however, within a few seconds Bonnie frowned as another contraction hit. She turned rapidly to Jacob, keeping her voice very calm.

'I think we've got a shoulder dystocia.' Jacob moved over to the bed immediately but Bonnie had things under control. 'Hayley, your second baby has got a little stuck—

their shoulder is stuck behind your pubic bone. Dr Layton and I are going to help you change position to try and get your baby out as soon as possible. I need you to stop pushing for a second until we help you into position.'

Jacob didn't interrupt at all. He just positioned himself at the side of the bed. Bonnie kept talking calmly and smoothly. 'We're going to do something called the McRoberts manoeuvre. I need you to lie on your back and pull up your legs as far as you can. Kerry will help on one side, and Dr Layton on the other. This will make it easier to get your baby out.' Kerry handed the little boy back over to his dad.

Bonnie gave a little nod to Jacob. 'Dr Layton is going to push down on your tummy when you have the next contraction. This should free your baby's shoulder. It might be a little uncomfortable.' Bonnie glanced at the clock. She had to keep watch. A baby's umbilical cord could become compressed with shoulder dystocia. If they didn't get the baby out in the next few minutes, Hayley would need to go for an emergency Caesarean section.

The contraction hit right on cue. Bonnie eased her hands in to give a gentle pull on the baby as Jacob attempted to press the pelvic bone and release the baby's shoulder. After a few tense seconds, Hayley gave a yelp and the baby slid into Bonnie's hands.

Kerry had already sounded the alarm and Sean was waiting with outstretched arms to check over the baby. He only took a few minutes. It was important. Babies who had shoulder dystocia could have damage to the nerves in their shoulder, arm and hand. Some could have breathing difficulties if their cord had been compressed. But after a few minutes Sean pronounced the baby well. 'Congratulations, Mum and Dad, here's your new baby girl.'

Hayley and Jordan beamed. Bonnie stayed in position. After a few minutes Hayley delivered her placenta and Bonnie did her further checks. 'Have you got a name for your daughter?'

Hayley nodded. 'Carly. We're going to call her Carly.'

Kerry came over with the other baby. 'Dillon and Carly. They're beautiful names for your children. Congratulations.' She handed Dillon back over to his dad. 'Dillon was six pounds twelve, and Carly six pounds four. Good weights. Sean said he'd be back to check them again later but there's no reason for them to go to Special Care.'

Hayley and Jordan smiled at each other. They were clearly in the new parenthood haze. Bonnie remembered it well.

Her heart sank a little—just as it always did at this stage. Robert, her ex, had never looked at her the way Jordan was looking at his wife. Robert had just looked permanently stunned. The same expression he'd had on his face when she'd found him in bed with her best friend. He hadn't been ready for marriage. With hindsight, they both hadn't.

Robert had been her boyfriend for barely a year when she'd fallen unexpectedly pregnant. His parents were traditionalists and had wanted them to get married. And now, Bonnie realised she'd been more swept away with the *idea* of being in love, rather than actually *being* in love. Maybe, at heart, she'd always known that Robert wasn't marriage material.

But what hurt most of all, despite her best efforts, was the fact he hadn't made any attempt at all to see Freya since they'd separated. It turned out Robert hadn't been father material either.

Cambridge was the chance of a new start. She didn't want to make the same mistakes again. She was determined not to get swept away in some ill-fated romance. Not when she had Freya to think about.

She loved her job. She always had. But sometimes, especially at an emotional delivery, she was struck by the connection between the parents of the new baby. Freya was everything to her. But sometimes it made her a tiny bit envious that she was missing out on something she'd never experienced.

It was pathetic really. Most people didn't get the fairy tale. Most people got relationships that were hard work—and she knew that. But it didn't stop her craving the impossible.

She tidied up in the room and got one of the domestics to make Hayley some tea and toast. Most women said that their post-delivery tea and toast was the best in the world.

Kerry tapped her on the shoulder. 'It's nearly your finishing time. I'm going to help Hayley with breast-feeding and will hand over to the next shift. Thanks for the help, Bonnie.'

Bonnie gave a smile. 'No problem, you're welcome.' She took the dirty laundry with her to the sluice, disposed of it and washed her hands again.

Jacob appeared at her back. 'I think that was one of the smoothest shoulder dystocia deliveries I've ever seen. Good call.'

Bonnie shook her head. 'That was pure luck. We both know things could have been different. I was actually breathing a sigh of relief as soon as that baby came out.'

Jacob rested his hand on the small of her back. 'Believe me, so was I. I didn't like the thought of a quick sprint down the corridor to Theatre.'

She could feel his warm hand through her thin scrubs. The warmth was radiating across the small of her back. When was the last time a man had touched her? She couldn't even remember.

She turned her shoulder just a little so she was looking up at him. She hadn't moved enough to let his hand fall. She didn't want it to break contact with her. 'Thank you, Jacob,' she said quietly.

'What for?' He tilted his head to the side. She was only inches away from those green eyes that sparkled with flecks of gold. This was the closest she'd ever been to him. She could see the tiny emerging shadow of stubble along his chin—even though she knew he'd shaved this morning. Her fingers itched to reach up and touch.

The weariness that had been on his face the first day she'd met him had seemed to gradually disperse. On occasion, Jacob still looked tired. But there had been something else that first day—a little despair? Jacob was still a mystery to her. The only thing she knew for sure was that he didn't have a woman in his life and for some reason that made her happy. Not that she'd ever admit that to anyone—not even Jessica.

'For not interfering,' she was whispering, even though there was no need. The rush and bustle of the ward was still going on in the corridor outside, but this seemed like a private conversation. 'For not coming over all "doctor" and trying to take over. For giving me a chance to do my job.'

He leaned forwards just a little. One inch. That was the space currently between them. She held her breath. If she breathed out right now, her warm breath would touch his skin.

But there was a problem. As she'd breathed in, she'd

breathed in *him*. Jacob. The faintest aroma of this morning's aftershave. The scent of his skin. She could almost swear she'd just breathed in a whole host of pheromones. What other explanation could there be for the fact she was feeling the slightest bit light-headed? She'd never been light-headed in her life.

'I'll always give you the space to do your job, Bonnie. From what I've seen you're excellent at it. I have faith you. The staff have faith in you. The patients have faith in you. You're a real asset to Cambridge Maternity. And I look after my staff.'

Her lungs were going to explode. She had to breathe out. She really did. Her insides were all over the place. It was the way he'd said it. The way he'd looked into her eyes and told her he had faith in her. She leaned back a little against his hand and tilted her chin up towards him. 'Thank you, Jacob.'

They froze. Neither of them moving. Their eyes locked together.

'Bonnie, can you just sign…? Oh, sorry.'

They sprang apart. It was stupid. They hadn't been doing anything but Bonnie could feel the colour rushing into her face.

Ellis, one of the midwives, was standing with a delivery note in her hand. Her eyes darted between them; it was quite obvious she was cringing and that made Bonnie do the same.

'That's fine, Ellis. I was just washing up after the twin delivery. Did you hear that things went well?' She was back into professional mode. She didn't even look back, just took long strides towards Ellis, taking the delivery note from her hand and walking over to the nurses' station, pulling a pen from her pocket.

She was trying to appear as calm and professional as possible. As if nothing at all had been going on between them. Because that was true. Nothing had been going on between them.

So why was her heart thudding against her chest and why did her cheeks feel as if they were on fire? And why was Ellis looking at her as if she would be the next topic of conversation on the hospital grapevine?

Ellis took the paperwork and disappeared back down the corridor. Bonnie sucked in a deep breath. What on earth was wrong with her? She'd almost wanted him to kiss her in the sluice at work. Even the thought of that sent a shiver down her spine—it was hardly the most romantic place in the world.

But it hadn't been about the place. It had been about the moment. The feel of Jacob's hand at the small of her back and the way she could see all the tiny lines around his perfect green eyes.

She squeezed her eyes shut. Even her thoughts were getting ridiculous. She had to speak to him. She had to try and understand what was going on. She had to draw a line here. She wasn't looking for any kind of romance. And definitely not with her new boss—no matter how much he just made her tingle. She spun around towards the sluice again.

But Jacob was gone.

CHAPTER FIVE

SOMETHING WAS DIFFERENT. Something had changed. And Jacob couldn't quite put his finger on what it was.

All he knew was he was currently sitting on his sofa watching an animated movie with a five-year-old. If someone had told him two weeks ago this was what he'd be doing he'd never have believed it.

'Who's your favourite dwarf?' whispered Freya. She'd insisted on the main light being turned off and eating ice cream as if they were at the movies. He'd never really developed a taste for ice cream but rocky road was hitting the spot.

'I like that one,' he said, pointing at the screen.

'He's my favourite too.' She jumped up and a big dollop of ice cream landed on his lap. 'Oops,' she said.

He shrugged and scooped the ice cream off his jeans with his fingers and dumped it in his mouth. Freya went into uncontrollable kinks of laughter.

All he knew for sure was that the big black cloud that felt as if it were permanently circling above his head had moved a little higher for the past two weeks. Maybe it was the fact that he was now in the waiting cycle. His treatment was over. He didn't feel quite so snappy. He certainly didn't feel so tired. And he was free to work with patients again the way he had before.

Something had definitely improved his mood. Even the junior doctors, who constantly got everything wrong and couldn't do the most basic of procedures, weren't annoying him as much as usual. He'd only thrown one out of Theatre the other day, instead of the usual four. People would think he was getting soft. He just wasn't quite sure if it was the treatment that had improved his mood or the home circumstances.

Living with Bonnie and Freya was certainly out of his normal experience. Freya had a way of winding him around her little finger. He wasn't quite sure if it was a five-year-old's mastermind plot, or if she did it purely unintentionally.

She jumped up from the sofa and over to her school bag, which was lying on the floor. 'Look at this!' she said as she pulled out a crumpled drawing. 'I made this for you at school today.' It was a painting of a man—with very big ears. He couldn't help it—he started to laugh.

She bounced back up on the sofa next to him. 'It's you. Do you like it?' Her little face was so expectant, just waiting for his approval.

He touched his ears. 'Are they really this big?'

'Yes,' she said without a moment's hesitation. 'Can we put it up on the fridge? That's where my mummy used to put my pictures.' She tugged at his hand and he let her pull him up and lead him through to the kitchen.

Bonnie was wiping a glass bowl clean as they walked through. 'Look what I made for Jacob,' Freya shouted as she waved the picture. 'We're going to put it up.'

Bonnie glanced at the picture and tried to stifle a laugh. 'I think that's lovely, honey,' she said. She raised her eyebrows at Jacob. 'Wait and I'll find you something to put that up with.' She opened a nearby drawer and pulled out a fridge magnet he didn't even know he owned. It seemed impolite not to put it up so he stuck it on the fridge.

Freya's little face was beaming. 'Come on,' she said, tugging at his arm again. 'My favourite song's about to start.'

He'd always loved his home. His sanctuary. His way of getting away from the outside world. But although his peace had been shattered, it was nowhere near as invasive as he might have thought.

He almost looked forward to coming home to them at night. And he couldn't work out why. Maybe it was the distraction. He didn't have time to think about the stuff hanging over his head. He didn't have time to consider what he would do if the test results weren't good—if the non-Hodgkin's lymphoma hadn't been halted in its tracks.

He didn't have time to remember how his mum had died of the horrible disease and how he could have the same future ahead of him. These were the things that used to spin around his head every night when he went to bed.

'Jacob, *come on*.' The little voice was impatient. He hadn't even realised that he'd been staring at Bonnie's backside in her snug jeans again. She spun around and gave a little smile as she put some cutlery back in a kitchen drawer.

She looked relaxed. She looked happy. She looked comfortable in his home. Something flipped over inside. He wasn't quite sure how he felt about all this.

She tilted her head to the side. 'Should I get us some

wine to see us through the rest of the movie?' She was smiling again.

He gave a nod as he let Freya lead him back through to the front room and he heard the clink of glasses being pulled from the cupboard.

Their *almost* kiss in the sluice would no doubt haunt his dreams tonight.

What had happened?

He knew it was something. It was definitely something.

There had been a tiny moment when…just *something* could have happened. He'd felt it. And he was pretty sure she'd felt it too. He'd seen it in her all too expressive eyes.

They'd spent the last week tiptoeing around each other. But that hadn't stopped the buzz in the air between them. It hadn't stopped the way their gazes kept connecting with each other.

He'd spent so long concentrating on his disease and trying to get well again that he was out of practice with all this. But even though it was winter, the temperature here was definitely rising.

It was official. Bonnie Reid was keeping him awake at night.

But why did that seem like a good thing and not a bad?

It was her day off and she was prowling around the house. She couldn't help it. This weekend she would be working on Saturday as part of her rota for the hospital. It was fine. Lynn was happy to have Freya for the day and planned to take her and her boys to London Zoo.

But Bonnie wasn't used to having time to herself. She'd cleaned what she could without offending the housekeeper. She'd learned very quickly what was unacceptable for her to do in the house. All her and Freya's laundry was washed and ironed and sitting in neat piles. The beds were made, the shopping done.

She gave a little shudder. The house was getting cold. There had been a dip in the temperature in the last few days and she wasn't quite sure how the heating worked in this house. She wasn't quite sure how Jacob would feel if he found out she was tampering with the settings on his heating. She walked across the front room, her footsteps echoing on the wooden floorboards, her hand running across the top of the mantelpiece.

There was an ornamental coal scuttle at her feet. She knelt down. It was filled with real coal. Jacob had said he hadn't got round to having the chimney swept.

She gave another shudder. Nothing would be nicer at this time of year than a real fire burning in this gorgeous fireplace.

She stood upright. That was what she could do. Jacob didn't seem to have any objections to a real fire. He'd just made it sound as if he hadn't got round to it. He wouldn't accept any money from her and, to be honest, it felt a little embarrassing. Maybe paying to have the chimney professionally swept would be a way to try and repay him a little for his kindness?

She didn't hesitate. This was the best idea she'd had in a while. She walked out to the hallway and dug around for the phone book. They were in the middle of Cambridge. There were lots of traditionally built houses around here. There must a local chimney sweep.

Jacob was on call. He might even not be home at all tonight. Sometimes he ended up just staying at the hospital if he was on call. As the consultant he would be called if there was any emergency with a patient. He'd already told her that he wasn't entirely sure that all the junior members of staff would page him. Some of them still seemed a little nervous around him. She'd tried not to laugh when he'd said that to her.

She picked up the phone and dialled. By the time Jacob got home tonight—or maybe tomorrow morning—she'd have a lovely fire burning in the fireplace, heating up the whole house and giving the place a more homely feel.

He'd love it. She was sure he would.

The first thing he'd noticed was the strange smell. Ever since Bonnie had arrived his house had smelled of those clean laundry candles that she insisted on lighting everywhere. They actually made his nose itch but he wasn't inclined to tell her.

She'd waved some red and green ones under his nose the other night and told him she'd bought some Christmas spice candles. If this was what they smelled like he'd be blowing them straight out.

She still hadn't picked up on his hints about Christmas. The main fact being he just didn't do it.

There was a strange noise to his left. It sounded like a sniffle. Or more like a sob.

He sneezed. Something was definitely irritating him.

'Jacob? Is that you?'

Bonnie. Her voice sounded panicked. He dropped his bag at the door and lengthened his stride, walking into his front room.

Or walking into the room that used to be his front room.

Bonnie was on her hands and knees on the floor, a basin next to her, scrubbing away at the floorboards.

Freya was sitting on a towel on the faraway leather sofa playing with her dolls.

He sucked in a breath at the sight of his perfect white walls.

They weren't perfect any more. There was a huge black streak that seemed to have puffed out from the fireplace and left an ugly, angry, giant-sized handprint on the wall.

Bonnie jumped up to speak to him. Soot was smudged across her cheeks and forehead, even discolouring her dark auburn hair. The front of her T-shirt was dirty, as were the knees of her trousers. 'Oh, Jacob. I'm so sorry. I thought I would have a chance to clean this up before you got home.'

He stepped forwards into the room and held out his hands. 'What on earth happened?'

Freya tutted from her sofa and shook her head. 'Naughty Mummy.' She fixed her eyes on Bonnie. 'Told you,' she said in the voice of someone at least fifty years older than her.

Tears streaked down Bonnie's face. 'I thought it might be a nice idea to get the chimney swept for you. You know—so you could come home to a nice warm fire. The house was so cold today. So I contacted a chimney sweep. And they seemed so professional. They even put a covering on the floor and some kind of plastic seal around the fireplace. But when he swept the chimney, there must have been a gap.' She turned to face the blighted wall again as her voice wobbled. 'And it just seemed to go everywhere. And they tried to clean up, they really did. And they've promised to come back tomorrow and re-paint the walls.'

He should be angry. But Bonnie was babbling. Just

as she had that first day he'd met her. Just as she did when she was really, really nervous and thought she'd just blown things.

It was kind of endearing. But he'd never tell her that. 'Okay,' he said quietly.

She looked confused. Another tear streaked down her smudged face. 'Go and get washed up. I'll finish the clean-up.'

He was too tired to be angry. He'd wanted to come home to a quiet house and rest. But the days of coming home to a quiet house were over. He could never imagine a house being quiet while Freya stayed there. She was questioning. She was curious. She was relentless.

Her head bobbed up from the menagerie of dolls she had accumulated on the other sofa. She shot him a smile. 'Hi, Jacob. How many babies did you see today?'

'Four,' he said promptly.

This had turned into a game. She asked every day. She frowned at him. 'Just four. Your record is six. You'll need to do better.'

'I agree.' He nodded towards Bonnie. 'On you go. Go and get showered. Freya will be fine.'

Bonnie still seemed surprised by his mediocre reaction. The truth was he was surprised by his reaction too. If he waited to see the chimney sweep tomorrow the re-action might not be quite so contained. But he wouldn't do that either.

He noticed the extra coal scuttle by the fire that contained wood-burning logs. Bonnie must have bought them to help light the fire.

When was the last time someone had done something like this for him? Sure, a few of his friends had offered help when they knew about his diagnosis. Hope and Isabel were the only two people—apart from his consultant—in the entire hospital who knew about his diagnosis. He'd worked with Hope for years and even though Isabel had only arrived a few months ago he'd known straight away she was completely trustworthy. When she'd caught him being sick in the sluice one day she'd just pulled the door closed and come over and asked what was wrong.

Both tried to help by feeding him various items of food. Hope had even tried to bake chocolate muffins for him and Isabel had handed him some tubs of beef casserole to stick in the freezer. Anything to get him to eat and keep his strength up. But he was embarrassed to say he'd only been minimally grateful. He was so focused on people not knowing what was wrong that he didn't really want to accept help.

This felt different. This was nothing about his illness. Bonnie knew nothing about that at all—and that was the way he liked it. The last thing he wanted to see on her face was pity.

This was something spontaneous. Something completely unique to him and her. Of course, she currently felt indebted to him. And that did kind of irk. But the fact she'd wanted to do something for *him*…just warmed him from the inside out.

He finished scrubbing the floor and carried the basin of dirty water back through to the kitchen, scrubbing his hands and turning the oven on for dinner. He put on the TV for Freya and headed upstairs into the shower. It only took two minutes to wash the smell of the hospital from his skin and hair, and pull on some jeans and a T-shirt.

As he headed back along the corridor Bonnie passed him on the stairs carrying Freya in her arms. 'Sorry,' she whispered. 'I made her dinner earlier and she's knackered. I'm just going to put her to bed. I didn't get a chance to put anything on for our dinner.'

Jacob noticed the circles under her eyes. He didn't want her to feel as if she had to do anything for him. 'How about I make it simple? Beans on toast?'

She smiled. It was the first genuine smile that he'd seen today. 'Perfect. Thank you.'

His culinary skills were just about up to beans on toast. He opened a bottle of white wine and spent a few minutes setting a new fire and lighting it. As his fingers touched the coal he was swamped by a whole host of memories. Last time he'd lit a fire he'd been trying to keep his shivering mother warm. She'd been at the stage when she'd been permanently cold, even though their house hadn't been cold.

Once she'd died, he'd never gone to the bother of cleaning out the fireplace and restocking it. Neither had his father.

The fire lit quickly. Probably due to the modern firelighters. By the time he'd finished the dinner in the kitchen and walked back through with them both on a tray, Bonnie was sitting on the leather sofa, mesmerised by the fire. She jumped when he set the tray down on the low wooden table. 'Give me a sec,' he said, before returning with the wine and two glasses.

Her freshly washed dark auburn hair was piled up in a loose knot on top of her head, with a few little curling strands escaping. She'd changed into her favourite jeans and a gold T-shirt with a few scattered sequins that caught the flickering flames from the fire. Her pale skin glowed in the light.

She sighed as he poured the wine and she settled the plate on her knees. 'I don't know if I deserve this.'

Jacob looked at her sideways. He couldn't hide the smile on his face. She seemed so despondent. 'I'm not sure you do either. But it's either we drink wine together, or we fight. Take your pick.' He held up his glass towards her.

She paused for a second before catching a glimpse of the laughter in his eyes, then lifted her glass and clinked it against his. 'I'm too tired to fight. I'll just drink the wine.'

They ate companionably together. Finishing the first glass of wine, then pouring another. Jacob hadn't bothered to put the TV or radio on. The only noise was the hiss and cracks coming from the fire.

Bonnie pulled her feet up onto the sofa, giving him a glimpse of her pink-painted toes.

'It's amazing, isn't it?'

He nodded. Watching the fire was quite mesmerising. He could easily lose a few hours a night doing this, particularly if he had a warm body lying next to him on the sofa. His guts twisted. Why hadn't he done this before?

'I'm sorry about the wall,' she whispered again.

His eyes fixed on hers in the flickering firelight. They gleamed in the orange and yellow light. He looked over to the black ugly mark on the wall and couldn't help but start to laugh.

It was hideous. But it could be fixed. By tomorrow it would be freshly painted and forgotten about. His shoulders started to shake, the wine in his glass swaying from side to side.

'What did you say when it happened?' He could barely get the words out for laughter.

She started to laugh too and shook her head. 'You've no idea. I was in the kitchen with Freya and I just heard this whooshing noise and a thump. The guy landed on his backside in the middle of the floor. He looked as if he was about to be sick.'

Now the laughter had finally started she seemed relieved to get it out. 'Then I came through and just burst into tears. I don't think that helped him.'

'I'll bet it didn't.'

He turned towards her on the sofa, his arm already stretched behind her head. It was only natural she turned towards him too.

'Please tell me you're not really mad with me.'

He shook his head and reached his finger up to touch her cheek. He didn't even think before he did it. It just seemed like the most natural act in the world. The act he'd wanted to do a few days before in the sluice room.

'I'm not mad at you. What you did was nice. It was thoughtful.' He gave a little shrug. 'I always meant to get around to it. It just never happened.' His voice tailed off a little. 'Other stuff got in the way.'

Her hand came up and rested on his bare arm. 'What other stuff?'

It was like a whole host of tiny electric shocks racing up his arm. He could feel the warmth of her skin next to his. All he wanted to do was grab her whole body and press it against his. Skin against skin.

'Nothing important. Work, that kind of stuff.' He didn't want to go there. Not with Bonnie. He didn't want to have any of those kinds of conversations with Bonnie. This thing between them. He didn't know what it was. But it seemed almost unreal. Not really acknowledged. Not really known by anyone but them.

She hesitated but didn't move her hand. She left it there in contact with his skin.

'I need some advice. I saw some other possible rentals today and one small flat that I could afford to buy. You need to tell me about the areas.'

The squeeze inside was so unexpected it made him jolt. He should be jumping for joy. But he strangely wasn't.

Sitting in the flickering firelight with Bonnie, watching the orange light glint off her auburn hair and light up her pale skin, giving her advice to leave seemed ridiculous.

It was just the two of them right now. In the glimmering light her bright blue eyes reflected off his. He was close enough to see the tiny freckles across the bridge of her nose.

But he wanted to be closer.

He licked his dry lips and watched as she mirrored his actions. This woman was going to drive him crazy.

'Where?' His voice was so low it was barely audible.

'One rental in Olderfield, one in Rancor and the flat is in Calderwood.' She named the prices for each.

He shook his head. 'Olderfield is not an area you want to stay in.' It was almost a relief to say those words. 'The price of the rental in Rancor is nearly three hundred pounds a month above any other. It sounds like a bit of a con. As for Calderwood—it's nice. It's fine. But it's the other side of the city. You'd need to change Freya's school again. Do you really want to do that?'

Everything he was saying was safe and rational. It was sensible.

But that wasn't how he was feeling right now.

He'd inched closer. And so had she.

It was almost as if an invisible force were drawing them together. Pushing them together. He could feel her warm breath dancing across his skin. The scent she'd put on after showering was pervading its way around him, wrapping round like a tentacle and reeling him in.

He had absolutely no wish or desire to resist it. None at all.

He was trying to read what was in her eyes. He was sure he could see passion burning there. She hadn't moved; she hadn't flinched. She just unobtrusively moved even closer, slotting under his arm as though she were meant to be there.

And for the first time it felt as if someone *was* meant to be there.

The flickering fire didn't just bathe the room and her skin in warm light. It made him feel different inside. It made him feel that the thing that was missing from this home might finally be there.

There was no time for talk.

He moved forwards, his lips against hers.

It was the lightest of touches. The merest hint of what was to come.

She let out a little sigh and her hand moved up to his shoulder, as if she was going to pull him closer.

The tiny voice came out of nowhere, cutting through the building heat in the room.

'Mummy?'

They sprang apart. Both of them realising what had almost happened. Bonnie was on her feet in an instant and out of the door, running up the stairs to the little voice at the top of them.

Jacob was left in the room. His breathing ragged and

his soul twisting like the ugly black mark on the wall. Was he mad?

What had he nearly done? She was a colleague. For a few minutes he'd completely forgotten about the little girl upstairs.

What could have happened next?

He stood up and flicked on the light, flooding the room with a bright white glare and dousing the flames in an instant.

It was time to pretend this had never happened.

CHAPTER SIX

'Wow, WHAT'S GOING on with Jacob Layton?' Kerry came through the theatre doors and walked to the sink, scrubbing her hands post-surgery.

Bonnie glanced over her shoulder as Isabel walked out of the theatre doors too, ripping off her gloves and gown and joining Kerry at the sink. 'I know.' The two of them exchanged glances and smiled at each other. 'I wonder what's changed his mood.'

Isabel's eyes met Bonnie's and an uncomfortable shiver went down her spine. 'What are you talking about?' she asked.

Kerry rolled her eyes. 'I dropped an instrument tray in Theatre. Usually, Jacob would have gone nuts and I'd have been flung out of Theatre.'

'Really?' Bonnie frowned. She'd heard of surgeons being extreme in Theatre. But she'd never experienced it herself. She certainly didn't like the thought of one of the obstetricians she worked with behaving like that. She wouldn't stand for it.

But Isabel and Kerry were still smiling at her as they finished drying their hands. 'What's that Scottish word you use to describe people who are grumpy or miserable?'

Bonnie was a bit unsure where this was going. 'Crabbit.' She used it quite a lot, along with a whole host of other Scottish words that were second nature to her, but seemed to leave the staff baffled.

Isabel and Kerry exchanged smiles again. Isabel deposited her paper towels in the bin. 'It's a good word. A very descriptive word.' She turned to her colleague. 'Kerry, would you say that Jacob's been crabbit lately?'

Kerry crossed the room. 'Nope. I'd say Jacob's had a whole new personality transplant. He didn't shout at all today. He just looked up and asked me to get him a new set of instruments. The whole Theatre was shocked.'

Bonnie frowned. 'Jacob normally behaved like that in Theatre?'

Isabel laughed. 'Not just Theatre. Labour suite, wards, clinics, the neonatal unit.' She held up her hand. 'Don't get me wrong, he would always switch on the charm for the patients, but for the staff?' She shook her head. 'Oh, no.'

Kerry put her hands on her hips. 'And both of you ladies haven't been here that long. A few years ago, Jacob was always Doctor Charming. But then just over a year ago he changed—practically overnight. He's been like a bear with a sore head ever since. Or he had been...' she turned to face Bonnie '...until a few weeks ago.'

Bonnie shifted uncomfortably on her feet. Two pairs of eyes were staring at her, smiling. 'I have no idea what you mean.'

Isabel walked past and tapped her on the shoulder. 'I don't know what it is you're doing. But all I can say is— keep doing it.'

Kerry nodded in agreement as the doors swung open again. It was Sean, the new obstetrician who'd arrived from Melbourne just a few weeks before Bonnie. 'Hi, ladies, sorry to interrupt. Isabel, can we talk?'

Something flickered across Isabel's face. It was the strangest look Bonnie had seen in a while. She couldn't quite put her finger on it. Something between complete avoidance and dread. It seemed that Jess Black had been right.

Isabel was super friendly and completely confident about the work she did. This was the first time that Bonnie had seen her look neither.

'It will only take a few minutes, Isabel.' Sean looked tired, but it seemed he wasn't going to be put off.

Her eyes flitted over to Bonnie. 'Didn't you want me to see a patient on the labour suite?'

'Eh…yes.' Bonnie knew avoidance tactics when she saw them. And there was no way she wasn't going to help out a colleague. Particularly when this might take the heat off her.

In a way it was good that people thought Jacob was more amenable. The question was—what had been wrong with him before? She had no idea. She and her daughter were living with a guy they hardly knew. She'd almost kissed him the other night! If Freya hadn't shouted…

She was crazy. She was plainly crazy. Jacob was her boss. Her brand-new boss. The last thing she should be doing on this planet was kissing the boss—no matter how much she'd wanted to.

She bit her lip. She was new here. She hadn't even had time to find her feet yet. Her new job was a big responsibility. *That* was where she should be focusing her attention.

She had Freya to think about. Her little girl had already been exposed to one disastrous relationship—there was no way she wanted to expose her to another. It was too soon. Far too soon.

It was time to focus on work—and only work. She wouldn't allow thoughts of Jacob to distract her from her job.

Sean disappeared back out of the doors, sighing loudly. Isabel's eyes flickered towards Bonnie. 'Thanks,' she said before putting her head down and disappearing out of another door.

Kerry folded her arms across her chest. 'This place just gets more interesting by the second.'

Bonnie gave a little smile and shake of her head as she headed to the door. 'Kerry, you have no idea.'

Jacob was feeling strangely nervous. One of the other obstetricians had been off sick for a few days and he'd covered their on-call rota. It meant that he and Bonnie hadn't really been alone together for the last few days.

The front room was back to normal. The walls freshly painted and bright white again. Except, the room wasn't back to normal. The room had changed. And the mood of the house had changed with it.

The temperature seemed to have dropped permanently in the last few days. It meant that every time he walked through the front door of his house, his feet turned automatically to the fireplace in the front room.

Bonnie was right. There was something about a fireplace. He was drawn to it like the proverbial moth to a flame. Last night he'd even contemplated buying a rug to put in front of it. He'd never really thought about soft furnishings before. He wasn't that kind of guy. He was all about the basics. The functional stuff.

Except that last night he'd spent an hour on the Internet wondering what colour rug to buy.

Now his fingers hovered over something else. Freya

had been really excited the other night when she'd seen the advert for the latest kids' Christmas film. It had been years since Jacob had gone to the movies. He'd still been in his early twenties.

He glanced at the film times before clicking to buy tickets. It was Tuesday night. Freya and Bonnie didn't do anything on a Tuesday. Monday was dancing, Wednesday was Rainbow Brownies. He couldn't believe that after a few weeks he actually knew this kind of stuff. It was all so alien to him.

Once he'd bought the tickets he looked for a restaurant. For the first time in his life, Jacob Layton picked up the phone to ask if his favourite place to eat had a children's menu. It had never crossed his mind before.

It was odd. This wasn't a date. This wasn't anything like that.

He just wanted to have some time away from the hospital, away from the house, and to spend a little time with Bonnie and Freya.

He was planning. He was being rational. But little voices in his brain were screaming at him. He didn't do this kind of stuff. Well, of course, he'd taken a woman to dinner before. The truth was he'd done that on *lots* of occasions. But incorporating a child into his plans? This was a whole new concept for him.

Bonnie appeared at the door. 'Jacob? Outpatients just phoned. Lisa Brennan, a thirty-three-year-old diabetic who is in for her twenty-week scan. They're having a few problems and wondered if you could go down. The sonographer is new and thinks there may be an anomaly but isn't quite sure.'

He stood up straight away. 'No problem. I'll go now.'

He paused in the doorway. 'I thought maybe we could do something tonight?'

A look of mild panic flickered across Bonnie's face and his stomach dropped. 'I mean, you, me and Freya. I was thinking about that new film she wanted to see. What do you think?'

He was babbling now. Doing the thing that he found so endearing in Bonnie. Why had she looked panicked? Did she really want to say no? Maybe he was reading things all wrong.

Her lips pressed together and after a few seconds the edges turned upwards. 'Freya would love that. It's a great idea.'

He brushed past her. 'Good. I'll book tickets and maybe we could grab some dinner first?'

He kept walking down the corridor as she gave the slightest nod of her head. He didn't want to tell her he'd already booked the tickets and the restaurant. That would seem presumptuous.

It was the oddest feeling. Jacob hadn't felt this nervous asking a girl out since he was a teenager. For a second, he'd thought she might actually say no.

As he turned the corner at the bottom of the corridor Bonnie was still standing at the office door with a smile on her face.

For a second he felt sixteen again. It was all he could do not to punch the air.

Bonnie was nervous—and that was ridiculous. She looked at the clothes laid out on her bed. Nothing seemed to suit.

'Wear the Christmas jumper, Mummy!' said Freya as she bounced in the room. 'We can match.'

Bonnie blinked. Freya hadn't been wearing that jumper a few minutes ago. She was going through a stage of changing her clothes constantly—and putting everything she'd worn for ten minutes in the washing basket.

She smiled. 'Well, I suppose it is officially December now.' She pulled the black jumper, adorned with a bright green Christmas tree and glittering red sequins for the Christmas baubles, over her head. As soon as she pulled it on she felt more comfortable.

That was what was wrong. She was fretting over what to wear as if this were actually a *date*. And it wasn't. But it had felt like that when Jacob had asked her. It had given her that warm, tingly feeling that spread throughout her body and stayed there all day.

Ridiculous. This was Jacob being polite and taking out his house guests. And if there hadn't been that soft, sizzling kiss a few nights ago that might have been a rational thought. It might have been brief but she couldn't get the feel of Jacob's lips out of her mind.

'Come on, Mummy.' Bonnie pulled on her favourite jeans and stuck her feet into her boots. She'd put makeup on this morning and had no wish to do it again, so just reapplied some lipstick. There. Ready.

Jacob was waiting for them at the bottom of the stairs as they walked down. The look of appreciation and smile he gave her made the little fire inside light up again.

'I can't wait to see this film,' chattered Freya. 'Three people at school have seen it already and they said it's brilliant. The princess dances on ice and the prince lives underneath the water.'

'Are you sure you're up for this?' Bonnie asked.

But he smiled. 'Oh, I'm sure. I'm sure in the next few days every adult will have seen this film too and it's all we'll hear about.' He opened the front door. 'I booked Paulette's Italian. Are you okay with that? I thought it would suit Freya since spaghetti bolognaise is her favourite food.'

She'd expected to go to the nearest fast-food restaurant. Jacob Layton was proving to be more than a little surprising.

It only took ten minutes to reach the cinema complex and the nearby restaurant. Dinner was almost a disaster. Freya was too excited to eat and ended up wearing most of her spaghetti rather than eating it. But the food was good and the company even better.

Jacob was careful not to talk shop in front of Freya— or ask Bonnie any difficult questions about being back in Scotland. He asked Freya about school and her friends, and Bonnie about her favourite things and how she was settling in.

She took a sip of her glass of wine. 'I love CRMU. The staff are really friendly. A few of them have invited me out—Isabel, Hope and Jessica. But it's difficult. If we were still at home I could ask my mum and dad to babysit. Going out in the evenings in Cambridge isn't really an option for me.'

Jacob hesitated. His fork poised just before his mouth. 'I could do it.'

She almost choked. 'What? No, I couldn't ask you to do that.'

'I mean, as long as I wasn't on call or anything. I mean, once Freya's had dinner and done her homework, there's really no problem. We could watch a film together and then it would be time for bed.'

Bonnie shook her head, glancing sideways at Freya, who seemed to have missed the conversation. 'That's so kind of you to offer. But no, Jacob, I wouldn't do that to you.' She paused for a second. 'I could always ask Lynn, the childminder. I'm sure she would say it was okay.' She put her hand around Freya's shoulder. 'But I'm just not ready to do that yet. We've had a lot of change in a short period of time. I'd like her to feel really settled before I start thinking about going out.'

Jacob nodded thoughtfully then shrugged. 'Okay. But the offer is there if you need it.'

'Is it time for the film yet?' cut in Freya, smiling, with her bolognaise-smeared face.

Bonnie glanced at her watch as she wiped Freya's face with a napkin. 'I think it is. Are you ready to go?'

Freya bounced out of her seat. 'I'm ready. Let's go and see the princess.'

Jacob paid their bill and helped Freya on with her jacket before they walked the short distance to the cinema. It was already busy, with numerous excitable children all waiting to see the film. The noise level was incredible.

Jacob winced. 'Is every kids' show like this?'

Bonnie nodded. 'Believe it or not, they do go quiet when the film starts.'

They collected their tickets and bought some popcorn, then filed into the cinema and found their seats. Freya changed seats three times. Sitting between them, then on one side of Bonnie, on one side of Jacob and back to the middle again. She leaned forwards as the film started.

In the darkness of the cinema something struck Bonnie. Freya had never been to the cinema with her father. Robert had always managed to find an excuse not to go on family outings with them and the cinema had rapidly become a treat for Bonnie and Freya on their own.

This was the first time she'd actually been at the cinema with a man since she'd been born. Regret twisted inside Bonnie. She should have chosen better. Robert had never lived up to the role of a father, and now here was Jacob, a single man with no experience of kids, bending over backwards to be accommodating towards them.

She wasn't sure what all this meant, but it was so nice to feel considered. She appreciated it more than she could ever say.

She reached over in the darkness, across the space where Freya leaned forwards, and slid her hand into Jacob's. He turned towards her, surprise on his face.

'Thank you for doing this,' she whispered.

He smiled and gave her hand a squeeze, circling his thumb in her palm.

He kept it that way for the whole ninety-minute film. And she let him.

CHAPTER SEVEN

THE HOUSE WAS looking truly magical. Freya was watching from the window, the excitement almost too much for her.

Today had been a quiet day. It was odd. It was a few days into December already and there were still no decorations in the house. Bonnie had always been the type to put her decorations up on the first of the month. Any later made her antsy.

Yesterday, a few tree decorations had arrived that she'd ordered online. Along with a personalised stocking for Freya and some Christmas candles.

This morning she'd had a look in some of the cupboards around the house, expecting to find a few cardboard boxes of decorations that she and Freya could put up. But there was nothing. Not even a single strand of tinsel.

Maybe Jacob hadn't bothered because he lived alone? He'd already told her he worked at the hospital most Christmases. He'd made a few fleeting remarks about not really doing Christmas. But nothing definite. Nothing that he'd actually explained.

So, this morning she and Freya had hatched the master plan. Jacob was working today. It was a Saturday and there were a few patients in the hospital that needed to be reviewed, so she was sure he would be kept busy.

It gave her and Freya time to visit the local hardware store and stock up on Christmas decorations. The kind that she'd always wanted to buy. Her credit card had trembled as she'd entered the store and fainted on the way out.

She'd never bought a real tree before. But the hardware store could deliver on the same day, and only an hour after they'd left the store the delivery driver arrived. He was great. He carried the tree up the front steps and into the front room. It had already been mounted for them and he made sure it was straight before he left.

Freya had been jumping for joy as they'd plugged the twinkling star lights in to check they worked before winding them around the tree. By four o'clock it was already starting to get dark. Bonnie pulled the blinds in the front room. She didn't want Jacob to see the tree from the street. She wanted him to come through the front door and get the full effect.

A thick green and red garland was wound up the banister on the stairs. Another, set with red twinkling lights, was adorning the mantelpiece in the front room. The fire was burning in the hearth and she'd switched off the main lights so only the twinkling lights and flickering flames warmed the room.

Freya wound her hands around Bonnie's neck. 'It's so beautiful, isn't it, Mummy?'

'Yes, honey, it is.'

She so wanted Christmas to be perfect for her daughter. It was beginning to look as if they wouldn't have found somewhere else to stay by then. Her ex hadn't even tried to make contact with his daughter—not even once—since they'd moved down here.

It was no real surprise. He hadn't bothered when they'd stayed in the same town. But she was worried about the effect on her little girl. How must it feel for Freya to know her daddy didn't love her? Not the way he should.

They finished unpacking the last of the deliveries. A carved wooden nativity scene that Freya helped set out on one of the side tables. Everything really did look perfect.

She heard a car door slam outside and Freya ran and peeked under the blinds. 'Jacob's coming. He's coming, Mummy.' She jumped up and down on the spot clapping her hands.

Bonnie couldn't wipe the smile off her face. She stood in the corridor, just at the entrance to the front room— waiting for him to appear.

It only took a few seconds. He walked through the front door, dropping his case and hanging his jacket on the coat stand.

'Hey, Jacob.' She smiled.

He smiled back. 'Hey, yourself,' then started to frown. He gave a little start, his eyes fixed on the banister behind her.

'We've got a surprise,' yelled Freya, running through the door.

Bonnie's skin prickled, her hairs standing on end. He didn't look happy. He didn't look anything *like* happy. Her blood felt as if it were running cold.

All of a sudden she got the feeling that she'd done something very wrong.

Jacob strode past her and into the front room, virtually ignoring Freya.

His face fell as soon as he walked into the middle of the floor, holding his hands out as he spun around, taking in the full effect of the room. She loved it. It was beautiful and really captured the spirit of Christmas with the flickering flames and twinkling festive lights.

Anyone would love it.

Anyone but Jacob, that was.

He looked as if he'd just been sat down in his worst possible nightmare. He walked over to the fireplace and tugged harshly on the beautiful green and red garland, pulling part of it free. 'What on earth have you done?' His voice was incredulous. 'Tell me you're joking. You've done this everywhere? This?'

He stared at the greenery in his hand, then dropped it to the floor. Freya's mouth was hanging open. She was stunned—as was Bonnie—but, what was more, she looked a little frightened.

He walked over and grabbed the tree, knocking some of the carefully hung red and green ornaments to the floor, one of them breaking with a crash. 'Who on earth said you could do this? What made you think you could decorate my house without my permission?' In a surge of anger he pushed the tree to the floor, scattering the decorations everywhere and making the lights flicker dangerously.

He was furious. Really furious. So angry he was trembling. Bonnie had never, ever seen Jacob like this. And although she was bewildered, she wasn't afraid; in fact, she was angry. But he wasn't finished. He leaned over the fallen Christmas tree and started yanking the tinsel from it. The harshness of his movements meant the sitting-room air and floor quickly filled with tiny ripped-off strands of multicoloured tinsel all around them. 'I hate this. I have to tolerate this stuff everywhere else—but not in my house!'

She walked over and put her arm around Freya's shoulder. 'What is wrong with you, Jacob? We wanted to do something nice for you—to surprise you.'

But it was almost as if he hadn't heard her. He was still shaking his head at the twinkling lights. He crossed the room and flicked the switch on one of the plugs, plunging that part of the room into darkness.

Almost as dark as your mood was her fleeting thought as he turned on her again.

'How dare you do this? Didn't I tell you I don't celebrate Christmas? I don't even *like* Christmas.' The words were said with such venom she actually found herself pulling back a little. But it only lasted a second. Because after that the red mist started to descend.

All the hours of work and preparation. The build-up of excitement between her and Freya all day. And he was ruining it all with some angry words and some hand movements. Destroying all their hard work.

She dropped her arm from around Freya's shoulder and stepped right up to his face. 'Oh, I get that. I get that you don't like Christmas. Enough, Jacob!' she snapped. 'You've made your point. You don't like Christmas. Well, pardon me for not being a mind reader. And pardon me, and my daughter, for trying to do something to say thank you for letting us stay. We won't make that mistake again!'

She turned at the sound of a little sob behind her and dropped to her knees, wrapping her arms around Freya's little body. She would kill him. She would kill him with her bare hands for his pathetic overreaction.

Jacob flinched. It was as if reality had just slapped him on the forehead and he realised the impact his reactions had had on Freya. For the tiniest second he seemed to hesitate, but Bonnie glared at him, furious with him for upsetting her daughter, and he spun on his heel and stalked back along the corridor, slamming the front door behind him.

The blood was pounding in her ears. She'd never been so angry with someone—not even her pathetic husband when she'd found him in bed with her so-called friend. Freya's shoulders were shaking and her head was buried into the nape of Bonnie's neck.

Over Christmas decorations? Really?

She didn't care that this was his house. She didn't care that on every other occasion Jacob had been a kind and hospitable housemate. This blew everything else out of the water.

He'd upset her daughter.

Jacob Layton was about to find out that hell hath no fury like an angry mother.

'Isn't it about time you went home?'

He lifted his head from the bar and the barman gestured his head towards the clock. The guy obviously wanted to close up.

The old guy shrugged. 'Can't be that bad.'

Jacob picked up the now-warm remnants of beer and washed them down. 'You have no idea.'

He looked out through the murky window. It had started to snow. He didn't even have a jacket. In his haste to leave the house he hadn't stopped to pick one up.

How far had he walked? He had no idea. He'd never even been in this pub before. Let alone nearly fallen asleep at the bar.

He gave the barman a little nod and shivered as he walked out of the door and the wind whistled around his thin jumper. With his suit trousers and business shoes it was hardly winter gear. But he hadn't stopped to think about much before he left.

That was the trouble. He *couldn't* think. He'd taken one look at all those Christmas decorations and a whole host of unwanted memories had come flooding back.

It was ridiculous. It was pathetic. He'd spent every year of his life around Christmas decorations.

But not in his space. Not in his home. In other places, they were bearable. In other places there were other things to do, other things to think about. At home, they would be right under his nose constantly—forcing him to think about things he'd long since pushed to the back of his mind.

The cold wind started to penetrate through his thin jumper, making him shiver. His insides were cringing.

Freya.

Her little face had crumpled and she'd started to cry.

He was ashamed of himself. Ashamed of his behaviour. He hadn't even stopped to think about her. And everything about that was wrong.

What embarrassed him even more was the fact that if it had been just Bonnie, he might not be feeling so ashamed. It had taken a five-year-old to teach him what acceptable behaviour was. What kind of human being did that make him?

The kind that had spent the last three hours in a bar, like some sad and lonely old drifter sitting on a bar stool alone, nursing one bottle of beer after another.

Pathetic. Was that really the kind of man he wanted to be? Was that the kind of man that would have made his mother proud?

All of a sudden he wasn't feeling the cold any more. All of sudden he was lost in distant memories as his feet trudged through the snow, his dress shoes getting damper by the second as the memories of his mother burned deep in his mind.

She had complemented his closed-off father beautifully with her calming good nature. She was always able to put a smile on his father's often grumpy face, or give a measured argument against his forceful opinions—skills that Jacob hadn't seemed to inherit.

If his mother had still been alive he would never have ended up at loggerheads with his father over his refusal to follow the family tradition into the military. His mother would have argued peacefully, but successfully, for his entry to medical school and the opportunity to pursue his own career options.

His father had never really accepted his decision—particularly when Jacob had opted to become an obstetrician. It wasn't heroic enough for his father. It wasn't front line enough, or pioneering enough. He didn't see the joy in bringing life into the world, compared with so many other specialities that frequently dealt with death. Just as well his mother had left him enough money, not only to put himself through medical school, but also to allow him the freedom to place a deposit on a house and have the option of being part of one of the finest universities and hospitals in the country.

She *would* be proud of him. She *should* be proud of him. She would love what her son had achieved.

But she would also expect him to treat everyone with the same respect he'd given her. With the love and compassion he'd given her.

The long street ahead was coated with snow. The orange streetlights cast a warm glow across the snow-topped cars. People spilled out of the pub ahead of him, laughing and joking. Full of cheer.

When was the last time he'd been in Cambridge city centre on a Saturday night? He couldn't even remember. Now he looked around him, Christmas was everywhere. Every shop window was decorated and a few of the flats on the main street had glistening trees in their windows.

He hung his head as the cold bit harder. Festive cheer. It should be spreading warmth through his soul. What on earth was he going home to?

His footsteps quickened as a horrible thought shot through his head. What if they'd left? What if they'd left because of his behaviour?

The beer sloshed around in his stomach. He hadn't eaten at all in the last few hours and that last thought made him feel physically sick.

The thought of going home to an empty house after a month wasn't at all appealing. It was strange how things had changed without him really noticing. *Please don't let them leave.* He would much prefer it if Bonnie was waiting at home ready to tell him exactly what she thought of him. He could take it.

He might even try and explain why he'd behaved like that—if, of course, she gave him a chance to speak.

The snow was getting heavier. It was kicking up under his feet and lying on his shoulders and eyelashes. His feet moved even quicker. How far had he walked?

It was a relief to finally turn into his street. Only a few windows were uncovered, letting their warm light spill out onto the snow-covered street. From a distance, he could see his tightly pulled white blinds.

He swallowed. His mouth had never felt so dry. Drinking beer certainly hadn't helped. More than anything right now he just wanted to know what lay behind his door.

He had to stop himself from breaking into a run. His brain was spinning. What would he do if they'd left? What would he say if they'd stayed? A thousand excuses and explanations were running through his brain. But somehow he knew they wouldn't wash with Bonnie.

Nothing but the truth would do for her.

He pulled his key from his pocket as he walked up the steps. He paused at the door. The house was silent. Not a single sound from inside.

The traditional door handle was icy cold. He pushed down on it and the door clicked open.

Relief. Pure and utter relief. If Bonnie had left, the door would have been locked.

He brushed the snow off his shoulders and hair and kicked it from his damp shoes.

Still nothing.

He walked silently down the corridor. The light was out in the kitchen and in the back sitting room. His stomach twisted. The green and red garland was gone from the stairs. There was no sign it had even been there.

He held his breath as he stepped into his front room. His completely bare front room.

All signs of Christmas were gone.

The tree. The lights. The garland. The nativity.

Just one small lamp was lit in the corner of the room, reflecting the bare white walls back at him. He'd never realised just how sparse this room was.

Bonnie was sitting on the sofa. She didn't even turn her head towards him. She was staring at the now unlit fire. Her jaw was set. In one hand she held a glass of wine, the fingers of the other hand running up and down the stem of the glass.

He braced himself, but she said nothing.

'Bonnie,' he acknowledged. An elephant had just decided to sit on his chest. At least that was what it felt like.

She didn't move, didn't flinch. It was almost as if he weren't even there.

He swallowed again. He really, really needed a drink of water. His mouth had never felt so dry. But he took a deep breath and sat down next to her on the sofa.

'Let me try and explain,' he said quietly.

'Oh, you'd better.' Her words dripped ice. Any minute now she was going to pick up the bottle of wine at her feet and launch it at his head.

Jacob had never really been lost for words before. This was a first for him. He didn't talk. He didn't share. Ever since his father had packed him off to boarding school once his mother died, there just hadn't been anyone to share with. Not like that. Not like the way he used to with her.

The truth was, he always felt that no one else had ever been that invested in him. Building walls around yourself as a child protected you as an adult. At least, that was what he'd always thought.

His behaviour tonight had been over the top. He had to explain. He hated what she might think of him right now. What Freya might think of him right now.

'I'm sorry I upset Freya tonight. I never meant to do that.'

'Well, you did. And it will be the first and last time.'

Bonnie's voice had no hesitation. The line was very clearly drawn in the sand.

'Let me be clear. Freya is my first and *only* priority. Every. Single. Day.'

He could feel prickles down his back. She was worse than mad.

'I know that.'

He leaned back against the sofa. This was going to take some work. He wasn't used to talking about himself. And he had no idea what Bonnie's response might be to his words.

For a tiny second he squeezed his eyes shut. They were still here. That must mean something.

He licked his dry lips. 'I haven't told you much about my past.'

Her fingers continued to stroke up and down the wineglass stem. It was almost as if she was using it as a measure of control. 'No. You haven't.'

She was wearing those jeans again and a soft woollen jumper. Right now he wanted to reach out and touch her. Right now he wanted to feel some comfort. Saying these words out loud wasn't easy.

'My mother died when I was ten.'

There. It was out there. The light in the corner flickered inexplicably and he heard her suck in a breath.

'She was the heart of our family. I was an only child and my father spent most of his life in the military. When my mother died it was almost as if all the life was just sucked out of us both.'

She turned a little towards him. 'What did you do?'

He shrugged. 'What could I do? I was ten. I'd spent most of my time with my mother. We'd shared everything. My relationship with my father had always been a little strained. I just think he didn't know how to relate to kids.'

As he was talking he'd moved to face her and as he finished his last sentence her eyebrows lifted. He knew exactly what she was thinking. Like father, like son. And he was struck by the realisation that was the last thing he wanted.

He fixed on her blue eyes. 'My dad sent me to boarding school.'

'Do those places even exist any more? I thought they only ever existed in Enid Blyton books.'

He shook his head. 'Oh, they exist all right. And they're just the place to send a ten-year-old whose mother's died.' He couldn't keep the irony or the bitterness out of his voice. 'I hated every second of it. The education part was fine. The school activity part was fine. But to go from living with your mother, to living there, with nothing really in between…' His voice tailed off.

'Why did he send you there?'

Jacob sighed. 'There was no one else to look after me. I'm an only child and so were my father and mother. Both sets of grandparents were already dead. My father had another posting abroad with the military and there was no question that he wouldn't go. He told me later that he'd always planned on sending me to boarding school.' He pushed up the sleeves of his wet jumper.

She tilted her head to one side. 'Had your mother stopped that?'

He shook his head. 'I have no idea.' He groaned and sagged back against the sofa. 'There were so many things that I wished I had asked her. So many conversations I wish I could remember. Most of it is just all caught up in here.' He waved his finger next to his head. 'Sometimes I think that things I remember I've just made up.'

'How did she die?'

Jacob hesitated, then took a deep breath. 'Cancer. Non-Hodgkin's lymphoma. It was brutal—it sucked the life right out of her.'

She licked her lips. 'Did you go to your mother's funeral?'

He nodded. 'It was full of people I didn't really know. No one really spoke to me. And because of the time of year it was bitter cold and lashing with rain. We were only at the graveside for around five minutes.'

A little spark of realisation shot across her face. 'When did your mother die, Jacob?'

This was it. This was the important part. He felt his eyes fill up and was instantly embarrassed. Men didn't cry. Men *shouldn't* cry.

But no matter how hard he tried not to, one tear escaped and slid down his cheek. His voice was hoarse. 'She died three days before Christmas. I came home to a house we'd decorated together, that would never feel the same again.'

'Oh, Jacob.' Bonnie's tears fell instantly, and she reached up to his cheek to brush his away. 'I can't even begin to imagine what that felt like.'

Now he'd started he couldn't stop. He felt safe. He felt safe talking to Bonnie. Someone he'd known only a month and invited into his home. There was nothing superficial about Bonnie Reid. She was all heart and soul. He'd never met anyone like her before. Or if he had, he'd never taken the time to get to know them.

It felt right to tell Bonnie about his mother and why his insides were so messed up about Christmas.

'I felt like when we buried my mother, we buried a little bit of ourselves. My father was never the same. I can't remember ever seeing my father smile once my mother died. Our relationship was non-existent. I'm embarrassed by it. I've no idea if he just couldn't cope. If it was all just grief. Or, if my mother had brought out another side of him, and when she died he just reverted back to how he normally was. All I know is that from the age of ten, happiness just didn't feature in our house.'

Bonnie's tears were free-flowing. 'That's awful. You had no one? No one else you could turn to?'

He shook his head. 'Christmas felt like a curse after that. That's why I hate it so much. I try not to be bitter. But it just doesn't evoke the happy memories in me that it does for others. I do have good memories of Christmases with my mother. But they were so long ago. Sometimes I wonder if they even existed.'

'Oh, Jacob.' Bonnie reached over, her hand stroking the top of his. She left it there and squeezed gently, the warm sleeve of her jumper touching his forearm.

It was the touch. The heat of her hand, coupled with the act of compassion. Something he hadn't felt in such a long time. Or maybe it was the relief?

The relief of reaching thirty-seven and finally being able to share with someone. It was as if a whole dark weight had lifted off his shoulders. He couldn't rationalise it. It didn't make any sense. But saying the words out loud, to someone who might actually understand, was a whole new concept for Jacob.

These last fourteen months had been so hard. The next few weeks probably the hardest while he waited for his results. The outcome of whether he'd come out the other side of non-Hodgkin's lymphoma, or he'd succumb like his mother. Bonnie and Freya had been good for him. They'd brought some light back into his life at a time when he needed it most.

Bonnie squeezed his hand again. 'You can't do that, Jacob. You can't take your feelings out on my little girl.'

He pulled his hand away and put them both up to his face, cringing. 'I know that. I'm so sorry. I wasn't thinking straight. I just came in, saw the decorations and it brought back a whole host of things I just wasn't ready for.' He put his head in his hands for a second. 'I overreacted. I *know* I overreacted. I'm sorry, I really am.' He turned to face her.

She was beautiful. Bonnie Reid was actually beautiful. Even with the harsh light in this stark white room, her dark red hair, bright blue eyes and pale skin made her the most beautiful woman he'd ever been close to. 'What can I do? What can I do to make it up to her? To make it up to you? I don't want her to hate me. I don't want her to be scared of me.'

Bonnie nodded slowly and met his gaze. There was a gentle smile on her lips. 'I can't tell you that, Jacob. You've got to figure that out for yourself. You're the adult—she's the child. You have to take some time to work through how you feel about everything.'

'How do I do that?' His voice was low. He couldn't tear his eyes away from her. All he wanted to do was reach out and touch her perfect skin—to join the invisible dots between the light sprinkling of freckles across her nose.

He wanted Bonnie and Freya to feel safe. To feel safe around him. Just as he'd felt safe to tell her about his past.

'What happened to your dad?'

He gave a little sigh. 'He died—two years ago of heart failure. Had a funeral with full military honours.' He raised his eyebrows. 'He would have been very proud.'

* * *

Bonnie bent down and lifted the bottle of wine. 'Why don't we have a drink together and just talk?'

He nodded, then smiled as he took the bottle from her hand and turned the label around. He raised his eyebrows. 'Did you open the most expensive bottle of wine that I had?'

She smiled and held up her phone. 'You bet your life I did. I looked it up online first. I was planning on finishing it before you got back. You're lucky I left you any.' She handed him a glass.

He poured the remaining wine into his glass and stopped for a minute, holding it between both hands. He was staring at the liquid in the glass. 'I'm just glad that you didn't leave,' he said quietly.

She reached over and put a hand on his back. 'I wanted to. I didn't even care that we had nowhere to go.' She shook her head, as if she couldn't quite understand herself. 'But I just couldn't, Jacob. Not like this.'

There was a silence for a few moments between them. Was she considering the same implications that he was? That what had started out as a temporary arrangement was becoming so much more?

He looked up through heavy lids. Now he'd come in from the cold, the heat of the house was hitting him in a big way. He'd gone from being frozen to the bone to feeling superheated in a matter of minutes.

Sensations of fatigue were sweeping over him. But his body was fighting it every step of the way. Fighting to hold on to the other sensations in his prickling skin. Those bright blue eyes were mesmerising. She didn't need to speak. It was almost as if he knew what she was thinking. Was he imagining this? He'd never felt a connection like this before.

'I guess not everyone leaves,' he whispered.

Bonnie took a long, slow breath and put her wine glass on the floor. Although her actions were slow and measured, he didn't doubt for a second that she knew exactly what she was doing.

As she turned to face him, one leg was pulled up on the sofa, tucking under her as she put her arms around his neck. 'No, Jacob,' she whispered. 'Not everyone leaves.'

His breath was stuck somewhere in his throat. He'd never told anyone what he'd just told Bonnie. Now she seemed connected to him—tied to him, and he didn't want that to end. The blood was roaring through his ears. The feel of the soft fluffy wool on the sleeves of her jumper pushed his temperature skyward.

But his self-defence mechanisms were still kicking into place. He'd lived his life too long like this for them to disappear instantly. 'But you did leave,' he murmured. 'You left your husband.'

He was fixed on her eyes. Fixed on the perfectness of her skin and beautiful auburn hair framing her face. She nodded. 'I did.' It was almost as if she sensed she had to tease him every part of the way. She gave a little smile, 'But I had exceptional circumstances—you know what they were.'

He reached over and touched her hair. 'Not really. Tell me about them. Tell me about Freya's dad.'

He could see her hesitation, see her sucking in a breath. He'd just shared with her. She now knew about one of the biggest influencing factors in his life. He'd barely scratched the surface with her.

Her eyes fixed on the floor. 'Robert was my boyfriend.

We were together about a year when I fell pregnant unexpectedly.' She threw up her hands. 'I know. Don't say anything. A midwife accidentally falling pregnant. The irony kills me.' Then she smiled. 'But Freya is the best accident that will ever happen to me.' She bit her lip. 'It's stupid really, and hindsight is a wonderful thing. Robert's parents were real traditionalists. So we got swept along with their ideals and got married before Freya arrived. The truth was Robert was never really the marrying kind.'

'But you married him anyway?' He gave a little smile. It wasn't really a question, it was a more a sympathetic observation. Bonnie didn't seem upset, just a little sad.

She started winding a strand of hair around her finger. She nodded. 'I think I was more in love with the *idea* of being in love, than actually *being* in love. In my heart of hearts, I never really pictured us growing old together.'

'And?'

She shrugged her shoulders. 'I was busy with work and juggling childcare for Freya. I kind of lost sight of being married. Robert was distant—distracted. I suspected something was going on. It made me mad. I came home early from work one day and found another car in the drive. I let myself into the house and found Freya playing downstairs. Robert was upstairs, in bed, with one of my closest friends.' She shook her head and sagged back a little. 'It wasn't my finest hour. The fact Freya was in the house. The fact it was one of my friends...'

Jacob raised his eyebrows. 'Oh, no. What did you do?'

She rolled her eyes. 'My "friend" ended up naked in my front garden after I'd marched her down the stairs. Robert's clothes were deposited out of the bedroom window—so at least she found something to wear.' She shook her head. 'After that, I just grabbed some things for me and Freya, packed up and went to my parents. I filed for divorce straight away.'

He was watching her closely. 'How did you feel?'

She paused for a second. 'It's probably a really awful thing to say—but I was more humiliated than anything else. Robert and I had been growing apart. I probably always thought we would come to a natural end. I just didn't expect it to be like that.' She gave a rueful smile. 'I wasn't exactly heartbroken about it. I might even have been secretly relieved it was over. But we lived in a small place. Every person in the town knew exactly what Robert had done to me. And pride is a terrible thing. I felt people staring at me wherever I went. I couldn't take it any longer.'

He nodded slowly. 'So you came to Cambridge?'

'I had to. I know you understand, Jacob. It's called self-preservation. It's the thing that makes you get out of bed for another day, even when you don't want to. I needed a change for Freya and me. I needed a chance of a new life for us both.'

He reached and brushed a thumb down her cheek. She was so wise. He'd never met anyone like this before. There was so much more to learn about Bonnie Reid.

He'd shared with her tonight, and now she'd shared with him.

'Thank you,' he whispered.

Her pretty brow furrowed. 'For what?'

'For not leaving tonight.' It was the thing that had bothered him every step of the way back home. It was the thing that he'd dreaded. That he'd expected. Because that was what he deserved. And he knew that. But Bonnie Reid had just surpassed all of his expectations.

His heart squeezed. If he'd left this room as she'd decorated it, things would have been perfect. The fire flickering in the fireplace, the tree lights twinkling all around them. But he'd destroyed all that and brought them back to his white, harsh, empty walls.

Bonnie Reid deserved better than that. Freya Reid deserved better than that.

She licked her lips. It was the tiniest movement—a subconscious movement—but it was all that he needed. He moved forwards, not hesitating, his lips connecting with hers.

She tasted of strawberries mixed with wine. The remnants of her perfume drifted up his nose, the feel of her jumper connecting with the delicate skin at the bottom of his throat. She didn't seem to mind his wet jumper. She didn't seem to care that wine sloshed from his glass as he wrapped one arm around her and tangled the other hand through her hair.

That hair. He'd wanted to touch it from the moment he'd seen it. It was silky, falling through his fingers easily. But he didn't want it to fall through. He wanted to catch it—just as he wanted to catch her. So he wrapped it around his fingers, anchoring his hand at the back of her head as the kissing increased.

She pulled back—and for a horrible second he thought she was going to say this was all a terrible mistake. But she didn't. Bonnie Reid was taking charge.

She moved, lifting the glass from his hand and sitting it on the side table, then, pushing his shoulders back against the sofa, she swung one leg over him, so she was sitting on top of him.

She put her arms around his shoulders again and looked him straight in the eye. 'There. That's better.'

'It certainly is.' He didn't hesitate. He pulled her closer, feeling the warm curves of her breasts against his chest. He slid his hands up and under her jumper. Her smooth, silky skin beneath his fingertips. Everything about this felt right.

Her smell. Her taste. Her touch. Her fingers skirted around his neck and shoulders, along the line of his jaw, scratching against his stubble, then through his hair, pulling his lips hard against her own.

His tongue played around the edges of her mouth as their kiss deepened. Suddenly, these clothes were too much; they were stopping him from feeling exactly what he wanted to.

He drew back and pulled his wet jumper and shirt over his head, then pulled her soft jumper off, throwing it on the floor with his own.

Her round full breasts were encased in a cream lace bra. She was breathing heavily now, her body weight on the most sensitive part of him.

He ran his fingers across her shoulder, reaching the pale skin at the bottom of her neck and then down, over her breastbone, between her breasts and down to her navel, resting just above the button of her jeans.

She sucked in her stomach—an automatic reaction but an unnecessary one. He loved every part of her soft curves.

His brain was screaming 'no' to him right now. But his body just wasn't listening.

He shouldn't be doing this. Bonnie and Freya were in a vulnerable position right now. This was only a temporary arrangement. Jacob Layton didn't form attachments. Not like this.

But everything about this felt right. Everything about

this had been simmering under the surface since his first meeting with Bonnie. Now it was exploding to the surface in volcanic proportions.

For his part, the attraction had just grown. The more he got to know her and Freya, the more he admired her. Her strength, her resilience, her determination to do a good job.

Her empathy with patients, her patience with staff. Her sense of humour, her stubborn streak and the way she answered back. Bonnie Reid was one of a kind.

And he was about to make the biggest mistake of his life.

Bonnie had already experienced one screwed-up partner. The last thing she needed was another. His hands stilled on her back.

Bonnie and Freya deserved a bright future. How could he give them one with his cancer history? That would always, permanently, hang over his head. He knew without asking that Bonnie would want more kids.

And he knew without thinking about it that he already believed the cancer was in his genes. He couldn't do that to a child. He couldn't do that to Bonnie and Freya.

'Jacob? Is everything okay?' She'd pulled back a little, a frown creasing her brow.

'Mummy?' The little voice cut through the emotions in the room.

Jacob froze. Bonnie did the opposite. She let out a little gasp, then flicked around, trying to locate her discarded jumper. She leapt off his lap and pulled the jumper over her head. Freya's voice hadn't sounded too close. She must be standing at the top of the stairs.

Jacob looked at his crumpled shirt and jumper, still

together, but lying at Bonnie's feet. 'Do you want me to come?'

She shook her head quickly as she started towards the door. 'No, no, it's fine. Let me deal with Freya.'

His last view was of the bottom he so admired in those jeans. He heard her padding up the stairs in her bare feet. 'Hi, honey. What's wrong? Let's get you back to bed.' He heard the noise of her sweeping Freya into her arms and the voices faded quickly.

Jacob leaned forwards and put his head in his hands. What was he thinking? How could he have explained to Bonnie why he'd stopped kissing her, without telling her about his diagnosis—the one part of himself he still wanted to remain private?

His stomach twisted. He knew none of this was right. But Jacob didn't share. It didn't feel normal to him; it didn't feel natural. Telling Bonnie about his mother had been the first time in his life he'd ever really shared.

But the cancer diagnosis? No. He didn't want her to look at him that way. With pity. With sympathy. With the 'I'm sorry there's a chance you'll die' expression on her face.

He never wanted anyone to look at him like that—let alone Bonnie. He'd only told two colleagues—ones he trusted explicitly—and that was only because he'd had to reduce his patient contact while undergoing his most intense treatments. If he could have got away with telling no one that was exactly what he'd have done.

He sighed and leaned back against the sofa, his bare back coming into contact with the leather surface. It wasn't comfortable, not against bare skin. Somehow he hadn't noticed with Bonnie on his lap.

He looked around the room. White, stark walls.

It had looked so much better before.

He could admit that now. He could try and be rational about things. It seemed a little easier now he'd told Bonnie about his mother dying at Christmas.

He winced as he remembered the look of their faces earlier when he'd started to tear the decorations back down. How stupid. How pathetic. How ungrateful.

He stood up and grabbed his shirt and jumper from the floor, walking through to the kitchen and dumping them in the laundry basket. He had a pile of clothes sitting on top of the tumble dryer. He grabbed a T-shirt and walked back through to the hall.

He had to find a way to make things up to Bonnie and Freya. He hated that Freya might be scared of him now. He had to do something to change that.

He pulled open the hall cupboard door and was nearly speared in the face with Christmas tree branch. A single red bauble rolled past his feet. She'd stripped the Christmas tree but obviously kept all the decorations.

He gave a smile of relief. That was where she'd stored them.

He glanced at the empty banister. He might not have got some things right tonight, but if he wanted to make it up to them he knew exactly where to start.

CHAPTER EIGHT

BONNIE RUBBED HER sleep-ridden eyes. She'd had trouble sleeping after last night's events. Freya had only woken up to go to the toilet and been a little disorientated. Once Bonnie had cuddled her back into bed she'd fallen asleep instantly.

But Bonnie's head had been spinning. She'd been shocked by Jacob earlier. But she'd also known there had to be a reason behind it. A deep-seated reason. And that was why she'd given him the tiniest bit of leeway.

Now she understood. It didn't excuse his actions, but she knew exactly how sorry he was—it had been written over every inch of his face. And when he'd shared about his mother she couldn't help but cry.

Her thoughts immediately went to Freya. She couldn't stand the thought of something happening to her and Freya being left alone. Who would love her the way she did? Certainly not her father. Something prickled down her spine. If anything ever happened to her, Freya would automatically go to her father. What kind of life would she have with him? The kind of life that Jacob had endured as a child?

Her skin tingled as Jacob entered her thoughts. Who

was she kidding? Had she just made the biggest mistake of her life?

Jacob had opened up to her. But there was still so much she didn't know about him—even though they were living under one roof. Maybe she was just being paranoid. But after living with an unfaithful, feckless husband, she wanted to go into any new relationship with her eyes wide open.

She'd been hurt. Freya had been hurt. She'd no intention of ever going down that road again. Self-preservation was a must. Even if any thought of him made her heart pitter-patter faster.

'Can we have breakfast, Mummy?' The little voice cut through her thoughts.

She turned and smiled at her little girl. She was blessed: Freya woke up each day in a good mood. She reached over and gave Bonnie a hug. 'I like it when you're in my bed, Mummy.'

She hugged back. 'I like it too. But it's only on special occasions. Now, what do you want for breakfast?'

'Toast and jam.'

'I think I can do that. Let's go to the toilet and wash our face and hands first.'

As they reached the top of the stairs she bent down to pick Freya up. It was just instinct—she'd done it most mornings since they'd got there. Freya wasn't used to stairs and Bonnie was always worried that she'd trip if she was still sleepy.

As she gathered Freya in her arms she realised something was a little off. It took her the first few steps to realise what it was. The red and green garland was wound back around the banister.

A smile started to edge around her lips. She kept

walking. Now she could hear, and smell, activity in the kitchen. Someone was cooking bacon and singing while they cooked.

As she reached the bottom of the stairs the twinkling lights from the front room attracted her like a magnet. She walked back into the front room.

Everything was back exactly where it should be. 'Look, Freya,' she whispered.

The tree lights were twinkling, the branches redecorated with tinsel and baubles. The nativity scene was back on the side table. The red and green garland for the mantelpiece was back in place. She'd no idea how he'd managed to patch it together—but she didn't really care.

The fact was, he'd done it.

'Mummy, our tree's back up,' said Freya. A smile had lit up her face. 'Does Jacob like it now?'

Bonnie nodded slowly. 'I think he must.' She couldn't stop smiling. He'd revealed part of himself last night but now he'd obviously made the decision to try and move on.

The house felt full of warmth. It was so much nicer with the Christmas decorations up; it felt much more like a home, rather than just a house.

She carried Freya through to the kitchen. Jacob was putting a pot of tea on the kitchen table. 'Oh, you're up, good.' His eyes skirted over to Freya; he looked wary. 'I've made breakfast. Sit down.'

Freya stared at the plate of bacon as Bonnie put her in one of the chairs. 'I don't want bacon. I want toast and jam.'

Jacob smiled at her. 'I thought you might say that.' He produced a toast rack stacked full of toast and a jar of jam.

Bonnie smiled as she sat down. Freya reached over and

grabbed a slice of toast. 'Can you butter this, Mummy?' Her eyes fixed on Jacob again. 'I like that the tree's back. I like the lights.'

A second of hesitation passed over Jacob's face before he pulled out a chair and sat down next to Freya. 'I do too. I think it was a good idea to get a tree for the house. Thank you very much. I'm sorry if I seemed angry last night. I was just a little surprised.'

Bonnie held her breath as she handed over the buttered toast to Freya and opened the jar of jam. She wasn't entirely sure how Freya would respond.

But Freya just shrugged. 'Can we watch cartoons today?'

It was that simple for a five-year-old. No stomach churning. No fretting. She just accepted what he said and was happy that the tree was back up.

Jacob and Freya continued to chat over breakfast. Today, it seemed, was going to be a quiet day in the house.

Jacob seemed more at ease. Maybe he was just getting used to having people in his house—or maybe talking about his mother last night had helped him a little.

She certainly hoped so.

It was so strange to see Freya chatting away with him. Even when they'd lived with her husband, breakfast had usually been their time together. Robert had rarely appeared at the breakfast table. And last night's events seemed to have been quickly forgotten.

They laughed together and something twisted inside her. She wasn't quite sure what it was. Fear? Envy? Confusion?

Jacob seemed comfortable this morning—but was she? She'd kissed him last night. If Freya hadn't interrupted it might have become a whole lot more. Bonnie didn't usually act on impulse—not when it came to men. But things with Jacob last night had just seemed so natural. So heated.

It made her want to catch her breath.

This was a new job. A new city. A new life.

Just how much change was she ready for?

Jacob felt as if he'd been holding his breath since last night. Ever since he'd kissed Bonnie and realised exactly the effect she had on him.

Part of him was sorry. Now he would always know exactly what he was missing. Part of him wasn't the least bit sorry. It had been a long time since he'd felt a connection to someone. The fact that Bonnie was a mother hadn't even entered his head.

If you'd asked him a few years ago if he'd ever have a relationship with someone who had children he would have said an overwhelming no. But he'd have been wrong. With the exception of last night, he'd liked being around Freya. It was surprising him—just as much as it was probably surprising Bonnie and Freya.

He'd noticed the way people were looking at him at work. For the last ten days he'd felt differently. He'd felt lighter. This morning he practically felt so light he could float away. The only thing that was still anchoring him to the ground was his test results.

Even if—and he prayed they would be—they were good results, it still wouldn't change other things for Jacob. The cancer would always lurk in the background, always a possibility of a recurrence. Always that uncertainty of whether it was familial and he could pass it on. Gene mapping wasn't quite there yet to give him that answer.

But these last few days at home had felt so much better. Putting up the decorations again last night had given him a lot of thinking time. It was time to put the negative associations that he had with Christmas to bed.

His mother would have hated him being like this. Feeling like this about a season that should be the happiest of times.

The look on Freya and Bonnie's faces this morning when they realised he'd put the decorations back up had been enough for him. He was sure he'd done the right thing. He'd also done something else. He was still to find out if it was right or not.

He pushed some tickets along the table to Freya. 'I found out about a little surprise. I was wondering if you and your mum would like to come.'

Freya stared down at the tickets. The words were obviously too complicated for a five-year-old, but the pictures told a good story. She pointed. 'Is that Rudolph? Can we go and see Rudolph?'

Jacob looked up at Bonnie. He was feeling hopeful, even though he should probably have run this by her first. She leaned over and spun the tickets around. 'Today? The Christmas lights, a visit to Santa *and* a chance to meet the reindeers?' Surprise and amusement, with a tiny bit of disbelief, mixed through her voice as her eyebrows rose.

He nodded carefully. 'What do you think? Would you like to go?'

Her face relaxed and she lifted her mug of tea to take

a sip. Her voice was quiet. 'I think that would be lovely. Thank you for thinking of us, Jacob.'

Her gaze met his. She was still thinking about last night.

He'd pulled back. She must be wondering why. Because the air between them still sizzled. It crackled. He still wanted to reach out and touch her cheek, kiss her lips. He just didn't want to be unfair.

He took a deep breath. 'I'll always think about you, Bonnie.'

Silence hung between them. It was probably the wrong thing to say. It almost seemed as if he were finishing something that had never started. Truth was, he didn't have a clue what he was doing right now. But the implication was clear. Bonnie was affecting him. He *did* feel something for her—even if he didn't know what it was.

But those words seemed enough for Bonnie; she gave a little smile and stood up. 'Come on, Freya, the Christmas lights and Santa visit aren't until three o'clock this afternoon. Let's have a lazy morning on the sofa.'

Freya jumped up in agreement and ran out of the kitchen towards the front room, leaving Jacob at the kitchen table, eyes fixed on Bonnie's backside in her pyjama trousers, trying to keep his thoughts in check.

'Is everyone ready?'

They were all practically standing in a line. Winter jackets, scarfs, gloves and wellington boots in place. Freya couldn't stand still. She had ants in her pants. She didn't care that the temperature had plummeted again and a mixture of sleet and snow was starting to fall. She just wanted to meet Rudolph.

'Will I get to sit on his back? Will Donner be there? And Blitzen? Is his nose really red?'

The questions had been never-ending since this morning.

Jacob smiled. 'I have no idea. This is all new to me.'

Freya frowned. 'Is it far? Are we going in the car?'

Bonnie shook her head. 'No. We're going to walk. That way, we'll get to have plenty of time to see all the Christmas lights.'

'Will Fraser from school be going to see Santa too?'

Jacob knelt in front of her. 'And who might Fraser be?'

Freya tossed her red hair over her shoulder. 'My friend,' she said matter-of-factly.

Bonnie suppressed a laugh. 'Welcome to my world, Jacob. Or rather the world of little girls—a new best friend every day. I just try and keep up.'

Jacob folded his arms across his chest and did his best to look severe. 'Fraser, eh? Well, if he's there you'll need to point him out. I'd like to meet this Fraser.'

Freya giggled. 'Can I get my picture with Santa?'

Bonnie nodded and bent to straighten Freya's hat. 'Yes, it's all arranged. Now, are you ready?'

She jumped up and down. 'I've been ready for hours, Mum. Let's go!'

It was the perfect afternoon. Cold without being *too* cold. A light dusting of snow everywhere. By three o'clock it was already getting dark.

Freya's little hand was in Jacob's. It was surprising how comfortable it felt. How comfortable *he* felt doing this. Bonnie had a cream woollen hat pulled over her auburn hair and a thick green wool coat. She looked perfect. Like something from a Christmas card.

He swung Freya up into his arms. 'Come on. Let's go and visit Santa and the reindeers. It won't be long until the lights get switched on.'

The prepaid tickets were the godsend. Thank goodness for one of the midwives in the special care unit. She'd mentioned buying the tickets last year and not having to wait in the freezing cold for hours with her young kids.

Freya only had to wait five minutes before she was able to jump on Santa's knee and tell him what she wanted for Christmas. She counted off things on her finger. 'I'd like a new baby doll, one that can eat and poop. I like to change nappies,' she said proudly.

Santa nodded in amusement. 'I think that can be arranged,' he said, nodding towards Bonnie.

She was leaning against Jacob. 'Thank goodness it isn't Christmas Eve,' she said. 'Last year Freya announced she wanted some board game when we visited Santa on Christmas Eve. It was the first time she'd mentioned it at all. And, of course, it was after five o'clock on Christmas Eve.'

He wrapped his arm around her waist. It was so easy to do that. 'What did you do?'

She shook her head. 'What do you think I did? I panicked!'

He watched Freya. She was saying to Santa Claus, 'We really need a house too. We've just moved down from Scotland and we still haven't found somewhere else to stay.' She looked up into the air. 'I mean, the house we're staying in right now is perfect. So, if we could have one just like it, that would be great.'

'You like where you stay?' Santa asked.

Freya sighed. 'It's the most beautiful house in the world.'

Something twisted inside Jacob. He'd always loved his house—even if he hadn't really made his mark on it. But to hear someone else say those words out loud? Say that they loved his house—that was special. It almost made him feel warm inside.

And for the strangest reason, it didn't send him into a mad panic. He wanted Bonnie and Freya to feel welcome in his home. He liked having them around.

Bonnie shifted a little as if she were uncomfortable.

'But it could be more perfect.'

Jacob turned at the sound of Freya's voice. She had his full attention.

'What would make it perfect, then?' asked Santa.

'A dog,' Freya said quickly.

Jacob burst out laughing. 'She doesn't seem to be letting this one go, does she?'

Bonnie laughed too. 'I'll have to buy her a stuffed one for Christmas. Or maybe one of those ones that bark? There's no way we could deal with a real dog. Not with me working full-time. It just wouldn't be fair.'

Jacob nodded. 'You're right. I've always considered getting a dog, but even with all the dog-walking companies, it just didn't seem fair to leave a dog by itself all day.'

She looked surprised. 'You've thought about getting a dog?'

'Of course.' He winked. 'I've heard they're not as complicated as women, or...' he looked over at Freya '...five-year-olds!'

Bonnie laughed as Freya jumped down from Santa's

lap and held out her hand towards him. 'Thanks, Santa, I'll let you know if I get what I asked for.'

Santa looked a little surprised and shot Bonnie and Jacob a smile as he shook Freya's outstretched hand. 'This is a very astute little girl. Merry Christmas to you all.'

They walked outside towards the reindeer pen and Bonnie pulled the bag of food they'd been given from her bag. One of the staff showed Freya how to hold the food in her hand and she screamed as a reindeer named Vixen slobbered all over her hand.

Without even thinking about it, Jacob stuck his hand in Bonnie's bag and pulled out the wipes that were sticking out, grabbing one out and wiping Freya's hand.

'Jacob?' He knelt down in front of her. 'Why don't the reindeers have red noses? Aren't they supposed to?'

He smiled. He loved the way Freya's mind worked. Her endless questions. Her five-year-old's logic. And her complete and utter belief in all things Christmas. This morning she'd shown him a website they'd been shown at school that would plot Santa's journey all the way around the world on Christmas Eve. They'd even been able to input the house address to let Santa know where they were.

He whispered in her ear. 'You've got to remember. It's not Christmas Eve yet. They don't fly until Christmas Eve, so they don't need their red noses until then.'

He could almost hear her thinking out loud. Finally she gave a little nod. 'Now I understand.'

His phone rang and he stood up and pulled it from his back pocket, looking to see who was calling. He glanced towards Bonnie and Freya and walked off to the side.

* * *

Bonnie looked up. It must be a work call. Jacob obviously didn't want to discuss a patient around them and that was fine.

Freya was still excited. In a few minutes' time it would be time for the countdown and switch-on of the Christmas lights. Bonnie held out her hand. 'Come on. The lights will be on in a few minutes. Let's find somewhere good to stand.'

The smells from the street vendors were wafting all around them. Roasting chestnuts, hot chocolate and mulled wine. The rich pine scents from the wreaths outside the nearby florist were mixing in with other aromas. Holly was intertwined amongst them and mistletoe hung from the door of the shop. Should she buy some?

Jacob was still talking. He looked worried; there were deep furrows across his brow. She crossed her fingers that there were no problems on the labour ward.

He caught her eye and turned away. Something twisted inside.

Now she was being stupid.

This was simple. This was just a nice day out between work colleagues—housemates. Because if she took that kiss out of the equation, there really wasn't anything else between them—was there?

In theory, no. But that wasn't the way she was feeling inside. And everything about that made her uncomfortable. After the nightmare of her ex-husband she'd vowed not to expose herself or Freya to anything like that again. She didn't need the hassle of the conflict.

Bonnie Reid fully intended to be a man-free zone. So what had gone wrong?

She hadn't even lasted a day. They'd moved in with Jacob their first day. How ridiculous was that?

From the initial grumpy meeting, Jacob had seemed to chill. She'd been nervous about staying there with Freya; the first few days she'd scoured the Internet for somewhere else.

But it was almost as if, after the first few days, he wasn't really in a hurry for them to move out. Anywhere she showed him he always had a reason for them not to move there. Too far out. Too rough. Not near a good school. And while it was helpful and informative, it wasn't actually inspiring her to move elsewhere.

She and Freya were getting a little too comfortable in Jacob's lovely house. It was almost starting to feel like home.

Jacob put the phone back in his pocket and spun around to face them. He walked over, picked up Freya and put her on his shoulders. 'This is where you'll get the best view,' he said, and she squealed with happiness as he swung her up.

But Bonnie's stomach was still churning. It was almost as if the phone call hadn't happened. It was almost as if he hadn't deliberately walked away from them and excluded them from his conversation.

A horrible chill crept down her spine. Jacob wasn't on call any more. His on-call duties finished at midday. Whoever had phoned him—it hadn't been about work. There were no patient confidentiality issues. So what didn't he want her to hear?

She didn't have time to think any further, because his arm was around her shoulders and he moved them forwards a little as Santa positioned himself on stage to make the announcement and turn on the lights.

Crowds had gathered all around them. They were

lucky Jacob had thought to buy them tickets. The area in front of the stage was crushed full of people. At the side, they could see the view all along the street. A perfect position to see the lights switched on.

Santa started cheering the crowd on. Some of the handlers had brought the reindeers out from the pen and positioned them behind him. The animals seemed completely unperturbed by the noise or the crowds. Freya, in the meantime, was clapping her hands with excitement.

'Ten, nine, eight, seven, six.' Bonnie joined in the countdown with the rest of the crowd. This was what she wanted for her little girl. To be full of the joys of Christmas and to enter into the spirit of things.

Moving down here had been hard. Emotionally hard. The separation in miles was the final nail in her divorce coffin, and one that she so badly needed. Everything down here was new. Everything down here was fresh.

Living in a town where Freya could have seen her father at any point, and been ignored by him, was too much for her. His lack of involvement hurt. It wasn't the issue of being both mum and dad to her little girl—that was without question. It was the carefully chosen words she had to find to explain why he didn't call—why he didn't visit.

And it didn't matter that moving to Cambridge gave Robert a perfect excuse for not visiting Freya. He hadn't needed one in Scotland. It just lessened the impact of him not being around. Freya was so caught up in her new home, her new school and her new friends that she hadn't even had a chance to miss him and that was a welcome relief.

Jacob looked over at her and squeezed her shoulder. 'Okay?'

'Yes.' She nodded, pushing away all the other little

doubts that had started to creep into her mind. It was one phone call. One. Nothing else.

Jacob wasn't Robert. And even if he was, it was none of her business. They were work colleagues—friends.

Santa finished the countdown, 'Three, two, one,' and flicked the switch.

It was magical. Like something from a movie. The Christmas lights started at the bottom of the street. Red, green and gold garlands strung across the road flickered to life.

It was like a Mexican wave. At points along the way there were bigger illuminations. A North Pole house, a multicoloured sleigh, a large pile of presents. The church halfway along the street had joined in. Multicoloured lights wrapped around the stained-glass windows and steeple lit up the dark night sky. A nativity scene in the churchyard, complete with shepherds and magi, was brought to life.

Freya loved every part of it. Every time another part lit she gasped with excitement. The lights were getting closer, finishing with the large Christmas tree in the middle of the square. The colours lit up one at a time, as if someone were stringing tinsel around the tree while they watched. First green, then red, then gold. Finally a large white twinkling star lit at the top of the tree as fireworks started to go off behind them. Cambridge really knew how to do Christmas.

One of the brass bands from the local schools started to play Christmas carols and Bonnie, Freya and Jacob joined in. By the time Jacob slid Freya off his shoulders an hour later her eyelids were heavy. Bonnie held out her arms to take her but Jacob shook his head. 'It's fine. We've still got quite a way to walk back.' She saw the tiniest flash of hesitation across his eyes, then he bent down and dropped a kiss on her lips.

Just when she thought she had things sorted in her head. Just when she'd convinced herself that what Jacob did was none of her business and she should forget their last kiss.

The kiss zapped everything back into his place. The taste of his lips and the feel of his hands sliding under her jumper and up her back.

'Come on.' He smiled at her. 'Let's get sleepyhead back home. It's getting cold out here.'

A few gentle flakes of snow started to fall around them. Freya had automatically snuggled into Jacob's neck and was already half asleep. Jacob kept his other arm around Bonnie and steered them both through the crowd and along the street.

Bonnie looked around. To everyone else, they must look like a regular family. Mum, Dad and little girl. Part of that terrified her. The other part pined for it.

She wanted Freya to be loved, to be part of a family. She wanted her little girl to have the relationship that she'd missed out on with her own father.

And Bonnie didn't want to grow old alone. She'd been stung by her cheating ex and it had made her wary. But it didn't stop her hoping that somewhere out there would be a man who would love and respect her the way she did him.

Would make her skin tingle and send pulses through her body from a mere look, a touch.

Trouble was, the only person who fitted the bill right now was Jacob Layton.

Could she really trust him with her heart? And with Freya's too?

CHAPTER NINE

JACOB STARED AT the letter in his hand.

This was it. The appointment he'd been waiting for. The one that could be the end of the big black cloud that had been hanging over his head for the last fifteen months.

His scheduled appointment was fourteen days away but he'd phoned and asked for a cancellation. He couldn't wait any longer to find out his results—good or bad.

Professional courtesy in the NHS went a long way. CT scan and blood tests tomorrow. Appointment with the specialist the day after.

His stomach twisted. Over the last few days he'd reverted to form and he knew it. He was snapping at people again, being grumpy at work.

All because of what was happening inside.

Something had hit him. Ever since he'd had that conversation with Bonnie and kissed her he couldn't think straight. His house was now full of Christmas decorations and happy, smiley people. And for the first time in his life he actually wanted to be a happy, smiley person too.

But he just couldn't be. Not with this hanging over his head.

The possibility of a real relationship—a real connection with someone—was there. But he felt as if it were slipping through his fingers like shifting sands.

Talking about his mother had been an enormous help. Sharing with Bonnie had given him a connection he hadn't felt since he was a young child. Bonnie was a woman he could trust. A woman he could love with his whole heart.

His grip tightened on the letter in his hand. So why hadn't he told her about this?

The truth was he wasn't ready. Cancer was a burden. Cancer was a relationship deal breaker. He was still at that uncertain stage with Bonnie. He didn't want to be a burden to her and Freya—particularly if the news he was about to receive was bad.

If it was, he would step back and fade into the background of their lives. He would probably stop making up reasons she shouldn't move to any of the properties that she'd shown him and help her and Freya take the next steps in their lives.

Above everything he didn't want Bonnie to feel sorry for him. To form a relationship with him out of sympathy or pity. He didn't want that kind of relationship.

He wanted the kind that had started to burn inside him already. The kind where she was his first thought in the morning and his last thought at night. The kind where he could walk into the labour suite and sense she was there without even seeing her.

The kind where her scent would drift across the room towards him and wrap itself around him like a magic spell. So the first face he would see would be hers and her smile would send him a thousand unspoken promises.

Bonnie and Freya had been badly let down before. He didn't want that for them again. And until he found out about his test results, he couldn't even begin to have the kind of conversations with Bonnie that he should be having.

Would she even consider their relationship progressing? How would she feel knowing that he'd had cancer? How would she feel about his position on children? She already had Freya, but Bonnie struck him as the kind of woman who'd want to expand her family. Could she be in a relationship with a man who didn't want to pass the risk of cancer—no matter how small—on to his kids?

So many unanswered questions. So many dangerous assumptions. Crabbit. That was how she'd good-naturedly described him the other day. It was a good Scottish word for him—because that was exactly how he felt.

Unsure. That was another word that described him right now.

He'd always spent his life knowing exactly who he was and what he wanted.

Bonnie—and Freya—had literally turned his world upside down.

'Jacob?'

He crumpled the paper in his hand and thrust it into his pocket. 'Yes?' Bonnie was standing at his office door. A furrow ran across her brow.

'Sean just phoned. Someone else phoned in sick for tomorrow. He wondered if you could cover the theatre list?'

Jacob hesitated. He'd never refused to cover for a fellow doctor before. His automatic default position was always to say yes.

But this was different. If he missed the tests tomorrow, he'd have to wait another two weeks before his routine appointment came up. There were another four obstetricians at CRMU. Sean had probably just asked him first as a matter of routine. He took a deep breath. 'No. Sorry, tell him I have obligations that I can't break. He'll need to ask someone else.'

Bonnie hesitated and took a little step towards him. 'Jacob?'

He shook his head. He couldn't have this conversation with her—not right now. He swept past her, before her light perfume started to invade his senses. 'Tell him to ask Isabel. I'm sure she'll oblige.'

He carried on down the corridor. One look from Bonnie's confused blue eyes was enough for him. He had to be so careful. She'd been hurt badly by her husband. He'd already done damage when he'd torn down the Christmas decorations. For the next two days it would be best if he could avoid her. He'd find a reason to work late tonight. And another reason to stay out of her way tomorrow. His tests were in the afternoon. Then he'd just have to wait twenty-four hours to find out his results.

He glanced at his watch. He needed to have a conversation with Dean Edwards about a baby in Special Care. He could go there. Bonnie would be tied up in the labour suite for the rest of the day.

He sucked in a breath as he pushed open the swing doors. Forty-eight hours. Forty-eight hours, then he'd know if his life was about to begin, or could be about to end.

CHAPTER TEN

SOMETHING WAS WRONG. She could feel it in her bones.

Jacob was avoiding her—and avoiding Freya. Last night he'd come home when they'd both been in bed. When she'd got up and gone downstairs to make a cup of tea and talk to him, it had been obvious he had other things on his mind.

It was painful. It was embarrassing to be around someone that had kissed her so passionately a few days before and now acted as though he didn't want her around.

Maybe it stung so much because she actually cared. She cared what Jacob thought about her.

And caring was the one thing she shouldn't be doing.

Jacob had told her about his mother. But there was something else he was keeping from her. And it made her uncomfortable.

She deserved better than that—Freya deserved better than that.

Worse than anything, she didn't even feel as if she could call him on it. They weren't even in a proper relationship. She had no right to ask where he was going, or what he was doing. She just had that horrible sensation of being taken for a fool.

It didn't help that she was staying in his house. In fact,

it made things ten times worse. If she'd met him through work and they'd maybe just shared a kiss, or gone on a date, she would be able to take a step back and distance herself.

Living under one roof made things a whole lot more complicated.

She tapped at the computer screen. It was only a few weeks until Christmas and the choices seemed even more limited than the last time she'd looked. Seven flats—all within her price range. All white, bland, soulless rooms in a range of buildings she wasn't sure she wanted to stay in.

Two in tower blocks. Three in areas that were less than salubrious. And that hadn't come from Jacob—a few of the other members of staff in the labour suite had recounted tales of staying in some of the surrounding areas. One looked in the same state as the motel she and Freya had stayed in, and another was nearer Freya's school but was a tiny one-bedroom flat.

She clicked on another that flashed by on the top of her screen. This time it was a beautiful two-bedroom flat well out of her price range. A large, spacious flat with original polished floorboards like Jacob's and the same bay-style windows dressed with the kind of curtains she'd imagined for his house.

She pressed the delete button quickly. She was being stupid. Even her house search reminded her of him.

She scribbled down the details of the tiny one-bedroom flat. She'd phone the agent later. How much space did she really need anyway? As long as the place was heated and didn't suffer from damp it would be fine. It had the essential ingredients. It was near Freya's school and it would be a place to call their own.

A tiny shiver crept down her spine. It had always been

her intention to find somewhere for her and Freya to stay. She'd allowed herself to be distracted by Jacob. She'd let herself be influenced by him when he'd told her everything she'd looked at was unsuitable. In a few short weeks, she and Freya had become comfortable in his home.

The sharp man she'd met on her first day had all but vanished. Once you scratched beneath the surface with Jacob Layton there was so much more. He was just good at hiding all the stuff that was really important. His sense of humour, his warmth, his vulnerability and his strength.

'Bonnie? Can you come and give us a hand? We've just been phoned. We've got a woman who is thirty-two weeks pregnant with twins coming in by ambulance. They think the babies are in distress.' Karen, one of the junior midwives, was at the door.

Bonnie clicked the window on the computer to close it and stood up quickly. 'No problem, Karen.' She walked out of the office and across to the treatment room to wash her hands and put on an apron. 'Which room are you preparing?'

Karen glanced over at the whiteboard. 'Room 3, I think. That's the biggest. I'll go and page the on-call obstetrician.'

Bonnie felt her stomach flip over. One of the obstetricians was off sick. There was every chance Jacob would now be on call.

She finished the final checks in the room just as the ambulance crew wheeled the patient in. 'Hi, Bonnie. This is Eleanor Brooks. She's thirty-two weeks pregnant with twins. Hasn't felt well the last few days and fainted in the street around thirty minutes ago.'

Bonnie moved over to the side of the bed and grabbed

the edge of the sheet as the paramedic pulled Eleanor over on the patient slide board.

'Hi, Eleanor, I'm Bonnie, the sister in the labour suite. Let me help you off with your jacket and we'll see how you're doing.'

Eleanor gave a nod and shrugged her shoulders out of her jacket, letting Bonnie pull it away as she lay back against the pillows. Her colour was poor and it only took Bonnie a few seconds to wind the blood-pressure cuff around her arm and start to inflate it.

Karen appeared again with the paperwork and spoke in a low voice for a few minutes with the ambulance crew.

'Eleanor, is there someone I can phone for you?'

Eleanor nodded towards her bag. 'My mobile is in there. My husband is John, but he works offshore on the rigs. You might not be able to get him. My mum's number is in there too. She lives in Cambridge.'

Karen glanced in Bonnie's direction; Bonnie gave her a silent nod. 'Is your husband up in Aberdeen?' She was calculating in her head how long it would take to helicopter him back from the rigs to the mainland, and then down to Cambridge. She blinked at the reading on the screen from the BP cuff. Karen's eyes widened.

'Have you seen your community midwife lately, Eleanor?'

Eleanor's blood pressure was unusually high. Any woman with a twin pregnancy was normally monitored quite closely. Eleanor shook her head. 'I had an appointment last week but she was off sick, and this week I wasn't feeling well enough to go, so I missed it.'

Karen scribbled a little note on the paperwork. 'I'll go and make these calls, chase up the obstetrician and arrange for Eleanor's notes.'

Bonnie gave a nod. 'Eleanor, can you tell me how you've been feeling this past week?'

'Awful.' The one-word answer said everything.

'Did you call your midwife for some advice?'

Eleanor sighed. Her eyes were half closed; it was obvious she was tired. Her legs and ankles were puffy. Bonnie bent over and gave the skin a gentle squeeze between her fingers, the imprint of her fingers clearly denting the skin.

'I didn't want to bother my midwife. I thought I'd feel better in a day or so. Everyone's had a viral thing lately. I was sure I had the same.'

Eleanor moved uncomfortably, ignoring Bonnie at her ankles and taking a little gasp of breath as she pressed her hand against her right-hand ribs.

'Eleanor? Are you having pain?'

Eleanor grimaced and nodded. The pain was too high up to be a labour pain, but it could indicate something else. The pain seemed to pass quickly and she relaxed a little. 'I've been tired. Really tired. But that's normal for twin pregnancies, isn't it? I've been feeling a bit sick too. I've had a headache for the last few days. I actually vomited twice yesterday—I've never done that before. And usually I'm peeing all the time, now I'm hardly peeing at all.'

Alarm bells were going off in Bonnie's head. Eleanor was showing some signs of pre-eclampsia. It wasn't that unusual in twin pregnancies, but Eleanor's condition seemed to be taking a dangerous turn.

She put her hand on Eleanor's arm. 'I know I've just got you into bed. But do you think you could manage to give me a urine sample? I know you said you're hardly peeing right now, but if you could squeeze something out that would be great.' She hesitated for a second. 'I'm also going to call the phlebotomist to take some bloods.'

Eleanor gave a little sigh and swung her legs around while Bonnie brought a commode into room. Right now, she didn't even want Eleanor walking into the separate bathroom. She wanted to monitor her at all times.

Karen came back into the room as Bonnie was helping Eleanor back into bed. She pressed the button on the blood-pressure monitor again. Karen held up some foetal monitors. 'I thought you might want me to attach these? And Sean is outside.'

Bonnie nodded as she wheeled the commode towards the door. 'Will you stay here until I get back?' Karen gave the tiniest nod of her head. They were both aware of the seriousness of the situation.

It only took Bonnie two minutes to dipstick the small sample of urine and put the rest in a collection bottle for the lab.

Once she'd washed her hands she went back outside. But Sean wasn't alone. He'd been joined at the desk by Jacob.

Her stomach flipped over. This was work. He couldn't avoid her—no matter how much he tried to.

Sean turned to face her. 'Can you give me an update?'

Bonnie nodded. Aware that Jacob still wasn't really looking at her.

'Eleanor Brooks is thirty-four. She's thirty-two weeks pregnant with twins. I've not seen her notes, but I'm assuming her pregnancy has been unremarkable up until now. She collapsed in the street earlier today. She has upper-right-quadrant pain, pitting oedema in her ankles, her blood pressure is one-sixty over one-ten. Pulse eighty-seven. I've just tested her urine and it's positive for protein.'

She watched as Sean scribbled some notes. 'There's more. She's had a headache the last few days, vomited twice yesterday and she's been very tired.'

Jacob frowned. 'Hasn't she seen a midwife at any point?'

Bonnie felt automatically defensive. 'She should have. She was last seen three weeks ago. The week after that, her midwife was sick, and last week she felt too unwell to attend. She didn't call in to speak to the midwife as she thought she just had a virus.'

Jacob started to swear under his breath. 'This is looking like HELLP syndrome. Do you mind if I come with you, Sean? We might need to do an emergency twin delivery.'

'Glad of the help,' Sean said quickly. He handed some blood forms to Bonnie. 'Can you get these done as an emergency?'

'No problem.' She took them as Sean and Jacob walked into the room to assess Eleanor. Five minutes later the ward clerk arrived with the notes and the phlebotomist answered her page. Bonnie flicked through the notes. Nothing untoward. All Eleanor's previous appointments had shown a healthy developing pregnancy.

The missed appointments were unfortunate. She just wished Eleanor had phoned her midwife when she'd started to feel unwell. Maybe her condition could have been picked up sooner. HELLP was serious. It could be life-threatening for both mother and babies.

Symptoms could be vague but it always started with pre-eclampsia. One of the crucial tests was the blood work and the quickest turnaround time from the lab

would be just over an hour. Eleanor was already showing some of the classic signs.

Sean and Jacob came out of the room, both talking
in low voices. The phlebotomist arrived, picked up the
blood forms and went to collect the samples that would
be needed.

'I think we should prepare and contact the anaesthetist
anyway. Give her an ace-inhibitor to try and bring her
blood pressure down and don't leave her alone.' Those
last words were aimed at Bonnie. It was the first time
his eyes had connected with hers.

There was something wrong—which was stupid, because she knew that already. But the look in Jacob's eyes?
It was almost blank. As if there had never been anything
between them, and there never would be.

Focus. She sucked in her breath. There was a patient to
deal with. But as soon as Eleanor's condition was under
control, Bonnie was definitely calling the letting agency.

She'd become too attached to him. *They'd* become too
attached to him, too quickly. It was time to take stock.
To take a breath.

She'd made a massive mistake with Robert. She'd married a man she didn't really love. When it came to men—
her previous choice hadn't been great. Could she really
trust her own judgement now?

Her heart was telling her one thing and her head another. It was all too much.

The phlebotomist appeared and waved the blood bot-
tles at them. 'I'll take these direct to the lab and ask for
the results to be phoned direct.'

Sean gave a nod. 'Thanks.' He turned to face Jacob.
'If I speak to the anaesthetist now are you free to assist
in Theatre if required?'

There was silence for a few seconds. The quiet made Bonnie look up. Jacob always responded immediately. He never hesitated over clinical care.

But this time he did. This time he glanced at his watch. She could see him swallow as if a million things were flashing through his brain. 'I'll need to make a call to try to delay something else.'

Sean looked just as surprised as Bonnie. 'No problem. I can always find Isabel. She's covering the other theatre list today—but we can cancel the routine procedures for an emergency.'

That was right. The other theatre list. The one that Jacob had refused to cover today because he had somewhere else to be. Where exactly was that?

A whole wash of memories flooded over her. Robert. Continually making excuses about where he was going or where he had been. The way he could never look her in the eye when he'd been telling her those lies. Her stomach was in knots. She hated that Jacob was following the same pattern. He could never know how much those memories and associations hurt.

Jacob wasn't Robert. He would never be Robert. But he was definitely hiding something. It made her question herself. It made her question her judgement. Her choices had been wrong before. It felt as if she could be walking down the same path.

Where on earth was he going? And why was he being so evasive about it?

Jacob waved his hand at Sean. 'It will be fine. Give me five minutes to make the call. Let's just try and make sure that if we need to take Eleanor to Theatre there are no delays and we're ready to go as soon as we get the blood results.'

Sean nodded towards Bonnie. His initial surprise had died away and now he just looked relieved that he didn't have to go and call Isabel. What was the deal with those two?

'I'm going to stay close by. Give me a shout if you need anything.'

Bonnie went back to the room to help Karen. It only took a few minutes to administer the blood-pressure drugs and start some IV fluids. Karen continued to monitor the babies and Bonnie set the blood-pressure cuff for every ten minutes.

Eleanor kept her eyes closed, occasionally wincing and touching her right side. It was a clear sign that her liver was affected.

Jacob seemed impatient. He was pacing up and down the corridor, and phoned the lab twice to harass them for the blood results. She'd never seen him quite so on edge.

On one hand, she knew that he was putting the care of Eleanor and her babies first. On the other, it was obvious he was anxious to still keep his other plans.

The anaesthetist, Laura, appeared and did a quick assessment. While Eleanor's current condition was serious she had no significant history that would cause any Theatre delays.

Laura was already dressed in theatre scrubs and tucked her hair into her hat as the phone rang. Jacob snatched it up, listening carefully before putting it back down. 'Her blood tests confirm thrombocytopenia and liver dysfunction.' These, combined with her other symptoms, meant that Eleanor could be at risk of liver rupture, uncontrolled bleeding or cerebral oedema.

'Let's go, then,' said Laura. 'I'll meet you in Theatre once you've spoken to Eleanor.'

Things moved quickly. Eleanor's mother arrived with news that her husband was already on the helicopter and had left the oil rig. It would still be hours before he arrived.

Eleanor's condition was worsening. She was beginning to get drowsy, so once Jacob had explained what was happening and consented her they prepared her for Theatre in a matter of minutes and whisked her down the corridor.

Jacob and Sean disappeared to scrub and Bonnie hurried back to the labour ward.

It was three long hours before she heard anything else.

Sean walked up to the nursing station and pulled his theatre hat off his head. His mussed-up hair and tired eyes said everything. She looked over his shoulder. 'Where's Jacob?'

Sean shrugged. 'As soon as we had stabilised Eleanor and the babies and everyone was happy he disappeared.'

She bit her lip to stop her saying what she actually thought. 'What about Eleanor and her babies?'

Sean nodded. 'Two girls. Both in SCBU. Three pounds, four ounces and three pounds, two ounces. Not bad for twins. One had to have a little support breathing and the other was fine.'

'And Eleanor?'

He sighed. 'She started bleeding out almost straight away. Her blood pressure plummeted and she had six units of blood and then some platelets. We caught her just in time.'

'What's happening now?'

'She's stable. Mainly thanks to Jacob. She's been transferred to ICU. They need to keep a careful watch for organ failure.'

Bonnie sighed. 'Poor woman. I hope she's going to be okay. Will you let me know how she is?'

Sean raised his eyebrow. 'Won't Jacob tell you?'

Bonnie felt colour rush into her cheeks. 'What do you mean?'

Sean seemed completely unperturbed. He leaned on the desk towards her, a cheeky grin on his face. 'You two had a fight? For a few weeks the world of CRMU thought you'd turned Jacob into Prince Charming. But now he's back to his usual lovely self. I take it Prince Charming has turned into a frog?'

Sean was good-natured. He was only teasing but she felt distinctly uncomfortable. She wagged her finger at him. 'If I find out you've been gossiping about me, Sean, I'll ban you from our tea room. Don't think I don't know who goes in there and eats all the biscuits and sweets.'

Sean pulled back in mock horror. 'Ouch. Tough sanctions.' He waved his hand as he started down the corridor. 'Don't worry, Bonnie. All your secrets are safe with me.'

She blushed again as one of the other midwives came out of a patient's room and raised her eyebrows at the comment. She pulled her phone from her pocket. Enough was enough. It was time to make that call to the letting agency.

'Mummy, where are we going?' Freya was looking at the photo on the laptop screen.

Bonnie took a deep breath. 'We're going to stay somewhere else, honey. This was only ever temporary. Jacob let us stay for a few weeks until we could find somewhere for ourselves.'

'But I like it here. I like staying with Jacob.' Freya stuck her chin out and folded her arms across her chest.

I like staying with Jacob too.

She knelt down in front of Freya. 'I know that, honey. But we have to find a home of our own.' She tucked Freya's hair behind her ear and turned the computer screen around to show her the flat she'd just reserved. 'It will be fine. Honestly, it's near to the school and you'll still get to see all your friends.'

Freya gave a nod and stared at the cases. 'Will we have a Christmas tree like Jacob's?'

No. Something tugged at her heartstrings. She didn't want to leave. She *really* didn't want to leave.

Jacob was being secretive. He'd kissed her, but never made any promises. He'd never even asked her and Freya to stay for Christmas. He hadn't asked them to leave either…in fact, he'd made lots of excuses for them not to leave. But it wasn't the same.

A distant, secretive man was not what she needed. No matter how much he made her heart flip over. It made her question herself all the time. She needed to protect her heart and her daughter's. They'd got too attached. Freya's reaction now just made her even more determined.

Tears were bristling in her eyes. 'We'll get another Christmas tree and I promise it will be just as gorgeous as the one we decorated here.' *Bang goes my limited budget.*

It was fine. She would make sure it was fine. Anything to keep Freya settled after all the disruption she'd exposed her to. She already had the ridiculously expensive doll and all her accessories that Freya wanted for Christmas. Blowing what little savings she had left on another set of Christmas decorations was an easy sacrifice.

The key turned in the lock and she heard footsteps coming towards the sitting room. Jacob. He opened the door and his face dropped as soon as he saw what they were doing. The flat was clearly visible on the laptop screen in front of them.

'Bonnie? Freya? What's going on?'

Bonnie could feel her heart beating against her chest. She hadn't expected Jacob to come home—not when he'd been avoiding them. She'd planned to write him a note, thanking him for his hospitality, but saying they'd found somewhere to stay and she'd see him at work.

She put her arm around Freya's shoulders. 'Oh, Jacob, I didn't expect to see you. It's just—' she held out her hand '—I think we might have outstayed our welcome. I've found somewhere for us to stay.' She met his confused gaze. 'I think it's time for Freya and I to move on.'

His mouth was slightly agape. He looked shocked. He looked a bit hurt. And everything about this was confusing her.

This was definitely the right thing to do. This was *absolutely* the right thing to do.

'I'll miss you, Jacob.' Freya's little voice cut through the silence. 'Thank you for letting us stay.'

Jacob knelt down opposite her. 'I'll miss you too, Freya.' His voice sounded hoarse. 'You…and your mother.' He didn't look up. He didn't look at Bonnie at all.

This was it. This was his chance to say something. To tell Bonnie that his feelings were every bit as strong as hers.

That he wanted to kiss her again—just as he had the other night.

That he wanted to spend more time with her and Freya. That he wanted to give this relationship a chance. That this actually *was* a relationship.

That she wasn't completely crazy, and he was as crazy about her as she was about him.

She held her breath. Waiting. Waiting. For something. For anything.

But nothing came. Jacob still couldn't look her in the eye.

'Freya, go and get your coat and shoes. We need to go to the shops.' Freya disappeared without a word.

He lifted his head. 'Why are you leaving? Why are you leaving *now*?'

It was the way he said the word. She stepped forwards, everything erupting to the surface. 'We can't be here any more. Freya's getting too used to being around you.' She lifted her eyes. 'And so am I.'

She gave her head a shake. 'This was a bad idea. You helped us out, thank you. But I have no idea what's happening between us, Jacob.' She held out her hands. 'I have no idea what *this* is.' She took a deep breath. 'I've found somewhere for us to go. We'll be out of your hair.'

'You have? Where? Is it one of those ones that you showed me?' He sounded automatically defensive—as if he were going to tell them not to go.

She shook her head. 'No, it's another. It's small, but in the area of Freya's school. It will suit us for the next few months until we can find something else.' She licked her lips. This was horrible. This was awkward.

There was a huge hand currently inside her chest, squeezing her heart hard.

Jacob looked at her again. There was a flash of something behind his eyes, which disappeared almost instantly. He looked down again.

'What's going on, Jacob? I know something's been bothering you the last few days. But you haven't said anything. You've been avoiding me. I thought we could talk about things.' Her voice was edged with hopefulness that he might actually respond.

He shook his head. 'There's nothing.' His voice was flat.

His dismissal made her mad. 'Don't say that. Don't say it's nothing. I know it is. Tell me. Tell me what's going on.' She was shouting now and she could almost see all his barriers being built up all around him. She bit her lip in anger and tried one last time. 'I thought we could share things. I told you about my past—and you told me about yours. At least I thought you had.'

She glanced towards the door, worried that Freya would reappear.

He sucked in a deep breath. It made him seem taller, his chest wider and more imposing. 'Not everything can be shared. Not everything is your business.' His words were clipped.

'Then we have to go,' she said quietly. 'I can't be around you, Jacob. I can't watch my little girl forming a closer attachment to you day by day when I feel as if you can't be honest with me.' She picked up her green coat. 'I've been down this road before.' Her eyes swept down to the floor and she gave a little shake of her head. 'I thought that this time I could trust my judgement.' She lifted her head and met his gaze. 'I guess I was wrong.'

There was silence for a few seconds.

'I hope you'll be happy,' he said quietly.

Something inside her died. That was it. Nothing else.

She'd been wrong. She'd been wrong about her and Jacob. There was nothing between them. A wave of humiliation washed over her.

She'd never felt like such a fool—not even when she'd found Robert in bed with her friend. Everything about this was different. With Robert, there had been no emotional investment left. With Jacob?

This hurt. This hurt so much it felt as if it could kill her.

Freya appeared at the door and she took her hand. 'Goodbye, Jacob.' Her voice was trembling. She just hoped he didn't notice.

She held herself straight and lifted her head before she opened the door and walked outside.

It was definitely time to go.

CHAPTER ELEVEN

JACOB TUGGED AT the collar of his shirt. It had never seemed tight before, but today it was cutting into him.

He hadn't slept a wink last night. Probably because everything about yesterday felt wrong and his house was…empty.

He shuffled on the seat and glanced at his watch for the hundredth time. He wasn't good at being a patient. Probably because he wasn't exactly that—patient. He watched as the door to the consultant's office opened and he sat up anxiously. The woman sitting next to him rustled her newspaper nervously as she was called in. He sighed and leaned back again.

That woman looked exactly the way he did—sick with worry. It was so strange being on the other side of the fence. This was exactly why he'd gone into obstetrics. He wanted to help life into the world. He wanted people to have joy in their lives.

Oncology services? Never. He hated having to give any expectant mother bad news. Imagine having to do this almost every day? He couldn't stomach that.

Right now he couldn't think about all the cancer success stories.

His insides clenched once again as he took some deep

breaths. Worst-case scenarios. That was all that was running through his head right now. Stepping back from colleagues, stepping back from the job that he loved so he could undergo another set of treatment. Feeling sick to his stomach for days on end. Forgetting completely about any chance of a relationship with Bonnie and Freya. Living the rest of his life alone.

It wasn't what he wanted. *None* of this was what he wanted.

But the way he felt right now? There was no way he could put this on Bonnie and Freya.

What he wanted was a fiery redhead and her adorable daughter.

The words he'd wanted to say yesterday had stuck in his throat. *Don't go. Stay with me, please—even though I'm not sure I can offer you a future.* He couldn't put himself out there—not until he really knew what he was offering.

But one thing she'd said had affected him more than others. Freya was becoming too attached. He felt it too. And it seemed entirely natural. As if that was the way it should be. Because the little part of his heart he hadn't blocked off *wanted* to feel like that. But right now, his brain couldn't even let himself go there.

He was finding it hard enough to deal with himself without having to worry about other people's feelings. He couldn't even begin to imagine forming a relationship with Freya, only for her to have to be told down the line that her parent figure had died.

He knew exactly what that did to a kid. He could never wish that on another.

His house had been hideously empty last night. It was

odd; it had never felt that way before. When he'd lived alone he'd never noticed the silence.

But last night he had. Every noise had seemed to echo through the empty rooms. Taking out one cup for coffee, or one glass for wine, had seemed pathetic. Finding Freya's plastic cup in the sink had made his hands shake and for a second he'd thought he might break down.

The pain he'd felt last night was familiar.

Bonnie had left. His mother had left. Not in the same way, of course. But he felt every bit as raw now as he had all those years ago.

The pressure of the waiting game was almost breaking him.

The hands on his watch moved oh-so-slowly. Ten minutes felt like two hours. He just wanted to know. Even if the test results were bad at least he could start making plans.

He jumped as the door opened and the woman came back out, a stunned expression on her pale face. Did she get good news, or bad?

'Jacob Layton?'

He was on his feet in an instant.

'Come in, please.'

For a second his feet were stuck to the floor, but he was too determined to get this part over with to let anything hold him back. He took long strides into the room, not waiting to be offered a seat, his eyes scanning the notes upside down on the desk. Trying to see if they would reveal anything.

The oncology consultant closed the door and took his seat opposite Jacob. Desmond Carter had looked after Jacob throughout his treatment. As soon as he'd been diagnosed, Jacob had looked for the best. Someone who would understand his need to continue to work and be able to tailor his treatment to his needs.

Desmond should probably have retired years ago. His hair was grey, his face deeply lined. But it appeared he loved his job as much as Jacob loved his.

He gave Jacob a little nod of acknowledgement. Another thing Jacob liked about Desmond Carter—he was a straight talker. He didn't give false platitudes and he told it like it was.

He glanced down at the notes in front of him. 'Jacob, let's talk about these test results.'

Bonnie was on edge. She was nervous about having moved to the new tiny flat just before Christmas. Nervous about the impact on Freya. Nervous about how she felt now she was out from under Jacob's roof.

It's temporary. She kept repeating the words in her head—hoping she might start to believe them.

She'd had to do it. Had to. She couldn't go on like this. Her insides had been so screwed up last night, praying, just praying Jacob might say something to her about how he felt. When it hadn't happened she'd spent the rest of the night crying into her pillow. Pathetic.

This was about her. This wasn't really about Jacob.

She was scared. Scared of putting herself out there and getting into a relationship with another man. She'd vowed to herself that if she ever got involved again, she would be absolutely sure. There wouldn't be a hint of doubt in her head.

But if Jacob couldn't tell her how he felt about her and Freya…then she was right. She was right to move out and give herself some headspace. Some time to make sure she could trust her judgement when it came to men.

The labour suite was busy today. All the staff kept joking about a power cut in Cambridge nine months before. And it certainly felt like that—she'd been catching babies all day.

But she hadn't caught sight of Jacob all day. It was probably just as well. He was bound to be avoiding her again. The further she pushed Jacob Layton from her mind, the better.

She finished stripping a bed in one of the rooms and walked along the corridor to the sluice. It was all hands on deck today; they even had a few midwives from some of the other areas helping out.

As she walked past the treatment room she glimpsed Isabel in a conversation with Hope.

Both had always been warm and friendly towards her—even inviting her to join them for dinner—and Jacob had mentioned that he was friends with both women. It struck her as a little strange. He seemed to hold them both in high regard, but she hadn't really seen him talking with either one.

'What's going on with Jacob?' Bonnie's footsteps stilled as Isabel's Australian accent floated out towards her.

They were drawing up a controlled drug for a pregnant woman in labour.

'How would I know?' answered Hope. 'I can barely get him to talk to me these days. It's a shame, but for a while we started to see the old Jacob again.'

Bonnie walked into the sluice and pushed the laundry into one of the baskets. She wasn't trying to overhear, but the two rooms were right next to each other with only a thin corridor leading to the sister's office separating them. She could still hear every word. She walked over to the sink to wash her hands.

'Do you think it's the cancer again?'

She froze. *What?*

Hope sounded serious. 'Do you think it's back? Oh, no. Don't say that. Not after everything he's been through.'

'Wouldn't he be due to get reassessed again? Some tests to see if the treatment's worked?'

The water was trickling in front of her but she hadn't moved.

Jacob. Jacob had cancer. *Her* Jacob had cancer and hadn't told her.

No. He couldn't possibly have. This couldn't be right. She held out her hands automatically, going through the motions of washing and drying them.

He hadn't lost his hair. It was short. But not missing. She hadn't noticed any marks on his skin for IV chemotherapy. He hadn't been sick around her. He didn't look sickly.

Really? Jacob had cancer? She finished drying her hands.

She couldn't help it. Her legs took her straight to the door of the treatment room.

'Jacob has cancer?' Her voice cracked. She could barely get the words out; her eyes were already filling with tears.

Hope and Isabel's heads shot around—a look of horror on both of their faces. They exchanged shocked glances.

Isabel took a step forward. 'Bonnie, I'm sorry. We didn't see you there.' She looked panicked. 'We should never have said anything.'

Her head was spinning. This almost felt as if it were happening to someone else.

Under any other circumstances she might think they were gossiping. But these women were Jacob's friends. They'd known him longer than she had and it was likely he'd taken them into his confidence.

'But you said it because you care—because Jacob is your friend.' Her heart was thudding against her chest.

Hope stepped forward too. She shook her head. 'Please understand, this happened long before you got here. We were both sworn to secrecy. No one else knows. Jacob didn't want anyone to know he had non-Hodgkin's lymphoma, or that he was undergoing treatment.'

Bonnie felt her blood run cold. Non-Hodgkin's lymphoma. The same type of cancer that his mother had died from. Oh, no. Poor Jacob.

She could be sick, right now, all over the treatment-room floor.

Hope touched her arm. 'Are you okay? You look terrible, Bonnie. I'm so sorry. I knew something was going on between you and Jacob. I just didn't know what. I guess I thought he might tell you.'

She started to shake, but whether it was from shock or disbelief she just didn't know. She took a long, slow breath.

Pieces in her brain started to slot into place. Now she knew why he'd been evasive. Now she knew exactly why he'd been acting the way he had. Everything made sense to her.

But he hadn't told her. And that hurt. It hurt so much she wanted to grab him and shake him.

Isabel stepped over next to them both. 'Bonnie,' she said carefully, 'I can see you're upset. I have no idea what's going on with you two—but I want you to know. You're good for Jacob. Up until a few days ago he was the happiest I've ever seen him. If you can help him, then please do.' She glanced at Hope. 'He's our friend. Above everything, we want him to be happy and well. Things that we've got no control over.'

She squeezed Bonnie's arm. 'I think you may be an influencing factor over one of those things.'

The tears welled in Bonnie's eyes. 'But he didn't tell me. He told me some things, but he never mentioned this at all.'

A worried glance shot between Hope and Isabel and Bonnie took another deep breath, trying to calm her frantic brain. 'But I think I know why.'

She turned on her heel and walked out of the door. The labour suite might be busy, but she wasn't looking after a patient right now and there were more than enough staff on shift.

Jacob had to be her priority.

Her footsteps halted a little on the way down the corridor. She'd spent the last two days fretting over herself. Thinking only about herself and Freya. She hadn't actually stopped to think that something might be wrong with Jacob. She'd challenged him. She'd asked him to tell her what was wrong. But not in a loving, compassionate way. She'd asked him in an angry, recriminatory kind of way. No wonder he hadn't told her.

She'd been too busy worrying about making a mistake again—focusing on the past instead of the future. How wrong she'd been. News like this put everything into perspective and made her realise exactly how precious life was.

She stalked past the midwives' station and opened the door of his office. He hadn't been around all day, but he was here now, sitting behind his desk.

Was he paler than normal? Were those dark circles under his eyes?

He jumped to his feet as soon as he saw her.

Now she could see him standing in front of her she could feel the adrenaline course through her. He could have told her. He could have told her the truth, couldn't he? Why hadn't he told her?

She'd been thinking a whole host of other things—she'd thought the worst of him. When she'd had no right to. Jacob had been nothing but kind and supportive to her and Freya. And she'd pushed him away with her own insecurities. But instead of reaching out to her, he'd pushed her away too. What were the reasons for that?

This man had wound his way around her heart. She'd seen another side to him, a warm and loving side. A side that showed her, even if he didn't know it, he was ready to move on with his life.

He'd lit something inside her that she hadn't felt in years.

'Bonnie? Is there an emergency? Is something wrong with a patient?'

He was ready to run to the attention of any patient that needed him. But what about her?

She closed the door quietly behind her and folded her arms across her chest. She would not cry. *She would not cry.*

But her heart was squeezing in her chest. Jacob had cancer. Jacob had the same cancer that he'd watched his mother die from. She already knew the damage that had inflicted on him as a child, and in turn as an adult. But she'd only known half the story.

What had the test results shown?

'Nothing's wrong with a patient, Jacob.'

Confusion flooded his face. 'Then, what is it?'

'Something's wrong with me.' She pointed her finger. 'Something's wrong with you.' Frustration was building in her chest. 'Why didn't you tell me you had non-Hodgkin's? Why didn't you tell me you had the same type of cancer as your mother?'

This not-crying thing wasn't going to work. The tears were threatening to fall any second.

His mouth opened but no words came out. He sagged down into his chair as if she'd just knocked the wind from his sails. 'Who told you?'

She pulled out the chair opposite and sat down. 'It doesn't matter who told me, Jacob. What matters is why *you* didn't?'

He still couldn't speak. He just shook his head for a few seconds, then put up his hands. 'How could I tell you, Bonnie? We've just met. I never expected this. I never expected to meet someone who would just—'

'Just what?'

His eyes met hers. There were no barriers in place. No shields to hide behind. 'Who would make me want to love again—to be part of a family again.'

She couldn't speak. A wave of emotion welled up inside her. This time a tear did escape, sliding down her cheek.

'I'm so sorry. I'm sorry I didn't stop to think what was wrong.' She shook her head. 'I just thought I was making a mistake again, that I didn't really know you that well.' She lifted her head and looked into his eyes. 'I felt as if I couldn't trust my judgement,' was all she could say. 'When all the time I knew what kind of man you were. I just didn't realise. I didn't think you might actually be sick.'

He stood up, walking around the desk and crouching down in front of her. He reached up and touched her hand, enveloping it with his. 'I had to wait, Bonnie. I had to know for sure. I couldn't put you and Freya through what I experienced as a kid. We'd only just met. I couldn't possibly expect you to sign up for that.'

She reached over and touched his cheeks. 'But you can, Jacob. I'm here for you. We're here for you. I don't care that you're sick. All I care about is that we're together.'

He reached up and brushed the tear from her cheek, taking one of her hands again. 'But why would I put someone that I love through that?' His face was serious. 'Two people that I love?'

The heat from his hand was rushing around her body. A whole host of tingles shooting straight towards her heart. 'You do?'

She couldn't help but smile. She hadn't been wrong. She hadn't imagined the connection between them. On one hand it was pure relief, on the other, she still couldn't understand why he wouldn't share with her.

'I do,' he said sincerely. 'I really do.'

She was fixed on his intense green eyes. 'Then why didn't you tell me, Jacob? You told me about your mum—why didn't you tell me about you?'

He ran one hand through his hair, giving his head a shake again. 'How could I tell you that, Bonnie? How can I declare love one minute, then tell you I've got a potential death sentence the next? What kind of man would do that to you? What kind of a man would do that to Freya?'

She held her breath. She understood. She understood exactly what he was saying but it still wasn't what she wanted to hear.

'So why couldn't we have that discussion, Jacob? I thought you didn't care about us at all. Why do you think I arranged to move out? Did you really think I wanted to?' She reached over and touched his jawline, feeling his smooth skin under her fingertips. 'Did you really think I would want to walk away if things were going to be tough? Because I wouldn't, Jacob. Not in a heartbeat. I love you. I don't care if it gets tough. I want to be the person by your side, holding your hand.'

His voice was quiet. 'But I don't want that for Freya. I don't want that for you. I watched my mother waste away before my eyes, the life just drained out of her. In the end, it wasn't a life at all. I could never do that to Freya. You've been through enough already.' He paused for a second then met her gaze again as he pulled his hand away from hers. 'I still can't.'

Bonnie leaned forwards; her face was inches from his. He could see fire spark behind her bright blue eyes. 'You don't get to make that choice any more, Jacob.' She pushed her hand up to her heart. '*I* do.'

He opened his mouth to speak again but she held up her hand. 'You've told me that you love me. You told me that you love Freya too. That's enough, Jacob. That's enough for me. I left because I doubted myself. I doubted my judgement. My past experience has made me untrusting, and I'm sorry for that.'

He pulled back. 'I can't do this. I can't let you do this. My mother had this cancer. I've had this cancer. I've got to assume that it's somehow in my genes. I can't make you any guarantees. I can't offer you what you want, Bonnie. Not when there's such a high risk.'

She stood up from the chair and faced him. 'What is it that I want?'

He frowned. 'Children. You'll want more children. This has to be in my genes. I could never, ever live with myself if I passed this disease on to our children.'

Bonnie looked furious. 'Have you asked me that? Have we had that conversation? What about what I think?'

He shook his head again. 'Look at you, Bonnie. You thrive on being a mother. You *love* being a mother—and you're fantastic at it. You were born to be a mother. I know that you want a whole house full of children. Don't pretend otherwise.' He pointed to his chest. 'And I can't give you that. I just can't.'

She blinked and he could see more unshed tears behind her eyes. 'I want you, Jacob. You and Freya. That's what I want. That's who I want my family to be. Can't we just work on that? Can't we just work on making a life together with what we have between us?' She stepped forwards, reaching up and cupping his cheek in her hand. 'Tell me about your test results. Tell me what happened. Good news or bad, I'm here for you. We're here for you. Just trust me enough to tell me.'

It was the first thing he'd noticed about her. Those bright blue eyes. And they were fixed on him with such an intensity right now that it felt as if a fist had closed around his heart and squeezed tight. He'd never felt like this. He'd never loved someone as he loved Bonnie. He'd never wanted to put himself on the line before. But Bonnie was everything. She didn't know. She didn't know he'd had good results. She didn't care. She still wanted to be with him.

For the first time he stopped to think straight. To let his heart rule his head. Every rational part of his brain had told him to back away. Every part of him that loved her didn't want her to be hurt.

But, for the first time, he could see himself building a life with Bonnie and Freya. A life that wasn't overshadowed with the thought of cancer recurring. A life that might actually be filled with love and hope.

And from the determined look in Bonnie's eyes it was exactly what she wanted.

His hand covered hers. 'My results were good, Bonnie. The non-Hodgkin's is in remission—for now. I'll need to keep having checks every six months for the next five years. There's always a chance it could recur.' As he said the words out loud he felt relief flood through him. He hadn't let that happen yet. He hadn't stopped to take a breath. The big black cloud that had been hanging over him for the last fourteen months had finally gone.

She didn't hesitate. She flung her arms around his neck. 'Oh, Jacob. That's fantastic.'

Her body was pressed against his. The warm angles familiar. The feeling of warmth, the feeling of love, the feeling of compassion were all here. All his for the taking. Could he really walk away from Bonnie now? When she'd told him no matter what his results she wanted to be by his side?

He stopped and pulled back, running his hand through her auburn hair. 'It is, isn't it?'

He was feeling lighter. And it wasn't just the diagnosis. It was the feeling of sharing. The feeling of having someone else invested in him. Of not having to face the future alone.

Bonnie's grin reached from ear to ear. 'It's better than fantastic.' She jumped up on him, her hands already around his neck, her legs now around his waist. The force sent him backwards against the wall and he started to laugh. Really laugh. Laugh as he hadn't in the last few years.

'Get rid of me now, Dr Layton,' she joked, her eyes gleaming.

This. This was what he wanted. This was what he'd wanted from the moment he'd seen her. Was he brave enough to reach out and grab it—just the way Bonnie had?

He was still smiling but he put on his most serious voice. 'Sister Reid, you seem to have put me in a compromising position.'

She tilted her head to one side. 'I have, haven't I? So, what are you going to do about it?' There was a challenge in her voice. 'I've already told you. Your choices are limited.' She uncoiled one hand from his neck and stroked her finger down his cheek. 'I think it's my job, and Freya's, to make sure that this year you have the happiest Christmas ever—*we* have the happiest Christmas ever.' The seriousness left her voice. 'So, what are you going to do, then?'

'Oh, that's easy,' he said as he adjusted her in his arms. 'I'm going to kiss you.'

And he did. Over and over again.

EPILOGUE

One year later

'ARE YOU READY, MUMMY?' Freya was bouncing up and down in her calf-length emerald-green bridesmaid dress.

Bonnie picked up her Christmas-themed bouquet and smiled. 'Oh, I've never been more ready. Let's go, gorgeous.'

They held hands and walked out of the hotel room to the top of the stairs. Jacob was standing at the bottom, waiting for them. In her honour, he'd dressed in a kilt. And she'd never seen a more handsome honorary Scotsman.

Her steps had never been surer as she picked up the skirts of her wedding dress and walked down the stairs to meet the man who made her complete.

Her last wedding hadn't felt anything like this. It had been beautiful, but she hadn't felt love in her heart and soul the way she did today. Jacob hadn't taken his eyes off her on her whole way down the stairs.

Her friends from the hospital applauded as she reached the bottom and she let out a nervous laugh. Jacob leaned over to kiss her. 'You look gorgeous,' he whispered.

'I don't think you're supposed to do that until after the ceremony,' she murmured back.

He smiled. 'Well, don't tell anyone. But I've got a really take-charge wife-to-be. She's taught me just to seize the moment.'

And she had. They'd spent the last year growing together as a family. Taking steps that she'd never have even considered a few years ago.

The celebrant gave them a nod towards the room where the wedding was to take place. The whole hotel was decorated for Christmas. A large Christmas tree was next to them at the bottom of the stairs and dark green and red garlands decorated the stairs. Twinkling lights glistened all around them. It really was the perfect setting.

'I'm not finished yet.' Jacob smiled.

'What do you mean?' she asked. This wasn't in the plans. But her tiny wave of panic disappeared in an instant. Whatever it was that Jacob wanted to do—she was sure she would love it.

'Before we start,' he said to their surrounding guests, 'I'd like to let you into a little secret.' He glanced at her. 'Bonnie and I have been keeping secrets from you—but even my future wife doesn't know this one.'

Her stomach flip-flopped. What was he talking about?

He pulled an envelope from inside his highland dress jacket. 'This morning, we received the news that we've been waiting for.' He gave her a smile that made her toes tingle. 'I haven't even had a chance to tell Bonnie yet, because I've been keeping with the wedding tradition of not seeing the bride before the ceremony.'

He held up the envelope. 'We got news this morning that Bonnie and I have been approved as adoptive parents.'

He bent down and picked up Freya. 'Do you know that little brother or sister we've been talking about?'

She nodded solemnly. 'Well, some time next year you'll get to be a big sister.'

'I will?'

'We will?' Bonnie could hardly contain her excitement. They'd been waiting for the final verdict. And this just made the whole day even more perfect.

A number of waiters appeared with trays of champagne that were quickly dispersed amongst the guests. Jacob handed one to Bonnie. He held his aloft. 'So, we've not even made it to the altar yet. But I guess I decided to seize the moment.' She could see the glint in his eyes as he spoke.

'Can I ask you all to raise your glasses? To the best Christmas ever and to families.'

Bonnie clinked her glass with his and took a sip, then wrapped her arms around him and Freya. 'You're going to make me cry.' She laughed. 'And we're not even married yet.' She gave her head a little shake. 'This couldn't be more perfect.'

His green eyes fixed on hers. 'Oh, yes, it could,' he said as he bent to kiss her. 'Happy Christmas, Mrs Layton.'

* * * * *

PLAYBOY DOC'S
MISTLETOE KISS

TINA BECKETT

To my husband, who is willing to drop whatever he's doing to sip hot cocoa and stare at the Christmas lights with me. I love you, honey!

CHAPTER ONE

JESSICA ANN BLACK was used to chaos. As she arrived at her fifth case of the day—a home birth—that was exactly what she found. Chaos.

Daphne's birthing coach—who was also her husband—was on the ground beside the bed, out of commission. The woman's mum was doing her best to calm her daughter, but the shaky voice and panicked expression said she was in over her head.

Taking a deep breath, Jess waded into the fray, her training kicking in. A senior midwife at Cambridge Royal Hospital, she wasn't called out to many home births, but she'd followed Daphne through two successful deliveries in as many years. When she'd begged Jess to see to this one as well, she hadn't had the heart to refuse. All had gone well with the other two, so she'd expected the same with the third.

Except it wasn't.

Daphne gripped the bed, panting in quick breaths. Hurrying over to her, Jess gave her mum's shoulder a gentle squeeze and asked her to see to Daphne's husband. Then she focused all her attention on her patient.

"I'm going to check you, love. Give me just a moment." Snapping on her gloves to measure her patient's dilation, she found instead the baby had crowned—head pressed tight against her fingertips.

Alarm bells flashed through her system, but she suppressed them. Jess had learned to school her features into bland indifference—no matter what she was faced with. So much so that the hospital often asked her to step in when there was a particularly tense or emotional situation. She somehow had the ability to defuse them.

Maybe because she had plenty of practice doing just that in her own family. Especially with her sister. Only it didn't always work, as she'd learned the hard way.

"How long have you been like this?" Jess grabbed several towels from the stack of clean ones Daphne had readied at her bedside and laid them just below the woman's bum.

"Hours." The word was accompanied by another moan.

Since Jess had only gotten the call fifteen minutes ago, she knew that wasn't true, but it probably did seem like hours to someone who was scared and alone. Well, she wasn't alone, but she might as well be.

This baby was coming much faster than the others had. Jess had left the hospital as soon as Daphne's husband rang her, but somewhere between then and now things had taken a turn, and Rick had fainted dead away. No wonder he'd panicked. Jess had always been here for this part of the delivery. He'd probably locked his knees and sent his blood pressure plummeting until he passed out.

She prayed the baby was still okay.

"You know how to do this by heart, Daphne. Your baby is almost here, so I need you to grab your legs and bear down on your bottom."

More panting. "I don't know if I can. Hurts so much more than the others."

Jess didn't stop to ask where the other two children were; hopefully they were with someone and not wandering around the house alone. She'd tackle that problem after she handled this one.

If she was good at one thing, it was taking things as they came at her—dealing with one task at a time in the order of urgency. And right now, they needed to get this baby out.

"You can do it, love, absolutely you can." She helped Daphne get into position and told her to wait for the next contraction and then push. Jess's phone was on the table next to her, the hospital's number already on the screen ready to be dialed at the touch of a button.

"It's here." Daphne groaned…or maybe the sound came from her husband, Jess wasn't sure, but her patient began bearing down as Jess counted in slow measured tones.

"Perfect. Take a breath and push again."

The baby's head slowly emerged, the characteristic shape from compression very much evident in this little one, which made her again wonder how long he or she had been stuck in the birth canal.

As soon as she delivered the baby's head, she instructed her patient to stop, while she continued to support the neck and prepared for the hardest part of the delivery: the shoulders.

Daphne had buckled down to work, her earlier panic gone as she concentrated on the job at hand.

"Okay, let's go at it again."

The first shoulder appeared, and Jess maneuvered it, easing it out. Then came the second. A little rotation to the left. There! Both were out. "One more good push, Daphne, and we should have it."

Out of the corner of her eye, she saw the woman's mother guiding Daphne's husband to a nearby chair. She called over, "Rick, put your head between your knees. Daphne is doing fine."

Her patient pushed again and, as she'd suspected, the baby—a girl—slipped right out and into her waiting hands. The newborn cried without any stimulation, making Jess go slack with relief.

"You've got a baby girl. Congratulations." Still holding the newborn, she used the tips of her fingers to pick another towel and draped it over Daphne's chest. She then placed the baby on it. "Love on her for a minute, while I cut the cord."

With no one to hand her any instruments, she reached into her bag and found clamps and scissors in sterile packages and ripped them open. She then clamped and cut the cord and delivered the afterbirth.

As soon as everyone was stable, and Rick was back on his feet and standing beside his wife looking rather sheepish, she pressed the dial button on her mobile. Daphne and the baby would need to be checked.

Expecting one of the nurses to answer, she tensed for a second when a low masculine drawl brushed across her ear. "Cambridge Royal Hospital, Dean Edwards here."

Dean Edwards. Special Care Baby Unit doctor and one of the hospital's most eligible bachelors. Definitely its most notorious from all of the whispered love-'em-and-leave-'em tales that floated through the hospital's corridors.

Forcing her voice to remain absolutely level and calm

even though her pulse had rocketed through the roof, she informed him of the situation and that she was arranging for transport to take the family to hospital. She asked that someone be there to meet them when they arrived.

"Will you be arriving with them?"

She hesitated, tempted for some strange reason to say yes. Shaking herself free of the urge, she said, "I have somewhere else to be, but I'll make sure they get off without any problems."

"I'll be waiting." The words sent a strange shiver through her. Almost as if he'd be waiting for her.

Ridiculous. Back to reality, Jess.

She still had her mum and dad's anniversary party to get through as soon as she left here. The last thing she needed was to be mooning over Dean Edwards. Besides, she needed all her wits about her, because the party meant she would be facing her twin sister, who she'd only seen a handful of times since Abbie's wedding day.

The day Abbie had married Jess's fiancé.

"You're still after him aren't you? You'd love it if something happened and we broke up."

Jess stood there in shock as her sister's furious words poured over her.

After him? The familiar accusation ripped open old wounds and laid them bare.

Hadn't it been the other way around six years ago? Martin had been Jess's fiancé, until Abbie—just like with everything else—had decided she wanted what her sister had.

"Just stop it, Abbie. I'm not up to it tonight." The pounding in her temples attested to that fact.

"Well, that's too bad. Because I have a few things I want to get off my chest, and since we're both here…"

Jess took a breath and reminded herself that they were at their parents' thirtieth anniversary party and that her sister was seven months pregnant with her fourth child. Throwing another brick on the restraining wall that held back her own bitter feelings, she tried again.

"Let's not fight, Abbie." She made her voice as calm as possible, trying to ward off the inevitable. "This isn't the time or place."

"Who's fighting? Certainly not me."

"No? It sure sounds like it. Those text messages weren't from me. Did you ever think about ringing the number, or asking Martin directly?"

Her sister had basically accused her of sexting her husband while he was away on business trips. It was ludicrous to have to defend herself against such a ridiculous accusation. Besides, she couldn't imagine Martin being stupid enough to leave incriminating texts on his phone for Abbie to find. There had to be another explanation. Unfortunately, Martin was away on yet another trip.

"I'm asking *you*, instead." Her sister's thunderous expression made her take a step back.

"You can well and truly have him, Abbie. I don't want him back."

It was on the tip of her tongue to say that she'd found someone else—that she was madly in love. But she didn't. Because there was no one even on the horizon. Madly or otherwise.

She hadn't gone out on a date in ages.

"Oh, really?" Her sister put a hand to her belly, disbelief written all over her face. "Well, you'd better make sure it stays that way."

Jess's teeth ground together, her anger rising. "That's enough."

"I still have a few things to make perfectly clear."

This was why she avoided being in the same room as her twin, going so far as to move from London to Cambridge. Those five minutes in the birthing suite—when her sister had arrived first—had set a pattern that continued to this day. Abbie had to be first in everything. Or at least look like it. She'd excelled at everything she touched, outdoing Jess whenever she got the chance. Her sister had even followed her to uni and studied midwifery, going one step further and making it look as if she'd had the idea first.

Abbie had the home and the family her mum had always wanted both her girls to have. Another source of contention, since her parents felt Jess poured too much of herself into her career.

But she loved her job. She wasn't substituting one thing for another. Nor was she worried about her biological clock running out.

She lowered her voice, aware that her mum was now looking at them from across the room with a frown. Time to put a stop to this. "This isn't a competition. It never was."

"You think I'm competing? With *you*?" Her sister took a step closer, crowding Jess against the buffet table, ignoring the guest who tiptoed around them, plate in hand. "Believe me, you'd know it if I were."

The problem was, Jess did know it. It was the reason she'd had little to do with her sister since agreeing to be her maid of honor—the day Martin had stood at the front of the congregation and watched the brides-maids glide down the aisle of the church. He'd spared her hardly a glance—eyes only for Abbie. That had been one of the worst nights of her life. Her sister had gloated openly, even as she'd claimed to be glad to leave be-hind her aspirations of becoming a midwife. Martin and Abbie's first child was born seven months later. She'd been "blissfully happy" ever since.

"Listen, Abbie, if I were going to send sexy texts to someone, it certainly wouldn't be to Martin."

"What is that supposed to mean?"

More anger flared inside of her. She couldn't believe her sister was doing this at their parents' party. They'd come all the way to Cambridge from their home in Lon-don just so Jess could attend—her crazy hours leaving her little time for holidays or anything else. Leave it to Abbie to try to ruin their efforts by thinking of no one but herself. Well, this time, Jess was going to call her on it.

The restraining wall she had so carefully erected burst at the seams, allowing words she'd vowed never to say to spew out in a rush.

"What I mean is Martin's gone a little soft around the middle, hasn't he? Besides, have you ever heard the expression *once a cheater always a cheater*?"

Her sister flushed bright red. "I can't believe you just said that. Martin loved me. What were we supposed to do?"

Jess could think of a few things, but the pain behind her eyes was growing, warning her that things were about to get much worse. The last thing she wanted to do was burst into tears in front of her sister.

She slid to the side to get away from Abbie and from

her own growing frustration. "Okay, I'm done. This is *not* the place to be sniping at each other."

"Sniping? Why, you…" Abbie clutched her stomach with both hands.

Jess rolled her eyes. Whenever challenged by any-one—her parents, her friends, her sister—Abbie always felt dizzy, or sick…or too exhausted to "have this con-versation".

"Let's just call a truce and go back to our own sides of the room, okay?"

"I think—" Her sister moaned. "I think something's wrong with the baby."

She suddenly realized all the color had leached from Abbie's face. Her sister had also reached out to grip the table, knocking over a tiered set of plates that held ex-pensive hors d'oeuvres.

Crash!

The china exploded on the ground spraying tiny crab cakes and stuffed mushrooms in every direction.

The whole room went silent, all eyes coming to rest on the twins. Jess's anger transformed to horror.

Because Abbie wasn't acting or trying to garner sym-pathy. Jess recognized the signs enough to know her sister was in labor.

And the baby was two months early.

CHAPTER TWO

SHE'D BEEN HERE for hours.

Dean Edwards had popped into Cambridge Royal's Special Care Baby Unit five times since his shift started to check on his tiny charges, and each time he'd spied her standing in almost the exact same spot with her shoulder propped against the wall staring at the row of cots.

Dressed in a red party frock that hugged her slender frame, she'd obviously come from some kind of celebration. Only she wasn't celebrating now.

In fact, she looked devastated, as if the baby she hovered over had passed away. But although tiny, the newborn was very much alive. And right now, those bloodshot eyes and tracks of mascara were doing a number on his gut, and he didn't like it.

Not much got to him in his thirty-five years. Except a woman crying. It brought back memories of unhappy times and unhappy people.

He'd been willing to let her stand there as he worked, but the increasing tightness in his throat finally drove him to clear it and cross over to her.

"She's going to be okay, you know." He kept his voice low and soothing, partly to avoid startling the sleeping babies and partly to keep her from realizing how her obvious grief had affected him.

She didn't even glance in his direction. "It's my fault she's here in the first place."

That made him frown. "Sometimes these things just happen."

"Do they?"

Light brown wounded eyes swung to meet his and the punch to his midsection was nothing like that earlier uneasiness.

"Yes." He leaned his shoulder against the same wall so that their faces would be level with each other. Long and lean, she was still a head shorter than he was. "And you need to get some rest. You can't do her any good, if you're exhausted."

Her eyes closed for a minute and her chest rose and fell before she looked at him again. "I'm not her mother."

Those words made his frown deepen. Had he detected a wistful note in her voice? "I know who you are."

"I'm Jessica…" She blinked, arms wrapping around her waist. "You do?"

Why so surprised? They'd spoken on the phone earlier today.

"Did you think you were invisible or something? If so, you should know—" he leaned in closer and lowered his voice to a conspiratorial whisper "—your invisibility cloak might need recharging."

That was the truth, because with her long blonde hair, soft caring eyes and a laugh that could melt the hardest of hearts, there was no way he could have missed noticing her from the moment she'd started working at the hospital. And because of that, he'd done his damnedest to avoid her. Until now. When he couldn't.

A trace of a smile appeared on her face. "Really? Because most times, I pretty much feel… Scratch that." She stood upright with a shrug. "Sometimes people confuse me with my sister. We do look quite alike."

The sister?

He'd seen her. Had been there right after her baby was born. And while there were obvious similarities in coloring and bone structure, that ended when you looked beyond, to what was inside. Maybe her sister's frown lines were due to worry about her child, but Dean didn't think so. Because Jessica's brows were smooth and clear. The only lines she had were little crinkles at the far corners of her eyes that spoke of smiles and laughter.

"Do you think so?" he asked. "Because I'm just not seeing it."

Up went delicate brows. "We're twins. *Identical* twins."

He couldn't stop himself from poking at what was evidently a sore spot. This woman revealed a lot about herself without saying much at all. "So you're saying not even your mother could tell you apart?"

"Of course she could, it's just that…" Another quick breath. "Some people can't."

Dean glanced at the babies across from him, a rare moment when they were still all snoozing away, the clicking of ventilators and beeping machinery the only sounds in the room besides the two of them. He'd like to keep it that way, if possible. These little ones needed rest. Lots of it. They weren't the only ones. Jessica Black looked well and truly exhausted, so much so that he was surprised she was still standing. She needed to take a break.

Against his better judgement, Dean was going to suggest she do just that.

"Have you been home yet?"

She shook her head, still staring at the cots. "I don't want to leave."

"I know, but you look like you could use some downtime—I know I could. Do you want to go somewhere and grab a bite? My treat."

Something about the way she'd blamed herself for her niece's premature birth made him want to find out why she would think something like that. The time he'd seen her sister beside the baby's incubator had given him pause. Jess had been there as well, but the sisters hadn't spoken a word to each other. In fact, the chill in the room had been almost palpable.

Instead of nodding or politely turning him down, Jess blinked. "Excuse me?"

Not quite the reaction he'd expected. "I was asking if you wanted to get something to eat."

"I heard what you said."

Okay, so coming over here to comfort her was evidently the wrong choice. She didn't seem to want it. Any of it.

Since he'd already asked, though, what choice did he have except to see this through to the bitter end?

"So, is that a yes? Or a no?"

"Oh, it's definitely a no. Not interested." She shook her head. "I may look like her, but I'm definitely *not* her. And your timing, by the way, is lousy."

Timing?

Bloody hell. Did she think he was trying to hit on her because she looked like her sister? If so, this day was just getting better and better. He'd heard bits and pieces of enough conversations to know that he had a reputation. An undeserved one. He was squeaky clean as far as keeping his professional life separate from his private. Beyond that, though, all bets were off.

He forced himself to glance at his watch and give her an easy grin, even as his back molars ground against each other. "Really? Because where I come from, timing is everything. And *this* is the time I normally eat supper. Not go to bed."

There were several seconds of absolute silence. When she looked at him again, her cheeks bloomed with red.

Maybe he should soften his words a little. "I promise this is about sitting down to a meal and giving yourself a much-needed break. Nothing else."

"Oh, Lord." She tipped her head back against the wall and closed her eyes. "I'm sorry. I just… I thought…"

Yeah, sweetheart. I know exactly what you thought. And she was partially right. With a roomful of sick babies, and after a particularly exhausting shift, bed was exactly where his mind was heading.

As in falling into it. To sleep. By himself.

"Supper," he confirmed. "I'll stay on my side of the table the whole time."

If anything, her color deepened. "It's been a difficult day. It was my parents' anniversary. And with Abbie going into labor in the middle of it, I'm not thinking straight."

All my fault.

Wasn't that what she'd said when he first came over to talk to her?

Suddenly he wanted to know why she blamed herself. "Which is why you need to get away for a bit. I know a great little place just around the corner that serves wonderful Indian cuisine. And it leans a bit to the fancy side, so you won't be overdressed." He allowed the side of his mouth to kick up again to reassure her.

She didn't smile back. Instead, her glance went to her dress and then back toward the row of special-care cots. "Are you sure she'll be okay?"

Instead of answering her, and since he couldn't give her any long-term prognosis at the moment, Dean took his stethoscope from around his neck and dropped it into his pocket. After washing his hands, he went over to the baby's incubator. He could feel Jess's eyes on him the whole time as he slid his hands through the holes on the side of the bed and stroked a tiny hand, checking the readouts on the stand next to the cot.

"She's stable." For the moment, although he knew that could change at any time. "She'll be watched carefully, but I can leave a call number for us at the desk if it'll make you feel better."

"Yes. It would. Thank you."

Dean wasn't sure why she wanted them to ring her rather than the baby's own mother, but he knew better than to ask.

Snapping off his gloves and discarding them, he motioned toward the door. "I'll just go hang up my coat and sign out. Do you want to meet me by the front door of the maternity unit?"

She nodded. "I'll let my sister know where I'm going." Without another word, she slid through the door of the SCBU and headed down the hallway, her red dress swishing around her hips in a way that made him rethink just how tired he was.

Too tired.

And she worked at the hospital.

A combination that had "do not touch" written all over it.

Dean had never been one to play by any set of rules except his own. But this was definitely one of them: don't get involved with any one female…and especially not one he worked with on a regular basis. Even though Jess didn't work on his floor and he didn't see her every day, it still counted. Getting too involved could get tricky. And ugly.

If ever he needed to stick to the game plan, it was now. He'd been able to abide by his inner rules in the past. And he could damn well do it now.

Jess recognized the place. All those rumors about Dean were usually centered around this particular restaurant—as in he'd been spotted here. More than once, and always with a woman in tow.

She swallowed. With soft lighting and half walls that divided the space into smaller clusters of diners, she could see why. The restaurant fostered an atmosphere of quiet intimacy.

For what? Discreet affairs?

Jess wasn't sure what madness had her sitting across from the playboy of Cambridge Royal, but something had obviously addled her brain. And from the way the hostess greeted him by name, eyes journeying over his tie and dress shirt—and the way he filled it out—as they came through the door, he'd been here many times before.

That brought up another question. The tie. Where had he come up with that? Did he keep one in his office just for spur-of-the-moment dinner dates? If so, it evidently got a lot of use. It would seem those rumors were true.

Which brought her back around to the insanity of being here. With him.

That argument with her sister and its aftermath had left her heartsick. Even her mum had shot her a couple of disappointed glances as they'd waited for the doctors to check Abbie over.

Had she done enough to avoid that confrontation? She'd tried to shut it down, but, in her desperation to get away, she'd been much harsher than necessary.

But the idea that she'd been engaging in some long-distance pillow talk with Martin while he was away on business trips was so ludicrous, she hadn't been sure how to answer her. Abbie didn't even have proof that Martin was engaging in anything of the sort. With anyone. Just some vague messages on his phone that could have meant anything.

Why hadn't Jess just walked away the second she realized her sister's temper was beginning to flare out of control? Instead, she'd stood there and defended herself in front of a roomful of guests. Moving the venue of the anniversary party to Cambridge had already made for a tense atmosphere, and by fighting with Abbie in the middle of their celebration she'd made things worse for everyone. Including that little one hooked up to machines in the Special Care Unit.

God. Her eyes closed as another shard of guilt stabbed through her stomach.

"Hey. You okay?"

Dean's voice had a gruff soothing quality as it drifted over her. One she'd never noticed before this second.

She blinked back to awareness. Exactly what did that mean? She only crossed paths with the man in those odd moments when their jobs intersected, which wasn't all that often. Her midwife duties kept her in one section of the hospital, while Dean's kept him in another.

But you noticed him. You know you did. How could you not with all that gossip about his exploits?

Yes. She'd heard those stories. Time and time again. Only no one she knew had actually claimed to have made it into Dean Edwards' bed. Or anywhere else, for that matter. But he'd been seen around Cambridge. And never with the same woman. The descriptions varied, but the pattern didn't.

"I'm fine." She toyed with her serviette. It was on the tip of her tongue to ask for the fifth time if he was sure it was all right to leave the baby, but she clamped down on it just in time to stop the question from emerging. The hospital would ring if there was any change.

The waiter arrived with a bottle and a question on his face. When Dean nodded, the man poured white wine into both of their glasses. Not that she needed to be drinking at a time like this. But it was only one glass, and, since she didn't keep any kind of alcohol in her house because of her dad, she didn't get to indulge all that often. Maybe it would stop the mad pounding in her chest at sitting across from the first attractive man in… well, since she and Martin had broken it off. Her sister might as well have poisoned the entire male species. Or at least made Jess feel like the consolation prize to anyone who might show some interest. Because when she was set side by side with her sister, Abbie was the one they'd chosen. Every. Single. Time.

She and Abbie might look alike, but their personalities were at opposite ends of the spectrum. Jess was the socially awkward one, the one who had trouble forming and keeping deep friendships, while Abbie was vivacious and outgoing, able to charm anyone she came in contact with. And her sister always got what she wanted.

And what she'd wanted was the very thing Jess had always dreamed of having. A place where she lived in no one else's shadow…where she truly belonged. At one time she'd equated that with having her own home and family.

When that possibility had been ripped away, she'd thrown herself into her job, doing all she could for her patients and their little ones. Maybe her parents were right. Maybe she was too dedicated. Looking at her tiny new niece had made her stomach churn with a longing she'd all but forgotten.

This was Abbie's fourth baby.

Jess had none. And no prospects of a serious relationship or any children in the near future.

She picked up her glass of wine, swirling the liquid to block the direction of her thoughts. Conversation. That was what she needed. Racking her brain, she tried to think of something that would break the growing silence. Something witty. Something that would make her feel a little less dull. Dean's eyes were now on her, a slight furrow forming between his brows.

Say something!

"I've never been here before. Do you come here often?"

Oh, no! Why had she asked that, of all things? A few seconds of silence followed the question before he spoke.

"Often enough."

His jaw tightened a fraction.

This was definitely where he brought his women.

His women?

She crinkled her nose at that thought. Wow, she was

really outdoing herself tonight. Worse, what if someone she knew was here? She sank a little lower in her seat, taking a sip of wine and swallowing it. "Really? It's my very first time."

Dean, who'd been in the process of lifting his glass to his lips, stopped with it midway to its goal. The furrow between his brows deepened, then he gave his head a slight shake as if clearing it and took a drink. A good-sized one if the movement of his throat was any indication.

Did he think she was flirting with him? She hoped not, because if he did, there was no telling what he might—

"What are you thinking about?"

Caught!

"My niece."

Those words brought her back to earth with a bump. Her niece's situation was the only reason she was sitting here in this restaurant.

Could the newborn sense the antagonism flowing between her and her sister, even in the SCBU? Abbie hadn't spoken to her since the baby's delivery, despite her mother's attempts at playing peacemaker.

Poor Mum. Some anniversary this had turned out to be.

He set his wine down. "You said it was your fault. You know that's not true."

"Abbie and I were in the middle of a row. She went into labor. If I'd just walked away…"

Would the outcome have been any different? Abbie had been bound and determined to have her say.

But surely Jess could have changed the direction of the conversation. Maybe. Her sister had always known exactly which buttons to push—which insecurities to choose—to get her going. Today had been no exception.

"Coincidence."

"Really? Stress can induce labor—you know that as well as I do." She paused a beat and then let the rest of it out. "She thought I was sending suggestive texts to her husband."

That got a reaction. Dean's eyes narrowed just a touch. "Were you?"

"No!" She fiddled again with the corner of her serviette. "I mean, Martin and I were engaged at one time, but once he saw Abbie—"

She couldn't finish the sentence.

Instead of pressing her for details, Dean chuckled.

That shocked her. "I don't see what's so funny."

"Well, not funny exactly. So your sister had her eye on your fiancé, and now that she has his ring on her finger, she's worried you might want him back."

That was it in a nutshell. It had been six years, but Abbie just couldn't let it go. It was one of the reasons Jess had moved to Cambridge in the first place, to get away from the constant haranguing and jealous questioning.

"I don't want him. At all."

"I can well imagine."

Which brought her back to the current dilemma. "I have no idea how to make her believe me."

The conversation paused when the waiter brought their food. Curried chicken with rice and vegetables served family style. Before she could lift a finger, Dean had taken her plate and dished up some of the fragrant food. Too bad she didn't have much of an appetite at the moment.

Once Dean had served himself, he had no problem

picking up where they'd left off. "So you think your sister is going to keep accusing you of trying to steal her husband...aka your ex."

Using her fork, she speared a piece of chicken. "She lives in London, so, once she goes back, I'm hoping it'll die back down. Or that Martin will be able to convince her we're not communicating behind her back."

"Mmm... I see." He popped a bite into his mouth and chewed. Swallowed.

Why was she even telling him any of this? And what was with her watching the man's throat? It had to be the way that sharp edge of his Adam's apple dipped, causing her eyes to want to follow it. All the way down to his... She jerked her eyes back to his face.

Dean continued. "No current love interest to throw her off the trail?"

"No." She hurriedly stuffed a piece of food into her mouth, even as she felt her face heat all over again. If he only knew how true those words were, he would think she was a complete washout when it came to the opposite sex.

In fact, the two of them should not even be having this conversation. She barely knew the man.

But what she did know of him... He was rumored to have a revolving bedroom door. Women in...women out. Swish, swish, swish turned that door.

"What if you did?" he murmured.

"Excuse me?"

He smiled at that. "You're not going to turn that cute little glare back on, are you?"

"Excuse... I mean, what?"

"That's better." He set his fork down and reached across to touch his fingers to hers. A shot of electricity arced through her hand and zipped straight up her arm. "I was just sitting here thinking. Maybe you should hand her proof of a conquest or two?"

It was said with a cheeky air that made her laugh. Not because it was funny, but because he said it as though it weren't such a stretch to imagine that she might have a long list of failed romances.

She didn't. She left things like that to her sister. And to men like Dean.

"I don't have any conquests."

His index finger brushed along hers, sending another shiver through her. "Do you always say exactly what you think, Jessica Black?"

"No." Although that wasn't quite right. She did tend to wear her heart on her sleeve, which was why her sister had always been able to zero in on what Jess wanted out of life—on which boy Jess liked. Then she turned on her million-kilowatt charm and took it for herself.

"Oh, I think you do." The low words curled around her midriff, squeezing the air from her lungs. "But maybe we can use that to our advantage."

"Um…we?"

"Mmm." He leaned across the table. "How about if we show your sister exactly how her little game is played."

"I—I have no idea what you're talking about."

"I think you need to show her you can round up your own men, thank you very much."

"Men? Plural?"

"Why not?"

Her gut churned. "How can you do that?"

"Do what?"

"Go to bed with hundreds of women as if it's nothing special."

His gaze hardened. "The hospital grapevine strikes again."

"It's not like you haven't been seen here. You have. The hostess knows your name, for heaven's sake." The words just kept pouring out. "I'm not judging. I just don't know how it's possible to have casual sex without feeling something…anything. Do the women just go along with it? Or do you simply stop ringing them after you've gotten what you wanted?"

The bitterness of everything that had happened with Martin came rushing back. The giving of her heart—her body—and then having him stop ringing her one day. Finding out he'd been seen with her sister and to have them show up at her door and spill the beans, that he'd been going out with Abbie while still engaged to her.

"What makes you think that the 'casual' in casual sex isn't on both sides? That the woman isn't just as interested in keeping things simple? Have you ever tried it?"

"Well, no." And she hadn't. Maybe that was why it seemed impossible to believe that two people could share a bed and then each go their separate ways the next day with no hurt feelings—no misunderstandings.

"Maybe you should. It's a hell of a lot different when neither party expects anything out of the arrangement other than a single night of pleasure."

The way his gravelly voice touched that last word sent a ripple through her midsection. What would it be like to have your physical needs met and then not expect anything further?

Maybe he was right. Maybe it wasn't as bad as it sounded.

And it could make her sister finally believe she was over Martin…that she'd been over him for a long time.

"Maybe I should."

One side of his mouth went up, and he leaned over the table. "Bet you can't."

She sat up a little straighter. If he could do it, surely she could. Unless he was calling her a prude. "Of course I can."

"Prove it."

Oh, no. This was not where she'd seen this conversation heading. "And how exactly am I supposed to do that? Are you going to hide in a cupboard and watch me?"

"No." A little of the mellowness in his voice had faded and a sharper edge had appeared. "But I can feel out the men. Make sure they're safe."

Jess could not believe she was even having this conversation. "So you would interview any prospective bed mate to make sure they aren't a serial rapist? Exactly where would this 'finding my own men' be done? A pub?"

One thing Jess was good at was sizing up personalities. Except how good had she been at sizing up Martin? Not great. Maybe she did need someone to help scope things out. Not that she was actually thinking of doing anything of the sort.

Was she?

Evidently she was.

"A pub is perfect," he said.

He didn't say it, but she got the distinct impression that that was where Dean picked up some of his prospective one-night stands.

Suddenly Jess was backpedaling like mad. She really

didn't think she could go through with it, but, since she'd criticized Dean, she could understand why he'd taken offense. Just because *she* didn't have casual sex once a week didn't make it wrong that he did. "And you would be what? My wingman?"

He tossed his serviette on the table. "Your wingman." He said it as if sounding it out. "I like it. I think that would work."

Oh, no, she had no intention of doing anything like what Dean was proposing. But the thought of letting the man see how much it bothered her...

What if she made it look as if she were going along with it? That way, even if she wiggled her way out of the dates, she could still tell her sister she was going out. Maybe it would even ease some of the bad feelings between them.

A thought came to her. What if Dean picked up a woman while she was there? The last thing she wanted was to see him walk out of that pub with someone. She had no idea why, but she didn't. "So let's say I agree to chat up three men—" she was careful not to actually say she would go on to have sex with these men "—then you have to do something as well. How about, you have to promise to leave the pub alone. Go without. See how the other side lives."

"So basically you would be the only one having fun?"

"Exactly. Think you can handle it?"

Dean leaned forward, one brow raised at the challenge. "Sweetheart, you've got yourself a bet."

CHAPTER THREE

DEAN HAD NO idea why he'd goaded Jess into that ridiculous bet. They'd gone to the pub twice so far and she'd easily found herself a partner both nights, slipping out of the place within an hour.

He wasn't sure why he'd done it. Or why he'd been so adamant about going with her. Maybe because it bothered him that she compared herself to her sister. And she did. He heard it in her words, saw it in the uncertain way her fingers twisted together when she talked about her.

And his own part of the bet?

Laughable, because she seemed to think he picked up a different woman every night.

It would be kind of hard to do his job if he spent all his nights having wild sex. Although he could think of one woman he might be tempted to make that sacrifice for.

Not that he would.

Especially since he'd promised that very woman that he would have no sex. At all. At least not for the next several nights.

"Dr. Edwards? Is everything all right?"

Sitting in a rocking chair in the corner and holding a tiny baby to his shoulder, he realized he'd zoned out for a few seconds. "Fine. I'm just getting ready to put her back."

His job didn't necessarily include cuddling his charges, but there was something about this one. Born to a drug-addicted mum, the little boy was off to a rocky start. But at least the child-welfare people had stepped in and insisted the mother clean up her act before allowing her anywhere near the child.

That was more than he had gotten when he was young. Then again, it was his father who'd had the addiction problem, not his mother.

He rubbed a few more gentle circles across the newborn's back. At least the baby had quieted down. When pregnant women took drugs, there were two victims. The baby's mother...and her child, who was now suffering through withdrawals—through no fault of his own.

Standing to his feet, he gave the nurse a quick smile before tucking the baby back into his cot. "Feel free to page me if this happens again."

She nodded, smiling back.

Young and attractive with curly brown hair and sparkling eyes, Deidre had made it a point to call him back whenever she had a particularly difficult case. He wondered if that was for the baby's benefit or hers. It didn't matter. He'd decided a long time ago it was better to leave his personal life at home and his professional life at the hospital. It was just better that way.

"You have such a way with them."

Did he? It seemed that anyone who offered these little guys a bit of love and affection would get the same response. And maybe that stemmed back to his childhood as well. He didn't want any of them to feel as alone as he'd once felt. And this particular baby had quieted down almost as soon as he'd settled into the rocker with him.

"I think it's just the body contact."

She raised her brows and went over to look at the now sleeping infant. "No, I think you just have the magic touch."

Not so magic.

He glanced at his watch, his jaw tightening. Tonight was the last night of his and Jess's bet, and suddenly the last thing he wanted to do was watch her walk out of that pub with yet another man. He'd made her ring him at home as soon as she arrived, and again after the man left her house, so that he would know she was safe.

Another thing he was nonplussed about. Of course she was safe. Jess was a grown woman and between the two of them they'd picked out the meekest, mildest-looking men they could.

Okay, that was probably all him, because Jess had talked to a couple of attractive muscular-looking chaps, but they'd made him uneasy.

Or was it just that he couldn't stand the idea of her spending the night with someone she might actually decide to go out with more than once.

Nope. That wasn't it at all. And just to prove it, tonight, he would let Jess pick out whoever she wanted.

And he wouldn't do a thing to stop her.

Having a wingman was the pits.

On their third and final outing, Jess was glad it was their last. Her days were spent with her niece, and her nights…well, her nights were Dean's. But not in the traditional sense.

As much as she wanted to skip out of the pub and go

home alone, Dean was always there. Always checking out the patrons. And, hell, if he didn't always steer her toward men that looked as if they were laced tighter than a corset. It was never the good-looking ladies' man, or anyone who was like Dean himself. No. In fact, whenever one of those types hit on her, somehow Dean was always there with a glare or a sharp word.

Why did he even care? Wasn't this all about the bet— about seeing what it was like to have a few nights of casual sex? That was what it had started out as.

Instead, Dean brooded. Off in the corner, he would nurse a glass of Scotch and watch her sit awkwardly at the bar. If he approved of whoever offered to buy her a drink he stayed put, if he didn't…well, if he didn't, he appeared next to her like an avenging angel and chased the man off.

So for the last two date nights—Jess had faked it. She pretended to leave with one of the pre-approved men and then bolted, feigning a headache or stomach virus. Maybe it was fortunate that the men were as nervous and unsure as she was, because it meant she went home alone.

Her one consolation was that Dean left by himself as well. At least, if he was keeping to his side of the bargain. From his grouchy demeanor at the hospital over the last couple of days, she'd say he really had slept alone.

Why that mattered, she had no idea.

She screwed up her courage for one last run, and went over to the bar, asking for a dark bitter ale—which she hated. Her friend Amy promised Jess would eventually get used to the stuff if she drank it often enough. Right now, she just wasn't seeing it. But it was cheap and Amy swore men were impressed by a woman who drank dark ale. Hmm. Her friend was single and pregnant, so while it might attract them, that was evidently all it did. Which might work in Jess's favor, actually.

She should probably give Amy a call and make sure everything was going okay.

Thank God this was the last night. Even Abbie and her parents had seemed surprised when she told them she had plans again this evening.

"Another date?" The hope in her mum's voice would have been comical had it not been so very far from reality.

She'd mumbled something that she hoped made sense and then slunk from the room and away from Abbie's suspicious eyes.

Sighing, she perched on the nearest stool and forced a sip down, glancing across the space and meeting Dean's eye. This evening he was in a snug black T-shirt and faded jeans, the combination doing a number on her tummy. She'd never seen him dressed this informally. He lifted his own drink—something that looked a whole lot stronger than hers—and gave her a mocking salute before taking a swig of it.

Why was he even here? Surely not to make sure she did what she promised. Because he didn't look particularly happy to be sitting there waiting for her to leave with her next victim. Or maybe he was just irritated that he wasn't going to take someone home himself. Either way, this wasn't fun anymore. Not that it ever had been.

Someone tapped her shoulder, and Jess turned her barstool to meet the smile of a blue-eyed ginger. "You're a fan of ale, I see."

The Scottish burr gave away his nationality, rolling

across her in a way that made her smile right back. "Not actually, but I'm trying to learn."

The man leaned forward and gave an audible sniff. "Dark Lady. Not a bad choice."

Okay, so maybe Amy was on to something. "Are you a fan?"

"I am now." Jess wasn't sure if he was talking about the ale or about her. She sized him up. Just how hard was he going to be to get rid of when it came time to leave?

When he covered her hand with his, she had her answer. She tensed, a trickle of panic beginning to gather in her midsection.

She didn't want to make anyone angrier than necessary. Especially a man like this one. She got the feeling he might be a little more difficult to shake.

Swallowing, she wondered if she could glance back at Dean and get his attention. They hadn't set up a signal in case she got in over her head. So maybe she should…

The back of her neck prickled just as her newfound companion's brows pulled together. His hand tightened over hers.

"I was wondering where you'd gotten off to, Jess."

Dean.

Had he read her mind? As much as she'd been thinking about sending out an SOS, what she really wanted to do was leave and get this whole bet thing over with. It had been beyond stupid. A time waster. For both of them. She never would be a casual-sex type of girl, no matter how hard he tried to convince her otherwise. It was all fun and games…until someone lost an eye—or their heart.

Not that she was in danger of that from this particular ale aficionado.

But from Dean?

Lord, she hoped not.

She spun around, suddenly deciding she didn't want or need his help. He'd decided he didn't approve of this particular man? Well, she would show him that, from now on, *she* made those kinds of decisions.

Up went her brows. She needed to cut him off before he got started. The last couple of times he'd wanted to get rid of a man who had his eye on her, he'd pretended to be her significant other.

"Mum isn't expecting us home until later." She smirked up at him, daring him to contradict her.

His response? A slow, knowing smile.

"Mum knows what we're like, when we're out on the town." He took the ale from her hand and set it in front of the Scotsman. "Enjoy."

The man let go of her, his possessiveness appearing to change to horror when Dean lifted a brow and said, "Dance with me…sis."

Then he whirled her into his arms and headed toward the floor where other couples were already moving to the beat of some slow song.

Jess couldn't hold back a laugh. "I can't believe you just did that. You've probably scarred that man for life."

There was no way she was going to admit she was relieved. Relieved she wasn't going to have to try to wave him off on her own.

"I can't believe you called me your brother."

"Serves you right for interfering."

He leaned back to study her face. "Did you want to leave with him?"

No, she didn't want to leave with him or anyone. But she'd gotten herself into a mess and wasn't sure how to get herself back out of it. "I thought we had a deal. I leave with three different men, and you leave with no one."

"I've changed my mind."

A warning tingle began at the back of her skull. "What do you mean you've changed your mind? Are you reneging on the bet?"

"Yes." The word brushed across her, and the tingle became a full-fledged shiver.

He pressed his cheek to hers and drew her closer. If the Scotsman wasn't scarred before at the way Dean had whisked her away, he probably was now.

Jess swallowed. "I'm not sure what you mean."

"I mean neither of us is leaving with a stranger. Not you. Not me." His hand tightened on hers just the way the Scotsman's had. The intimate contact filled her with alarm, but a completely different kind of alarm. Because she liked it.

"Well, you not leaving with someone was kind of the point, wasn't it?" Although her voice sounded as shaky as her legs felt, she managed a smile.

"I'm forfeiting. As of now."

So he *was* tired of frittering his nights away with nothing to show for it in the end. She should be glad. Because that meant she didn't have to pretend to leave with anyone now.

But she wasn't glad. And she wasn't quite sure why. "You're a free man. I assume you already have someone in mind."

"I do."

Jess turned her head, trying to figure out who the lucky woman was.

He tucked his fingers under her chin and shifted her face back toward his. "You're wrong. Are you so oblivious about what you do to a man like that?" He nodded in the direction of the bar where she'd sat a few moments ago.

"I'm not sure what you mean."

"He wanted to take you home with him."

"Oh." Of course she knew that, but then again people in places like this probably weren't particularly choosy. After all, they were here for the same reason that Dean probably came here. To find a companion for a night of sex.

He chuckled. "You really don't have any idea, do you?" His fingers left her chin and trailed up the line of her jaw. "There's only one woman I'm interested in leaving with."

"Who?" The trembling in her legs came back full force.

"Let's just say I'm thinking some *very* unbrotherly thoughts right now."

Her? He wanted to leave with her. Why?

Wasn't it obvious? Casual sex, remember?

It was on the tip of her tongue to give him a resounding yes and leap into his arms. But whatever had been niggling in the back of her head grew as she thought through the implications. He was tired of playing the wingman...tired of his little hunger strike. And now he was hoping to break his fast. What easier target than the person he'd coaxed into taking this ridiculous bet in the first place? The person he'd dared to have casual sex with three different men. How easy would it be for Dean to be that third man?

It had nothing to do with her at all. She could be a plastic mannequin for all he cared.

Casual sex, indeed. Maybe that was good enough for

him, but it wasn't for her. He might think her a prude, but she didn't care anymore.

Hurt surged up from somewhere inside her—a large festering lump that threatened to burst open in front of everyone in the pub.

"I don't think so, Dean. I have no clue what put this idea into your head, but you can put it right back out. If you want someone to pass the night with, you'd better keep on looking. Because this girl is leaving this whole scene. Alone."

With that, Jess yanked free of Dean's hold and stomped out of the pub and into the night.

CHAPTER FOUR

THE BABY WASN'T BREATHING.

The second the newborn was placed in his hands, Dean went into full crisis mode, belting out orders, even as he raced through possible treatment options, ruling them out one by one. Exhaustion pulled at his limbs, but at least he was able to put that fiasco with Jess last night out of his head. For now. He had no space for anything but what was currently happening in this room.

The victim of a drunk driver, the newborn's mother had been fatally struck as she crossed an intersection to go to work. CPR at the scene and efforts to resuscitate at Cambridge Royal had proved unsuccessful. The decision was made to put mum on life support and do an emergency C-section in an effort to save the baby, even as a grief-stricken husband waited outside the surgical suite.

"Let's bag her." He laid the baby on a table and a manual resuscitator was placed in his hand.

"Come on, sweetheart." The words whispered through his skull, with each squeeze of the Ambu bag. The tiny chest rose and fell. There was a heartbeat, but, so far, no effort at breathing on her own.

Going through his mental checklist, he had one of the nurses take over the bagging so he could test reflexes. He was gratified to see there were at least some reactions, though not what he would have liked. But babies' brains weren't fully developed. He'd seen some amazing recoveries in newborns even more premature than this one.

Most had not been deprived of oxygen for this long, however.

He glanced at his watch. Five minutes since delivery.

"Stop pushing air for a moment and let's see what we've got."

The nurse lifted the BVM and the whole world stopped breathing. At least Dean did. Then there was a gasp. And the kick of a small leg.

Suddenly the baby's face screwed up tight, and she let out a squeaked puff of air. Her lungs reinflated, and it became a full-fledged cry. Joined by another. Then another.

The sense of relief couldn't have been greater if it had been Dean's own flesh and blood lying on that metal table. Because at least the new father wouldn't have to mourn two deaths. And the baby's mum, still on a ventilator behind them, might be able to save more lives through organ donation, which was what her husband said she would have wanted.

"Let's take her down to Special Care to do the rest of the workup." The sooner they got her into one of the incubators, the better for her tiny lungs. They would monitor her for a while to make sure she kept breathing and remained stable.

The second they arrived on the ward, Dean noticed Jess's sister was in the room, seated beside her baby's incubator, but she didn't have exam gloves on. Nor did she have her hands through the openings so she could touch her baby's skin. Instead, she just sat there slumped forward. Glancing at the observation window behind him, he spied Jess. Her face was turned away as if she were staring at something down the hall. Maybe she just couldn't face looking at her sister.

He hadn't spoken with Jess since that disastrous scene last night at the pub. Why the hell had he pulled something like that?

He had no idea.

Turning his attention back to his newest charge, he directed the staff as they hooked the newborn up to the monitors and checked the baby's oxygen levels. So far, things were looking more hopeful than they had for the last half-hour.

"Let me know if anything changes."

Satisfied that everything was under control with this particular baby, he headed over to where Jess's sister sat and greeted her. When he asked if she wanted to interact with the baby she shook her head. "I don't want to do anything that would hurt her."

Something in her face tightened, and her eyes strayed toward the window.

Ahhh…so she did know her sister was there. When he turned his attention in that direction, he noted that Jess was now looking at both of them. And something in her stricken expression made his chest ache. Surely they could put what had happened between them last night aside—for a little while, at least. He motioned her inside. Jess hesitated, and he wondered if she might ignore him for a second, but, finally, she pushed through the door and slowly headed their way.

"I don't want her here." The low, angry words made him blink. The ache in his chest tightened even further.

These two women might look alike, but he'd been right earlier. The resemblance began and ended there.

"She's your baby's aunt," he said.

"And she caused this." Her hand swept around the room. "All of it."

"She caused *all* of these babies' problems?" He knew what she meant, but he wanted to hear her actually say the words. To say that she blamed Jess for what happened.

The woman's head jerked as she looked up at him. "Of course not. But my baby is here because of her."

When he realized Jess was close enough to have heard the ugly words, his heart hardened into a rock. The same rock he'd carried as a child when his father's anger had come at him and his mum in the form of ridicule or through his fists. But when Jess made to turn around and flee, he reached out and caught her by the wrist before addressing Abbie again. "No. Your baby is here because she was born too early. Nothing more. Nothing less."

The nurses working on the other baby threw them a curious glance, but he didn't budge. Jess had worried herself sick over her niece as evidenced by her vigil over the incubator that first night. And the way she made sure the nursing staff had her mobile number and made them promise to ring her at the first hint of trouble.

It took repeated tugging before he got her close enough to slide his arm behind her back and hold her in place, and even then she looked as if she wanted to crawl under the nearest rock. Or the nearest incubator. But he was not going to let her run away the way he'd once done. She was going to stand and face this particular bully head-on. And unlike Dean when he was a child, she would not have to do that alone.

Right on cue, Abbie's glance cut from one to the other before settling on the point of contact between the two of them. "Exactly what is going on here?"

Beneath his hand, Jess squirmed, and he was quite sure she wanted to ask him what the hell he thought he was doing. But she didn't. Nor had she made the slightest effort to defend herself in the face of her sister's ire.

Something swelled up inside of him—an urge to protect that was both familiar and foreign. Time to put someone firmly in her place. And he thought he knew the perfect way to do that. He was pretty sure Jess was going to kill him later, but he'd deal with that fallout when the time came.

He allowed his arm to drop, and when he glanced at her face, it was pink. Very pink. And it looked good on her.

One of the nurses came over to tell him the baby he'd worked on was settled in and seemed stable. "Good, thank you. I'll keep an eye on her for a while."

With that, the pair left the room, leaving just Dean, Jess and her sister.

Abbie again addressed them. "Does someone want to tell me what's going on?"

Here went nothing.

"I take it Jess didn't tell you?"

Two pairs of brown eyes swung to look at him.

"Tell me what?"

He draped his arm back around her shoulders. "Don't be shy, sweetheart. Tell her."

Jess's mouth popped open, eyes widening in horror. "What?"

"I'm sure they've wondered where you've been the last couple of nights."

"Dean…" The warning in her voice was unmistakable. But he'd come too far to turn back now.

"Jess and I have been going out." It wasn't exactly a lie. They had been going out to the pub, after all. Her sister didn't need to know that Jess had turned him down flat as far as anything else went.

"Going out. You expect me to believe that?"

Anger pumped through his veins at the open disbelief in Abbie's voice. Suddenly, he was very sure he was doing the right thing.

And if this little farce got out? Well, worse things had been said about him—at least from what he'd heard here and there.

Leaning down to her ear, he whispered, "I'll explain later. Just play along."

Out loud, he said, "It's recent. We're keeping it quiet. For now." Another half-truth. Their going out had been recent. And he was pretty sure Jess wanted it kept quiet.

Jess didn't agree. Or disagree. But a little of the sneer left her sister's face.

"So what you said at the party… All of those texts Martin got wasn't about you trying—"

Jess finally found her voice. "I've told you that. Many times, Abbie. Martin and I have been over for a long, long time. He loves you. Not me."

So it was true. Jess had once been engaged to Abbie's husband. And Abbie thought her sister still had the hots for him.

He looked at her with new eyes. If he had to choose between the sisters right here right now, there would be no question as to who he'd go with.

Jess. Hands down.

"I guess I owe you both an apology, then."

"No, you—"

Dean squeezed her shoulder to stop the words. Abbie did owe her an apology, from what he'd seen. A big one.

"But as for the baby…" The woman's glance went back to her child. She leaned forward a little. "What's that on her leg?" She pointed at the incubator and tapped the side of it. The newborn startled for a second, then relaxed.

"What?" Jess shook off his hand and moved closer.

"There. That red thing on her calf."

There was a small red mark the size of a thumbprint on the side of the baby's leg.

The relief on Jess's face was almost comical. "It's just a little birthmark. A port wine stain. It's nothing."

"A port what?" Abbie trailed her fingers over the Plexiglas side as if tracing the mark. "Will it go away?"

"Probably not, but it's nothing serious. I promise."

There was a pause before Abbie spoke again. "I don't want people to make fun of her."

There was a note of sadness—or maybe it was fear—in her voice. It made Dean take a closer look, seeing something of himself in her words. Had Abbie been made fun of at some point by someone? It would explain some of that angry defensiveness she seemed to carry around with her. He'd had a little of that himself when he'd been younger. More so after his dad went to prison and his mum took off for parts unknown when he was just sixteen.

Dean had been angry all right. Angry at his parents. Angry at the group home he'd been placed in. Angry at life in general. Until he'd learned to harness that anger and put it to good use. And that included not pinning his hopes on any one human being. At some point, they all let you down.

"I'm sure they won't," Jess said. "Why would they?"

Her sister sniffed as if she was not about to listen to anything Jess had to say. Then she stood. "I think I'll go back to my room. I'm knackered."

She'd still made no move to touch her baby, and that bothered Dean more than he wanted to admit. Everyone had his or her own way of dealing with emotional pain, but to shut off physical contact with her own child?

Well, hadn't he wished from time to time that his father had cut off physical contact? But he hadn't. It had taken putting Dean's mum in hospital that last time to keep the man from hurting them again.

"Do you want someone to walk you back to your room?" he asked.

Abbie shook her head. "I can manage. You'll ring me if there's any change?"

Dean might have thought the words were meant for Jess, except she was looking directly at him. Ignoring her sister just as she was ignoring her baby. "Someone will. Yes." He was not going to let her use him to wound Jess even more.

She left the room without so much as a thank you or another glance at her child.

The second she was gone, Jess dropped into the seat her sister had just vacated. "Oh, my God, why on earth did you do that?"

He wasn't sure why, himself. Maybe the urge to protect was overdeveloped in him—the result of having no one to defend him as a child. That could also explain why he'd felt such a strong need to help the most vulnerable of humans: newborns in crisis.

"Well, it wasn't a total fabrication. We do have The Pub." He said it as if it were some special shared memory, rather than a total washout.

She actually smiled. "Did you have any luck after I left?"

Dean hadn't stuck around. He'd followed her…staying far enough behind for her not to notice, but close enough to know she made it to her car without that big Scot following her.

"I decided to stick to the rules, after all."

"Oh." She blinked a couple of times as if surprised. "Well, anyway, thanks for what you did a few minutes ago. It wasn't necessary, though. It didn't seem to matter to her one way or the other, except maybe she finally believes I'm not after her husband."

"Oh, it mattered. She just wasn't going to let you see it."

If anyone knew, he did. How many times had he hidden his feelings from his father? Dean had stood there and let the man do his worst without crying or pleading for him to stop. Because he'd learned to detach himself from what was happening to and around him. As a result, he'd learned to keep his emotions tucked away to the point of *almost* denying he had any.

Except when he did foolhardy stuff like pretending to be someone's significant other for no good reason. And it had been foolhardy. Because dancing with her at the pub, getting to know the way her eyes crinkled when she laughed affected him on a level he hadn't known existed. Maybe because he'd never bothered to truly get to know the women he dated.

Like that thin streak of gray he'd noticed over the past couple of nights when she'd tucked her hair behind her ears. It almost blended in with the rest of the blonde strands, but not quite.

"Where did you get this?" He couldn't resist touching the silky lock now.

"The gray, you mean?" Her smile widened. "A llama at a petting zoo decided to get a little too friendly with my hair clip when I was a kid. It yanked the clip—and a good hunk of my hair—out and chewed on them for a while before deciding they weren't so great, after all. When the hair grew back, it was white."

He ran the bleached-out tresses between his fingers. "Your sister doesn't have this, then."

"No, she doesn't." She gave a slight shrug. "It's my own personal souvenir."

A visible reminder of past hurt. Thankfully his own past remained invisible to the world, even if the aftermath still bubbled up inside of him from time to time. It was one reason he hadn't wanted to work with toddlers or young children. His suspicious mind would probably jump to conclusions each time a boy or girl presented with a broken arm. Or a broken heart.

No. This was where he belonged.

Jess leaned forward and glanced at her niece, the act tugging her hair from his fingers. "I never even noticed the spot on her leg before," she murmured.

"Because it's not important."

"It is to Abbie."

His fingers itched to give her hand a reassuring squeeze. He curled them into a ball at his side, instead. "It may fade with time."

"My sister has always tried so hard to be perfect. She's incredibly disciplined about everything she does."

"And you're not?"

She shrugged. "I don't expect everyone around me to live up to a certain set of expectations."

"You expect yourself to live up to them, instead."

She paused. "Maybe." She glanced up at him. "Can I hold her?"

Dean nodded. "Of course. Only for a minute or two, though."

It took a little doing to manage all the tubes and wires, but the second the baby was placed in her arms, Jess was in love. From her little pink cap to the teeny-tiny nappy, Marissa Fay Stewart was as perfect as could be. She didn't stir other than to twitch a shoulder as she settled into place.

Jess cuddled her with one arm while she stroked a gloved thumb down the newborn's leg. She didn't understand why Abbie didn't want to stay by her cot. Why she didn't seem to even want to hold her baby. Was she just afraid?

Her sister was a good mother to her other three children. At least from what she'd heard from her parents—the kids were all happy and well-adjusted. Maybe that was it. It had to be a huge adjustment to add another child to their family. Her sister would come around.

She touched the little mark on her calf, just barely visible from where she sat. "She's gorgeous."

"She is." Dean agreed with her without hesitation. When she glanced up at him, though, his eyes weren't on the baby. They were on her.

Her face heated and she ducked her head again, hoping he didn't notice the way he affected her. This was why almost every female in the hospital swooned over him, including some of the babies' mums.

Well, Jess wasn't about to be one of those women. Not even a pretend one. If what he'd said was true, that her sister believed his little charade, then they were going to leave it at that. No need to take it any further.

The sound of something tapping on the viewing glass across the room caught her attention and things went from bad to worse. Martin stood there waving at her. Why wasn't he with his wife?

She clenched her teeth at her own stupidity. Maybe he'd already been to Abbie's room. He must have ended his business trip early when he heard the news.

Dean gave her a questioning look.

"It's the baby's father. Martin."

"The same Martin who left you for your sister."

She cringed, but it was true. Hearing it said out loud though brought back a whole host of awful memories. But Dean was no longer beside her, he was striding toward the door, letting in her ex...her sister's husband.

"I was in Tokyo, and had a dickens of a time finding a flight out. How is she, Abbie?"

Jess froze at the mistake. Before she could say anything, though, Dean moved beside her. "Look again."

Her ex glanced at her. "Oh, hell, sorry, Jess. You were holding the baby, and I just assumed..."

"It's okay. Abbie's tired. She's in her room. I take it you haven't been to see her yet?"

"I thought I'd find her here, actually." He squatted down beside her chair. "Is the baby okay?"

The tears that hadn't come earlier now stung her eyes. "She's tiny. But perfect."

"And Abbie? Is she all right?"

"Yes. She's upset, naturally, but she's doing well physically." She decided to leave out the details of what had transpired, pretty sure someone would soon enlighten him as to her part in the ordeal.

He touched the baby's head. "She looks like you two."

A hand came to rest on her shoulder, and Jess stiffened when she realized it was Dean. A trill of apprehension went through her, and, as much as the rational part of her brain was yelling at her to shake off his touch, she just sat there without a word.

Martin noticed as well and slowly climbed to his feet. He held out a hand. "Sorry. I'm Martin Stewart, the baby's father. And you are?"

"Dean Edwards. Your baby's doctor. And Jess's significant other."

What? *What?*

Her entire body suddenly went numb. Dean had just upped the ante from a few casual dates to being involved in a more intimate relationship. Without her permission.

Oh, Lord, she did not want to do this. What if Martin jumped to the conclusion that they were living together?

Except her parents were staying at her house.

Significant other could mean any number of things, though…right?

Her ex was slow to respond, but he finally brought his eyes back to her. "This is a surprise, Jess. Do your folks know?"

Oh, no. Martin had never been great at keeping secrets. And if the way she'd found out about his preference for her sister was anything to go by, her parents were about to get the shock of their lives.

"Please don't say anything. We've been keeping everything kind of hush-hush. I didn't want to take away from Mum and Daddy's anniversary celebration."

"Of course." He glanced down at the baby again. "Can I hold her?"

Well, at least one of the baby's parents wanted to.

Just then the newborn shifted in her arms and stretched, giving a chirping cry. All of her misgivings left in a rush. "She's waking up."

Tiny blue eyes squinted up at them, as if not quite sure what to make of this big new world. Jess leaned over and kissed her little forehead and then carefully stood, minding the tubes and glancing at Dean. "Is it okay?"

"Yes. Just for a moment."

Martin slid into the chair, and Jess carefully placed his baby into his arms. Like the expert he was by now, he rocked her and murmured little endearments, already forgetting anyone else was in the room.

Jess took the opportunity to grab Dean's arm and pull him out of earshot. "What were you thinking?" she whispered.

"Just wanted to reinforce our story. To make sure Abbie bought it."

"Bought it? It's a little over the top, don't you think? What if my parents find out?"

One side of his mouth kicked up. "It wasn't just for Abbie's sake. I wanted to make sure your brother-in-law knew he couldn't go back in time."

"Go back in…" She glanced at Martin and then rolled her eyes. "What is wrong with you people? He's married to my sister. They're happy together."

"Which is why your sister is so worried about what's going on behind her back."

"Nothing. Is. Going. On."

He tugged a stray curl that had gotten loose from her ponytail. "Your sister might just think otherwise.

Only now, she and everyone will assume it's going on between you and me."

The man had a point, and she hated him for it. And as soon as the baby was well and on her way home, she and Dean were going to abruptly end their so-called relationship, making sure everyone in her family knew that it was she who'd done the dumping this time.

And as soon as that happened, things could go back to the way they were before. When life was sane…and maybe just the tiniest bit dull.

CHAPTER FIVE

"So where is he, and why have we never met him? Or even heard about him?"

The impatience in her mum's voice came through loud and clear. Far from solving all her problems, it seemed she and Dean had stirred up a firestorm. "We've been waiting for years for you to finally decide to invest in something besides your career."

Her jaw tightened. This was the same argument they'd had on many other occasions. They thought she didn't want to get married because she was too busy with her job. Her mum was wrong. Jess did want a family. She wanted to feel as if she belonged to someone as more than a mere shadow of her sister. But she'd never met the right man, and, after Martin, she'd found it much harder to trust than she used to.

It was easier not to argue the point, though. She'd been there and done that, and it had solved nothing.

"I didn't want to ruin your party, Mum."

"Ruin it?" She glanced over at her husband. "We would have had something else to celebrate, right, Norman? Instead, I had to hear about it the day before we return to London. From Martin, no less."

So much for her ex keeping things quiet.

Right now, though, the look in her dad's eyes made her heart ache. Unlike her mum, her dad had always been the master of giving unconditional love—the type that forgave any transgression. He didn't fuss or join in to castigate her with how she needed to "find a nice boy and settle down". He simply came over and dropped a kiss on her head. "I'm happy for you, love. We both are."

"Oh, Daddy." Unable to stop herself, she threw her arms around his neck and hugged him tight. She couldn't undo what had already been done. Not yet, anyway. Once things died down a bit, she would quietly click that chapter shut and tell her parents it was over between her and Dean.

Somehow.

"So why didn't you say something?" Her mother's crisp voice pulled her back from her father's arms.

She wasn't sure what her mum wanted to hear and was loath to say more than she absolutely had to.

"With the party and Abbie's pregnancy and then…" She shook her head, unable to bring up the painful subject of what had happened at the party. "Well, things have just been hectic."

"We'll want to meet him, of course. It seems your sister and Martin already have." She sat in one of the two slipper chairs in Jess's cottage, her face softening. "Finally. Both of my girls are going to get their happy-ever-afters."

Oh, Mum. Not yet. Not yet.

But she hoped someday she would be as happy as her parents seemed to have been these past thirty years. A lot of that had to do with how easygoing her dad was.

"Tonight." Her mum said the word with a finality that made her blink.

"I'm sorry?"

"I'm going to fix my special shepherd's pie and you'll invite him to dinner. I intend to meet my future son-in-law."

"We're not engaged. We're just…" She took two steps back, horror welling up her throat. This was getting too far out of hand.

"No matter, I want to meet him. What better way than to chat over a meal? Besides, I'm sure he'll eventually propose. Why wouldn't he?"

Um…maybe because he didn't love her. Heavens, how was she going to get out of this?

Her parents had been staying at her little cottage, and her mum had done most of the cooking for the last week and a half. But this? No. She couldn't bring Dean into what could become a powder keg. Even if he had been the one to start it. "Dean probably has to work."

Her mum frowned. "You don't know his rotation schedule?"

Caught in her first lie, she tried to recover. "It's not that I don't know it, it's just that I…"

Don't know.

She did the only thing she could. "I'll ring him and see if he can come." Misery pulled at every word. She was hoping, at the very worst, she could get by with a quick introduction at the hospital along with a smile and a peck on the cheek that was halfway believable. Not a full-blown meal. Where people might actually have to talk. In depth. For hours.

She blamed Dean. And he was going to get an earful the first chance she got.

"Perfect," her mum said, the fingers that had been drumming on the arm of the chair finally going still.

"Why exactly did Martin mention it?"

Her mum smiled. "I heard him and Abbie talking about you, and... Martin let it slip while visiting her room. You know how he is at keeping secrets."

Yes. Unfortunately she did know. All too well. He had barely been able to contain himself when he and Abbie had shown up on her doorstep as a united front. He'd apologized, multiple times, but said he'd fallen in love.

Which was quite funny, considering he'd professed his love to Jess a week before that.

"Ring him now, won't you? Now that we know Marissa Fay is out of the woods, it gives us even more of a reason to get to know your young man."

"He's not my young man, and she's not exactly out of the woods."

Alarm clouded her mother's face. "Did something change?"

"No, Mum, she's doing fine." She couldn't bring herself to put a negative spin on the baby's prognosis just to worm her way out of an uncomfortable situation.

"Well, then?"

Her dad seemed to sense something was afoot, because he laid a hand on his wife's arm. "Gloria, maybe this isn't the time."

Her mum looked closer at her. "You two aren't fighting already, are you?"

No. Because they didn't know each other well enough to argue. Although they'd had a bit of a row at the pub the other evening. "Of course not."

Left with no choice, she pulled her mobile phone out of the pocket of her scrubs, just in time to realize she didn't even know Dean's mobile number... She'd rung his home phone the other times. So she couldn't very well ring him directly.

Damn. Now what did she do? Claim she had no coverage?

No, because one of them could simply check their phone and offer to let her use it. So she did the next best thing. She pressed the button that would connect her with the hospital's main number. She recognized the woman who answered. Gulping back a bubble of dismay at involving anyone else in this charade, she simply said, "Madeline, this is Jess Black. Would you mind terribly paging Dr. Edwards and asking him to give me a ring?"

"Sure. What's the number?"

Her face heated as she was forced to reel off her mobile number, knowing her mum was going to wonder why Dean wouldn't already have it programmed into his phone. She rang off and swallowed again before turning back to her parents. "He might be with a patient, and I didn't want to disturb him."

Except her mobile buzzed almost immediately. Assuming it was him, she took a deep breath and pressed the button. "Hi, honey."

"Well, hello, there…honey." The low mellow voice on the other end of the line was rife with amusement.

Her teeth clinked together a couple of times before she got up the nerve to continue. "It seems the cat is out of the bag, thanks to you and Martin. He told my parents. About us."

"Ah. I have to admit, I'm a bit disappointed. I thought that 'honey' meant you were actually growing fond of me."

"I am. I mean…well…" She couldn't believe this was happening. Any of it. "Mum and Daddy are leaving *tomorrow*—" she put a subtle emphasis on that word before continuing "—and are anxious to meet you. She thought you might like to have dinner at my place tonight. I told her I wasn't sure of your schedule and that you're extremely busy, so you probably have to work—"

"I would love to come. Tonight, was it?"

"What?" The word came out as a high-pitched squeal, her heart galloping out of control. She'd given him the perfect out, and he'd completely ignored it. Was he that dense? Or was he simply laughing at her discomfiture?

"I said I would love to come to dinner."

Yep. That smug amusement was still there, coloring every word he spoke.

He was getting his jollies at her predicament, was he? A predicament he'd helped create.

"You're sure you don't *have to work*?" She was a little less subtle this time.

"Positive. I'm off duty. Free as a bird."

Damn him.

"I guess that works perfectly, then. Six-ish?" She glanced toward her mother, who nodded before reaching for her father's hand and gripping it tight, her own triumph evident.

Time to make Dean pay a little bit for not bowing out. "I'll save the story of how we met, then, for tonight. I know how much you adore telling that funny bit about the lake. About how you fell in, and I had to rescue you."

"Brat."

"No more than you…honey."

"I'll see you tonight. I take it I have carte blanche on that story, then?"

She had a feeling that not only had the cat been let

out of the bag, but the genie had just been released from the bottle. "I trust you to stick to the pertinent points."

"Always. I need to go—I still have a few patients to see." There was a pause, then he came back. "I guess I'll see you tonight, sweetheart."

Ack! Even though she knew he was just trying to make her fidget—and he was doing a good job of that— the words still made a funny little pinging happen in the center of her chest. She decided to ignore it. Especially since she was the one who'd started the whole endearment thing.

"See you tonight." As she hurried to mash the button to cut off the call, she could have sworn it ended with Dean's laughter.

Despite the way he'd teased her on the phone, Dean wasn't all that sure about doing this dinner thing tonight. But he'd given his word. He pulled into the driveway of a small cottage, then checked the address again. This was the place.

The beige paint with its crisp white gingerbread trim reminded him so much of Jess that it made him smile. He couldn't see the sister living in a minuscule place like this, but Jess? Absolutely. This fit her to a tee. And the image of coming home to something like this...of that sturdy wooden door opening and a couple of happy kids rushing down the walkway to greet him, made a pang go through his gut. It would be so very different from the loneliness and never-ending fear he'd experienced as a child.

As if by magic, the door did open. But it wasn't children who stood there, but the woman he'd just been sitting here thinking about.

Jess. Dressed in jeans that were tucked into brown boots and a long beige sweater that hugged her curves, she looked homey and, oh, so different from the way she dressed for work. She was as quaint and welcoming as the cottage. Except for that nervous frown.

Over their little deception? *His* little deception. He was to blame for this entire thing, and he could see it wasn't going to be without consequences.

He'd put Jess into an untenable position. No one wanted to lie to their parents. But her sister had pushed just the right buttons, and he'd instinctively stepped in between her and Jess in a figurative sense. If he'd had more time, he might have come up with something a little less drastic though.

Which brought up another point. Were Jess's parents so unused to seeing her with a man that they assumed this was something special? From the way she'd acted about their bet a few days ago, maybe that was indeed the case.

Staring. He was staring.

Clicking open the door to his car, he exited, giving her a little salute as he retrieved something from the passenger seat. Two sets of flowers. One for Jess and one for her mum. No need to make anyone suspect things weren't what they seemed in paradise.

He'd never bought a woman flowers in his life, not wanting anyone to think he planned on sticking around after a night or two.

But this was safe, right? Jess knew it was all a charade. Easily ended. Once her parents and her sister left, that would be that.

He made it up to the front door, making sure his eyes stayed glued to her face, no matter how much they might want to roam over that delectable figure. Once he arrived, though, and handed her one set of flowers, he glanced behind her and noted her mum was watching from a few yards behind Jess.

What better excuse to…?

He placed one hand on her shoulders and squeezed slightly, watching her eyes widen and her nostrils flare as he drew close and pressed his lips to hers, allowing his mouth to graze across them and then continue along her cheek.

She shivered as he reached her ear, and he couldn't hold back a smile. "Relax," he whispered. "Mum is watching."

With that, he released her, waiting for her to step back. Which she did, but it was in a stumbling rush that had him reaching out to grip her wrist to steady her. He threaded his fingers through hers to keep her next to him. He had a feeling all she wanted to do was disappear into the inner depths of the house. Not something a woman in a serious relationship would do.

He tugged her closer as he turned his smile onto the woman who looked so much like her. "Mrs. Black. Thank you again for inviting me." He held out the second bouquet, watching her smile as she accepted it with a look that might have been relief.

"Please call me Gloria. I can't tell you how glad I am to hear that you and Jess are together." Her smile reached her eyes this time. "I'll just go put these in water. Would you like something to drink?"

"Just a glass of wine, please. Red, if you have it."

Gloria looked confused for a second, then Jess cleared her throat. "I don't keep alcohol in the house, Dean, remember?"

Bloody hell. That was something he should know. "Of course. I should have brought a bottle with me. How thoughtless."

"It's fine." If anything, Jess's voice was even tighter. "It's better for Daddy not to have it sitting at the table, anyway."

A chill went through him. Jess's dad was an alcoholic?

Memories of his own father's battle went through his head. Only his fight hadn't just been against the bottle. It had been against his wife and son once he'd slugged down his nightly quota and lost sight of his soul, or whatever it was that had kept the hounds of hell at bay.

Once released, they'd slashed and torn at everything within reach.

Had Jess experienced any of that horror?

From the look on her face, that would be a no. So her dad wasn't a mean drunk.

"My grandfather," she said in a low voice as her mum turned to go back into the kitchen. "He abused my dad and his other kids until he died of cirrhosis. Daddy doesn't want anything to do with alcohol, so none of us drink in front of him."

That was funny because Dean allowed himself the occasional drink for the exact opposite reason: to prove he could control his usage when his father hadn't been able to.

Speaking of control…

"Your grandfather never hurt *you*, did he?" There was a tension in Dean's jaw that he didn't like. Images running through his head that he liked even less.

"He died before I was born." She touched his arm.

"Daddy's nothing like him. Please don't mention any of this."

Not a chance. He never talked about his own parents. To anyone. He'd buried that part of him so deep it rarely ever came to the surface anymore. Except at times like this. Unlike Jess's grandfather, his dad was still very much alive. At least he thought he was. He hadn't spoken to the man since the day he went to prison. In fact, he hadn't heard from his mum in a long time either. This was the first time he'd thought of either of them in years.

Damn.

A mixture of churning emotions boiled up from somewhere inside, threatening to reach the surface.

The sooner he got out of there, the better. He didn't want to accidentally say something at the table that might bring back painful memories. For Jess's dad. For himself.

Her dad came out of the kitchen wearing a ruffled apron that could only belong to his daughter. The queasy sensation stalled, and then subsided.

"Sorry for the frilly gear," the other man said. "I've been telling Jess she needs to buy some gender-neutral things if I'm to do much cooking."

Dean brushed the words aside with a smile, reaching out to shake her father's hand. His grip was solid, putting Dean at ease almost immediately. He wasn't the alcoholic. But he had experienced what it was like to be at one's mercy.

They had something in common. And he got the feeling that Jess's father would have kept his family safe from anyone or anything that threatened it.

"Norman Black. Nice to meet you."

"You as well. I'm Dean Edwards."

Jess made a little sound in her throat, hands gripped tightly together. "So what are we having?"

"Shepherd's pie, remember? Your mum did the majority of the work tonight. I simply made the salad."

Shrugging out of his coat when Jess reached toward it, Dean let her hang it up by the front door, where several others were—one he recognized as the coat she'd worn to the Indian restaurant and to the pub. With a quick flick she draped his over the top of that very one.

A peculiar flash of awareness crept up his spine. He shot her a glance to see if she'd done that on purpose, but she was already moving farther into the room, laughing at something her dad had said. He threw another look at the winter gear and then shrugged. They were just coats. Not a metaphor for anything else.

"I think Mum is ready." She was back at his side. "I hope you like shepherd's pie." There was an uncertainty to her voice that made him take a closer look.

"Adore it. My mum didn't seem to…"

He'd almost said that his mother didn't like to cook, unless she knew her husband was on his way home. And that was only because she knew what would happen if dinner wasn't on the table when he arrived.

"She didn't seem to…?"

"Nothing. She was just never keen on fixing things that didn't come from a tin."

"Did she work?"

He shook his head, blasting himself for even going there. And he wasn't sure why he had. There was just something about Jess that invited confidences, shared secrets…and aroused his protective instincts, evidently.

Besides, hadn't she just finished sharing a pretty big secret of her own—about her grandfather's drinking?

It was human nature to want to mirror what someone else did.

He wasn't quite satisfied with that explanation, but, since they were now in Jess's minuscule dining room, he didn't have time to formulate any other theories.

And his growling stomach reminded him that he'd skipped lunch. Something smelled delicious.

Right on cue, Gloria hurried out of the kitchen. "Jess, would you put some ice in the glasses and get the drinks ready please?"

"Is there anything I can help with?" he asked.

She waved him away. "No, just have a seat. I've put you to the left of where Jess normally sits."

Another thing he didn't know about her. Before he had to guess, Jess went around the table and picked up a glass. "What would you like to drink? Something fizzy?"

Okay, so that was where he was to sit. *Thank you, Jess.*

"Just give me whatever you're having."

Soon they were all situated around the table. Needing a drink of something stronger than the water he'd been served, he sucked down a mouthful, only to have bubbles assault his throat. He swallowed in a hurry, fighting the need to cough. Losing.

Jess laughed. "I wondered why you wanted tonic water. You normally hate it."

He jerked around to stare at her before realizing she'd simply hazarded a guess. She didn't know he hated it. Or why. There was no way she could know that when his father had sat at the dinner table guzzling whatever his liquor du jour had been, a too young Dean—wanting to be like his dad—had begged his mum for whatever his father was drinking. She'd served him tonic water, instead, and pretended it was the real thing. By the time he'd been old enough to know what was going on and to equate the drinking with the abuse, he'd hated his "grown up" drink.

He was not about to admit that now, though. So he took another sip, albeit a more cautious one this time, forcing the cold fizzy liquid to sit in his mouth for a second before swallowing it down in a rush. "Just trying to develop a taste for it, that's all."

Something that was never going to happen.

Gloria reached for his plate and placed a generous portion of the meat pie on it. "Well, isn't that sweet? That's true love for you. I can't tell you the number of things that Norm has learned to like for me."

Another pang went through Dean's chest. This was what love was supposed to be like. Unfortunately, it didn't usually work out that way. Look at his folks. Or even Jess's sister and her husband, for that matter. Fighting and bickering seemed to come with the territory. As did problems like drinking and abuse and jealousy.

No, thanks. He was glad he'd steered clear of all that. His life was fine just the way it was.

Jess took his plate from her mum and put it in front of him. Then she covered his hand with hers. "Dean does all kinds of nice things for me. Don't you, honey?"

He almost choked again, but not because he had anything in his mouth. It was because of the image that suddenly went through his head. He *could* do all kinds of nice things for her, if she let him.

Not going to happen.

Not in this lifetime. And not in the next. Besides, he'd tried to take her home for a fun-filled night of sex, only to have her turn him down flat. Something Dean wasn't used to. It still stung to remember the way her eyes had sparkled with anger as she'd turned and walked away from him.

Although as she started to withdraw her hand her fingers slid along his in a way that made his skin heat and caused certain muscles to tighten in warning. Had she done that on purpose?

Before he could think it through, he turned his hand over and stopped her fingers from leaving his, smiling when he heard her soft intake of breath.

She wanted to play games, did she? She had no idea who she was dealing with. He was a tactical expert when it came to this kind of war. "I love doing things for you." He put a wealth of meaning into those words, smiling when sudden color flared along her cheekbones and slid into her hairline.

Her mum's brows went up. She'd certainly gotten it.

"I have to admit, Jess, I'd almost given up hope. I'm so glad you've decided that work isn't all there is to life." She handed a plate to Norman. "They're almost as cheeky as we were at their age."

Cheeky wasn't exactly the word he would use. Lustful. Needy. Wanting. Those were all terms that described him right now.

He wanted her. In spite of the fact that she didn't seem to want him in return.

They were simply playing a part. A part that would end the second her family went home to London.

But that didn't stop him from wishing he could take her back to his place and see just how far they could take this little charade.

"We were, weren't we?" her dad said.

Jess tugged at her hand, and this time he let her go. Besides her mum was now dishing out the rest of their food and making sure everyone had what they needed.

Not by a long shot. But this was the hand he'd been dealt. And from where he was standing, it looked as if two things needed to happen. One, he needed to get laid. Two, Jess needed a whopping dose of self-confidence. Maybe they should both head back to the pub and grab the first available partner to satisfy those needs. Except they'd already tried that and it hadn't worked. He was actually lucky she'd turned him down, because Dean didn't date people from work. Ever. Too messy. Too complicated. He preferred things simple and to the point.

Jess was neither.

So yeah, his moment of weakness that night at the pub could have turned into a major disaster.

Digging into his food to take his mind off Jess, he wasn't surprised at how good it tasted. What did surprise him, though, was how comfortable her father seemed to be in the kitchen. None of this expecting one person to get everything to the table while the other slouched on the sofa doing nothing.

"Delicious. Thank you so much for inviting me."

"I just wish Jess would have told us about you sooner." Gloria sent her daughter a look of reproof.

"Nothing to tell." Jess half muttered the words.

Her mother either didn't hear her or was ignoring her. "So tell us a little about yourself, Dean."

This time it was Dean who stiffened. He'd expected to be asked about the "falling into the lake" story Jess had threatened him with over the phone. Not something about himself personally. "What would you like to know?"

"Are you as fixated on your job as Jess is?"

"Mum, please." Jess sounded miserable.

Hoping to defuse the situation, he said, "I think most medical professionals are pretty dedicated."

Norman covered his wife's hand with his own. "Of course they are. When did you realize you wanted to be a doctor?"

When? The day he decided he wanted to help *fix* people instead of breaking them. But he wasn't about to say that. "I think it's every child's dream at some point. With me, it just seemed to stick."

"And you and Jess met at the hospital?"

This time it was his daughter who answered. "Yes. We work in different wards, but see each other from time to time."

Yes, they did. Except that Jess hadn't expected Dean to even know who she was. There was something about that that bothered him. Really bothered him.

He'd joked about her invisibility cloak, but now he wondered. Did she really think she was that invisible? He'd noticed her from the time she'd started working at Cambridge Royal four years ago. The way her blonde ponytail swished from side to side as she walked. The way she had of lifting a hand to wave at colleagues instead of simply nodding to them.

The way she smiled as she looked down at her patients.

He'd noticed all of that? When?

He realized everyone was staring at him. "Sorry?"

"My dad asked what our most romantic date was."

The sardonic tilt of her brow told him he really should have thought this through a little better, or at least planned for the obvious questions. Hmm…well, they wanted romantic? He would give them romantic.

"Well, after the 'falling in the lake' bit that Jess mentioned, we seemed to hit it off. I think our most memorable afternoon was when I took her for a nice little hack in the countryside. Just the two of us on horseback. We took a hamper of food. And—"

"You took her out for a hack?" Her dad interrupted him, and he could have sworn the steady gaze now held a hint of suspicion.

And Jess. Well, she looked just plain horrified. He had a feeling he was about to find out why.

Gloria took up where Norm left off. "Jess is afraid of horses. Has been ever since she was thrown from a pony when she was young."

"I—I got over it. Dean helped me see there's really nothing to be afraid of." Except she looked pretty afraid right now.

Perfect. He had to choose the one thing Jess was terrified of, and her dad had called him on it.

"Well I, for one, would love to see some pictures of that. Wouldn't you?" Norm's question was aimed at Jess's mum.

"Definitely."

He and Jess had two choices. They could either come clean and tell the truth—which meant her sister might start back up with the accusations—or he could continue to do his best to make this look real.

"I don't have any of those shots with me at the moment." His mind scrambled to find a solution. "I know you're leaving tomorrow—perhaps I could email them to you?"

"Perfect. We'll be expecting them." There was definitely an edge to the words this time.

Jess glanced at him, a frown on her face, but she didn't contradict him. Instead, she said, "I'll have Dean send them to me, and then I'll forward them to you. How does that sound?" She dropped her fork onto her almost empty plate. "Well, I need to save room for some of that delicious custard tart you made, Mum."

The rest of the evening revolved around small talk and chatter about some of the cases they'd worked on. Somehow, though, he didn't think her dad was going to forget about those pictures. Which meant he and Jess were going to have to do some creative maneuvering. Like editing a photo to show her on a horse?

No. That wouldn't work.

He was going to have to actually get her on one and snap a few pictures.

And if he couldn't talk her into it?

Well, he was going to have to, because if they didn't do something and fast his impulsive decision was going to wind up coming back and biting him right on the ass. Which would be fine, if it were only him. But he didn't want Jess to pay the price for his mistakes.

No, he was going to have to sweet talk her into agreeing. And unlike at the pub a few nights ago, he was going to have to make sure she said yes.

CHAPTER SIX

"You want me to do what?"

Surely Jess hadn't heard him correctly. Dean wanted her to get on a horse? Her dad was right. She was afraid of horses. Terrified of them. They were huge and all kinds of scary.

"Just for a couple of pictures."

"I think I'd rather just tell my parents we've decided not to see each other anymore."

Dean leaned against the door of his car as they stood in front of Jess's house. Dinner had actually gone quite well, except for that one hiccup. "Your sister will still be in town after they leave, I assume. Are you going to tell her we broke up as well?"

She closed her eyes. If she did that, she could almost guarantee the arguments would start right back up. And Abbie would probably claim that she'd broken things off with Dean because she was still secretly in love with Martin. They would be back to square one. Unless she and Dean could keep up the pretense until her sister left.

When would that be?

"I really am afraid of them."

"I know this bloke—"

"This *bloke*? Well, that certainly puts my mind at ease."

Dean grinned and reached for one of her hands, threading his fingers through hers. "How about if I promise to ask him for a very nice horse?"

"Is there such a thing?" She rolled her eyes. "Why didn't you just tell my dad you'd taken me to the Bull Run in Spain? Or that we'd done the polar plunge while visiting Russia? Those would be more believable than the idea of me on a horse."

"It would be a little harder to get photographs of one of those events, don't you think?" He carried her hand to his mouth, placing a kiss on her knuckles that made her stiffen. "For your dad's benefit. I don't think he's fully bought into our little love story."

"This was such a huge mistake." She glanced toward the front window of the cottage, just the same. Were her parents really watching them to see if they were truly dating each other? She'd sensed some definite tension from her dad, but assumed it was the normal protective instincts that most fathers had for their daughters. He'd certainly been angry enough at Martin when he'd switched his attentions to Abbie.

"You've already gotten through the hardest part," Dean continued. "Having dinner with them."

"Really? You're not the one who has to get on the back of a crazed animal and hope it decides to let you live."

If anything, his smile grew. "You're being a bit melodramatic, don't you think? We'll climb on a couple of docile horses and take a few snapshots. It'll be over before you know it."

"Is that what you tell your patients?"

He tugged her closer, until she found herself up against him, his hands at her hips. "My patients are too little to understand anything except a cuddle and a full tummy."

The image of Dean cradling one of those tiny pree-mies made her heart squeeze. He would make a fantas-tic dad, if he could ever get past the need to jump from one woman to another.

She just had to make sure he remembered this was strictly make-believe.

Before she could say anything, though, his nose nuz-zled the skin just below her ear. Electricity shimmered along her nerve endings. "Dean, what are you doing?"

Her voice came out far too shaky for her liking.

"Your dad is standing at the window watching us," he whispered.

"He is?" Her instinct was to crank her head around again and look at the house. Instead, she found a palm cupping her chin and holding her in place.

"Trust me. He's there." His lips touched her cheek, and this time instead of the hum of electricity, her mus-cles reacted with a violent shudder that swept from her toes to the top of her head. "It's just a pretend hack. We'll stay close to the barn. I promise."

"I… I…" Her thoughts were careening around in her head—a terrifying mixture of fear and need, each vying for supremacy. "I guess I can try."

"That's my girl." He brushed his nose against hers. "In the meantime, let's give your father something to ponder while he waits for those pictures."

With that, his lips slid against hers. Once. Twice.

It's just pretend.

And then, proving she didn't really believe that at

all, she reached up on tiptoes and pressed her mouth hard against his.

Dean went totally still for all of five seconds, then his arms wrapped around her waist and he hauled her tight against him, head tilting. Suddenly the pretend kiss became something that was very, very real. And she had no idea how to stop it. Or if she even wanted to.

This situation had turned on its head so completely it wasn't funny. The last thing Dean would have ordinarily wanted was for the father of one of his dates to catch him necking with his daughter. But this was no ordinary situation.

And neither was this kiss.

Dean didn't care who was watching him, because with Jess's arms wound around his neck and her lips open beneath his there was a raw primitive feel he never would have associated with this particular woman.

Her ex had given this up? For someone Dean had come to view as a shrew?

His hand cupped the base of her skull and turned her head just slightly. Just enough for him to really settle his mouth against hers.

Well, Daddy dearest would probably not need those pictures after seeing this.

Except he *wanted* to take Jess to his friend's stable. Wanted her to be willing to try something different, to do something wild and crazy and maybe even a little terrifying.

Like this kiss?

Definitely. His tongue surged forward, finding no resistance at all, just a warm moist place he never wanted to leave.

And damn if she didn't make this sexy little sound in the back of her throat. The one that whispered for him to keep going, to press her hard against the side of the car and take it all the way to the finish line.

Somehow he didn't think her dad would be as kosher with him doing his daughter right here in the garden, no matter how much Dean might want to.

So he eased her back, a curse running through his mind. Rippling through his body.

Her lips remained slightly parted, her breath coming in and out in cute little gusts that made him want to drag her into the bushes and finish what he'd started.

He leaned his weight against the car door, pressing his forehead against hers. "You okay?"

"Huh?" Slowly her arm unwound from his neck. "Oh. Um…yes. Fine."

She didn't sound fine. Her voice trembled and there was a quality to it that made him wonder exactly how often she'd been caught necking in front of her dad.

Probably never, from the sound of it. Her mum's comment about Jess being all work and no play…was that based on reality?

Hell, he wasn't thinking straight right now.

Blowing out a breath, he stroked the back of his fingers along her cheek. "As good as that was, I'd rather leave with all of my teeth intact."

Jess tilted her head for a second, and then, as if realizing what he was talking about, gave a nervous chuckle. "I don't think he would knock them *all* out."

The woman was a complete enigma. The unexpected heat of that kiss had hit him right between the eyes. And then her shy teasing afterward brought out every protective instinct he possessed. If he'd been her dad, he'd have come down that pavement like a raging bull, pulling Dean off her and sending him on his way.

Releasing her, he leaned forward and gave her cheek a quick kiss, finding it warm from her blush.

Or maybe from her reaction to finding herself in his arms.

Back away, Dean.

Maybe it would have been better to have saved this part of the act for her sister and brother-in-law.

He could always do it again.

That thought made something curl low in his gut. Some warm anticipation that made him plan crazy, impulsive things.

Impulsive…like his father?

That kiss had certainly blown out of control far too quickly.

But he hadn't hurt her. Or anyone else.

He forced himself to say it again. "Are you okay?"

"Yes." She nodded and took a step back, pushing her hair back from her face. "Yes, I think I am."

It sounded as if she'd just been handed a revelation. But what kind of revelation? Of how good it felt to be thoroughly kissed in front of your house? Or that she never wanted to repeat it?

He already knew which side he was camped on. The do-it-again-soon camp.

"So you'll let me know if we need to nudge your dad in the right direction again."

"And what direction would that be?"

"Toward believing this—" he motioned between the two of them "—is real."

It had felt real to him. A little too real.

She shook her head. "If he doesn't believe it by now, I don't know what more we can do to convince him."

There was no way he was going to touch that. Because if he did, he'd tell her to slide into his car and he'd take her somewhere and show her.

"Pictures. We still need pictures."

Yes. That was the answer he was looking for.

"I don't know…"

He reached out to slide his thumb along her cheekbone. "No getting out of it now."

"Okay."

Her capitulation had happened far too easily. Or maybe she was still as stunned as he was by what had happened between them.

Whatever it was, she was keeping it to herself, because she took two more steps back, and then, with a murmured goodbye, turned and headed up the walk. Sure enough, he was positive the edge of one of her lacy curtains had just dropped back into place as her dad…or maybe her mum…decided the show was over.

And yet, the energy in his body was still humming with possibility.

Even though that possibility was now opening the door and going inside her house.

A day later, and despite her best efforts, Martin finally cornered her in the hospital corridor. She'd just finished a difficult delivery and was hoping to call her friend Amy and remind her that she was due for a checkup, since she'd missed her last appointment.

He stood in front of her, not exactly blocking her path, but almost. "I know all of this has been tough on you—not to mention Gloria and Norm—and I wanted to say I'm sorry for how Abs is acting. She's not herself at the moment."

Hmm…her sister hadn't "been herself" since they were teenagers. Surely there were other twins who weren't best friends. "She's in a strange hospital with caregivers who aren't her own. It's natural for her to feel out of sorts."

"She's taking it out on you, though. And for that I'm sorry."

"Don't be. She's worried about the baby." In reality, that was what Jess hoped it was, although Abbie hadn't shown quite as much interest in this child as she had when her other three had been born. She'd doted over each of those in turn.

But she'd barely visited Marissa while she'd been in hospital, even though her room was just down the hall from the SCBU. Martin, on the other hand, had been a constant figure there, ever since his arrival in Cambridge, even getting to know the nurses and speaking with Dean on several occasions. That made her nervous. One slip and Dean could make the situation between her and her sister that much worse. The last thing she needed was for Abbie to start back in on her about her ex.

Dean's plan had worked. So far.

But it hadn't made Abbie want to spend any more time with the baby.

"She's had a traumatic experience," Jess continued. "Maybe she just needs some time to heal physically and emotionally.

Could her sister be suffering from some form of PTSD? That hardly seemed likely, but maybe her blaming Jess for the premature birth was a way of making herself feel better. In reality, neither of them was to blame. At least Jess kept telling herself that.

And so did Dean. On a regular basis.

He'd stuck by her side with a glue-like tenacity that made her edgy. In fact, she was surprised he hadn't popped out of the woodwork by now with some murmured endearment—although she did notice he was careful around the nurses and staff, for which she was grateful. Because the monikers he chose for her were peculiar. Especially one of them, which made her squirm.

My girl.

She was not "his" and never would be. The first time he'd said it—in front of her house when she'd agreed to climb on a horse—she'd passed it off as a "good girl" kind of thing. But it seemed the words had stuck. In his defense, she had called him honey. But she'd done that with a sardonic edge.

There was nothing humorous about the term he was using.

And she wished with all her might he would stop. Wasn't there something called a self-fulfilling prophesy? She didn't want to start believing those words could, should, or would become true. Ever.

Martin's voice reminded her of his presence. "Where's Dean? Maybe he could talk to Abbie. Or maybe even prescribe her something."

The thought of Dean going and talking to Abbie alone made something in her cringe, even though it was ridiculous. Old fears, however, were hard to banish.

But if she was worried that Abbie was going to try to flirt with Dean, she needn't bother. Dean wasn't hers.

That's my girl.

For some reason, she didn't think Dean would have

ever done what Martin had done. Why she thought that she had no idea. Martin had been the last boyfriend she'd lost to Abbie, but he hadn't been the only one.

Dean's not your boyfriend, fiancé, significant other or anything else. Not really.

Abbie couldn't steal something Jess had never had.

"I think that's something you should discuss with Dean and Abbie, not me."

A voice came from behind her. "What should I discuss?"

Jess whirled around to find the man in question standing just behind her, his brown hair rumpled as if he'd run his fingers through it many times. His eyes looked tired. In fact, he looked flat-out exhausted.

"Hard day?" The words had come out before she'd had a chance to think things through.

"Pretty bad." He reached down to link one of his fingers with her, making her tense up. "I just want to settle down on the couch with a cuppa and you."

Ugh. He was laying it on pretty thick. She'd almost gotten used to his teasing over the last day or two, maybe because he restricted it to when they were around her family. But maybe she should talk to him about easing up. "I think Martin wanted to talk to you about Abbie."

Martin's face had slowly infused with red as they'd stood there. "It's not important. It can wait for another time."

"But Abbie—"

"Just needs some time to recover. Rest. You said it yourself."

Dean tilted his head. "Is something worrying you? I can take a quick look before I head out."

"It can wait until tomorrow." He looked as if he was

going to turn around and leave, but then he took a deep breath. "I held the baby for a while today. She seemed more alert."

"She's getting stronger."

Martin's eyes closed for a second. "Thank God. I'll be sure to tell Abbie."

"Has she been down there yet today?" Dean voiced what Jess had been thinking.

"No. Not today. Maybe tomorrow." Martin's voice didn't sound any more sure than Jess's had been when she'd gone to visit her sister today.

Not that she'd said much. To her, anyway.

Unwilling to let Martin walk away without her saying something, she pulled her hand from Dean's grip and touched her ex's sleeve. "You've got my mobile number if you need me, right?"

He nodded. "Yes. And, Jess…" There was a short pause. "Thank you for everything."

"You're welcome."

With that he started back down the hall toward her sister's room.

When she turned to face Dean again, he looked even less happy than he had a few minutes ago.

"What?"

"Should you be doing that?"

Confusion made her blink. "Doing what?"

"Encouraging him to ring you."

"Is there a reason why I shouldn't?"

He took a step closer. "I would think that would be obvious. Your sister is already suspicious. Asking him to ring your mobile…"

He thought she was encouraging him in a romantic way?

Confusion turned to anger. Why did everyone assume she was up to no good? Her sister. Her mum, during the party. And now Dean. "I only asked him to ring if he needed something." She swallowed when that didn't come out quite right and tried again. "If he or *Abbie* needed something, or if he was concerned about the baby. Besides, my whole family now believes we're a couple. Thanks to you."

"You seemed happy enough to go along with it at the time."

She had been. But she was thinking more and more that this had been a mistake. It would be in everyone's best interest to get those pictures, show them off to her family, and then go back to seeing Dean as little as possible. Which made her wonder why he'd wandered down to her part of the hospital in the first place. "Was there something you wanted?"

"As a matter of fact, yes. I spoke with my friend. The one with the horses. And he said we can come over anytime. We just need to let him know so that he can have our horses tacked up and ready to go."

Ready to go. She doubted she would ever be ready. But she could do this. If she could survive her sister's betrayal and now her accusations, she could surely survive sitting on a horse for a few seconds. It would be over before she knew it.

Ugh. Weren't those the same words that Dean had used? Right before he'd called her "his girl".

"I have the next couple of days off, so maybe the sooner we do this, the better." She glanced at his face, again wondering at the tired lines beside his mouth. "Did something happen with a patient?"

"No. Just had some personal issues come up."

Personal. As in another woman?

Oh, great. She hadn't thought of that. That she might be cramping his style as far as his love life was concerned. "If you want to go out with someone, I don't want to stand—"

One side of his mouth went up. "It's not a woman. Although it might be a hell of a lot easier if it were."

She flinched. As hard as she'd tried to remain stock-still, those words had hit her hard.

"Hey." He wrapped warm fingers around her upper arm and edged her down the hallway until he came to an unoccupied room. He ducked inside, still towing her behind him.

"I don't understand."

"I don't suppose you do." He looked torn, as if part of him wanted to explain what was going on and the other part didn't.

"It's my father," he finally said. "It appears he's just been released from prison. They've lost track of him and are afraid he might show up here at the hospital."

CHAPTER SEVEN

HE WASN'T SURE why he'd told Jess about his father. Maybe because he wanted her to be prepared if the man suddenly burst into the hospital looking for him.

Damn. The last thing he wanted to see was that part of his past. It was also the last thing he wanted Jess to see. In spite of the tension between her and her twin, Jess's home life was so…normal. Her mum seemed a little prickly at times, but her parents had been married for thirty years, for God's sake. And he'd bet his life that her father had never once lifted a hand to his wife or daughters.

Flipping a pencil into the cup on his desk, he felt as if he was caught in a vat of quicksand. Telling her had probably been a mistake. And yet if he hadn't…

Did he even know what his father looked like after all these years? No. But if he knew the man, one of the first things he'd do was head for the nearest pub. After that…

He stood. It would do no good at all to sit here and brood. He'd arrived early to work this morning so that he would be able to leave early and take Jess to the horse stable, and then they were off to an ice-skating rink that wasn't far from where his friend lived. Maybe between the stable and swirling around on the ice, her family would believe they were indeed a pair.

And he'd bet that Jess could use a break.

Speaking of Jess's sister, he wanted to make a quick stop at the SCBU and see how Marissa was doing this morning. He made it halfway down the hall and caught sight of Abbie at the nurses' desk talking with one of the special-care nurses. Deidre…perfect.

Abbie half turned toward him and her mouth shut in a hurry, the pink hue that was so common to Jess's cheeks seeping into Abbie's. Did she not want him to hear their conversation?

If so, it was none of his business. Except Deidre was also staring at him.

He nodded at her as he arrived, only to have her nod back and then hurry away. Abbie was now fidgeting with her sweater.

That was right. She'd been released from hospital as of this morning. He'd only seen her in a hospital gown until now. She appeared a little softer somehow. More human.

Looks could be deceiving, however.

"How is the baby?"

Abbie glanced at her hands, which were splayed across the nurse's desk. "I was heading there now. Do you want to walk with me?"

Dean immediately went on alert, but covered it with a smile. "I was going there as well. Shall we?"

He dropped into step beside Abbie and waited for whatever she wanted to say. Because it was pretty obvious something was on her mind.

It didn't take long.

"I think I may have let the cat out of the bag."

Every muscle inside of him went taut with tension. Had Jess told Abbie about his father and the worry that he might come to the hospital? He hoped not. It wasn't exactly something he wanted broadcast through the gossip chain. He still wasn't even sure why he'd told Jess about it.

Maybe because his first reaction was to protect those he cared about from whatever his father might do.

Which meant what? That he cared for Jess?

Of course he did. As a friend and as a colleague.

So why hadn't he told Deidre or any of his other work acquaintances?

He ignored the question and focused on Abbie. "And what might you have let out of the bag?"

"I happened to mention you were dating my sister to a couple of the nurses, and they seemed surprised."

Relief washed over him. As bad as that was, it seemed a whole lot better than everyone finding out about his father or his childhood.

His focus narrowed. Actually it wasn't better. And he was pretty sure Jess would agree with him. "We were trying to keep that quiet, actually."

She nodded. "I guess I realize that now, from people's reactions. But I… I was just so surprised that Jess was actually seeing someone that it just came out."

Did she really expect him to believe that? Or was she fishing for information, as Jess's dad had seemed to do. And what could he use for an excuse? It came to him just as they reached the door of the special-care nursery. "We haven't made things official yet, so I didn't want her to be bombarded by a thousand questions."

"I guess I can understand that." Abbie's voice held more than a tinge of curiosity.

They arrived at the SCBU and he held open the door and waited for her to go in. She had the grace to look slightly sheepish. "I won't say anything else, then."

"Thank you." He eyed her. "Let me help you hold your baby."

"Oh, but…" Her voice died away as if she couldn't really think of a good excuse to refuse.

What was wrong with her? His mum had never been very maternal, but he'd always assumed that was because she'd lived in fear for so many years. Had his life really started out like this? Had his mum been at all eager to hold him as a child? She'd never had any other kids.

Well, this baby was going to get at least one good cuddle from her mother before she left the hospital.

"There's a chair right in front of her cot. If you'll slide into one of those gowns hanging on the pegs and then get yourself settled, I'll check her over and then let you hold her."

"Very well. Let's make it quick, shall we?"

Dean frowned. Jess might let her sister run roughshod over her, but Dean was not about to let her do it to him. He took his time checking the baby's color and checking the obs the nurse had posted on the chart. Abbie and Martin's baby was very lucky. She was strong and healthy. Too small to be released, but there was no reason to think she wouldn't go on to have a very normal life.

Glancing to the side, he noted that Abbie had donned the requisite gown and was perched on the very edge of the plastic chair. "Go ahead and scoot back so that you're comfortable before you hold her. It'll be a lot more difficult for you to get settled once she's in your arms."

Abbie pushed herself to the very back of the chair.

She didn't look more comfortable, though. That was neither here nor there as far as he was concerned.

Carefully opening the top of the special cot, he checked the wires and tubes to make sure nothing was tangled, then, sliding one gloved hand beneath the baby's neck to support it and the other beneath her nappy, he lifted her up, holding her close to his body and absorbing that quintessential baby smell as he pivoted on his heel. Abbie was still sitting exactly as she had been... hands clasped together in her lap.

"Hold out your arms, and I'll place her in them."

There was a pause of two or three seconds before she actually did as he requested. "Ready?"

She gave a curt nod.

Dean set the baby into the crook of Abbie's left arm and waited to make sure she had her before moving away.

"She doesn't look like him." Her voice was small. Quiet. So quiet he thought he must have misunderstood her.

"I'm sorry?"

"Nothing." She seemed to come to herself. "Babies don't always look like their parents when they're this small, after all."

"Not always. No." A sense of foreboding rose up. Something was wrong with this picture, but he had no idea what it was. When Jess had held the baby, it had seemed so natural. She'd looked down at her niece with such an expression of love that it had taken his breath away. There was none of that emotional vibe with Abbie. In fact, she seemed almost repelled.

Kind of like his mum had been with him?

But Abbie had other children. Children she seemed to love dearly.

It wasn't up to him to understand anything except the physical health of these tiny, helpless beings.

Deidre poked her head into the room. "Dr. Edwards? One of Dr. Granger's patients has eclampsia. She's not due for almost three months. They're asking for you."

"Are they inducing?"

"Her blood pressure is too high. They're going to take the baby now."

The sense of foreboding he'd had a moment ago was nothing compared to the way his heart jerked and sprinted at a rate that he recognized.

Far too early. If they were going to take the baby it meant the mum's life was in imminent danger. His job was to do what he could for the baby. "Tell them I'm on my way."

Deidre ducked back out of the room.

"You can't leave me here alone with her!" The panicked voice came from the chair.

Abbie. And she sounded more than dismayed. She sounded petrified.

He glanced down and saw he was right. Her eyes were wide with fear, her tense fingers tightening on Marissa's tiny frame.

"I'll send the nurse back in. I'm sorry, but I have to go." Giving her no further chance to object, he turned and headed out of the door. He asked Deidre to check in on Abbie as he went down the hall.

When he arrived at the surgical suite he shoved his arms through a gown and scrubbed in. The interior of the room held the sort of ordered chaos he'd come to expect. As his mind picked apart what was what, he saw that he'd arrived just as obstetrical surgeon Sean Anderson was making a vertical incision in the patient's lower abdomen.

Not good.

It meant they weren't worried about scarring or anything except getting that baby out as quickly as possible.

He moved into position. "Baby's obs?"

Sean glanced his way for a second, but didn't slow his pace. "Heart rate is good, but there was no time to administer anything to speed maturation of the lungs. I don't know what we're going to find."

He nodded, but knew better than to say anything else. They were in a fight for the life of the mother. Saving both mum and child was always the goal. All he could do was his best once the baby was born.

Sean opened the uterus and reached inside. Out came a perfectly formed baby boy. So tiny. So damned tiny.

His heart seized as they clamped and cut the cord, not even trying to get the baby to breathe.

"She's bleeding. I need some suction in here!" Sean handed the preemie off to him, caught up in the struggle to get the mum's bleeding under control. Eclampsia's high blood pressure put the patient at risk for heart attack or stroke. When medication didn't work, the only solution was to remove what was causing the spike in pressure: the baby.

The nurses assigned to the infant rushed with him to the table, everyone having his own job. They suctioned the mouth, administered oxygen, rubbed the baby with towels…anything to get him breathing. Nothing. Listening to the baby's heart, he found the rate slow. Too slow. "We need to intubate, right now."

There were two battles being fought in the room.

One to save the life of the mother. And one to save the life of her baby.

In the background, he vaguely heard Sean still yelling out orders to those on his team. His own team of nurses worked with a timed precision that made him proud on one level. On another, he wondered if it would be enough.

Once the intubation tube was in place and oxygen was pumped directly into the lungs, he waited until another nurse had the feed electrodes pasted to the baby boy's chest. They turned on the monitor. The straight line turned to spikes. But they were shallow. And still too slow. Only ninety beats per minute when it should have been at least a hundred and twenty.

A quick test of reflexes found the baby did indeed have them. But for how long? At just over six months, it was iffy as to whether the baby would even survive the night. But he was determined to give the infant the best possible chance. "Let's get him over to SCBU and see about those lungs."

The baby was just over twenty-four weeks and weighed in at only one pound two ounces. Twenty-five was the normal threshold for viability, but, as rare as it was, he'd seen babies this premature make it.

He glanced back at Sean. They were suturing the mother. Their eyes met. "How's the baby?"

"I won't know for a while. Mum?"

"The bleeding's under control. Blood pressure is coming down already. I think we've rounded the corner."

That might be true for Sean's patient, but for his own tiny charge that corner was still far in the distance. He could only hope the baby held on long enough for them to reach it.

* * *

"My parents left yesterday."

Pulling into the driveway of Dean's friend's house, Jess could already see several horses out in a nearby pasture, while another one stood at the fence line next to the car just to their right. Heavy vapor poured from its nostrils with every puff of air, making the creature look like a dragon from a fairy tale. He might as well be breathing fire, from where Jess sat.

"I don't think this is a good idea." In fact, Jess was sure it was a very bad idea. As was the brilliant one to go ice skating after this was all over.

Assuming she survived the first ordeal.

Her white skates from her teenage years were tucked into the boot of Dean's expensive car, along with his own black ones. Somehow she couldn't see him twirling around at an ice rink. He just looked too broad. Too strong.

Okay, so she would live. She had to, because that was definitely one picture she wanted to see. Of Dean weaving to and fro, making patterns in the ice.

"You're going to do fine."

Right. That was easy for him to say. "Just look at that one. He seems ready to take down anyone who ventures too close."

Dean glanced over at where she was pointing and laughed. "That's Thor."

"Thor?" Her head jerked around again to look at the pure white horse. She noticed no one else was around him. In fact, another fence stood between this horse and the rest of the herd in the distance. "Are you serious? That's his name?"

Dean nodded. "Yep. Because he swings a pretty serious hammer."

She closed her eyes to shut out the twin plumes of steam that were still emerging with the beast's every breath. "Oh, God. I don't even want to know what that means. Has he kicked anyone *recently*?"

"Kicked?" His head cocked to the side. Then he smiled again. "No. And you probably *don't* want to know why he's called that. Let's just say his mares haven't lodged any complaints."

Heat flashed up her face, along with relief. "Oh. So he's not mean."

"Not at all. For a stallion, he's pretty much a pussycat."

Somehow, she wasn't seeing it. She scrunched further down into her winter parka, hoping the dark fabric proved true to its promise that it could go from earthy to elegant without a hitch. Because right now, this was about as earthy as she could imagine getting.

"Let's go say hello," he continued.

"Oh. I'm fine. I'm sure he won't think me rude if I just sit this one out."

He gave her another grin. "It's a perfect photo op. We can shoot one of you standing next to him."

"Next to…?" Her eyes widened. "Oh, no, I don't think so."

"You'll have to shed your coat, of course. The pasture is still green enough to pretend it's autumn, if that's what one is expecting to see."

He acted as if he hadn't heard her at all. "I said, I don't think so."

Tweaking her nose, he popped open the door and exited his vehicle. "It's okay. I promise."

He came around and held open the door for her. Unfortunately, the day wasn't as chilly as it could be. In fact, it felt more like a typical autumn day than mid-December. So much for her hope to be snowed out. There wasn't even a damned cloud in the sky.

Let's get this over with.

When she got out and stood next to Dean, he fingered her hair for a minute, startling her. She jerked her head to look at him, but he just shrugged. "Just thinking it was a good thing you didn't wear a hair clip."

Did the animal bite? There were still a good couple of meters between her and Thor. "How about I stand here and you get a quick shot?"

Just then someone came out of the house. Dean smiled and crossed over to the man, who had to be pushing fifty, shaking his hand.

"Good to see you both." He glanced at Jess. "Is this her?"

"It is indeed. Jess, this is Clifton Mathers. Cliff, my friend Jess Black."

His friend. At least he wasn't introducing her as his girlfriend. But why would he?

"Nothing to be afraid of, missy. Dean told me to make sure to give you one of our mildest mounts."

"As mild as Thor?" The words just came out of nowhere.

Cliff shook his head. "No, I've got a little bitty thing picked out for you. One of our ponies."

"A— A pony?" All she could think of was the beast who'd tossed her over its shoulder as if she were nothing more than a hunk of fairy floss years ago.

"She's a tall pony. You'll suit her just fine."

Great. The combination of pony and tall did not make her feel any better.

Dean nodded at the fence. "I thought we might get a shot of us with Thor."

She'd so hoped he'd forgotten about doing that.

"I think Thor would be delighted," Cliff said.

Delighted. Well, at least one of them would be.

Dean waited until she shed her jacket, then handed his phone to Cliff. He eyed her when she made no move to walk over to the fence. Did he think she was just going to skip over there and hug the animal? Not bloody likely.

Unwilling to look like a total fool, she finally allowed herself to be tugged toward the white horizontal slats that made up the fence line. If she'd hoped Dean would keep his body in between her and the horse, she was soon disabused of that notion when he let go of her and moved to the other side.

What had she been thinking?

What had started as a quick fabrication by Dean to get her sister off her back had turned into a huge production that now included her parents.

Why did Dean even care what her sister thought?

Worse, he'd warned her that Abbie had talked to a couple of the nurses.

That made her swallow. She did not want to go down as a tick mark on a list of this man's known conquests. She'd already had that happen once with Martin. Theirs had been a whirlwind affair and engagement. But once he'd met Abbie, that had been it. He had no longer been interested in her.

"Love, you need to scoot in a bit closer so I can get all of you in the picture."

Cliff was speaking to her.

Closer? She gulped and peeked to the side. There was scarcely a meter between her and the horse as it was. She plucked up a few more ounces of courage and then sidestepped twice. A warm current of air gusted across her neck.

Ugh! The animal's breath—not to mention she was probably within reach of those huge white teeth now. "Could we do this quickly?"

Dean reached over and took her hand, giving it a re-assuring squeeze. It almost worked.

Then, something warm and rubbery touched her neck, just above the collar of her light sweater, and brushed across it. She froze, waiting for a set of equine chompers to latch onto her. But they didn't. A curious snuffling sound met her ears.

She chuckled. She couldn't help it. The animal's lips tickled. And he certainly didn't seem to want to hurt her.

A few of her muscles relaxed, and she glanced side-ways to find one of the horse's deep brown eyes fas-tened on her. And the expression in them seemed…kind.

She and the horse continued to stare at each other, his neck curved in her direction, grassy breath sliding across her cheek with every breath he took. A sense of awe filled her.

"Wow." It was the only word that came to mind.

"Perfect." Cliff's voice broke the spell, and she blinked back to herself. "I got some great shots."

He had? When?

Dean came around the front of the horse and nudged the animal's head away from her. "See? Not so bad." His murmured words came right before he dropped a quick kiss on her mouth.

He pulled back almost immediately, but it was too

late. Her lips tingled and a strange twitchy sensation came to life in her belly muscles.

Boneless.

That was what she felt. She stiffened her knees and forced them to hold her upright. It was just a quick friendly kiss of reassurance, like that hand squeeze had been a few minutes ago.

Except she could almost guarantee that friends didn't make each other feel like that. As if she wanted him to linger and reassure her some more.

She'd even forgotten about Thor's presence beside her—although he was back to snuffling around her sweater, his horsey lips blubbering and vibrating almost as much as her legs.

Thor's antics had put her so at ease that when it actually came time to sit on a pony's back—and Cliff was right, this particular pony was taller than the one from her childhood—it was all anticlimactic and dull. They got their pictures with no incidents and the next thing she knew they were back in his car and driving to the ice-skating arena.

Dean handed over his phone and told her to scroll through the pictures, to see if there were any good ones.

In the first few shots, even Jess could read the fear on her face, but as she continued scrolling she saw a change take place. At around the twentieth photo, she swallowed. Cliff had captured the moment Dean's lips met hers. The angle was perfect, showing that her eyes were closed and that she seemed to be leaning into that brief touch.

Damn. If she could see that, then…

Maybe she could figure out how to delete it before Dean came across it on his own. But just as her finger hovered over the screen his hand came over hers, stopping it. "If you're doing what I think you are, don't. I did that for the benefit of your parents."

Horror washed over her. The kiss had been staged?

How could she be so stupid? She'd actually believed...

With lightning speed she ran through the rest of the pictures without really seeing them and then handed the phone back. As if he realized something was wrong, he touched her cheek. "Hey. Just because it was planned, doesn't mean I didn't enjoy it."

Far from reassuring her, it only made her feel worse. He had no problem kissing her and enjoying the physical pleasure without ever letting that pleasure seep any deeper. But as their failed bet had proved, she wasn't nearly as adept at keeping things light and easy as he was.

If she was going to survive the next couple of weeks, though, she was going to have to figure out how Dean managed it. And then she needed to copy him step for step.

Otherwise, this man could very well break her heart.

CHAPTER EIGHT

JESS'S SKATES SCRAPED across the ice, bringing her to a halt right in front of him. She hadn't said anything about being an expert skater. But she was. And the healthy pink flush to her cheeks was a welcome sight after the pale translucence her skin had had in those first few days that her niece had been in the SCBU.

"Having fun?" he asked. He had to admit that he was. In spite of the news of his father's release from prison, and his concern about the preemie of their eclampsia patient, Dean was having a good time.

And most of it was due to the woman in front of him. This was why he didn't do relationships. He'd learned the hard way that if you got too attached to a person, they would go away. His dad had gone to prison for beating his mother—which was a good thing—but it was damned hard to obliterate your feelings for a parent, no matter how heinous his behavior might be.

And then his mum. As soon as she'd recovered from that last beating, she'd decided she'd had enough of the whole ugly scene. Dean had been sixteen. Legally old enough to be emancipated, if they'd gone before a magistrate. But had his mum done that? No. She'd simply cut him loose and left him behind saying he was old enough to be on his own. After all, he'd already been working and had been almost through school.

And yet he still loved his mother, even after all these years, even if he hated the choices she'd made along the way.

"I'm having a wonderful time," Jess said. "At least skating is one thing I'm not afraid of."

"We should take some pictures here as well. After all, that's why we came, isn't it?"

A shadow fell across her face, the first since they'd put their skates on a half-hour ago. Jess was head and shoulders above him as far as skill levels went. But that didn't mean he hadn't liked watching her skim across the ice like some kind of professional athlete. He'd even seen a few of the men on the ice watch her as she flew past.

She wasn't going to pick anyone up here, though. Even though their bet was over and done with, he wrapped an arm around her waist and reeled her in. Jess gave a quiet squeak. "What are you doing?"

He leaned in close. "Making sure everyone knows that you're mine for the day."

But not for the night. Which brought him back to that failed bet. Worst decision in history. He should have offered himself up for her little experiment at the very beginning, and been done with it. No more suppressed instincts. No more wondering what it might have been like if they'd fallen into bed together.

He was an expert at keeping his emotions out of any sexual encounters. He couldn't say the same of Jess, which was what had ultimately stopped him. One of his biggest rules had always been to make sure the woman knew where things stood and what she could expect once the night was over.

There were women out there who could do that—despite what Jess thought. He'd met them. Slept with them. And everyone was still friends. Well, maybe not friends, but they could exchange a friendly smile and a few words of greeting if they happened across each other later.

Yep, it would be different with Jess.

As if she sensed his thoughts she pulled back, throwing him a quick smile. "I'm actually not anyone's. For the day, or otherwise."

With that, she whisked past him, doing an expert spin and then settling in to skate with easy grace, hands behind her back, eyes half closed as if soaking in everything she could.

He found himself doing the same. And since he was still standing in the same spot he'd been a few minutes ago, he forced himself to move, feeling like a lumbering oaf compared to Jess's lithe movements.

She passed him again with an amused wave. A flicker of irritation went through him, this time. Maybe they should have stayed at Cliff's house and settled in for a visit. But he'd wanted to do something that Jess would find fun, rather than stressful. The pictures had just been an excuse.

Instead, it was Dean who was stressed. Other couples held hands and moseyed around the rink and a small group of men stood on the outside perimeter watching the skaters—a few of them, the ones who'd eyed Jess earlier, probably wondering if she was single. Well, hopefully they'd gotten the message when he'd put his arm around her.

Jess, however, didn't seem to care if anyone was

ogling her from the sidelines. Well, then, he would just force himself not to care either.

"Helloooo…"

She was back, this time turning around and skating backward so that she faced him. "I just thought of something. If you're in a hurry to get back, we can take a few pictures and leave. I know this wasn't supposed to be a real outing, just a photo op."

"I'm fine. I haven't been away from the hospital in ages, other than to go home to sleep. It feels good to be out in the real world." Something came to him. "But we do need some pictures. Better to do it now while there's still plenty of light and people."

He took her hand and pulled her toward the railing across from them, heading straight toward one of the men who'd been staring at her. With an easy smile he held up his phone. "Would you mind shooting a few shots of us as we go around the rink?"

The way the man's face fell would have been comical, if he hadn't been so obvious about his stares. The rental skates on the ground beside him said that he might even have gone out onto the ice in an attempt to reel in his catch once he'd singled one of them out. Wasn't that what Dean would have done?

Possibly. Hopefully he wouldn't have been quite so cold-blooded about the whole thing. It was one thing to engage in conversation that led to something else. It was another thing entirely to sit there like a predator, hoping to find a likely target.

Something inside of him whispered a protest. Was he certain he wasn't like that?

Yes. Definitely.

"Sure thing, buddy." The man's accent marked him as American. "Just let me know how it works."

How it works is this: you stand there and take pictures and leave Jess the hell alone.

Dean showed him how to operate the camera function, hoping that the man didn't just take off with it. Again, he had the idea that the bloke was just hoping to score a little something extra while on holiday. Well, he'd have to look elsewhere.

"Thanks." He tossed the American one final glance before taking to the ice with Jess in tow. Soon, she turned the tables, however, pulling him along at a speed that was a bit faster than he was used to.

"Don't forget you have an amateur on your hands."

"That's hard for me to believe. I think you're an expert."

In other things, was her inference. His irritation spiked a bit higher. It was one thing to have had that chat and bet about casual sex, it was another thing entirely to have her act as if it were a communicable disease that she had no intention of catching. Did she really think she was immune?

He moved behind her and wrapped his arms around her waist, his skates moving to the outside of hers and coasting. "Wh-what are you doing?"

"The man's taking pictures, remember?"

"Pictures. Right."

He leaned in and nuzzled her neck, feeling like old Thor and seeing exactly why the horse had engaged in a little love talk of his own. She smelled wonderful. And her skin was soft. Silky...

Someone sliced past, throwing them a quick glare. It was then that Dean realized the coasting had slowed to a crawl and that they were almost standing still, people flowing around them.

He ignored them. Pictures. He wanted her father to buy into their story.

The problem was, Dean was starting to buy into it himself. He kissed her ear. Her cheek. Slowly moving along it until he reached the corner of her mouth. Suddenly Jess spun around on one skate. But not to get away. No. She was now facing him. Looking up at him as if she wanted nothing more than for him to…

And so he did. He touched his mouth to hers, glorying in the chill that clung to her lips, the scent and taste of the hot cocoa she'd drunk before coming out on the ice. The combination surrounded his senses.

He gripped the edges of her parka and drew her closer. Using her skill on the ice to hold himself up. At least that was what he told himself. In reality, he just wanted her against him. Wanted to slide his hands beneath all of those clothes and feel the warm skin of her stomach…her breasts.

That was what finally pulled him from his trance. He'd done this to prove she wasn't entirely immune. Well, hell, it seemed he was the one who'd caught something. And he'd better figure out a cure and quick.

He drew back. "I think he's probably gotten enough."

Jess gasped, looking as if he'd just slapped her. And rightly so. It was the second time he'd pretended a kiss was all about the pictures, when in reality it was all about her. About the way she made him feel. But if she thought he was the king of casual sex, now was the time to play the part.

"I'm sure he has." Her eyes turned frosty. "Time to go see, isn't it? Actually it's past time. And I think I'm ready to call it a day, if you don't mind. If you'll send me copies of the pictures, I'll forward them to my parents. And that'll be that. Thank you for bailing me out, but you're now off the hook."

He didn't want her to just run back to her rabbit hole and disappear, as much as he knew that was exactly what should happen. For his own peace of mind.

"If I remember right, I put myself on that hook, not you." Well, that made no sense at all, but it was the only thing he could think of.

Dean let go of her jacket and took what he hoped was a casual step back, only to have his skates suddenly shoot out from under him, landing him straight on his ass.

CHAPTER NINE

"I HAVE TO go home."

Abbie stood over her baby's cot, gripping some kind of small bottle.

"What do you mean you have to go home? What about Marissa?"

"Mum rang me this morning. Jerry is in hospital. He has pneumonia."

Jess's heart dropped. Her four-year-old nephew. "Oh, God, I'm sorry. What about Martin?"

Her twin's head turned in her direction for a second, but there was no accusation in her eyes for once. "He'll come with me, of course, and then it's back to work for him tomorrow."

"Already?"

Abbie nodded. "He cut short a business trip to come to Cambridge. There are some things he needs to tie up before he can officially go on paternity leave. He didn't expect the baby to…arrive when she did."

Guilt surrounded Jess once again. "I'm so sorry for what happened."

"I think I'm being punished." The words were spoken with a quiet resignation that gave Jess pause.

Her sister had been quick enough to blame her for this last week. What had changed?

"Why would you say something like that?"

"Two of my children are now sick." She shifted the bottle from one hand to the other. Jess tilted her head and peered at it a bit closer.

Concealer.

Was she putting on makeup here in the SCBU? When she moved her glance back to her sister's face, all that met her were dark circles and mussed hair. Her sister was always so sure of herself. So careful about her appearance.

Something seemed off.

Well, she had two children in hospital. Any mother would be frantic—feeling torn between the two of them, whether to stay or whether to go.

Jess laid her hand on the top of the special-care cot. "You're not being punished. And I'll keep an eye on her, Abbie. If anything at all comes up, I'll ring you immediately."

"Every day. Please ring me every day."

One of the other babies cried and a nurse came in to check on him before Jess could move. "I will. She's so very precious, isn't she?"

She looked down at the tiny human, eyes tracing over the rise and fall of her chest. The kick of a little leg. The one that had...

The birthmark. It was gone. Jess leaned a little closer.

No. It wasn't gone. That was what the concealer was for. All traces of compassion rushed away like a torrent. "You put makeup on her leg? What is wrong with you, Abbie?"

Abbie dropped into the chair and covered her face

with her hands. The other nurse finished what she was doing and then retreated to the far corner, probably wanting no part of what was likely to be a drama of the first order. It always seemed to be, where her sister was concerned.

"I…" Abbie tilted her head back to look at her, and Jess was shocked to see tears. "You have no idea what I've done."

Were they still talking about the concealer? Her sister had mentioned being punished. Did she think the birthmark was part of that?

"What is it, then?" And where in the world was Martin? Shouldn't he be here with his wife, if they were leaving?

She handed the bottle to Jess. "It's not what you think. I don't want the baby to pay for what I did."

"You didn't do anything. And you can't cover up her birthmark. It's just a tiny spot. I don't understand why it's such a big deal."

Her sister sighed. "Martin works so much. It seems like he's always off on some business trip. I used to wonder if he was coming to see you."

"Of course he wasn't. I would never do that to you. Or to anyone." Something churned in her stomach, and she wasn't sure she really wanted to hear any more.

Abbie's mouth tightened. "You always were the perfect one."

"Please don't."

"I'm sorry." She stood up and seemed to pull herself back together. "Martin is packing my things now, and we leave in two hours. You'll ring me?"

"Of course." She handed the bottle back to Abbie. "I know you're not asking me to put this on her."

"No. It was just stupidity on my part." She curled her fingers around the concealer, knuckles showing white. "I'll let you know when we arrive in London."

"And please let me know how Jerry is. Give him a gentle hug from his Aunt Jess."

She needed to make more of an effort to visit her nephews. Even if she and Abbie didn't always get along, the boys shouldn't have to pay the price.

"I will." Abbie unexpectedly wrapped her in a tight hug. "I'm sorry. For everything. I hope someday you'll understand."

At the moment, Jess didn't understand anything, except that her sister was hurting and for the first time was letting her share that burden just a little. Feeling a little weepy and out of sorts herself after what had happened with Dean on the ice two days ago, she put her arms around her sister and squeezed her right back.

There was hope. There had to be. For Abbie. And for her.

Isabel Delamere was posting a flier of some type on the staff board. An Australian obstetrician who'd been seconded to Cambridge Royal Hospital, Isabel had quickly become a part of daily life in the maternity unit.

Dean moved in to take a closer look at the paper. Something about a staff Christmas party. His brows went up. "Haven't we had a couple of those already?"

She smiled at him. "A couple. But one was for prospective adoptive parents in Aaron Cartwright's program. Hope Sanders and Bonnie Reid helped organise it. But we haven't had anything for just the staff yet. A few people felt we needed a more adult type of party."

When Dean's brows crept even higher, she laughed.

"Not that kind of party. Just a fancy venue with pretty frocks, flashy tuxes and lots of festivity." A shadow passed across her face. "Some of us could really use that right about now."

She was right. He'd been tense for the last couple of days, ever since that kiss with Jess at the ice-skating arena. He'd spent that night in bed, his imagination exploding at what might have happened had he just kept his mouth shut.

As a result he'd become more and more irritable. And frustrated. He'd found himself in the strange position of lusting after someone he shouldn't have.

He knew it would be the worst kind of mistake. But that didn't stop his head from picturing it, in explicit detail.

Speak of the devil. Here she came. Head down as if she were going to power past him without a glance. Except that Isabel called out to her, waving her over.

And over she came. Shoulders hunched. Arms stiff at her sides. As if heading to an execution.

Isabel nodded at the poster. "We're quite late getting this under way, but were hoping you could help spread the word." The other woman touched her arm. "And maybe even get us a head count? You'll be there, right?"

Looking at the writing and the bright image of a huge fancy Christmas tree, Jess drew in a quick breath. "It's at the Sarasota?"

"Yes, super posh, so wear something fancy." Isabel waved a sheaf of papers. "Well, I have more of these to get up. If you could let me know how many you think can make it, that would be fab. I expect to see you there." With that, she was off on her next mission.

Dean studied Jess's face. It was as if she couldn't stop staring at the poster. "What is it?"

"That's where my parents had their anniversary party." Light brown eyes closed, and she swallowed. "I'll never be able to forget that night. Or what happened."

Moving closer, he looped an arm around her shoulders. "I'm sorry."

"I can't go. I know it'll disappoint Isabel, but—"

"I think you should go."

"What?"

"Face it head-on. Replace bad memories with something more pleasant. Otherwise, every time you hear the hotel's name, you'll associate it with what happened."

If anyone knew that, it was him. Just like the tonic water he'd forced himself to down at Jess's place. It had ended up being a good thing, the newer memory supplanting some of the ones from his past. Maybe Jess could do the same thing. Replace a bad memory with a not so bad memory. "I'll go with you, if it'll help."

When storm clouds formed in her eyes, he shook his head. "Not for a photo op, but as a friend. If you get there and realize you can't handle being there, we'll leave." He stepped in front of her and tilted her chin. "No one should have to face something like this alone. Not if you don't have to."

The air seemed to crackle between them for several seconds, and then she drew a big breath. Nodded. "Thank you. I think I'll take you up on it." She paused. "If you're sure?"

Letting go of her, he took a step back, afraid he might be tempted to lean closer and capture that satiny mouth with his.

"Very sure." Maybe this would help ease the tension

between them and drop them back on safer ground. He grinned, a sense of relief flowing through him. "I haven't worn a tuxedo in ages. This gives me a good excuse to put on something besides a lab coat or scrubs."

Jess glanced down at her own blue medical garb and smiled up at him. "It will be fun to let my hair down for a while."

Her blonde hair was pulled back in its customary ponytail, that gray streak looking like an exclamation point that had been tipped on its side. Bold. Unapologetic. She could have dyed it to go with the rest of her hair, and yet she let it run free—like an inner wild child who refused to be tamed or subdued.

He liked it. Glad that she'd left it natural. He took his thumb and ran it over the narrow strip of hair until he got to the elastic in back. "Isabel said the party would do everyone some good. She might be right."

Before he could even think about what he was doing, he touched her cheek and continued, "Don't worry, we'll make sure Marissa is well cared for while we're there."

She bit her lip. "That reminds me. Abbie is going home. One of her other children is ill." He listened without speaking as Jess filled him in on what was happening in short choppy phrases.

"She did what?" He couldn't help but interrupt when she mentioned her sister had put makeup on the baby. "Why would she? There's always a danger of contamination."

"I know. And she acted oddly once I'd realized what she'd done. Like she wanted to tell me something, but changed her mind."

"What do you think it was?"

"I have no idea. But I have a feeling it has to do with Martin."

At that, Dean frowned. Surely Abbie wasn't accusing her sister of going after him again. "How so?"

Reaching back, she tightened her ponytail. "She talked about him working so much. I think she suspects he's having an affair. But then she talked about the problems with Marissa being a punishment for something. Something *she'd* done."

"If she thinks Martin is the one having the affair…" Another staff member murmured an apology as they went to move past them to look at the flier. Dean eased Jess over to the side.

"Maybe she feels like she drove him away somehow." Jess glanced toward the ceiling. "I have no idea. I told her I'd look after Marissa until she gets back. She's written up a power of attorney so that I can make medical decisions for the baby, if something terrible happens. I just hope I don't have to. I want her to grow and thrive."

"It's what we all want. For each and every one of those babies."

Including the preemie from the eclampsia case. So far the baby was hanging in there, despite the odds.

"You're incredibly good at what you do." Jess's soft voice held a sincerity that made him swallow.

"Thank you. We all do our best."

"No. I think it's more than that. You have a drive that I don't see in every doctor. Yes, they care about their patients, but there's something different about the way you go about it."

Too close. He didn't want her looking inside and seeing his own shattered childhood. Or realizing how scared and alone he'd felt during his years at home.

As devastated as he'd been by his mother's abandonment, in a way it had come as a relief. He'd become self-reliant. No longer depending on anyone other than himself.

Staring at the one woman who might be able to see beneath his flirty, carefree mask, he forced himself to push it on a little tighter. "I'm just doing what I was trained to do. Helping my patients get the very best medical care available. Nothing more. Nothing less."

Less. Now there was a good word. One that was beginning to sound better and better.

As in seeing less of Jess.

And as soon as that Christmas party was over, he was going to retreat to his own little self-reliant corner, and this time he would make sure he stayed there.

CHAPTER TEN

"You two look adorable together. You have no idea how long your father and I have waited for this."

Her mum's voice made tears spring to her eyes. Staring at the upper right-hand corner of her computer where a slideshow of the shots she'd sent were blinking past one after the other, she had to admit, it all looked far too real.

The pictures of them beside Thor had a spontaneity that she certainly hadn't felt when she'd been standing there. But her face was pink, her teeth digging into her lower lip, while Dean's eyes held a mischievous glow that transported her back to that day. He'd just finished telling her where the horse's name had come from. And Cliff had caught the moment perfectly.

And the ice skating. Dean had handed his phone over to that stranger and they'd staged another scene. This one had him standing behind her, arms wrapped around her waist. Jess's head was tilted back so that she leaned against his shoulder. If she closed her eyes, she could almost smell that earthy, manly scent that had drifted past her nose as she'd stood within the circle of his arms.

She'd wanted him in that moment. Desperately. The fact that she would just be one more woman on an ever-growing list hadn't seemed to matter. It was getting harder and harder to convince her body that sleeping with him would be a big mistake. Especially now, when she couldn't quite remember why that was.

"Well, don't marry us off just yet." What else could she say? They weren't getting married. Ever. And there really wasn't a need to keep pretending. Abbie had already left and so had Martin.

But they had to come back to get the baby, didn't they?

"Even I can read the writing on the wall." Her father's smile came through the video chat. They'd convinced him, evidently.

Unfortunately, she'd almost convinced herself as well, which would be a royal disaster. She did not need to get caught up in the fairy tale Dean had spun for her family. If she did, she might never be able to free herself again.

An image of Dean crouched in the corner of an enormous web, waiting to devour her, came to mind.

Only when he climbed toward her—making his way along the sticky fibers of the trap he'd spun—he didn't have the menace of a spider...but that of a lover. The same man who'd held her on that ice, his strong arms binding her to him. What if sleeping with him set her free from that web? Because what was really holding her there were all of those *what-would-it-be-like?* thoughts that kept going through her mind.

Like the ones filling her mind right now.

No. Can't happen.

He only wanted to satisfy his physical needs.

And she didn't?

Hmm...maybe putting a stop to his advances at the pub hadn't been such a smart idea, after all. What better person to teach her about casual sex than the king of casual sex: Dean Edwards?

What would be so terrible about that, really, if they both knew where things stood?

That wasn't what she'd thought all those nights ago.

She shook her head to clear it, realizing her parents were still staring at her.

The writing. Her dad had said he could see the writing on the wall.

"We're not going to rush into anything. We're both busy people."

"Not too busy to get married and have a family, surely?" her mum protested.

She had a point as far as that was concerned. Jess didn't make much time for her personal life. Ever since she and Martin had broken things off, she hadn't wanted to date or do anything else for that matter. Which was why she allowed herself to be talked into working extra shifts. She was so knackered on most nights she went home and fell right into bed—alone.

And forty years from now, would she be settled into the same routine? Or maybe she'd have ninety-nine cats to keep her warm in bed.

Dean had been so sweet after her reaction to the Christmas party's venue. He could have easily found a date for the evening. Instead, he'd offered to go with her and leave whenever she'd had enough. He'd put her feelings ahead of his own.

Would he be as attentive in bed?

Jess shivered. She had no doubt he would be an excellent lover. How else would he have gotten the reputation he had? If he were a jerk about things afterward, surely she would have heard about it? But no. Women swooned over him.

"We're trying to play things by ear, Mum. These things can't be hurried."

Her mother made a scoffing sound. "Your sister has quite a head start on you in the department of providing us with grandchildren."

Jess tensed. "You're getting way ahead of yourself."

Maybe her mother sensed something in her voice, because she came back with, "Of course I am. But speaking of children, how is my newest little granddaughter?"

"She's doing wonderfully. We're going to try to give her her first bottle this afternoon."

"Abbie will be so pleased to hear it."

Her father had gone silent in the background, but he was looking at her through the computer with a slight frown on his face, even as the pictures of her and Dean kept flashing by in another window of the screen.

Oh, no. She knew that expression. He was about to ask something tricky.

She tried to head things off at the pass. "How is Jerry doing? Is he still in hospital?"

"He is. He's quite ill, actually." Her mum waved her hand in front of the screen when Jess's eyes widened. "His life isn't in danger, of course, but you can just tell he's poorly. Abbie did the right thing in coming home."

"It couldn't have been an easy decision." Her sister's behavior that last day still puzzled her. The whole putting makeup on the baby's leg and then those enigmatic words about being punished. But at least she finally seemed ready to make peace with their own personal past.

"It wasn't. All she talks about is going back for the baby once Jerry is well enough."

"Marissa will be here for a couple more weeks, I should think. She still has a bit of weight to put on."

"Jess." Her father's voice pulled at her. "Are you happy?"

The question was so far removed from what they'd been talking about that it took her brain a moment or two to untangle the words. Once she did, they hit her between the eyes. She squirmed in her seat, hating that she was deceiving them like this. She should have just taken whatever Abbie dished out…except that Abbie was making not only herself miserable, but everyone around her. Going along with Dean's fib had seemed a small price to pay at the time. But it had grown into this gargantuan monster that required more lies to keep the original one from being discovered.

"He's a good man." Words very much like the ones she'd said as she'd stood in front of that poster for the Christmas party. And it was true. Dean had been a good sport. It didn't hurt that he was also a great kisser. The memory of his lips moving across hers in front of her house came to mind. And then at the pub. On the ice.

She wanted to kiss him again. Wanted to find some measure of satisfaction in his arms.

Should she? He'd offered to leave the Christmas party early if she wanted to. What if she asked him to leave for a completely different reason?

Would he say yes?

After what she'd done at the pub? She had no idea.

"I didn't ask that." Her dad wasn't going to let this alone evidently. "I asked if you were happy."

Yes. She was. This time with Dean had brought her joy. He was fun, sexy, brave. And watching him cradle Marissa in those big hands had done a number on her heart. She was happy to have spent this time with him. Even if it never went any further.

"Yes. I'm happy. Does that satisfy you?"

Her mum sighed. "I can just see the love in your eyes when you say that."

She could? Then Jess had better smack it right back out of there. She didn't love him.

Like him? Yes. Lust after him? Um, double yes.

That was what she'd been doing just moments ago. Lusting. Was she going to do something about it?

Maybe. For one night of hot sex.

Warmth swept along her inner thighs, setting areas to tingling that needed to remain still and quiet. She was on the phone with her parents, for goodness' sake.

"I'm sure Dean will be thrilled to hear you say that." She didn't roll her eyes. At least not outwardly. But inside? Oh, yes, they were rolling all around like those fake glasses with the googly eyes.

Suddenly superstitious about everything that had happened, she crossed her fingers behind her back and hoped the universe took pity on her situation. The last thing she needed was for it to look down at her and decide to give her exactly what she deserved.

"Well, I'd probably better go. I need to go shopping for a dress for the Christmas party and I have a shift in the morning."

"Christmas party?" Her mum's brows went up. "This is the first I've heard of this."

"It's for the hospital staff. They're having it at the same hotel as your anniversary party, actually."

"Such a beautiful place. Are you going with Dean?"

Finally. One thing she was not going to have to lie about. "I am."

"Well, we definitely wouldn't want to keep you from shopping. Pick out something that will knock him dead."

"Not too dead," her dad interjected with a smile. "We want him alive and well." His voice turned serious. "After that business with Martin, I'm glad you've found someone."

Her heart ached all over again. Her dad had never quite forgiven her ex for breaking off their engagement, although he hid it well. But Jess saw glimpses of it every once in a while. Just a flash of narrowed eyes or a frown when he listened to his son-in-law, but she'd caught it, just the same.

"Dean's a peach, all right." She forced a bright smile. "I've got to run, though. Chat again soon?"

"After the party, if not before." Her mum planted a kiss on her husband's cheek. "We'll want to hear every detail."

If Jess got the nerve up to do what she was thinking of doing, there would be at least one part of the evening her parents would never hear about.

Because she *had* made up her mind—at least she hoped so. She just needed to drum up the courage to follow through.

She was going to back Dean into a corner at that very posh hotel and ask him to spend the night with her. She did want a fling. A real one. Not with just anyone—and certainly not with some stranger from the pub—but with Dean. Maybe then she could stop obsessing about the man.

He did casual sex on a regular basis, so there'd be no chance of him getting the wrong idea about where they were headed afterward. Right?

So it was settled. She would do it.

And then she'd just hope and pray he didn't do what she'd done at that pub…and turn around and walk away.

She was feeding the baby.

Dean stood back against the wall and watched with interest, a lump forming in his throat. Jess didn't know he was here—not yet, anyway—he'd seen her through the window and quietly entered the SCBU through the side door. All her attention had been on the tiny infant cradled in her arms, cooing and talking softly to her. "Good girl. Mummy is going to be so happy to know you're drinking from your bottle."

A few of the tubes had been removed this morning, once they knew for sure that the baby's suck reflex was going strong. Using a gloved pinkie finger, Dean had been thrilled when the infant's head had tracked the path of his finger, trying to root around and latch on. The next step had been to introduce the real thing.

And the baby had done it. She'd latched onto the bottle's teat and started sucking with enthusiasm.

That wasn't the only good news. The baby born to the woman with eclampsia was also improving in small steady increments. In fact, that baby was in the cot right next to Marissa's. Dean had come to check on him.

Jess murmured again and the knot in his throat tightened further. She was going to make such a good mother. Unlike his own, who'd been so young that she hadn't known her own mind. Or how to protect herself—and Dean—from the drunken fool she'd married.

He hadn't heard anything else about his father since he'd received the news that he'd been let out of prison. The one good thing was that his mum was long gone. He'd never be able to hurt her again. And Dean would make sure the man didn't get close enough to anyone he cared about to hurt them either.

Exactly who would that be? Dean had no one. And that was how he wanted to keep it.

His gaze traveled back to Jess, and he realized her light brown eyes were no longer focused on the baby. She was staring right at him, a question written in her gaze.

"What?" he mouthed.

She shook her head.

Quietly moving over to where she sat, he crouched down beside her. "How's she doing?"

Jess smiled. The sight almost knocked him over. There was a radiance to her eyes and a soul-searing happiness in the softness of her face that spoke of a woman in love.

He swallowed. No one had ever looked at him like that.

And even though he knew the expression was for the minute creature she held in her arms, he could pretend for just a few seconds what it might be like to have had a mum like this one.

Only Jess wasn't a mum. And this wasn't her child.

He shook himself back to reality.

"Brilliantly," Jess murmured. "Just look at her."

In order to stop staring at the woman, he did as she asked and glanced down at the baby. With a tiny tuft of light hair on her head and blue eyes that fixed on Jess's face, she sucked with quiet enthusiasm. A drop of white appeared at the outer corner of her lips and he reached for Jess's arm where the burping rag had slipped and used it to carefully dab at the speck.

On impulse, he leaned over and kissed the baby's head, smiling when she shifted as if irritated by the interruption. When his attention moved back to Jess, he was surprised to find her eyes moist.

"Are you okay?"

"Just happy that she's getting stronger."

"We all are."

She pulled in a deep breath. "Yes. Of course. So did you get yourself a tux? The party is just days away."

"I already have one."

Her lips tightened slightly. "I imagine you go to quite a few fancy parties."

"Not so many, no. I bought the tux for a friend's wedding before I realized that most people simply rent and return them. I figured since I had it, I could use it whenever I needed one for a fancy dinner." His brows lifted. "Don't think I've used it twice since then, actually."

"Oh." The tense lines beside her mouth eased. "Well, I bought a new dress and a killer pair of shoes."

"Killer, eh?" He had no idea what that meant, but he was imagining sky-high heels and a very short hemline. Not a very realistic idea, however. "I thought your red one was quite nice."

She crinkled her nose. "That wasn't the happiest night of my life. I've decided to retire that frock to the back of the wardrobe. No, the one I bought is blue and gold. It's very festive."

And because he couldn't curb his curiosity about her footwear he decided to ask. "And your shoes—are they gold as well?"

"Yes. Strappy. With a dangerously high heel."

After the way she'd murmured those words, that wasn't the only thing that was becoming dangerously high. And in the Special Care Baby Unit, of all places.

"And how do you plan to walk in those dangerous heels?"

Her teeth caught one corner of her lower lip for a few seconds before releasing it. "Oh, I don't plan on walking."

Bloody hell. And the dangerously high areas were getting higher.

She laughed as if guessing exactly what he was thinking. Minx!

"I don't plan on walking," she said again. "I plan on dancing."

"Dancing? Well, I hope your dance card is empty, because that is something I would like to see."

Her index finger reached up to stroke across the baby's forehead. "In all honesty, I just want to keep from breaking my neck."

"You seemed pretty competent out there on the ice. Unlike someone else we both know."

"Hmm…you *are* the one who fell, aren't you? Well, as long as you don't take me down with you, we should be fine."

He couldn't hold back the smile. The woman was sexy as hell with a side of realism that made him want to do all sorts of crazy things. "We'll just have to help each other stay on our feet, then."

"I was hoping you'd say that, because if you could see these shoes…"

If she didn't stop talking about them, he was going to have a real problem when he stood up to leave. Time to bring himself back to earth. "Do you think you'll be taller than me?"

"Ha! I don't think they make shoes that tall."

The way she said that made something in his stomach curl. He could have sworn there was a grudging admiration…or maybe even attraction…tucked inside those words.

He might just have to find out.

But not here. Not surrounded by ill children.

Once that Christmas party came around, though, he was going to have to see if the woman was all talk and no action. Or if she'd changed her mind and decided they wouldn't make such a bad pair, after all.

His phone went off, and he glanced down at the screen. It was the maternity unit. "Duty calls," he said. "Can you get her back in her cot without help?"

"I got her out by myself so I think so." She nodded toward the door. "Go on. We'll be fine. If I have any trouble, I'll call a nurse."

With that, Dean climbed back to his feet. But not without throwing one last glance behind him at the woman who was beginning to infiltrate his dreams. And worse, he had a feeling tonight's dreams were going to include a certain pair of high strappy sandals, and, if he wasn't mistaken, he'd be plotting all kinds of ways to get her out of them.

Just then, Jess's phone went off. With a frown, she glanced down at the readout. "Oh, no."

He had his hand on the door, knowing he needed to go. "What?"

"I'm being called down to Maternity as well. It's my friend Amy. I'm her midwife, and she's in crisis."

They arrived in a chaotic maternity unit just as the baby was delivered by C-section. Although the baby was obviously full term, the newborn was blue and limp with no reflexes. No heart rate. The nursing staff were already administering chest compressions. Leaping into action, he went to work intubating the baby and pushing air, while Jess stood in the background looking shell-shocked.

"What happened?" he bit out.

Isabel looked up from where she was still working on Jess's friend, who was under general anesthesia. The floor was littered with bloody towels. "Grade three placental abruption. Worrisome fetal heart rate that bottomed out just as we were going in. We're taking her uterus."

"Oh, God." Jess's startled cry echoed what they were all thinking.

Taking the uterus to save the life of the mother. Even as they worked on the baby, he ached for Jess's friend, who might not only lose this child, but would never carry another.

Fifteen minutes went by in almost complete silence as everyone continued to work at a feverish pace. They administered adrenaline, hoping to stimulate the baby's heart.

"Come on…come on…" He could hear the frustration in his voice. He realized Jess was standing over him as he willed the newborn to respond.

This time, it wasn't going to work.

Time to call a halt…

Wait. A blip went across the monitor. Then another one. Another.

Everyone paused, staring at the machine, which had gone from almost a flat line to a trio of beats. The jumbled rhythm began to take shape, growing more and more regular with each second.

There! Sinus.

"Keep bagging him. We're getting something."

Jess's voice came from beside him. "I can't believe it."

Abruptio placentae sometimes struck without warning. It was always an obstetrical emergency and depending on the amount of placenta that separated from the wall of the uterus the outcome could be good for both mother and baby, or it could be catastrophic.

"We're not out of the woods yet." They'd have to do an EEG to get an idea of brain function, but his heart was going.

Dean bit out a few more instructions to the team. He was in no rush to move the baby right now. Not until he was a little more stable. Until then, they needed to get him on a ventilator. Dean made the call.

He glanced at Jess. "Are you okay?"

"Amy's my friend. I was going to call her to remind her that she'd missed her last appointment."

"You're her midwife?"

Jess nodded. "She insisted, even though I didn't think it was…" Her eyes closed, and she leaned against his arm.

"She's special to you, and you wanted to be there for her. Neither of you could have predicted this would happen."

She glanced over at the table, where two doctors were still operating on Amy. "What am I going to tell her?"

"The truth. That no one could have foreseen this. It's not her fault. Or yours."

He was a great one for giving that kind of advice.

He'd convinced Jess to lie to her parents and sister about their relationship.

To keep her from being hurt.

And why was that? Because of his own past? Because of the way he'd been hurt by his biological family? Jess's case was very different from physical abuse. But he knew from experience that words sometimes wounded just as badly and left terrible scars—scars that might not be visible but that were there just the same.

Jess scrubbed her palms over her eyes. "What if she doesn't make it?"

"Let's not go down that road, yet." He paused. "Does Amy have family here?"

"No. She's all alone. This is her very first baby." She swallowed. "It looks like it'll be her last, if he survives."

He squeezed her shoulder and then released it. "There are other ways. We both know that."

"Yes, but that's not going to make her feel any better right now." She licked her lips. "I keep thinking this could be Abbie lying there. That the baby could have been Marissa."

"But it's not. They're both fine." He glanced back as another doctor came into the room. Within a few minutes, they'd gotten the baby hooked up to the ventilator and orders were written up for the other tests.

"She's going to want footprints made…just in case."

"I'll order it."

Jess's brown eyes were rimmed with moisture. She drew a stuttered breath. "Thank you. This means a lot to me."

"I'm going with him. I'll let you know as soon as I know something."

"I want to come with you."

"Are you sure you don't want to stay until she's out of surgery?" He nodded toward Amy.

"I can't do anything for her right now." She looked up at him. "Except for this."

They had footprints made as the newborn was rushed from one department to another. When they'd finally gotten him to the SCBU, two hours had gone by.

They went to check on Amy and found Isabel just wrapping things up. "She's still out. We've given her three units of blood," Isabel said. "Who's the next of kin?"

"She doesn't have any that I know of. I'm her friend. I'm listed as her contact person."

They were evidently pretty close friends. You didn't just hand something like that over without a lot of trust on both sides.

With her family the way it was, Dean was glad she had someone to talk to. He'd never even thought to ask about who her friends might be or if she even had any. Maybe because Dean had always been kind of a lone wolf, never really forming those kinds of relationships. Nor had he ever felt the need to.

And judging from the way Jess was hurting for her friend, he wasn't sure he really wanted to. He'd cried into his pillow from time to time at the boys' home after his mum had left. But it was always when no one could see. By the time he was eighteen, the tears had stopped. He couldn't remember a time since when he'd really cried.

Maybe it was a good thing he didn't do relationships.

"You'll let me know if anything changes, right?" Jess turned toward him. "I'm going to stay with her for a while."

"Are you sure?" Even as he said it, there was something inside of him that urged him to stay as well. Which was exactly why he needed to leave. Now.

"Yes. I want to be here when she wakes up."

And who would be there for Jess?

Not him. It couldn't be. He headed for the door, but just before he went through it, he stopped. Went back over to her. He wanted to kiss her cheek, but the doctors were still there finalizing things. He settled for gripping her hand for a minute. "Ring me if you need me. You've got my mobile?"

She nodded. "Thank you. I will."

As he made to leave once again a part of Dean that was centered squarely in his chest hoped that she would.

CHAPTER ELEVEN

DEAN WAS TALKING to someone on his mobile. Propped against the wall of one of the hallways, he didn't look happy. She couldn't hear the conversation, but he appeared to be doing more of the listening than the talking. Anything he said was short and curt, lips thin, face tight. She started to back away, when his eyes met hers, and he motioned her over.

Great. She'd been on her way to see Marissa this morning. Amy had finally regained consciousness last night and had sobbed in weak, tired squeaks that broke Jess's heart. The baby was still hanging in there, and they'd gotten news that there was brain activity. And the baby was already breathing on his own. All hopeful signs. Even so, it had been awful telling her friend what the doctors had had to do to save her life.

Feeling tired and just a little sad, she made her way over to where Dean was, noticing that he was doing his best to get off the phone.

"I'm not interested in meeting."

His tone was so grim, she wondered who in the world he could be talking to. Had one of his female friends decided to get too clingy and was demanding he turn a one-night stand into something more?

The thought made her cringe, especially after what she'd been thinking of doing.

"Who I'm seeing is none of your business."

Wow. Now that was harsh.

Jess gave a quick wave and mouthed, "See you later," only to have him reach out with his free hand and catch her by the wrist.

"Well, I really wish they hadn't given you this number."

His eyes darkened ominously for a second or two. "You're not my father. You stopped being that a long time ago."

Oh! It wasn't a woman. It was his father. Dean had said his dad had been released from prison and might try to see him. She'd almost forgotten.

What had he been in prison for? White-collar crime? Or something worse? For Dean to say the man was no longer his father, it had to be something quite serious. Or maybe Dean was just angry that his dad had broken the law. He seemed to be a very by-the-book kind of guy. Except when it came to relationships. And lying to her parents.

That still stunned her when she thought about it. She had no idea what had made him step up that day and claim to be her significant other, but he'd done her a huge favor. It had stopped the haranguing and nagging from both her sister and her mother, and those comments about how driven she was by her career.

Which she wasn't. Not at all.

Wasn't she? She'd thrown her heart and soul into her job, going as far as to further train in crisis management—which was why she was often called in on difficult cases. And she was good at her job. She loved it.

But was it enough? She'd thought so once she'd gotten out from under her mum's thumb. But when she'd started in again during their visit, it had made Jess doubt herself.

As did Dean.

Even as angry as he seemed right now, the man was gorgeous. And she could see herself falling for someone like him under the right circumstances.

Which these were not.

"Please don't ring me again." With that, his thumb hit a button on his mobile and evidently disconnected the call. He let go of her hand and dropped his phone back into the pocket of his lab coat. "Sorry about that."

She wasn't exactly sure why he'd called her over there. "That was your father, I take it?"

"Mmm, no. Didn't you hear? I don't have one of those."

Her heart ached to hear the rough edge that still clogged his voice.

"You may not like whatever the man has done, but he is still your dad."

Another sound came from the back of his throat. "Don't think so. And it's probably best not to assume you know him."

That made her blink. "Sorry. I was only trying to—"

He leaned his head against the wall. "Damn it. I'm sorry, Jess. I have no right to take my anger out on you."

"What did he do, anyway, that landed him in prison?"

He turned to look at her. "He put my mum in the critical care unit."

"He what?"

"He hit her. Until she broke."

Her heart froze for a second, and then pounded back into a chaotic rhythm. "God, Dean. I'm so sorry. I never would have guessed. Did she divorce him?"

"I don't know, actually. She left town almost as soon as she got out of hospital."

She swallowed. So his dad had gone to prison, and his mother had left. How old had Dean been when all of this happened? "Were you grown and gone?"

"Not quite. And I have no idea why I'm telling you any of this. Sorry. I actually wanted to say I'd be happy to pick you up for the Christmas party."

The event was the day after tomorrow, but she wasn't ready to let go of the other subject quite so easily. "Are you going to see him? Your dad, I mean."

This time he smiled. "You don't believe in beating around the bush, do you?"

"You once said I say exactly what I think, so why hold back now?"

"No, I'm not planning on seeing him. Ever."

It was none of her business, really, but something made her say, "Maybe he's changed or wants to apologize for what he did?"

He seemed to mull that over for a few seconds. "It's too late for any of that. If he wants to start his life over, he can do it without me."

Jess could understand exactly why he would say that. She'd tried to do that with her sister at one time. It was why she'd moved away from London, so that she could get a fresh start.

Without the shadows from the past crowding in.

She was still nervous about going to the hotel where her sister had gone into labor. Maybe if she arrived with Dean, it would make things easier.

"I get it. Believe me. And as far as the other subject goes, yes, I would appreciate you picking me up. As long as you don't mind leaving if it gets to be too much."

"Absolutely. We can make a secret sign. When I see you flash it, I'll know it's time."

Something in her heart warmed that he would be willing to do that for her. "What kind of sign?"

He glanced down at her feet. "You said you were going to wear some killer heels. Maybe if you reach down and slide your finger under one of the straps as if they're uncomfortable. It would also make a handy excuse for leaving."

"Good thinking. I like it."

"Great. So how about six-thirty? That should get us there in plenty of time for the buffet line to open."

"Sounds good. You already know where I live."

"I do."

Jess couldn't believe she'd had such doubts about going to the party with him. Now it seemed like the perfect solution.

Except for one thing.

She'd toyed with asking him to go home with her, but he might prefer someone else. She needed to at least give him an out, if he wanted one. "What if you meet someone there that you'd like to get to know a little better? Should we have a sign for that? I mean, I don't want you feeling like you're stuck with me."

"I won't."

Did he mean he wouldn't meet someone he might like or that he wouldn't feel stuck?

As if reading her mind, he slid his fingers under her chin. "We won't need a second sign."

"O-okay." Suddenly very aware of the masculine

scent that was weaving through her senses and that there was a nurse at the far end of the hallway, she backed up a step. "I need to get back to work."

Something else popped into her head. "And I'm sorry about your dad. And your mum."

"Thank you, but it was all a long time ago. Water under the bridge, as they say. I need to get back as well. I'll see you Friday evening, if not before."

With that, Dean headed down the hallway, nodding at the nurse as he passed her. Jess turned as well, suddenly forgetting where she'd been going when she'd spotted him. Maybe because she couldn't quite wrap her head around the fact that she was going to the Christmas party with the playboy of Cambridge Royal.

And if nothing else went right for the rest of the day, that was enough to make her smile.

Talk about a prophecy coming true…nothing else went right. Although Amy's baby, Matthew, was still holding his own, three other labors had turned into full-blown emergencies. She'd barely had time to go down and visit Amy and then Marissa. Then Jess's sister had rung in the middle of one of those emergencies and had bullied her way through the system until one of the nurses had pulled her from the room to take the call.

It had not gone well. Jess, at the end of her rope, had almost lost her temper and undone the tentative truce she and her sister had forged.

All she could think of at the end of the day was that the Christmas party had better be pretty damned good. Because she was looking forward to it far too much. And looking forward to seeing Dean in that tuxedo?

Yes. That also worried her a little bit. He'd become

far too intuitive where she was concerned, and this little voice inside of her said that she might even be falling for the man. That would be a disaster.

And what about that idea of a fling she'd entertained over the few days? Could she do it and not want more?

That wouldn't happen, because Dean wouldn't let it. So even if she did the unthinkable and got a little too attached, she had him to drag her back to reality. Which was a good thing, really.

She got her bag out of her locker as her shift ended, vowing she was just going to take things one day at a time and see what happened. In the meantime, she had some walking to do. If Dean expected her to be wearing those sexy shoes she'd purchased, she'd better work on breaking them in.

Dean pulled up in front of Jess's house and gripped the steering wheel. His bow tie felt a little too tight all of a sudden. He hadn't seen her since that ugly conversation with his father—who'd tried to ring him several more times over the past day and a half. Dean had let all of the calls go to voicemail. He had no desire to talk to the man. Or to see him.

But he did want to see Jess. He'd never wanted a home or a family, but there was something about her that made him feel utterly comfortable in her presence. Maybe because the woman was who she was. She didn't try to play games or say things she didn't mean—except to her parents, and that was his fault for initiating the whole fake dating thing.

Nothing to do but get out of the car and ring her buzzer. He sat there for a moment longer staring at the cozy little cottage, wondering what Jess was doing right now. She was the punctual type, so he didn't see her still rushing around the place putting last-minute touches on her hair or makeup.

Was she sitting on the couch waiting for him to come to the door? Was she calmly sipping a cup of tea?

She was calm. He couldn't quite picture her losing her temper the way she said she had at her parents' anniversary party.

And yet, she'd gotten angry with him at the pub, so he knew she was capable of it.

Actually, he liked that unexpected flash of fire. Maybe that was what drove her sister to provoke her. There was something satisfying about knowing he could wring a reaction out of her when nothing at work seemed to.

Ridiculous. Why on earth would he want to rattle her?

And why was he just sitting here like a stooge?

He exited the car and headed up to the door. Pressed the buzzer.

As he'd suspected, the door opened almost immediately. And his eyes almost fell out of his head.

She was dressed in a deep blue dress that looked like something a Greek goddess would have worn; the garment was gathered into tiny pleats at her waist with a gold sash. The neckline was bound with the same type of gold edging that went on to form wide straps at her shoulders.

The woman was gorgeous. Beyond gorgeous.

It was quite cool outside, so she must have a wrap of some kind inside the house.

Even as he thought it she opened the door and motioned him in. "I was just finishing a cup of tea. Would you like one?"

Mystery one solved.

Mystery two...her footwear. The long dress covered her shoes, so he had no idea what they looked like. It didn't matter, he'd see them before the night was through, because she'd eventually have to throw him that signal, right?

Judging from the added height, though, they had to be quite tall. He stepped inside. "No, thank you, on the tea, but take your time. We still have half an hour before things really get under way."

"Let me just get my coat and put my cup in the sink, then. Have a seat, I'll be right back."

When Jess turned to head toward the kitchen, his breath stuck in his throat. The band that formed the straps of her dress dropped past her shoulder blades and traveled halfway down her back, before meeting in the middle, exposing a large expanse of pale silky skin.

How could the woman even wear anything underneath it?

You will not look when she comes back.

Of course, when she did, that was the first place his eyes went. Bloody hell. How had he missed that? The fabric was loosely draped over her breasts, but when she reached for a minuscule handbag and a jacket, he caught sight of a distinct pucker.

That meant nothing. She could just have a thin bra on.

Only his body didn't think so. It was coming up with all kinds of interesting images, none of which were doing him any good.

Why did this woman have such a dramatic effect on him? Dean prided himself on being maybe not as cool, calm, and collected as Jess was, but he considered himself a pretty "in control" kind of guy. Maybe because he'd never wanted to be out of control as his dad had been when he'd been drinking. Or feel out of control the way his mother must have felt whenever he'd come home drunk.

Jess blinked at him, a fleeting look of uncertainty going through those brown eyes. "Something wrong?"

"No." He was acting like an ass. "You're beautiful. Absolutely stunning."

Not very poetic, but true.

She curtsied. "Thank you, kind sir." Her eyes swept over him. "You look quite dapper yourself."

Taking the jacket from her, he held it out so that she could slide her arms through, her scent spiraling up and knocking another cog from his senses.

Suddenly, he had to know. "Have you practiced our signal?"

"I'm afraid I might fall over if I try anything funny in these." With that, she lifted up the hem of her dress and showed him what she meant.

And he could see why she had her doubts. The shoes fit the style of dress she was wearing and made her look tall and lean.

Statuesque. That was the word he wanted.

The sandals were exactly as she'd said they would be, gold with thin straps crisscrossing over the top of her foot and then wrapping around her ankle. To say they were high was an understatement.

He cleared his throat. "Maybe I should be the one making the distress signal." And he could see himself making it right about now. Because he was definitely in distress.

Jess laughed and let her dress fall back down, covering those devastating shoes. "A little different from my no-nonsense hospital gear."

"I'm seeing a wardrobe review in the future once they catch a glimpse of you."

Her hair was caught up in some kind of fancy clip at the back of her head and that streak of gray was on prominent display. He stepped closer and slid the backs of his fingers up the silky strands. "This looks quite fashionable." He loved that little quirk about her. In fact, he loved a few too many things about the woman.

"It only took a minute, really."

And all he could think of was how it would only take a minute to undo the clasp and let her hair fall down around her shoulders in glorious disarray. Or to wake up to find it across his pillow.

He needed to shut down this line of thought right now. Before he decided they didn't need to go to any staff Christmas party. They could have their own little party right here. Right now.

Except he'd already seen what Jess thought of that idea. And he couldn't imagine her settling for less than everything either. She deserved it.

He just wouldn't be the one to give it to her. He needed to remember that. He'd had a phone call that underscored all the reasons why he'd stayed out of relationships over the last fifteen years. He dropped his hand back to his side and took a deep breath.

"Are you ready?"

She nodded. "As ready as I'll ever be."

She handed her coat to the attendant with a murmured thank you.

From the way it was decorated it might have been a

completely different hotel from the one her folks had had their anniversary party in. The ballroom was spectacular with arching pillars that shimmered with twinkle lights. Draped satin tablecloths covered the buffet tables, which held a stunning array of food. To the left of the tables, a bar offered up what looked like every type of drink imaginable.

She sent a memo to herself to not go near it. Not because of her grandfather. But because of Dean. He was doing a number on her senses that alcohol couldn't touch. But mixing the two could create an explosion she wouldn't be able to control. And right now, with his hand on the small of her back as he guided her into the room, lighter fluid was slowly being trickled across the kindling in her head. One spark and up she'd go.

Isabel waved to her from across the room, lifting her glass in salute, but even from this distance her friend seemed a little distracted. Or maybe that was just Jess. And when Dean's thumb found the bare skin just above the back of her dress and skimmed across it for a second, that distraction grew. Then his hand lifted. He leaned down. "Doing okay?"

Was he kidding? She was so far from okay that it was laughable. But there was no way she was admitting that to him. "So far, so good. It looks a lot different than it did during my folks' anniversary party."

That night would never be quite banished from her memory, nor would the guilt, but her sister had seemed a little softer just before she'd left for home—even if they had almost argued on the phone a couple of days ago. Her mum was also a bit more mellow. Whether she had Dean to thank for that or not, she wasn't sure. At some point in time, she would have to set them all straight.

But that day wasn't today. And it probably wouldn't be tomorrow.

Marissa had grown over the last three weeks and was getting stronger by the day. A few more ounces, and she would be transferred to the regular nursery.

So much had happened. Her opinion of Dean had changed entirely. And after hearing him talk to his father… Well, she never would have guessed he'd had such a difficult childhood. He seemed so confident and self-assured as an adult.

His past made her and her sister's squabbling seem petty. And her parents had never hit their children. Mum had been a bit critical at times, yes, but maybe that had spurred Jess's success in her chosen field. And that hard-won calm she was known for might have come from being able to take a step back from whatever was being dished out to her.

"Do you want something to drink?" Dean's voice broke in.

"Tonic water, if they have it."

She smiled, remembering Dean's violent reaction to the drink at her parents' meal. Something clicked into place. "Why do you dislike it so? Does it have something to do with your dad?"

"Hmm." The little humming sound vibrated against her ear. "Yes, actually. I was a little kid who wanted to be all grown up. Didn't quite work out the way I expected."

Her heart ached for him. But his tone had cooled, a clear warning not to pursue this subject any further.

She modified the question she really wanted to ask. "So what *do* you drink nowadays?"

He laughed, sending a shiver over her. "I drink the real stuff. Just to prove I can."

"Since you're a successful doctor, I'd say you have."

"I'll get our drinks. Wait here."

While he was gone, Jess took the opportunity to glance around, feeling kind of out of place. Work was frenetic, and she knew most of these people in a professional sense, but, outside of Isabel, Hope, Bonnie and a few of the other hospital staff, she didn't have a lot of close friends. As if reading her thoughts, Isabel appeared at her side, giving her a quick hug.

"You look fantastic," her friend said.

Isabel was clad in a long green dress that suited her complexion and figure to a tee; Jess returned the compliment. "That dress is to die for. And those earrings… beautiful." Silver chandelier earrings with glittery green stones dangled almost to her shoulders.

"I told you this was going to be a very grown up party."

"No kidding. How did you all pull this off?"

"Teamwork is the key. I had a lot of help."

Jess scrunched her nose. "I'm sorry I haven't been around to lend a hand."

"You've had a few other things on your plate, love, with your sister and niece." Her friend nodded toward the bar, where Dean was currently waiting for their drinks to be poured. "All those rumors are rubbish, aren't they?"

God, she was so glad to be able to tell someone. "Yes. It was a stupid ploy to get my parents and sister to stop asking me when I was going to settle down and have children."

Isabel looked as if she was going to say something and then shook her head. "Just a warning, then. A little batch of mistletoe has been making its way around the ballroom. I've been circling the room to make sure it doesn't find me."

An old flame from Isabel's past had appeared at Cambridge Royal without warning a couple of months ago. She hadn't told Jess much about Sean Anderson, other than the fact that she was dismayed by his presence.

"Did Sean come?"

The other woman's glance darted to the left to the far side of the room, past where dancers floated to the sound of a small chamber orchestra. "Oh, he's here. I'm trying to stay out of his way as well, so if I rush toward you with a look of panic in my eyes, can you stash me beneath one of the buffet tables or something?"

Jess laughed. "Of course I can. You'd just better hope that Sean, the mistletoe and you don't converge at the same place at the same time."

"Not a chance." Isabel shuddered. "I'm keeping my eye on both of them. So far, so good."

Dean appeared at her side, drinks in hand. Isabel greeted him and then turned back to Jess. "Don't forget about that warning. Converging is to be avoided at all costs."

"I won't forget."

Then her friend was off in the opposite direction of Sean, who Jess could swear watched her go when she glanced in that direction.

"What kind of converging are we supposed to avoid?"

"Someone smuggled in some mistletoe, and we're supposed to be watching for it."

One of Dean's brows went up. "And avoiding it, I take it?"

"Yes."

"Would that be such a tragedy? I can remember a time

or two when some mistletoe might have been in order." Lazy amusement colored his tone.

Jess squirmed, her face heating. "We didn't have an audience then." Oops, except they had that time at her house. "Well, not one that wasn't planned."

"That's true. And you played your part quite well on that occasion." He handed her the glass of tonic water.

Ignoring his comment, she nodded at the glass in his hand. "What did you end up getting?"

"Whiskey." He swirled the amber liquid in his tumbler and then glanced up with a frown. "It'll be my only one, if you're worried about making it home safely."

"Not worried at all." From what she gathered about Dean's father, he was not angling to be anything like him. "Have you heard from him again?"

"No." He took a quick sip just as the sound of clapping came their way.

Jess glanced to see what was going on and spied the mistletoe being held over the heads of two unsuspecting victims who were being urged to kiss. A quick peck was the result.

"I hope it stays on that side of the room." She took a sip of her water, finding it distasteful all of a sudden. Because of what Dean had told her about his aversion to it?

"What's that face for?"

She laughed. "Just wondering exactly why I've always drunk this. It's quite awful, isn't it?"

"Am I winning you over to the dark side?"

"Maybe the enlightened side."

"Do you want me to get you something else?"

She shook her head. "I'm a lightweight. I'm good with a sip or two, but after that things start going downhill."

"I can't imagine you tipsy." One side of his mouth went up in a half smile.

"It's not a pretty picture, believe me."

Another bout of clapping occurred, still on the other side of the room.

His smile disappeared. "It normally isn't."

She really should try to be more sensitive.

"I'm so sorry your dad hurt you." She touched his arm, trying not to picture Dean as a little boy who was frightened of the man who'd fathered him. "You talked about not wanting me to face my sister on my own. You shouldn't have had to face what he did on your own."

"It's in the past." He held out his drink. "Since you're only good with a sip or two, do you want to share mine?"

Suddenly feeling as if she did indeed need something stronger than her fizzy water, she accepted the drink, letting him take her glass and set it down on a nearby table.

The tumbler was heavier than she expected, and there was an imprint on the side of it—from Dean's lower lip as he'd sipped? A tingle ran over her and, feeling slightly naughty, and very sure that Dean wouldn't realize what she was doing, she turned the glass slightly and drank from that very spot.

God. The smooth whiskey burned her throat as it went down, but it was nothing compared to the scorching heat that went through her when she caught Dean's eyes on her.

He knew exactly what she'd done. She saw it in the flash of awareness in his gaze, the slight flaring of his nostrils. The way his gaze traveled across her throat, and continued downward. Her toes curled in her fancy shoes and panic washed through her.

She was playing with fire. This man was more perceptive—and far more dangerous—than any other man she'd gone out with, including Martin. *Especially* Martin. Dean was an expert at playing these games, while she was a hopeless novice.

But that didn't mean she didn't want to experience what he had to offer at least once. He'd made casual sex seem like the best thing imaginable.

Well, she wanted some of what he was offering, and it wasn't the liquid in this glass.

Feeling a slight dizziness that had nothing to do with liquor, she slowly raised the drink back to her mouth, holding his gaze this time as she took another tiny sip, allowing her lips to remain on the glass much longer than necessary.

Dean's mouth tightened, and he plucked the glass from her hands. "You're going to need that magic signal, Jess, if you keep that up. Only I'll be the one you need rescuing from."

Yes. She wanted that. Wanted to have to be rescued from him.

Dean raised the tumbler to his nose and inhaled deeply, sending another shudder through her. Could he smell her on the glass? Then he drained the drink and set it aside on the table. "Dance with me."

He held out his hand.

She shouldn't. She'd already warned herself that she was becoming enamored of him. Did she really want to be toyed with and then dumped as Martin had done with her?

No. But she couldn't be dumped if she walked away after one night. No strings. No promises. Just hot sex with the sexiest man she'd ever laid eyes on.

Decision made, she put her hand in his. "Aren't you afraid people are going to talk even more?"

"If they're going to talk, we'd better make it worth their while. We can always set everyone straight later." He drew her against him. "Besides, do you really care what they think?"

No. She didn't. Sure, some of them would gossip for a few weeks, but once she and Dean parted ways the talk would die down, and they'd move on to something juicier.

Placing her hand on his shoulder, she allowed him to ease her onto the floor where others were dancing. This was the second time she'd found herself on a dance floor with him, and it was every bit as heady as the first time. Only this time she wasn't worried about him using her to break some sexual fast, because she was thinking she might like to do a little fast breaking of her own.

With Dean. Who would keep things easy and un-complicated.

They could probably even remain friends afterward.

Who was she kidding? Stay friends? They weren't even friends now.

Except he'd stepped in and bailed her out when her sister was playing the bully. Had been a great sport when her dad had insisted on evidence that they were indeed seeing each other. If they'd been seriously dat-ing she might even have liked to go out on that hack with him when spring came. Except they weren't, and never would be.

One of her heels tipped sideways for a second, but Dean immediately tightened his grip, preventing her from falling.

"I told you I wouldn't be doing anything fancy in these shoes."

A low laugh met her ear. "And I knew I would love them as soon as I saw them."

Little pebbles of regret gathered in her stomach. This was what she wanted someday. A partner who would catch her when she stumbled, who would walk beside her through life.

Close your eyes and don't think, Jess. Just feel. That's all tonight is about.

Her fingers slid from his shoulder to the lapel of his tux and curled around it. Just beneath the expensive fabric, his muscles flexed against her touch. Because he liked it?

She hoped so. If this night didn't end with them going back to his place—or hers—she was going to be disappointed. No, more than that, because Dean had been tossing around little innuendos from the time he'd picked her up. Surely all of that word play was geared toward a goal. She only hoped she knew what it was.

Dean turned her, and she opened her eyes to make sure she wasn't about to career into someone and caught sight of Isabel.

She was standing next to Sean Anderson, and neither of them looked very happy. In fact, when she tuned her ears, she could swear they were in the midst of a heated argument, although she couldn't hear the words past the orchestral music. Just then a sprig of green was placed over the arguing pair's heads, and the rhythmic clapping began. This time she could hear the "kiss her, kiss her, kiss her" coming through loud and clear.

Oh, no! The converging her friend had been so anxious to avoid. Mack Trimble, the male nurse who was holding the mistletoe over the pair with a mischievous grin, received a death glare from Isabel for his trouble, then she turned and stalked away from both him and Sean. Even from here, Jess could see a muscle working in Sean's jaw, but he didn't go after her. He stood there for another minute or two, totally ignoring Mack, who, along with the crowd, realized they weren't getting any satisfaction this time.

Her eyes met Mack's and in slow motion she watched as his brows went up. Horror streamed through her as the man made a beeline toward them.

"We need to get out of here." Jess had barely squeaked out the words when Mack was on them. The shorter man was barely able to hold the sprig high enough to reach over Dean's head. The chanting began anew, people seemingly unfazed by the rebuffing they'd received from their last attempt.

A wave of heat surged into her face and she was pretty sure it had turned bright red. Dean, on the other hand, didn't seem mortified in the least.

"Too late," he murmured. "Maybe we should give them what they want."

"But what about—?"

His lips covered hers, cutting off whatever she'd been about to say. And right now, Jess wasn't even sure what that was.

Vaguely she heard the beginnings of an "ooooooooh" from the partygoers because this kiss was no peck and release as most of the other ones had been. Dean's lips remained in place, his fingers going to the back of her head as if meaning to hold her where she was. Ridiculous. She wasn't going anywhere. As surely as electricity held its victim a prisoner of its force field, Dean's sheer presence kept her in place.

The fingers at his lapel tightened until she was hanging on for all she was worth.

Then Dean was gone and the spell broke. A huge ball of laughter went through the ballroom and she realized they'd been kissing long enough to have gathered the attention of a whole lot of people.

Mack, pleased to have gotten so much bang for his buck, bowed and wiggled the mistletoe, pointing it at person after person, only to have them wave him away. A minute or two later, the revelers went back to doing whatever they'd been doing before the excitement started.

She caught Isabel's eye from one of the nearby groups. Her friend mouthed "sorry" and then disappeared, ducking through another cluster of folks.

"I can't believe you did that," she snapped.

One brow went up. "Did you want me to stop?"

Lie. Say you did. That this was a big mistake, and that he needs to take you home pronto.

"I want you to take me home…" There. She did it. She'd gotten the words out. Only there were more consonants and vowels swirling behind the ones she'd released, forming words and sentences that she was powerless to stop. "I want you to take me home and finish what you started."

CHAPTER TWELVE

DEAN'S BREATH RUSHED from his lungs at her words. They were standing in the middle of the dance floor, where he was still reeling from that kiss. Evidently, he hadn't been the only one affected.

And if she was asking him for what he thought she was, Dean was only too happy to oblige. He'd been fighting his attraction for her from the moment he saw her with her niece tucked in her arms, and he was tired of warning himself away from her.

Maybe this wasn't a bad thing. Jess didn't just tickle his lust and then make him want to run as soon as it was satisfied. This was more than that. For the first time in his life, he found himself wanting to make love to a woman and maybe even stick around afterward.

That thought was enough to make his gut clench. Not enough to make him back out, though.

Hell, he couldn't sort all of this out now. That could happen later. Once he got her out of those shoes.

Or maybe not.

Maybe she would stay in them the first time.

He didn't want any misunderstandings about what his intentions were. "If we leave now, it's not going to be for a quick roll in the hay. I'm going to keep you there all night."

Jess didn't bat an eye. "Who said I was letting you leave before I'm done with you?"

The fires he'd banked time and time again flared to life. He touched the toe of his dress shoe to the sandals hidden beneath her dress. "I want the shoes left on."

They were standing in the middle of the dance floor, no longer moving. Instead, they were staring at one another.

Jess smiled. "Then I want yours on as well."

A mental picture of both of them in bed with nothing on but their shoes made him laugh. "Touché."

He threaded his fingers through hers. "Shall we continue our bargaining someplace that's a little more… private?"

"Definitely. Because I have some demands of my own."

His flesh gave a twitch that bordered on painful at that. He was rapidly getting the feeling that Jess's reputation for remaining cool and levelheaded only extended to the workplace. There'd been hints of something simmering below the surface on other occasions. Right now, he was only too ready to find out what that might be.

"In that case…" He towed her through the crowd of dancers not caring that people would talk. They'd been talking about him from the day he'd arrived at Cambridge Royal. For once, they would get it right. He was taking Jess home for exactly the reasons they thought he was. "My place…or yours?"

"Where do you live?" Her words came from behind him.

"Farther out than you do."

"Mine, then."

"I like the way you think." They reached the door and the bellman took his valet ticket, opening the door for them.

"Your vehicle will be here momentarily, sir."

He didn't want to have to wait a moment, or even a second. Nodding at the man, he regretted not being able to go and get his car himself and be on his way.

What was with this sudden impatience? He was normally all about the slow buildup of anticipation. Instead, his skin felt prickly and tight as if he were going to split apart.

She shivered against him. "My coat. I forgot it."

Glad to have something to take his mind off his thoughts, he said, "I'll get it."

He draped his tuxedo jacket around her shoulders and waited for her to slide her arms through it. She then handed him her coat-check ticket. "I'll be right back," he said. Once he was in line, his mobile phone, which he'd muted for the party, vibrated in his pocket.

"Damn." He half muttered the word, wondering if he should just ignore it. What if it was the hospital, though, and something had gone wrong with Marissa or one of his other patients? Not something he was willing to risk.

He pulled the instrument from his pocket just as he reached the coat-check attendant. He handed her the ticket and turned away to check the screen on his phone.

It was a number he didn't recognize. He scrolled through his recent calls to see if he could place it and saw a few more like it. It hit him. It was his father.

His teeth ground against each other. No. He was not going to let the man ruin tonight the way he'd ruined plenty of nights in his childhood. He shut the caller down with the press of a button and then went through the screens until he found the block feature and activated it for that number.

Retrieving Jess's coat and doubly glad they were going to her house in case his father somehow tracked down his address, he noted that his car was finally waiting in front of the hotel. The last thing he wanted was for his dad to show up at his door while Jess was there— or, worse, if he was fresh from a binge of drinking and snogging.

He got outside and accepted his keys from the valet and pressed a few bills in the man's hand. When Jess started to shrug out of his jacket he shook his head, his reasons for being here slamming back through his gut. "I like seeing you in it. Keep it on."

Her smile washed away the last remnants of doubt about doing this, especially when she snuggled deeper into the garment as if she liked the feel of it.

He hadn't lied. He liked seeing her in it. Imagined her wearing his white dress shirt the next morning as they ate breakfast, her nipples just visible...

And thoughts like that would get him into an accident before they'd even arrived at their destination.

He held open the door and waited until she was in before moving around to the driver's side and climbing into the vehicle. "Music?"

She leaned her head against the headrest. "I'm good."

He found his fingers going to her nape, his thumb stroking over that contrasting streak of hair. "I have no doubt of that, Jess."

"How do you do that?"

"Do what?"

"Infuse everything I say with a meaning that makes me want you."

"Do you—" his blood pumped through his veins "—want me?"

"Yes. And I don't want music. Or anything else. I just want to get home and get what you promised."

Maybe the impatience he'd felt earlier wasn't all that unusual, since she seemed just as anxious as he was. The thought reassured him. His one-night stands normally had an expiration date of twenty-four hours. Never before had he gone out with a woman and then waited weeks to sleep with her. That had to be why he felt so off balance right now. As soon as he did this and got Jess out of his system, he'd be fine.

Except he wanted to make one thing perfectly clear.

He started up the car and pressed the accelerator, the powerful motor responding instantly. "I still want the shoes."

"You've got them."

With that, he put his father out of his head and the vehicle into fast motion. He agreed with her wholeheartedly. All he wanted was to get to her house, shut her front door and start doing some of the things he'd imagined doing for the last three weeks.

As soon as her driveway came into sight, Jess breathed a sigh of relief. When Dean's hand hadn't been on the gear shift as he'd maneuvered through traffic, his palm had rested just above her knee, his thumb stroking wicked paths along the outside of her thigh. Her leg was covered by her dress, but it might as well have been bare skin from her reactions. She was sure that he was going to notice her squirming pretty soon as the heat inside of her bubbled to the surface time and time again. In fact, if he'd suggested pulling to the side of the motorway and taking her right there, she didn't think she would have uttered a single word of protest.

He didn't get out right away. Instead, he turned to her, a question in his eyes.

"I haven't changed my mind, if that's what you're worried about."

"Not worried. Just curious."

"About what?"

He paused as if not quite sure how to ask. "About how your experience with your pickup men went. Was your time with them as easy as you thought it would be?"

It was on the tip of her tongue to shrug and say "of course," since that was probably what he expected. But she couldn't. For some reason, the words just wouldn't come.

So she shook her head. "I wouldn't know."

"I don't follow."

"I didn't go home with either of them. I chickened out."

His fingertips went beneath her chin as he eased her around to look at him. "Why did you pretend you did, then?"

"I thought you might think I was pathetic."

"Pathetic? Never." He leaned over and pressed a light kiss to her mouth. "And since we're baring all, I have to say I'm glad you didn't bring them here."

"You are?" Surprise went through her. She'd thought for sure the truth was going to scare him off. After all, he was looking for exactly the kinds of encounters he'd bet she couldn't have. And he'd been right. At least until tonight. Until the crazy want inside of her drove her to do something so totally out of character that it scared her.

"Yes. Because I want you all to myself, and I don't want you comparing me to those other two men."

She should be insulted. Angry. It was the classic double standard, but she couldn't bring herself to be. Because somehow she didn't think he said that to many women. Did that make her special in his eyes?

She didn't know. And she'd better not care one way or the other, unless she wanted him to take off out of here like a bat out of hell.

Forcing a grin and rolling off the first quip that came to mind, she said, "Then you'll have to compete against my imaginary lover, who sets the bar pretty high."

"Ah, but imagination is nothing compared to the real thing, I promise."

Oh, she had no doubt about that. Dean was going to bring her to explosive heights, if all those little tastes during the last three weeks were anything to go by. And suddenly, she didn't want to wait any longer to see if she was right. "Are you ready?"

"More than ready. I didn't want to leave this house when you came down the hallway this evening in that dress. Maybe I should have just kept you here, instead of going to the party."

If he had, she wouldn't have stopped him.

"Then we need to make up for lost time."

"Sweetheart, no time with you could ever be lost." With that he exited the car and moved around to open her door, retrieving her jacket from the back.

She'd almost forgotten that she was still wearing his tuxedo coat, but had to admit she loved being surrounded by his scent…with the fact that he'd been wearing it all evening.

Fumbling in her little handbag for the keys to her front door, she finally found them, her hands shaking with nerves. How the hell was she supposed to slide it in the lock?

As if sensing her thoughts, he took the key from her fingers and unlocked the door, holding it open for her to pass through.

Once she did, she reluctantly shed his jacket and started to hand it to him, only to have him wave it off. "I won't be needing that."

Gulping, she hung it on a peg by the front door and deposited her handbag on a small entry table. Dean laid her coat over the top of his with a smile. "Seems to be becoming a habit."

"What is?"

He shook his head and then laid his hands on her shoulders, drawing her close. "Being in this house and wanting to kiss you."

With that he leaned down and did just that, his lips sliding over and over hers until she was trembling with need. Still he made no move to deepen the kiss, instead reaching behind her head and plucking the decorative clip from her hair and letting the locks fall around her shoulders.

"Better," he whispered. "Because now I can do this."

He twined a strand of her hair around his finger and something in her belly tightened. No man had ever been that fascinated by her streak of gray before. At least not like this. It was as if he couldn't stop himself from touching it. All she wanted, though, was for him to touch her.

All of her.

So she decided to kick-start things into motion. Reaching up, she tugged on one of the ends of his bow tie, watching as it came undone, her eyes taking in the strong column of tanned skin just above it. His Adam's apple dipped for a second as he swallowed. That alone gave her the courage to push the ends of his tie aside and undo the first button of his crisp white shirt, then the next.

The finger holding her hair flexed, tightening on the locks.

"Jess, what are you doing?" The words were whispered from somewhere above her head.

Smiling, she reached up and nipped his chin. "And I thought you were the experienced one. Or do you normally do this dressed?"

"Not usually. But with you, anything's possible."

The words sent a shiver through her. How was he able to make her feel so special, as if he hadn't done this a million times in a million different ways?

Two more buttons popped free of their holes. A swath of skin came into view, along with a pec that was surprising on a doctor.

More surprising was when he released her hair and grabbed her hands. "I think that's enough for now." He reached down and swooped her into his arms. "Bedroom?"

Looping her arms around his neck, she nodded toward the hallway. "Down there and to the right."

Dean set off in that direction, his strides eating the distance in seconds. He kicked open the door to her room, and she crinkled her nose at the girliness of the space. She'd never identified it as such before, despite the soft colors and a ruffle here and there, but this man's raw masculinity made it seem far more froufrou than it was.

Moving to the bed, he leaned down and laid her on it. She'd expected him to drop her so she'd tensed, waiting for the bounce of the mattress. Instead, he followed her down, his white shirt and black trousers looking out of place against her lavender spread…but in a good way. He went up on one elbow, tracing the skin just above her collar bone. "How does this little beauty fasten? I've been looking for a zipper all night long."

"Y-you have?" The thought that he'd been thinking about how to get her out of the dress the entire time at the party made her mouth go dry.

"I have a feeling every man in that room was looking for the same thing, and damning me to hell for being the one to leave with you."

He was lying. He had to be. The thought that it might be a line he fed to woman after woman made the delicious ache that had been spreading through her belly loosen its grip just a bit.

"I always knew you were a smooth talker."

A slight frown appeared between his brows, and she thought for a second she might have spoiled things for both of them. "It's the truth, Jess. I don't think I've ever wanted to rush quite as much as I do right now. And yet another part of me is begging me to hold on for as long as possible."

He leaned down and feathered tiny kisses along the skin he'd been tracing a few seconds earlier. "I think a compromise might be in order," he continued. "Think we can satisfy both sides?"

As in doing this more than once? "Oh, yes."

"Zipper?" He came up and stared at her face.

"On the left hand side. It's hidden."

Fingers walked along her hip, heading up until he reached the side of her breast, his thumb strumming over it, but not quite reaching the most sensitive part. He tugged on something. "Ah, here it is."

Down the fastener went in a steady, insistent fashion until it was at the upper part of her thigh. Cool air brushed against her. The same digits that had opened the zipper now ran over the skin he'd laid bare.

She couldn't suppress the tiny moan that welled up in her throat.

As if that sound triggered something, Dean stood, staring down at her as he quickly undid the rest of the buttons of his shirt, tugging it free from his trousers and then tossing it over a chair that was beside the bed. When he went for the fastening on his trousers, she wanted to sit up and take over, but to do that would mean the front of her dress would fall to the side and expose her.

Was that so bad?

So she did it, levering herself into a sitting position, one hand gripping the loose body of her dress and holding it against her.

His eyes narrowed for a second, maybe thinking she was drawing things to a halt.

Nope. Not happening. Not at this point.

"I want to do that," she whispered, eyes on the zipper in front of her. He was hard and ready just beyond that barrier, from the way the fabric bulged to capacity.

"Hmm… I could take that one of any number of ways, but I think we'll leave those delectable options for another time."

With that, he reached a hand in his pocket and pulled out his wallet. "But you can get something ready while

I finish what I started." His teeth flashed white as he referenced her earlier words.

He unzipped, leaving her to hold her dress in place with one hand while she flipped open his wallet to try to find what she knew he wanted. Only her glance kept straying up to where he was now toeing off his shoes.

"Jess, you're not trying very hard." His trousers dropped to the floor, leaving him just in boxer briefs—black silky fabric probably designed to help his trousers lie flat. No chance of that, because there was nothing "flat" about him right now. "I think you might need two hands."

Her eyes widened. Just how big was the man?

His chuckle brought her attention back up. "I was talking about the wallet. I think you might need two hands to find what you're looking for."

Oh, Lord, she was such a ninny. Only if she let go of her dress…

It would serve him right.

She let it drop the same way he'd allowed his trousers to fall away. The shoulder straps kept the garment from sliding completely down, but they did nothing to prevent the one side from baring her breast.

Dean's rough intake of breath said he'd expected her to chicken out. Well, maybe he was going to learn a thing or two about her tonight.

Peeking inside the money compartment, she slammed it closed again when quite a few bills came into view.

"It's there, in the little pocket just below the cards. It's hidden, just like the zipper on your dress."

Jess tried to concentrate, but it was just so hard when Dean was standing there in a pair of briefs and nothing else. He'd already taken off his undershirt and socks.

There! As he said, it was hidden. At first it looked like a row of stitching, but when she rubbed her thumb over it, it separated. She reached in and found a wrapped condom. Disappointment sloshed through her. Only one. And he'd said…

"There are a couple more in the inner pocket of my trousers."

Ack! The smile in his voice said he knew exactly what she'd been thinking.

She could think him presumptuous or any number of things, but right now all she felt was glee. He'd hoped this would happen just as much as she had.

"And now there's the little matter of that dress."

She smiled back up at him feeling like a goon. "And those shorts."

"Then I suggest we do something about both of those. Right now."

CHAPTER THIRTEEN

JESS SAT UP, her hair streaming down her naked back, and all Dean could do was stare.

He was still off balance. His skin still felt just as tight. Sleeping with her had changed nothing.

And yet the woman had rocked his world. More than once. More than twice. He'd slipped a couple of extra condoms into the pocket of his tuxedo, in the wild, unlikely chance that he actually got to make love to her. And that was what it had been. Not that first time. Maybe not even the second. But that third slow, heated rush had sent a bolt of realization through his chest.

He loved the woman.

That was why he'd been in such a hurry. Why even after making love to her multiple times, it still wasn't enough.

Those uneasy sensations weren't going to go away. Not now. Not in two weeks. Probably not ever.

Hell! How could he have let this happen?

Maybe it hadn't been a matter of letting it happen. Maybe it was meant to happen. With her and only her.

Why couldn't he find happiness with someone? Did his upbringing preclude that? Did his father really wield that much power, even now?

Maybe not.

Jess tossed a lock of hair over her shoulder and sent him a quick glance, blinking in uncertainty at something she must have seen in his gaze. He whisked away his thoughts. He could figure all of that out later. "Are you okay?"

"Okay?"

"Are you feeling all right?" Wow. He was actually at a loss for words. Impossible. It had never happened before.

Then again, he'd never quite been in this position before, where he hadn't tiptoed out the door at the first opportunity.

She wiggled that delectable bottom for a second as if trying things on for size.

He couldn't stop the smile that came to his face. She'd seemed perfectly happy with his size…and with everything else. Those little cries of pleasure, the way she'd gripped his shoulders as he'd moved above her…

Damn, he could have sworn he'd used up every last one of his wildcards, but she was doing something to him all over again. Casting a spell from which he didn't want to wake.

"I'm feeling a little shaky."

Ditto, sweetheart.

He sat up as well and kissed the spot where her shoulder met her neck, a place he'd discovered had the ability to make her arch up. Right on cue, she tilted her head and pushed toward his touch, so he increased the pressure, using the sharp edges of his teeth to scrape across the sensitive nerve endings.

"I have to get up for a minute." She reached across the bed, fingers gripping the dress he'd taken off her.

He circled her wrist with his fingers. "Use my shirt."

His flesh was tightening all over again, and he was all out of condoms. But he wanted to see her slide her arms through his shirt, knowing she didn't have a stitch on beneath it.

She stood, the muscles of her buttocks curving in a way that made his mouth go dry. She pulled the garment off the chair and slid it on. She threw him a look over her shoulder, her delicate brows arching. "And my shoes?"

"On. Definitely on." His voice came out rough and gravelly. She'd indulged him, leaving those high sandals on throughout their lovemaking. When she came back to bed, though, he'd unbuckle those delicate straps and take them off, kissing his way across her arches.

You are in a whole lot of trouble here, Dean.

Maybe he should run out to the nearest local store and pick up some more supplies. But there was a little part of him that was afraid if he left now, she would never let him back in.

And he definitely wanted back in.

If he was going to do this, though, he was going to do it right. And that meant making sure she was as taken with him as he seemed to be with her.

"Next time, then, you have to keep your shoes on," she said.

Dean chuckled and relaxed against the pillows, enjoying watching her totter toward the bathroom, his shirt billowing around the bottom edge of her ass. And since she'd made no move to button the shirt up, he could only imagine what the front of it looked like.

He'd find out when she came back.

And maybe by then he'd figure out how to tell her

he wanted more than just one night. Breaking his own hard-and-fast rule about no repeat sex.

He definitely wanted repeats. For as long as she'd give them to him.

Jess was in the shower when the call came. It was Isabel.

"You need to come to the hospital right now."

He sat up. "Is there an emergency?"

"It's your father. He's here."

Damn the man. Couldn't he take a hint? Well, this time he was going to be even more direct. Ugly words came to mind, and he grabbed at them. "Tell him I'm not interested in seeing him."

He was sorry to have to drag his friends into this mess, but he needed to make sure the man understood that he didn't want him in his life.

"Dean." Something in Isabel's voice sent a chill up his spine. "You need to come. Right now."

Her words had him leaping out of bed and looking for his clothes. He could still hear the water running in the shower, but all thoughts of taking up where they'd left off fled. Was his dad drunk again? If so, he should probably have just told Isabel to have the police pick him up and throw him in jail until he sobered up. But he couldn't. Because something inside of him warned him this could be worse. A lot worse.

So much for the man no longer holding any power over him.

He scribbled off a note, telling Jess he'd had an unexpected emergency come up and had to leave. He knew he should knock on the door and say a proper goodbye, but he knew that was what it would be. All the reasons he played things loose and easy came rushing back to him. Not just because his mum and dad had been such train wrecks, but he'd seen what diving into something impulsively could lead to.

Not violence, he would never hit Jess…he wasn't his father. This was about his mum. When she'd left, it had cut him to pieces and left him in a state he never wanted to revisit.

Isabel's phone call served as a chilling reminder of everything that could happen…of everything that *had* happened.

Thank God he'd never said anything to Jess about his thoughts earlier. If he had…

God, if he *had*…

No. This was how it had to be. He would leave the note. Jess would think he was doing what he always did: playing around and then dashing off. It was better for both of them. And hadn't she said she wanted to see what casual sex was like? Well, this was pretty much how it went.

And right now, he hated everything that went along with it.

He dropped the note onto the bedside table knowing that he needn't worry about her locking him out of the house when he left—because he was locking himself out. For good.

Dean was taking some time off. At least that was what Isabel had said. Jess's emotions ran the gamut. One second she was furious with him. The next, she felt like crying.

She still couldn't believe his dad had committed suicide. He'd parked his rental car behind a building and attached a hose to the exhaust pipe, trapping the other end in the driver's side window. He'd barely been alive when they'd brought him in. But it was only his body—that conglomeration of organ systems. He'd been brain dead. Dean had been the one to ultimately decide to discontinue life support. It had all been over by the time she'd come in to work the next day, thinking the worst and finding it to be true. His note had told her nothing.

Anger swept back over her. After all they'd been through together, he could simply shut her out? Without any hesitation?

Why not? Hadn't Martin done exactly the same thing?

Except she'd believed it would be different for her this time. Somehow.

She'd tried to ring him for hours after she heard the news, but the calls had gone straight to voicemail, and he'd never once rung her back. A week had gone by since he'd left her house…since his father's death and she'd still heard nothing from him.

It would be obvious to any normal person. He didn't want to talk to her.

Why would he? She was no more special than any of the other women he'd been with.

Except she could have sworn…

Shutting down that line of thought, she shifted Marissa in her arms and rocked her, trying to absorb some little measure of comfort.

That was all she wanted to do nowadays. Work and be with this tiny baby. And pray that the hurt would eventually go away.

Please let it go away.

How stupid could she be? She'd done exactly what she'd told herself not to do. She'd fallen in love with the man.

Well, never again.

Dean had told her how he liked his relationships, but had she believed him? No. And here she was, nursing a heart that was in far worse condition than when Martin had left her.

She leaned her cheek against the baby's downy head. "Why can't I just accept it? It's over, Mari."

Not that it was ever there to begin with.

And those shoes? Buried at the bottom of the rubbish bin, where they belonged. She'd chucked her broken heart in beside them. Only that traitorous organ, unlike the shoes, hadn't stayed buried. It had climbed up and out and was now thumping out a painful rhythm within her chest.

But if she was hurting, she could only imagine what Dean was going through. As much as he'd said he didn't want to see his dad, it had to have been a terrible blow to have him go the way he had. Was he feeling guilty? Relieved? Angry?

She had no idea.

Because Dean didn't let anyone in. Ever.

Oh, she might have fooled herself for a moment or two and thought that he was opening up just a crack. The opening had been minuscule, though, not nearly wide enough for a person to squeeze through. And now he'd slammed it shut again.

Was he alone?

Moisture pricked the backs of her lids. The thought that he might be drowning his sorrows in someone else's arms…

A shaft of pain went through her.

"I don't care." She whispered the words to her baby niece, rocking a little harder as the infant continued to sleep. Tears spilled over, and she struggled to blot them with her shoulder before the special-care nurse saw her and asked what was wrong.

She couldn't tell her. She couldn't tell anyone.

Everything had gone according to plan. She'd had a fling with the man, just as she'd wanted. And yet here she sat, gutted, because in the end she'd wanted more from him. So much more.

"Jess?"

She started at the voice that came just over her shoulder. Her head jerked toward the sound, and she found her sister standing there. Abbie took one look at her face and knelt beside the rocking chair. "What's wrong?"

In a totally uncharacteristic move, her sister threaded her arm through Jess's elbow and squeezed. "Is it Marissa?" She stared at her baby's closed eyes.

"N-no, she's fine." Except the words escaped on a half sob.

"Here, let me take her." The tubes had been removed as Marissa had gotten stronger, so it was just a matter of shifting her into her mum's arms. Abbie sat on the floor, curling her legs beneath her as she held her baby—really held her. She leaned down and breathed her scent as if trying to memorize it, and then kissed her tiny forehead.

This just made Jess's tears come harder. She should be telling her sister to get up off the floor, it wasn't sanitary, but all she could do was stare at them, half in wonder at the change in Abbie and half in pain from what she herself had lost.

You couldn't lose what you never had. Wasn't that what they said?

Just then, her sister looked up. "I'm so sorry, Jess. For everything I've put you through."

She had no idea what her sister was talking about. "It doesn't matter."

It didn't. Her relationship with her sister was the last thing on her mind right now.

"Is there somewhere we can go? Where I can keep holding her, but get some privacy? I need to talk to you."

The only privacy she wanted right now was the privacy of her own bedroom, where she could sob into her pillows until there was nothing left. Except even that final sanctuary had been invaded. Because everywhere she looked, she saw Dean: how ridiculous he'd looked sitting against those ruffled purple pillow shams—and how absolutely wonderful it had been to have him there.

The tears flowed with no signs of stopping. She took a shuddering breath and tried to force back the tide.

"Wait here." Somehow her sister managed to get herself up off the floor, still holding her baby, and went over to the nurse. She must have said something because in a minute or two Abbie was back, and, with Marissa still in her arms, led Jess down the hallway to one of the empty rooms.

Abbie sat on the bed and motioned for her to join her. Jess grabbed a couple of tissues from the bedside table and mopped up her eyes. How pathetic was she? Crying over yet another man who didn't want her?

"Tell me."

Jess looked at her, seeing the dark circles under her sister's eyes, the fact that she wasn't wearing any makeup. Even her hair looked softer and more natural.

She drew herself up tall, knowing the other shoe was eventually going to drop. It always did. Well, this time she wouldn't be drawn into a war of words. She was too tired. Too heartsick. And all of those past problems with her sister were nothing. Nothing, compared to what she was facing.

Sucking in another deep breath, she shook her head. "I think maybe it's you who has something to tell me."

"Okay, then, I'll go first." Abbie hesitated, and then looked her in the eye. "Martin and I have separated."

"What?" Of all the things she might have expected her sister to say, this was not it.

Shifting the baby in her arms, Abbie feathered her fingers across the tiny forehead, down her nose as if she was just now discovering the wonder of the little creature she'd brought into the world.

"I had an affair. Martin was traveling so much and I was sure he was seeing you. I was angry and afraid. It was just going to be the one time. I never meant it to go any further than that. But one time turned into two and pretty soon I wasn't sure what I wanted anymore. Until Martin came home from his trip, and I decided I loved him and wanted to make it work." Her eyes closed for a second or two before reopening. "I broke it off with the other man and thought things could go back to how they were before."

Jess could guess the rest…the reason why her sister had refused to bond with her baby, why she'd been so hateful, throwing those accusations at her at the party. "Then you discovered you were pregnant."

"Yes." Abbie sighed. "I thought I could handle it all on my own. Pretend it was Martin's and that he would never find out. Only it ate me up inside. I was afraid I was starting to hate the baby. And then I went into labor at the party, and I almost lost her. That mark on her leg, it was like a permanent reminder of what I'd done. Of what I'd put her through during my pregnancy."

Jess put her hand on Abbie's shoulder. "I'm so sorry. I had no idea."

"I was looking for a fight that night."

"Does Martin know?"

"Yes. I told him. He wants to work things out, but I asked him to move out…told him I needed to come here and see the baby. I need time to think things through."

"The other kids?"

"They're at Mum and Daddy's house."

Jess had to say it. "Martin loves you, Abbie. You shouldn't try to go through this by yourself."

Something swirled in her memory banks, clicking and processing those last words, even as her sister continued to talk.

"I know now what you must have felt like when you found out Martin was cheating on you. I feel like I failed him. So terribly."

Was that what Dean had felt like when he'd discovered his father had tried to take his life? That he'd somehow failed the man? It was the other way around. His father had failed him. Time and time again.

And now he—just like Abbie—was probably sitting somewhere trying to get to grips with everything that had happened.

Inside her head, the processing finally stopped and a formula appeared. *No one should have to face something like this alone.*

Wasn't that what Dean had said to her when she didn't want to go to the party at the hotel? He'd said she shouldn't have to face it alone. That he would face it with her.

But what had Dean done? He'd done exactly what he'd told her not to do.

"You need to go home. Or, better yet, ring Martin and tell him to come here. I'm sure Mum and Daddy are thrilled to watch the boys. Jerry? Is he okay?"

"He's out of hospital. But after what I did…" Abbie's eyes, so like her own, were wounded and uncertain.

Dean was probably telling himself that exact thing. He'd rebuffed his dad in the hallway, had told him never to ring him again.

There was no way Dean—or anyone—should have to deal with something like that on his own.

Jess needed to find him. If for no other reason than to reassure him that he wasn't to blame for what had happened to his father any more than she was to blame for what had happened to her friend Amy. Somehow she had to make him see that.

She could be his friend. Even if she could never be anything else.

Digging the keys to her house out of the pocket of her scrubs, she handed them to Abbie. "Stay at the cottage. There's plenty of food and supplies. Light a fire and talk this through with Martin. Just the two of you. I won't be there, so it'll be perfect."

"Where are you going?"

"I have a little unfinished business of my own to take care of."

"With Dean?"

She nodded her head, determination growing in her heart. "Oh, yes. With Dean."

CHAPTER FOURTEEN

HE STOOD AT the grave site of his father, the mist from the rain blinding him to everything around him, which was probably a good thing, since he didn't have to wonder if the moisture on his face was caused by the weather or by something else.

He'd made such a mess of things. Not only had he handled things terribly with his dad, but with Jess as well. He'd seen the emergency phone call from the hospital as his sign that things with her weren't meant to be, and that he needed to get the hell out. Yet she was still all around him.

Even here.

He'd purchased a simple grave marker for his father, although he wasn't sure the man deserved it. Maybe his dad had grown to be sorry for his actions. Dean would never really know what had gone through his father's head while in prison, or even in those last couple of weeks of his life.

He should have at least agreed to see him. Hear him out. Maybe then he could have washed him from his system once and for all.

And Jess? Had he done any better with her? He'd taken off, tossing off a casual note in his wake, just as his mum had done all those years ago. And although his thumb had hovered over the answer button on his mobile phone, he'd let her calls go straight to voicemail. Only when they'd stopped coming had he acknowledged the ball of regret that had lodged in his gut with each missed call.

The ball that was now the size of a boulder.

He knelt beside the grave and traced the lettering he'd had inscribed. A name and date of birth and death. No "beloved father" because, in the end, they'd been strangers.

And his mum? Did she house the same regrets? Maybe the time had come to try to find her. He should at least let her know that the abusive man who'd tormented her all those years ago was gone.

And what about Jess? He sat there, not really sure what to do about that.

He loved her. Beyond anything he could have ever imagined. And yet he'd taken off without a word of real explanation.

Didn't he owe her one? To tell her the truth, that he was messed up in the head right now, but that he cared about her? That he wanted to see her again?

She'd probably slam the door in his face—and with good reason, after what he'd done. But he owed her closure.

The kind of closure he'd never been given by his parents. In the end, how did he know his father hadn't tried to give that to him? Unless Dean wanted to perpetuate the kind of negative cycle he'd lived through, he needed to break it once and for all.

His finger dipped into the period at the end of the inscription that symbolized the end of his dad's life. He could at least put a punctuation mark on the end of his encounter with Jess. For both of their sakes.

Unless...

Unless she could find it in her heart to maybe stick with him for a little while. Feel out their relationship. Maybe she could even grow to care about him.

He glanced down at his shirt, water dripping off the end of his chin. But first, he needed to go home and put on some dry clothes. Something in his heart came back to life as he climbed to his feet with one last glance at the small stone below him.

Maybe this wasn't the end. Maybe it was a beginning.

If so, there was only one way to find out.

Jess rang Dean's doorbell one last time. He wasn't home. Scrolling through the personnel records hadn't been the wisest thing to do. She should have just rung his mobile again and left a message asking for a meeting. Except Dean hadn't returned any of her other phone calls, so she didn't hold out much hope that he would return this one.

It was harder to slam a door in someone's face than to ignore a ringtone. At least that was what she'd told herself as she'd pulled into the driveway, trembling with nerves.

The rain didn't help. It wasn't a downpour, but a dreary mist that echoed what her heart had felt over the last week.

Had it only been a week since they'd spent the night together?

Yes. And yet it could have been yesterday. Nothing had changed.

In her way of thinking, Dean at least owed her a straight explanation. Maybe he'd gotten phone calls in the past from other women and had used the same technique, but Jess wasn't other women. She was the one with the reputation for calmly handling difficult situations.

She didn't feel quite so calm now, however.

She felt cold and miserable…and wet.

It appeared Dean's stonewalling might just work, after all.

She'd done a lot of thinking as she drove over here. No woman at the hospital had ever admitted going to bed with the man. So that put her in a different class, because she knew plenty of women who'd leap at the chance to go out with him, not to mention sleep with him.

If she was going to go down, she wasn't going to do so without a fight. Not like some desperate hanger-on, but simply a woman who wanted to hear it straight out: that he didn't feel anything for her and would prefer to leave what had happened between them in the past.

She wasn't going to get that chance right now, evidently. There were no lights on in the house. No car in the driveway. This was something she was going to have to tackle another time. Until then, she'd have to find a hotel or something, because Abbie was at her house probably waiting for Martin to arrive.

Turning around, she flipped the hood of her slicker up and trudged back into the rain, squinting her eyes to keep the water from running into them.

She'd just reached the driver's side door of her little car, when headlights swept into the lane, heading straight for her. The vehicle pulled to a stop behind hers, blocking her exit, but just sat there for a moment or two, engine idling.

What the…?

Then the lights went out and, although it was the middle of the day, she had to squint yet again to help her eyes adjust to the sudden gloom.

The door opened and out stepped the man she'd been longing to see.

Dean.

He looked as damp and miserable as she did, although…

Something. Something in his eyes made the breath catch in her throat.

He slammed the door shut and walked over to her, staring down at her. "You're here."

Trying to place the inflection in his voice, she failed. She had no idea what he'd meant by that. Was he irritated? Well, at least he hadn't said, "It's you. What the hell are you doing here?"

She decided to play it as neutral as possible. "Yes, I am."

"I was going to come find you."

The breath that had been trapped inside of her whooshed back out. He was? Why? She swallowed and then forced the words out. "I was coming to find you."

One side of his mouth went up, erasing a bit of the taut grimness that had been on it a second ago. "You succeeded."

"Yes." Now she was stuck. She had absolutely no idea what else to say. Maybe she should start with what she knew and then move to the questions afterward. "I heard about your father. I'm sorry."

"Thank you. It was a shock. I blamed myself." His smile had faded, and Jess mourned being the one to chase it away.

"It wasn't your fault."

One of his shoulders lifted and dropped, but he didn't respond to her statement. Maybe coming here hadn't been such a good idea. Except he'd said he'd been getting ready to come find her. She had to know why. "You didn't answer any of my calls that day, so what did you want to see me about?"

There was a longer pause this time. Then his voice came through. "It was a mistake for me to leave you that night. I needed you."

Oh, God. Those words were an arrow straight through her heart—a wonderful piercing barb that exploded into a rainbow of colors, obliterating the gloom. "I'm here now."

Dean took a step forward and wrapped her in his arms. "Yes, you are." His chin came to rest on her head, making her eyes burn.

This was the time. If ever she was going to risk it, it needed to be now. "I need to tell you something."

"Tell me you're not leaving." The words rumbled above her head.

"No. I have no plans to leave, although you may want me to when I tell you what's happened."

"Are you pregnant?"

Was there an edge of hope to those words?

"No. It's only been a week. And we used protection, remember?"

"Protection sometimes fails."

The irony of it struck her right between the eyes. Yes, it did. She'd done her damnedest to protect her heart, to wrap it in layer after layer of latex and shield it from him. Only her attempts had failed miserably. He'd somehow gotten past her barriers and reached inside of her.

"In a way it did." She leaned back and looked into the

face of the man she loved, needing to see his eyes when she said the words. "Remember all that talk about casual sex? It wasn't. Casual, that is. At least not for me."

"Not for me either." The smile was back. Wider this time. "I love you, Jess. I don't know exactly when it happened, but it wasn't because of the sex—although that was pretty phenomenal. It was before that."

Jess's throat closed completely, trapping all the words she wanted to say inside of her. Her mouth opened and shut as she tried to force something…anything out.

Dean went on. "A few days after my father died, I realized I couldn't go on shutting myself off from the world, or I'd risk ending up like him. You're the first person I've truly felt anything for since my mum walked out on me all those years ago."

She found her voice. "I love you too, only I've been afraid to admit it. And when you wouldn't ring me back, I assumed you simply didn't feel the same way. That you just wanted me to stop. But I had to hear you say the words."

"Hell, I'm sorry, Jess, for putting you through that." He dropped a kiss on her head.

"Actually my sister was the one who helped me make the decision to come find you."

His arms tightened around her. "Your sister?"

"Yes. We had a long talk. I even brought along my new shoes, since you seemed quite fond of them. I hoped they might sway your opinion. They're in the car. I can get them if you'd like."

He slid to the side and wrapped his arm around her back, then started walking toward his front door. "I don't need the shoes, Jess. Or the dress. I just need you." A wicked gleam came to his eyes. "But first, we need to get you into something dry."

"That reminds me, I still have your shirt."

"I have other shirts. But the dry I'm thinking about is my bed." He paused for a moment when he reached the front door. "We can talk about marriage and rings later. Right now I just want to enjoy walking through every step of the process."

Marriage? He was thinking about marriage?

"I want the same thing."

Dean unlocked the door and swung it open. Then he swooped her into his arms and carried her across the threshold. "But that doesn't mean we can't practice some of the finer points."

As he turned and kicked the door closed Jess wrapped her arms around his neck, reveling in the fact that this man loved her and she loved him in return. She was looking forward to showing him exactly how much… far into the night and for as long as he would let her.

EPILOGUE

DEAN SMILED AS Jess handed him a large festively wrapped box and then perched on the arm of the couch right next to him. Facing the fireplace—and a Christmas tree brimming with presents—he was surrounded by Jess's relatives. Her mum and dad had come down to spend the holidays with them in Cambridge, as had her sister and her family.

He wasn't used to spending so much time with a group of people like this, but he had a feeling it could grow on him. There'd still been no word from the private investigator he'd hired to look for his mum, but that was something he no longer had to face alone. Jess had been right there with him, every step of the way. Whatever came of it, they would handle it. Together.

Abbie and Martin had evidently made their peace, from the way she was folded in his arms as they watched their children scurry to and fro. Loving touches and the bright glow in their eyes as they looked at each other said things were on the mend. It was the same with Abbie and Jess. Old hurts and irritations would probably surface from time to time, but for now all was peaceful. Marissa had been released from hospital a week ago and was now tucked into a portable cot to the side of the tree, sound asleep. Unlike Jess's nephews, who bounced with excitement over getting the rare opportunity to unwrap presents before it was even officially Christmas.

Tugging the bow on the gift Jess had given him, he marveled at how well things between the two of them had gone. So much so that, despite saying that he wanted to wait on marriage and relish the steps leading up to it, his impatience had gotten the better of him. But that gift—safely tucked in his jacket pocket—would come later, far from the eyes and ears of the rest of her family.

He opened the box and parted the tissue paper inside to find a white dress shirt. When he glanced up, he found her eyes alight with wicked amusement. Over the past week, she'd worn a wide array of his shirts, looking just as mouthwatering in each and every one of them. "I like it," he murmured. "Thank you. I'll have to try it on a little later."

Color swept into her face as she caught his meaning. Because he did indeed intend to try it on—her, that was—as soon as he gave her his own wrapped gift.

He slung his arm around her waist as the kids bounded toward the tree to see who else had a present hidden beneath it. Glancing up, he found her watching him. "Love you," he murmured.

"Love you too."

Jess's parents—especially her mum—seemed a little softer and sweeter as they watched their children and grandchildren laugh and carry on. Their hands had found each other's and clasped tight.

Their happiness seemed in keeping with the holiday, known for its love and gifts.

He squeezed Jess just a little bit tighter, knowing that

being here with her was the greatest gift he could ever hope to receive.

It was enough. It was more than enough.

And he planned to savor each and every moment of it, for the rest of his life.

* * * * *

HER DOCTOR'S CHRISTMAS PROPOSAL

LOUISA GEORGE

CHAPTER ONE

'ODDS ON IT'LL be the Pattersons. She was telling me the other day that she missed out on winning it a couple of years ago, so she's going to cross her legs until the twenty-fifth. No hot curries, or hot baths and definitely no hot sex for her.'

You and me both, girlfriend. Obstetrician Isabel Delamere tried to remember the last time she'd had anything like hot sex and came up with a blank. It was all by design, of course…working in a maternity unit was enough reminder of what hot sex could lead to—that and her own experiences. But every now and then she wondered…what the hell was she missing out on?

Plus, how could she possibly be lonely when she spent all of her waking hours surrounded by colleagues, clients and lots and lots of wriggling, screaming, gorgeous babies?

Sighing, she wrote *Patterson* down on the First Baby of Christmas sweepstake form and added her five-pound note to the pot. 'If mum has her way there's no way that baby's coming until Christmas Day. She's set her heart on the hamper, and between you and me they don't have a lot of money. I think she needs it.'

'I admire your optimism…' Bonnie Reid, one of

Isabel's favourite midwives—and new friend—at the Cambridge Royal Maternity Unit, added her contribution of a large box of chocolates and a bumper pack of newborn nappies to the crate of donations that threatened to overshadow the huge department Christmas tree and wooden Nativity scene. With a heavy bias on baby items, some gorgeous hand-knitted booties and shawls, and heaps of food staples, whoever won would be set up for the next year. 'But when I saw her yesterday that baby was fully engaged and she was having pretty regular Braxton Hicks contractions, so my bet is that baby Patterson will make a show well before Christmas Day.' Bonnie stepped back and surveyed the decorations, her lilting Scottish accent infused with wistfulness. 'Oh, I do love Christmas.'

Me too. Isabel dug deep and found a smile. Well, in reality, she loved being with her sister at Christmas; they shared a very special bond. This last year here in the UK had been the longest they'd spent apart, and the prospect of Isla doing all the traditional celebrations without her bit deep. Especially…she sighed to herself…especially when Christmas had always been so full of memories.

Isabel slammed back the sadness and tried to immerse herself in the here and now rather than thinking of her sister back in Melbourne on the other side of the world, all ripe and ready to have her first baby. She wondered whether the Melbourne Maternity Unit was taking similar bets. Maybe Isla would win the Aussie sweepstake? Now that would give the rest of the department something to giggle about: the head midwife winning with a Christmas Day baby! 'So, go on, then, who will it be?'

'Who will what be?' A deep male voice, redolent with her beloved Aussie tones. The sound of home.

The sound of heartbreak.

Isabel inhaled sharply.

Sean.

And even if the man had been mute she'd have known he was behind her simply because of the full-on reaction her body had any time he was in the vicinity. Every tiny hair stood to attention. Her heart rate escalated. Palms became sweaty. Seventeen years on and she'd managed to deal with it…when she didn't have to face him every day. She'd almost erased him from her heart.

Almost. She'd come to the other side of the world to forget him. And she'd managed quite well for close to nine months until he'd turned up, out of the blue, and those feelings had come tumbling back. The memories…and his questions… Questions she couldn't bear to answer.

Somewhere a phone rang. Somewhere voices, raised and harried, called to her. 'Dr Delamere. Please. There's been an accident…'

Oh, God. She was shaken from her reverie but her heart rate stayed too high for comfort. 'Isla?'

'Isla? No,' Bonnie called over from the nurses' station. 'Susan Patterson. Motor vehicle accident. They're bringing her in to ER. Heavy vaginal bleeding. Mum shocked. Foetal distress. ETA five minutes.'

'What? No! We were just talking about her.' Without even looking at Sean, Isabel jumped straight into doctor mode. 'Right, Bonnie, sounds like a possible abruption. Get Theatre on alert. I'll meet the ambulance down in the ER.'

'I'm coming with you.' Sean was heading towards the door.

Only when hell freezes over. 'No. Sean, absolutely not.'

Silence.

She realised that all the eyes of the staff were on her. No one knew about their history, and for as long as there was breath in her body no one was going to. 'I mean… thank you very much for your offer, Dr Anderson, but I'll be fine.'

He shrugged, following her into the corridor, into more quiet. 'I'm in a lull here. Everyone's discharged or doing well, I don't have a clinic until two o'clock. Are you really saying you couldn't use an extra pair of hands? I have done this before, you know.'

'Yes, I know.' She also knew what a talented and empathetic obstetrician he was, she just didn't relish the prospect of spending any time with him. But she had to give this mum everything she had and an extra pair of confident hands would definitely help. 'Okay. But this is my case, my theatre, my rules.'

'Of course. If I remember rightly, it was always your rules, Isabel. Right down to the bitter end. In fact, I don't remember having any say in that at all.' He gave a wry lift of his eyebrow as they hurried towards the emergency room. 'This one time I'll abide by them. But once we're out of there then…'

She stopped short. 'Then, what?'

'Then I change the rules to suit me.'

She shrugged, hoping upon hope that he couldn't see through her recalcitrant façade to the shaking, smitten teenager she still felt like when she was around him. 'Do what you want. It won't affect me. At all.' *Liar.* It seemed as if everything he did affected her. Just being here. Breathing. In Cambridge. Goddamn him.

Isabel threw him a look that she hoped told him where exactly to shove his rules, and strode straight in to Resus. She would deal with Sean Anderson…later… never, if she had her way. 'Now, Susan? Crikey, love, what on earth has been happening?' She took hold of her patient's hand.

Mrs Patterson was lying on a trolley, tears streaming down her cheeks. Pale. Terrified. Her voice was barely audible through the oxygen mask over her nose and mouth. 'Thank God you're here, Isabel. I'm so scared. I don't want to lose this baby. Please. Do something.'

'I will. I just need some details then we'll make some decisions. And we'll be quick, I promise.' She'd have to be. If it was a placental abruption, as she suspected, both mum and bub were at serious risk. Outcomes weren't always positive. And well she knew. Too well. Isabel examined Susan's belly for the baby's position and well-being. Then she tightened an electro foetal monitor belt over the baby bump. 'Has anyone called Tony?'

'I did.' Jenny, the paramedic, filled her in on further details. 'He's on his way. Grandma's looking after the toddler. They were in the car at the time of impact. Hit from behind. Susan felt a tight pull in her belly. Possibly from an ill-fitting seat belt, but there's no visible marking or bruising on the abdomen. I have normal saline through a wide-bore IV in situ. Moderate vaginal bleeding. Blood pressure ninety over fifty and dropping. Baby's heart rate jittery and at times…' She pointed to her notes and let Isabel read. The baby's heart rate was dipping, a sign of foetal distress. Mum was clearly shocked. Judging by the blood staining her clothes the baby needed to be out. Now.

'Okay. Thanks.' Isabel turned to the ER nurse that had appeared. 'I need you to cross-match four units of packed cells. I need clotting times, usual bloods and that portable ultrasound over here as quick as you can.'

Susan's hand squeezed in Isabel's. 'But I wanted... I wanted to hang on...two more weeks....'

'I know, but these things happen and we just have to deal with them as best we can.' Isabel gave Susan a quick smile, positioned the ultrasound machine in front of her, squeezed jelly onto the probe and placed it over Susan's tummy. 'I'm just going to take a quick look.' Baby was okay—distressed, but alive. Isabel exhaled deeply. Thank God.

She looked over at Sean and saw his reassuring smile. She gave him a small one back. They both knew that at least some of the immediate anxiety was over.

But the placenta was, indeed, partially separated. The baby was at serious risk and mum's blood loss was not stopping. Despite the desperate urgency Isabel needed to be calm so as not to frighten mum too much. 'Okay, Susan, we do have a problem here, but—'

'Oh, my God. I knew it...'

'Sweetheart, we'll do our best. It'll be okay.' Isabel prayed silently that it would. 'Your placenta is failing, I think the car impact may have given it a nasty jolt or tear and there's a real risk to the baby if we don't do something soon. As you know the placenta is what keeps baby alive, so we have to take you to the operating theatre and do a Caesarean section. I need your consent—'

'Where's Susan? Susan? Where's Susan?' A burly-looking stocky man covered in dust pushed his way in, steel-capped boots leaving grubby imprints across the floor. 'What the hell's happening?'

Isabel scanned the room for Sean. But he was there already, his hand on Tony's forearm, gently slowing him down. 'Are you Tony? Here, let me bring you over. It's a lot to take in, I know, mate. There's a few tubes and lines and she looks a little pale. But she's good.'

'She is not good. Look at her.' The room filled with the smell of beer and a voice that was rough round the edges, and getting louder. 'Is that…? Is that blood? What's happened? What about my boy? The baby! Susan! Are you all right?' Then his tone turned darker, he shoved out of Sean's grip and marched up to Isabel. In her face. Angry and foul-mouthed. 'You. Do something. Why are you just standing there? Do something, damn it.'

Isabel's hand began to shake. But she would not let him intimidate her. 'I'm doing the best I can. We all are. Now, please—'

'No need for that, mate. Come away.' Sean's voice was calm but firm. At six foot one he was by far the bigger man. Broader too. And while Tony was rough and menacing, Sean was authoritative. There was no aggression, but a quietly commanded respect and attention. 'We're going to take her to Theatre right now, but first we need to know what we're dealing with. Yes? Have a few words with Susan, but then we need to get moving. I'll show you where you can wait.'

'Get your hands off me.' Tony pushed his way to the trolley. 'Susie.'

'I'll be fine, Tony. Just do as he says.' Susan started to shake. 'I love you.'

'If they don't—'

Sean stepped forward. 'As I said. Come with me. *Now.* Let's have a quiet word. Outside.' He bustled Tony out of the room.

'He's not a bad man.' Isabel's patient's voice was fading. Alarms began to blare.

'I know, I know, he's scared, is all.' Thank God Sean was able to contain him because the last thing Isabel needed was a drunk father getting in the way of saving a mother and baby. 'Now we need to get you sorted, quickly.' Isabel nodded to the porter. 'Let's go.'

She all but ran to the OR, scrubbed up and was in the operating theatre in record time. Sean, somehow, was there before her. 'So we have a crash C-section scenario. Your call, Izzy. Whatever happens, I've got your back.'

'Thank you.' And she meant it. Well drilled in dealing with emergencies, she felt competent and confident, but having someone there she knew she could rely on gave her a lift. Even if that lift involved her heart as well as her head.

Within minutes she'd tugged out a live baby boy. Floppy. Apgar of six. But, with oxygen and a little rub, the Apgar score increased to ten. As occurred with every delivery Isabel felt a familiar sting of sadness, and hope. But she didn't have time for any kind of sentimentality. One life saved wouldn't be enough for her. Placental abruption was harrowing and scary for the mother but it was high risk too. That amount of blood loss, coupled with the potential for complications, meant they were perilously close to losing her.

'Blood pressure's dropping…' The anaesthetist gave them a warning frown.

'Hang on in there… I just need to find the tear.' Isabel

breathed a sigh of relief as she reached the placenta and started to remove it. 'Attagirl.'

Within an hour they'd managed to save Susan's life too, although she had hung close to the edge. Too close.

And now…well, now that dad was with baby, her patient was in recovery and the rest of the staff had scarpered, Isabel was alone. Alone, that was, with the one person she never wanted to be alone with again. Rather than look at him she stared at the words she was writing. 'Well, Sean, I don't want to keep you while I finish writing up these notes. Thanks, you were a great help. Things could have turned nasty with Tony.'

'He just needed me to explain a few things. Like how to behave in an emergency department. But I get it. The bloke was worried. I would have been too if I was losing my wife and my baby.'

Guilt crawled down her spine. How would he have been? At seventeen? Quick-mouthed and aggressive? Or the self-assured, confident man he was now? She stole a quick glance in his direction. 'You wouldn't have acted like that. So thanks for dealing with him. And for your help in here.'

'It wasn't just me. We almost lost them both, but your quick thinking and nifty work saved both their lives. Well done.' He threw his face mask into the bin, snapped his gloves off and faced her. 'You look exhausted.'

'Gee, thanks. I'm fine.' She didn't feel fine. Her legs were like jelly and her stupid heart was still pounding with its fight-or-flight response. She looked away from the notes and towards the door. Flight. Good idea. Easier to write them up in the safety of her office, which was a Sean-free zone. Snapping the folder closed, she looked up at him. 'Actually, I've got to go.'

'Wait, please.'

She stepped towards the door and tried hard to look natural instead of panicked. 'No. I have a million things to do.'

'They can wait.' His tone was urgent, determined. He was striding towards the exit now too.

'No. They can't.'

'Isabel. Stop avoiding me, goddamn it!'

He was going to ask.

He was going to ask and she was going to lie. Because lying had been the only way to forge enough distance between her and the one thing she had promised herself she could never do again: feel something.

She calculated that it would take precisely five seconds to get out of the chilly delivery room and away from his piercing blue-eyed gaze. For the last two months she'd managed to steer clear from any direct one-to-ones with him, shielding herself with colleagues or friends. But now, the things unsaid between them for almost seventeen years weighed heavily in the silence.

He was going to ask and she was going to lie. Again.

The lies were exhausting. Running was exhausting. Just as getting over Sean and that traumatic time had been. She didn't want to have to face that again. Face him again.

His scent filled the room. Sunshine. Spice. His heat, so familiar and yet not so.

Seventeen years.

God, how he'd matured into the sophisticated, beautiful man he was destined to be. But wanting answers to questions that would break her heart all over again... and his.

She made direct eye contact with the door handle and started to move towards it again.

'Izzy?'

She would not turn round. Would. Not. 'Don't call me that here. It's Isabel or Dr Delamere.'

'Hello? It's not as if anyone can hear. There's only you and me in here. It's so empty there's an echo.'

'*I* can hear.' *And I don't want to be reminded.* Although she was, every day. Every single day. Every mother, every baby. Every birth. Every stillborn. Every death.

She made it to the door. The handle was cold and smooth. Sculpted steel, just like the way she'd fashioned her heart and her backbone. Beyond the clouded glass she could make out a bustling corridor of co-workers and clients. Safety. She squeezed the handle downwards and a whoosh of air breathed over her. 'I'm sorry, Dr Anderson, I have a ward round to get to. I'm already late. Like I said, thanks for your help back there.'

'Any time. You know that.' His hand covered hers and a shot of electricity jolted through her. He was warm. And solid. And here; of all the maternity units he could have chosen… This time it wasn't a coincidence. His voice was thick and deep and reached into her soul. 'I just want one minute, Isabel. That's all. One.'

One minute. One lifetime. It would never be enough to bridge that time gap. Certainly not if she ever told him the answer to his question.

'No, Sean, please don't ask me again.' She jabbed her foot into the doorway and pulled the door further open.

Then she made fatal error number one. She turned her head and looked up at him.

His chestnut hair was tousled from removing his

surgical cap, sticking up in parts, flattened in others. Someone needed to sink their fingers in and fluff it. So not her job. Not when she was too busy trying not to look at those searching eyes. That sculptured jawline. The mouth that had given her so much pleasure almost a year ago, with one stupid, ill-thought-out stolen kiss, and...a lifetime ago. A boy turned into a man. A girl become a woman, although in truth that had happened in one night all those years ago.

Onwards went her gaze, re-familiarising herself with lines and grooves, and learning new ones. Wide solid shoulders, the only tanned guy in a fifty-mile radius, God bless the sparse Aussie ozone layer. Toned arms that clearly did more working out than lifting three-kilogram newborns.

His voice was close to her ear. 'Izzy, if it was over between us... If everything was completely finished, why the hell did you kiss me?'

Good question. Damn good question. She'd been brooding over the answer to that particular issue for the better part of the last year, ever since he'd crushed her against him in a delivery suite very similar to this one, but half a world away. It had been a feral response to a need she hadn't ever known before. A shock, seeing him again after so long, turning up at the Melbourne hospital where she'd worked. He'd been as surprised as she had, she was sure.

Then he'd kissed her. A snatched frenzied embrace that had told her his feelings for her had been rekindled after such a long time apart. And, oh, how she'd responded. Because, in all honesty, her feelings for him had never really waned.

Heat prickled through her at the mere memory. Heat

and guilt. But they had to put it behind them and move forward. 'Really, Sean? Do you chase most of the women you kiss across the world? It must cost an awful lot in airfares. Still, I guess you must do well on the loyalty schemes. What do you have now, elite platinum status? Does that entitle you to fly the damn planes as well?'

His smile was slow to come, but when it did it was devastating. 'Most women aren't Isabel Delamere. And none of them kiss like you do.'

'I'm busy.'

'You're avoiding the issue.'

She held his too blue, too intense gaze. She could do this. Distract him with other issues, deflect the real one. Get him off her back once and for all. She was going away tomorrow for a few days. Hopefully everything would have blown over by the time she got back. *Like hell it would.* She could pretend that it had. She just needed some space from him. 'So let me get this straight. You turn up out of the blue at the same place I'm work-ing in Melbourne—'

'Pure coincidence. I was as shocked as you. Pleas-antly, though. Unlike your reaction.' The pressure of his thumb against the back of her hand increased a little, like a stroke, a caress.

She did not want him to caress her.

Actually she did. But that would have been fatal error number two. 'Then after I leave there you turn up here. Also out of the blue? I don't think so.'

'Aww, you missed a whole lot out….where I didn't see you or have any contact with you for many, many years. As far as I was concerned you were the one that got away. But also the one I got over.' At her glare he shrugged shoulders that were broader, stronger than she remembered. 'I put you out of my mind and did exactly what I had planned to do with my life and became a damned fine obstetrician. Then one day I turn up at my cushy new locum job at Melbourne Maternity Unit and bump into my old…flame. I never dreamt for a minute you'd be there after hearing you'd studied medicine in Sydney. I assumed you'd moved on. Like I had. But then, Delamere blood runs thick with the Yarra so I should have realized you'd be there in the bosom of your… delightful family.' He gave a sarcastic smile. Sean had never got on with her hugely successful neurosurgeon daddy and socialite mother who ran with the It crowd in Melbourne. 'Well, in that sumptuous penthouse apartment anyway. Cut to the chase—the first chance you get: wham, bam. You kiss me.'

'What?' She dragged her hand from under his and jabbed a finger at him. 'You kissed me first. It took me by surprise—it didn't mean anything.'

'No one kisses like that and doesn't mean it.'

He'd pulled her to him and she'd felt the hard outline of his body, had a crazy melting of her mind and she'd wanted to kiss him right back. Hard. Hot. And it had been the most stupid thing she'd done in a long time. Not least because it had reignited an ache she'd purged from her system. She'd purged *him* from her system. 'And now you're here to what? Taunt me? Tell me, Sean, why are you here?'

'Ask your sister.'

'Isla? Why? And how can I?' There was no way Isla would ever have told Sean what had happened. She'd promised to keep that secret for ever and Isabel trusted her implicitly. Even though over the years she had caught Isla looking at her with a sad, pitiful expression. And sure, Isabel knew she'd been badly scarred by her experiences, they both had, but she was over it. She was. She'd moved on. 'Isla is back home in Australia and I'm here. I'm hardly going to phone a heavily pregnant woman in the middle of the night just to ask why an old boyfriend is in town, am I? What did she say?'

'It was more what she didn't say that set alarm bells ringing. I asked her outright why you had suddenly gone so cold on our relationship, she said she couldn't tell me but that I should ask you myself. Between her garbled answers and your sizzling kiss, I'm guessing that there's a lot more to this than you're letting on. Something important. Something so big that you're both running scared. My brain's working overtime and I'm baffled. So tell me the truth, Isabel. Tell me the truth, then I'll go. I'll leave. Out of your life.'

Which would be a blessing and a curse. She was so conflicted she didn't know if she never wanted to set eyes on him again or…wake up every morning in his arms. But if he ever found out why they'd split up option two would never, ever happen. He'd make sure of it. 'It doesn't matter any more, Sean. It was such a long time ago.'

'It matters to me. It clearly still matters to Isla, so I'm sure it matters to you.' He leaned closer and her senses slammed into overdrive. Memories, dark, painful memories, rampaged through her brain. Her body felt as if it were reliving the whole tragedy again. Her heart rate jittered into a stupid over-compensatory tachycardia, and she squeezed the door handle.

It was all too much.

In her scrubs pocket her phone vibrated and chimed 'Charge of The Light Brigade'. She grabbed it, grateful of the reprieve. The labour ward. 'Look, seriously, I've got to run.'

'Doing what you do best.' He flicked his thumb up the corridor, his voice raised. 'Go on, Izzy. Go ahead and run. But remember this—you walked away with no explanation, you just cut me adrift. Whatever happened back then wasn't just about you. And while I've thought about it over the years it's hardly kept me awake at night, until Isla hinted at some momentous mystery that she's sworn not to talk about, and if it involves me then I deserve to know why.'

Isabel glanced at the phone display, then up the corridor, where she saw a few heads popping out from rooms, then darting back in again.

She looked back at Sean. She thought about the dads in the delivery suites, so proud, so emotional, so raw. How they wept when holding their newborns. She thought about Tony, who'd have fought tooth and nail for his son, even if it had riled every member of hospital staff. She thought about the babies born sleeping and the need for both parents to know so much, to be involved. They cared. They loved. They broke. They grieved. Both of them, not just the mums.

So damn right Sean deserved to know. She'd hidden this information for so long, and yet he had every right to know what had happened. And once he knew then surely he'd leave? If not because it was so desperately sad, but because she had kept this from him. He'd hate her.

But the relief would be final. She'd be free from the guilt of not telling him. Just never, *never* of the hurt.

She opened her mouth to say the words, but her courage failed. 'Please, just forget it. Put it behind you. Forget I ever existed. Forget it all.'

'Really? When I see you every day? Forget this?' He stepped closer, pinning her against the doorway, and for a moment she thought—hoped—he was going to kiss her again. His mouth was so close, his scent overpowering her. And the old feelings, the want, the desire came tumbling back. They had never had problems with the attraction; it had been all-consuming, feral, intense even then. It was the truth that she'd struggled with. Laying bare how she felt, because she was a Delamere girl after all, and she wasn't allowed to show her emotions. Ever. She had standards, expectations to fulfil. And dating Sean Anderson hadn't been one of them. Certainly carrying his child never was.

His breath whispered over the nape of her neck. Hot. Hungry. Sending shivers of need spiralling down her back. He was so close. Too close. Not close enough. 'What's the matter, Izzy? Having trouble forgetting that I exist?'

And what was the use in wanting him now? One whiff of the truth and he'd be gone.

But, it was time to tell him anyway.

'Okay. Okay.' She shoved him back, gave herself some air. She made sure she had full eye contact with him, looked into those ocean-blue eyes. She was struggling with her own emotions, trying to keep her voice steady and level, but failing; she could hear it rise. 'We had to finish, Sean. I didn't know what to do. I was sixteen and frightened and I panicked. I had to cut you out of my life once and for all. A clean break for my own sanity if not for anything else.' She took a deep breath. 'I was pregnant.'

He staggered back a step. Two. 'What?'

'Yes, Sean. With your baby.'

CHAPTER TWO

'WHAT?' THIS WASN'T what he'd expected at all. Truthfully, he'd thought she'd been embarrassed about being seen with him. A lad from the wrong side of the Delamere social circle with two very ordinary and dull parents of no use to the Delamere clan. Or perhaps a bit of angsty teenage intrigue. Or possibly some pubertal mental health issues. But this...?

He was a...father?

Sean's first instinct was to walk and keep on walking. But he fixed his feet to the floor, because he had to hear this. All of it. 'Pregnant? My baby? So where is it? What happened?' Two possibilities ran through his head: one, he had a child somewhere that he had never seen. And for that he could never forgive her.

Or two, she'd had an abortion without talking it through with him. *His child*. Neither option was palatable.

She followed him back in to the OR and looked up at him, her startling dark green eyes glittering with tears that she righteously blinked away. With her long blonde hair pulled back into a tight ponytail she looked younger than her thirty-three years. Not the sweet delicate creature she'd been at school, but she was so much more, somehow. More beautiful. More real. Just…more. That came with confidence, he supposed, a successful career, Daddy's backing, everyone doing Miss Delamere's bidding her whole life.

But her cheeks seemed to hollow out as she spoke. 'I lost it. The baby.'

'Oh, God. I'm sorry.' He was an obstetrician, for God's sake, he knew it happened. But to her? To him? His gut twisted into a tight knot; so not everything had gone Isabel's way after all.

She gave a slight nod of her head. Sadness rolled off her. 'I had a miscarriage at eighteen weeks—'

'Eighteen weeks? You were pregnant for over four months and didn't tell me? Why the hell not?'

So this was why she'd become so withdrawn over those last few weeks together, refusing intimacy, finding excuses, being unavailable. This was why she'd eventually cut him off with no explanation.

She started to pace around the room, Susan's notes still tight in her fist. 'I didn't know I was pregnant, not for sure. Oh, of course I suspected I was, I just hadn't done a test—I was too scared even to pee on a stick and see my life change irrevocably in front of my eyes. I was sixteen. I didn't want to face reality. I…well, I suppose I'd hoped that the problem would go away. I thought, hoped, that my missing periods were just irregular cycles, or due to stress, exams, trying to live up to Daddy's expectations. Being continually on show. Having to snatch moments with you. So I didn't want to believe—couldn't believe…a baby? I was too young to deal with that. We both were.'

He made sure to stand stock-still, his eyes following her round the room. 'You didn't think to mention it? We thought you'd be safe—God knows…the naivety. You were pregnant for eighteen weeks? I don't understand… I thought we talked about everything.' Clearly he'd been mistaken. Back then he'd thought she was the love of his life. He'd held a candle up to her for the next five years. No woman had come close to the rose-tinted memory he'd had of how things had been between them. Clearly he'd been wrong. Very wrong. 'You should have talked to me. Maybe I could have helped. I could have… I don't know…maybe I could have saved it.' Even as he said the words he knew he couldn't have done a thing. Eighteen weeks was far too young, too fragile, too underdeveloped, even now, all these years later and with all the new technology, eighteen weeks was still too little.

The light in her eyes had dimmed. It had been hard on her, he thought. A burden, living with the memory. 'I spent many years thinking the same thing, berating myself for maybe doing something wrong. I pored over books, looked at research, but no one could have saved him, Sean. He was too premature. You, of all people, know how it is. We see it. In our jobs.'

'*He?*' His gut lurched. 'I had a son?'

She finally stopped pacing, wrapped her arms around her thin frame, like a hug. Like a barrier. But her gaze clashed with his. 'Yes. A son. He was beautiful, Sean. Perfect. So tiny. Isla said—'

'So Isla was there?' Her sister was allowed to be there, but he wasn't?

'Yes. It all happened so fast. I was in my bathroom at my parents' house and suddenly there was so much blood, and I must have screamed. Then Isla was there, she delivered him…' Her head shook at the memory. 'God love her, at twelve years of age she delivered my child onto our bathroom floor, got help and made sure I was okay. No wonder she ended up being a midwife—it's what she was born to do.'

He wasn't sure he wanted any more details. He had enough to get his head around, but he couldn't help asking the questions. 'So who else helped you? There must have been someone else? An adult? Surely?'

'Evie, our housekeeper.'

'The one who turned me away when I came round that time? Not your parents?' He could see from Isabel's closed-off reaction that she hadn't involved them, just as she hadn't involved him. He didn't know whether that made him feel any better or just...just lost. Cut off from her life. After everything he'd believed, he really hadn't known her at all. 'They still don't know? Even now?'

'No. Evie took me to a hospital across town and they sorted me out. Because I was sixteen the doctors didn't have to tell my parents. I never did. They were away at the time, they wouldn't have understood. It would have distressed them. The scandal—'

'Of course. We always have to be careful about what our Melbourne royalty think.' He didn't care a jot about them now and he hadn't back then. They'd cosseted their daughters and he'd struggled to get much time alone with her despite his best efforts; over-protective, she'd called them. Of course, he knew better now. But even so, Isabel had been nothing more than a pawn in their celebrity status paraded at every available opportunity, the golden girl. The darling Delamere daughter who couldn't do any wrong.

No...that wasn't what he'd believed at the time, only the intervening years had made him rethink his young and foolish impression of her. When they were together he'd come to love a deep, sensitive girl, not a material-istic, shallow Delamere. But then she'd cut him off and he'd been gutted to find out she was the same as her par-ents after all. But this news…and to keep it to herself all that time. Who the hell was she? 'And that's why you broke off our relationship? That's why you sent my ring back to me? No explanation.'

She fiddled with her left ring finger as if that ring were still there. 'I didn't know what else to do, to be honest, I was stressed out, grieving. I'd lost my baby. It felt like a punishment, you see. I hadn't wanted him, but then, when I lost him I wanted him so badly. And seeing you, telling you, would have brought back all that pain. I wasn't strong enough to relive it again.' She'd walked towards him, her hand now on his arm. 'I'm sorry, Sean. I should have told you.'

'Yes, you should have.' He shook his arm free from her touch. He couldn't bear to feel her, to smell her in-toxicating scent. To see those beautiful, sad eyes. And to know that she'd let him live all those years without telling him the truth.

He forced himself to look at her. To imagine what must have been going through her head at that time. The fear, the pain, the confusion. The grief. It must have been so terrifying for a young girl. But still he couldn't fathom why all of that had been a reason to shut herself off from him. To keep all this from him.

She looked right back at him, not a young girl any longer. She was a beautiful, successful woman with tears swimming in her eyes—tears that did not fall. She wiped them away. It was the first time he'd seen any emotion from her in the months that he'd been here. Now, and when she'd kissed him back in Melbourne. There had been a few emotions skittering across her face back then: fear mainly, and a raw need. 'Please, Sean. Please say something.'

He didn't know what to say. How to feel. Right now, he was just angry. Empty. No...just angry. It was as if a huge chunk of his past had been a lie. He should have known about this. He should have been allowed to know this. 'I've spent all these years wondering what turned you from being such a happy, loving girlfriend to a cold and distant one literally overnight. I thought it was something I'd done and I went over and over everything until I was lost. Or that you'd had a nervous breakdown. Or that I wasn't good enough for you. I tried to see you but had the door closed in my face so many times I gave up. You refused to answer my calls. I tried hard to understand what was happening. In the end I just presumed your parents had somehow found out and banned you from seeing me.'

'They wouldn't have done that.'

'Wouldn't they? You weren't exactly thrilled at the prospect of telling them we were an item. *Let's keep it a secret,* you said. *Our secret love.* It seems you had a lot of secrets back then, Isabel.'

She flinched, so she must have remembered saying words he'd believed at the time were heartfelt. 'I didn't want to cause you any pain. There wasn't anything you could do. I thought it would be for the best, for both of us. Just put it all behind us.'

'I could have grieved, Isabel, I could have helped you with that.' He held her gaze. 'So was it? For the best?'

She shook her head. 'No. Not for me, anyway.'

'And not for me, either. I'm sorry, Isabel. I'm sorry you had to go through that, I know how hard it must have been. But…' And it was a hell of a big *but*…what was he supposed to do now? Why hadn't she told him? Even though she'd lost their baby, did that mean she'd had to throw their love aside too? He couldn't think straight. Just looking at her brought back hurt, and more, stacked alongside the fact that he'd been a dad. He'd had a son. And he hadn't even known.

Words failed him. 'I can't imagine your state of mind, you're right. But one thing is for sure. If I'd known something like that that deeply involved someone else, someone I'd professed to care about—to love, even—I'd have mentioned it.'

She hung her head. 'It was a long time ago. We have to move on, Sean.'

'Easy for you to say, Isabel.' He was loud now, he knew his anger was spilling into his voice, his face, but he didn't much care. 'You've had many years to get over this. It's in your past. But this, this is my present right now. So you'll excuse me if I take a little time to come to terms with it all. I had a son? Wow. It would have been nice to know that.'

'Oh, yes? Well, it was horrible. I was distraught, traumatised. I was a young girl, for God's sake.' Her voice was shaky now, like her hands. 'You know what makes it all so much worse? *You.* Seeing you brings it all back, and I don't want to think about it any more. It hurts. Okay? It hurts, so I wish you'd never found me.'

You have no idea what she's been through, Isla had said when she'd encouraged him to come all this way to confront Isabel. *Don't hurt her.* No? He didn't want to do that. He didn't want to make her relive that pain.

But he didn't want to be with her either. Right now

he didn't even want to breathe the same air as her. Not after this.

A difficult silence wrapped around them like the foggy December day outside.

Her hand covered his. 'I didn't mean to hurt you, Sean. I'm sorry for leaving you to wonder all those years.'

'Yeah. Well, so you should be. Keep out of my way, Isabel. I mean it. Keep out of my way.' And without so much as looking at her again he stalked out of the room.

'You've had a major operation and a big shock to your body. Three units of blood. That's an awful lot to get over.' Isabel gave Susan Patterson what she hoped was a reassuring smile. Twenty-four hours post-op many patients felt as if they'd been hit by a truck. But because they always, always put their babies first they tried to recover far too quickly. 'The good news is, you're making an excellent recovery. Your blood pressure is stable and your blood results are fine. We're going to move you from High Dependency back to the ward so you can be in with the other mums, and we'll bring baby up to be with you. He's ready to leave SCBU now. Between you both you've kept us on our toes, but things are definitely on the way up. He's a little fighter, that one.'

'He's got a good set of lungs, I'll give him that.' Susan gave a weak smile back. Kicking back the covers, she tried to climb out of bed. But when her feet hit the floor she grabbed onto the bed table for stability. She was still a little pale, and Isabel made a note to keep an eye on that. It wasn't just haemoglobin she needed to watch, it was Susan's desire to do too much too soon.

'Hey, there's no hurry. Rest easy. I'll ask a nurse to

come help you have a shower. That scar's in a tricky place, so you need to support it when you move. And remember, Caesareans do take longer to recover from, so don't expect too much from yourself.' Glancing at the chart, she realised Susan's baby was still listed as Baby Patterson. 'Have you thought of a name for that gorgeous wee boy yet?'

Doing as she was told, Susan sat down on the side of the bed; a little more colour crept into her cheeks. 'We had thought about something Christmassy like Joseph or Noel, but as he was early we had to change all that. If he'd been a girl I'd have called him Isabel.' Her cheeks pinked more. 'After you, because you did such a great job of saving us both. But instead we thought we'd choose Isaac. It has the *Is* in it—and that'll remind us of you. I guess you get that all the time?'

Isabel felt her smile blossom from the inside. 'Actually, not very often at all. It's very nice of you. Thank you. I'm honoured.'

'Oh, and Sean as a middle name. After Dr Anderson.'

Sean. Of course. Why not? She forced the smile to stay in place. 'Oh. Lovely. I'm sure he'll be thrilled.'

And she'd got through ten whole minutes without thinking about him, just to be reminded all over again.

Last night had been filled with internal recriminations that had intensified in direct proportion to her wine consumption. From: she should have told him years ago, to…she was glad she'd kept that pain from him, to…how dared he be so angry? She'd been the one going through the miscarriage. She could choose who she disclosed that information to.

But the way he'd looked at her had hurt the most. He'd shut down. Shut her out. The light and the vibrancy that she'd always seen in him had been extinguished. He hadn't even been able to look at her. And that had been her fault.

And now…now that she thought about it, she realised that he had a very disturbing effect on her. Even after all the intervening years she still found just looking at him made her mouth water, made her heart ache for more. Thinking about that kiss made her…

'Isabel? Dr Delamere?'

'Oh, sorry. I was miles away.' Now she couldn't even focus on her job properly. First and last time she'd let that happen. It was Maggie, one of the ward clerks. 'I have a message from Jacob. He wants to see you in his office, as soon as you can.'

'Oh, fine, thank you.' Isabel turned to excuse herself from her patient. 'I'm sorry, Susan, but Jacob's the boss around here, so I'd better get going. I'm off to Paris tomorrow for a conference with him. But I'm so glad we managed to get you on the road to recovery before I go.'

'Paris? Lucky you.' The new mum looked almost wistful.

'No. You have a husband and a lovely family. I'd say you are the luckier woman right now.' Isabel tried to put all thoughts of Sean out of her mind. Once upon a far-away innocent time she'd dreamt of having what Susan had: a husband and family. But the thought of risking her heart again left her more than cold. Terrified, in fact. She just knew she couldn't survive that kind of loss again.

So seven days away from Sean would be the perfect antidote. She could lose herself in the bright lights and the Christmas markets and the lovely amazingness that she'd heard Paris was—oh, yes, and she had work to do, at least, for the first few days. 'I'll pop in this evening,

Susan, to make sure you're okay before I head off. In the meantime, be good and rest up.'

Thinking about which boots to take with her to Paris…and deciding, oh, what the hell, she'd take all three pairs…she sauntered along the corridor to Jacob Layton's office. She was just about to tap under the Head Obstetrician sign on his door when she heard voices. Two men. Not happy.

What should she do? Knock and enter? Wait?

Ah, whatever, she'd been summoned, so she knocked.

'Isabel.' Jacob opened the door with a frown. He seemed flustered. Not his more recent relaxed self, but more a throwback to the days when he used to have the nurses quaking in their boots. Maybe things hadn't been going so smoothly with him and Bonnie. But they seemed fine, beyond happy even. Or…worst-case scenario, maybe he was sick again? The man had a habit of keeping too much to himself and not allowing others to share the load.

'Hi, Jacob.' Instinctively she put her hand out to his arm. 'Are you okay?'

'Yes. Fine.' He stepped back from her hand, looking a little alarmed. No, embarrassed.

'Are you sure? You look—'

'I'm absolutely fine. In all respects.' Not one to expand on anything personal, he gestured her to come into the office. 'But I need to talk to you…both.' He nodded towards Sean, who was standing at the far side of the office, looking out of the window, hands thrust into his trouser pockets. Everything about Sean's manner screamed irritation. Anger.

He turned. 'Isabel.'

'Sean.' So they were down to monosyllables. Okay,

she could live with that for the next five minutes. But, dang it, her heart had another idea altogether and tripped along merrily at the sight of him standing here in a dark-collared shirt and asset-enhancing charcoal trousers, all grumpy and angry and so very, very gorgeous. Why did he have to look so damned delicious?

He always looked delicious to her, she realised, with a sudden pang in her tummy. Even when he was angry. But that wasn't important, couldn't be important.

'Look. You're not going to like what I'm going to say. So…' Jacob beckoned them both to sit down '…I'm just going to cut to the chase, here.'

'Why? What's the problem?' Something inside Isabel's gut tumbled and tumbled. She looked from Jacob to Sean and back again.

Sean shrugged. 'We are. Apparently.'

Jacob shook his head. 'I'm sorry to say, I need to talk to you about an incident yesterday. An argument, be-tween the two of you.'

Blood rushed to her cheeks. Isabel couldn't believe it. She'd never had so much as a frown about her behav-iour, never mind being involved in an 'incident', as if she'd been rude or unprofessional or worse. It had been a private conversation, opening her very shattered heart. 'Someone complained about it? A patient?'

'No, not a patient.' Her boss looked a little red-faced. 'This meeting is unofficial and won't go down on your records, unless…well, let's just say, if you can resolve this situation amicably…'

'What situation?' Uh-huh. Of course. Sean hadn't been happy about what she'd told him yesterday, he felt betrayed and now he wanted to get his own back by get-ting her fired? Surely that was too underhanded even for him? That would be callous and bullying and very unlike the Sean she'd known. But she didn't know him now, really, did she? They'd been apart too long. He wouldn't…would he? She turned to look at him. 'Did you make a complaint, Sean?'

His blue eyes fired black. 'Don't be ridiculous. Of course not.'

Jacob's hands rose in a calming gesture. 'No, no, it wasn't Sean. It wasn't a complaint. *I* overheard a lot of arguing yesterday in the OR. Raised voices. Personal things were said. It made for unpleasant listening—which, I might add, was unavoidable and a few other people overheard too. The staff now think they're going to have to work in world war three, dodging bullets flying between you two.' Jacob leaned towards Isabel. 'I know I've been difficult, I know I can be a grouch, but I hope I never had cause to raise my voice or make everyone feel as if they couldn't work with me.'

He'd been sick, poor man, and had wanted to keep that to himself. He'd told no one and borne the weight of the department's needs along with his illness. He deserved a bloody medal. And yes, he'd been grumpy too, but things had changed—in his love life, mainly—and he was a lot happier now. And well again. The atmosphere in the department had become much more relaxed, until…

'So are you saying that people don't want to work with me? That it will be awkward?' Because of Sean? This was ridiculous. Never, ever, had her private life interfered with her work. Never. She was a professional. Her work was her life and she would not let anything get in the way of that. Damn Sean Anderson. Damn him for making her life hell all over again.

'No,' Jacob continued. 'I'm saying that I can't have my top obstetricians in such discord. You need to be able to assist each other, to work together at times. I want a harmonious atmosphere when I come to work. Not Armageddon. My staff deserve that, the patients certainly deserve that and so do you if you're going to do the job well.'

Sean nodded, and his reaction was surprising. 'Things got a little heated, I admit. It won't happen again.' She'd expected him to level the blame at her, but instead he wore it. He continued, 'We will be back to situation normal as soon as we leave this room. You have my word on it.' But Sean didn't look at her and she knew from the tightness in his shoulders and the taut way he held his body that he was livid, and only just about managing to keep it together in front of the boss.

And he was right, of course. They had to be normal and civil with each other, for the sake of their colleagues and their jobs. Their patients deserved the utmost professional conduct, not two senior doctors fighting over something that happened years ago.

But still…she didn't know if she could face him and be normal. Not after the way he'd looked at her. And definitely not after the kiss that still haunted her.

She needed time away from him, that was the answer. Although, she ignored the nagging voice in her head that told her that seventeen years apart from him hadn't made a huge difference to her attraction to him. This time she'd make it work. She'd erase him from her life. She'd go to Paris and teach herself all things Zen and meditate or something, she'd learn the huffy aloofness of Parisian women, she'd become sophisticated…

and she'd come back immune to his generally annoying attractiveness.

'Yes, you're both right. Things got out of hand and it won't happen again. You and I are off to Paris tomorrow, Jacob, so we can all put this episode behind us. When I get back things will very definitely be back to normal.' She felt better already.

Jacob scraped his chair back and stood, signalling the conversation was coming to an end and that he now wanted them to act on their word. 'Actually, Isabel, I need to talk to you about Paris. Unfortunately, something's come up and I can't go. I'm going to have to leave you to do the presentation on your own. I'm sorry.'

'Oh. Okay.' Not so bad. Paris on her own would be wonderful. Perhaps she could play hooky a little and do some sightseeing? Have a makeover?

Her boss scrutinised her reaction. 'You'll be fine, don't worry.'

'I'm not worried at all. It'll be great. But I thought you wanted to schmooze the SCBU ventilator manufacturers for some discounted prices?'

'I'm sure you can manage that just fine.' He started to walk them both to the door. 'And Sean will be on hand to help.'

Isabel screeched to a halt. 'What? Sean? What?'

Sean looked as incredulous as she did. 'What the hell…? Absolutely not. No way.'

Jacob shook his head to silence them. 'I need two representatives over there to handle the schmoozing requirements and networking meetings. You're both rostered on over Christmas when we're short-staffed, and currently we're a little top heavy—no one tends to take leave just before Christmas, it's a vacation dead zone.

So, it makes sense to send you together. I'll have the documentation transferred into your name by the end of today, Sean, and a synopsis of who you need to speak with and when. Who knows? A little *entente cordiale* might do you both some good.' Like hell it would. 'Really, I don't care. I just need two reps there and a harmonious atmosphere here. Got it?'

'No.' Isabel's mouth worked before her brain got into gear.

'No?' Jacob stared at her.

'I mean, yes.' No. She couldn't go with Sean. Four nights in Paris with her ex-lover who could heat her up with one look and freeze her bones with another. She needed space from him, not to be banished to a damned conference hotel with him. 'This is—'

Ridiculous. Painful. Harmful.

So, so stupid.

But if they couldn't sort it out amicably it would go down on their employment records—and who knew what else, a warning? No way. She wasn't going to let this ruin her, so yes, they needed to sort it out once and for all. But that meant she was going to be stuck with him in the famous city of love with harsh memories and increasing desires and a whole lot of tension, trying to sort out a situation that was far from normal.

'That is, if you don't kill each other first. Now, I'm running late for another meeting, so if you'll excuse me.' Jacob's word was final. 'Play nicely, children. I'll see you when you get back.'

CHAPTER THREE

'WHO THE HELL has a symposium just before Christmas?'
Sean lugged his duffle bag onto the train, threw it onto
the overhead rack and sat down opposite Isabel.

Angry as he was with the whole situation, he couldn't
help but note that she looked as pulled together as any
self-respecting Delamere girl would be. A dark fur-
trimmed hat sat on her head, her straight golden hair
flowing over her shoulders. A smattering of mascara
made her green eyes look huge and innocent, and her
cheeks had pinked up from the bitter north-easterly that
had whipped around them as they stood on the Eurostar
platform. A red coat covered her from neck to knee. At
her throat was a chain of what looked like diamonds.
They weren't fake. He knew her well enough to be sure
of that. She looked like an Eastern European princess
rather than a doctor.

And, despite himself and the rage still swirling round
his gut, he felt a pull to wrap her in his arms and warm
her up. *Damn it.*

She barely took her eyes away from the glossy magazine she was reading. 'It was originally planned for Sep-
tember, but had to be postponed because of a norovirus
outbreak at the hotel the day before it was due to start.

That's smack in the middle of conference season so all the other appropriately sized venues were already full. This was the only time they could rebook it. So we're stuck with it.' Now she lifted her head and glared at him. 'Like I'm stuck with you. But I won't let that spoil my time in Paris.'

She was angry with him? 'Whoa. Wait a minute. Let's backtrack a little…you're pissed with me because of what exactly? Because I don't remember me keeping any secrets from you for the last seventeen years.' The train was beginning to fill. People were taking seats further down the carriage, squealing about Christmas shopping, so yes, he knew this wasn't the time or the place.

But she answered him anyway, her voice quiet but firm. 'Sean, I apologised for that and I cannot do anything about it. You want to keep going over and over it, feel free but it won't change a thing.'

Her eyes clashed with his in a haughty, assertive glare. She was not going to move on this, he could see. But he could see more than that too. He could see how tired she was. How much she was hurting. How the proud stance was a show. And he felt like a jerk. She'd been through a traumatic time and had achieved so much despite it.

And how she had him feeling bad about this whole scenario he couldn't fathom.

Dragging a book from his backpack, he settled down. It would get easier, he asserted to himself, being with her. He'd get over the swing of emotions from anger to lust. He'd get bored of looking at her. Surely? He would stop being entranced by that gentle neckline, the dip at her throat where the diamonds graced the collarbone. He'd get tired of the scent…expensive perfume, he guessed, but it was intoxicating nonetheless, sort of exotic and flowers and something else. *Her…*

Now, where was he…? Ah, yes…neonatal emergencies…distraction therapy.

As the train jerked to depart she closed her magazine and gazed out of the window. Luckily the seats beside them were free; they had the four-berth area to themselves. 'I've never been to Paris before.'

For a minute he thought she was talking to herself, then he realised it was actually an attempt at a civil conversation. Fine, they were in a public place. He could do civil just to get through the two-and-a-half-hour journey. But that would be as far as it went. 'It's a great place. I went a few years ago, when I did my gap year. I travelled around Europe for a bit.'

An eyebrow rose. 'I didn't know you did a gap year?'

'There are lots of things you don't know about me, Isabel. There are years and years of my life you know nothing about, and you've spent the last couple of months that I've been here running in the opposite direction whenever I'm around too. Hardly surprising you know nothing at all.'

'I know.' Tugging off her coat and hat, she plumped up her hair and looked at him. 'I'm sorry. After what I told you yesterday you'll understand that I just couldn't deal with you being back in my life again.'

Guilt could do that to you, he mused. 'And now?'

She shrugged a delicate shoulder. 'Now I don't have a choice. Thanks to Jacob.'

'Indeed. So let's make a deal, shall we?'

'Depends what it is?'

'We'll attend this conference as a team to represent the department. But after that, in our downtime, you don't get in my way and I won't get in yours.' That should do it. No cosy dinners, no shared intimacies. He could revisit some old haunts, discover new ones. On his own. He stuck out a hand.

'Fine by me.' She took it, her eyes widening at the shot of something that zipped between them as their palms touched. Heat burnt her cheeks as, with equal force, it seared through him, wild and unbidden, shocking in its intensity. For a moment she locked eyes again with him; this time he saw fire there. Then she let go and wiped her palm down her trousers as if trying to erase any trace of him from her skin. 'So, what are you going to do? In Paris? Do you have plans?'

'Oh, we're doing polite chit-chat? The ever-so-charming Delamere dialogue?'

All heat extinguished in a second, her glare intensified. 'Gosh, you really do hate me and my family, don't you?'

'Isla's sweet.' He let the insult by omission sit with her for a moment. What was that line between love and hate? He knew he was straddling something of equal measure. He wanted her, and he didn't want her. Too much either way, it was disturbing. 'I was actually referring to the way you smooth over any difficult social encounter. How easy it is for you to glide seamlessly from one meaningless subject to the next.'

'Then you don't know me at all either, Sean. You think you do, but whatever misapprehensions you have about me, they're wrong. I'm not like my mum and dad. I never was. I used to hate being paraded in front of the cameras and the elite with a begging bowl for whichever charity they favoured that month. Don't get me wrong,

I loved the causes they were fighting for, but I always felt awkward and embarrassed to be there.'

He kept his face passive. 'I thought I knew you. I always believed you were polar opposites to your parents.' And even though he'd consoled himself over the years that she had just resorted to Delamere type and turned her back on him, here she was challenging him. Because he'd seen her in action, the compassion and the dedication. Truth was, he didn't know her at all now, not really. He knew what she'd once been, but the young, bright Isabel Delamere didn't exist any more—he was learning that very quickly.

And the other unpalatable truth was that he was intrigued by her. He'd found out her secret and should have packed his bags—job done, history exposed—and put her and Cambridge behind him. But now he was in forced proximity with her and, well…she was a whole new fully realised version of the girl he'd known—a more professional, more intense, more dedicated version. It wouldn't hurt to learn just a little bit more. For old times' sake. 'I guess the Delamere name would have helped your job prospects no end, though.'

They were interrupted briefly by a waiter bringing the Chablis and cheese platter Sean had ordered on boarding.

Even though they were at loggerheads she still accepted a glass of wine from him. Took a sip. Then answered, 'Just like you I got where I am by sheer hard work. My name didn't open any doors for me. Once out of the State of Victoria no one's heard of Daddy—well, a few have but no one cares. He's a neurosurgeon too, which isn't very helpful to someone who wants a job in obstetrics.'

'It can't have hindered you, though.'

She shook her head. 'Whatever you want to believe, you clearly have it all worked out. But in reality I'm just bloody good at my job. I certainly don't have to prove myself to you; my competence is between me, and my patients. Who, I might say, have ranged from a pre-eclampsic mum in Kiwirrkurra, to a too-posh-to-push minor British royal and everything in between. So get off your high horse, Anderson, and give me a break.'

'You worked in Kiwirrkurra? I didn't know that. Impressive.' Kiwirrkurra had to be one of the most remote areas in the country so up-to-date technology and equipment would have been lacking, not to mention the barren, dry heat that shrouded the place. Not many would have been able to cope with the workload and unpredictability of outback medicine. It was the desert, for God's sake; somehow he just couldn't imagine Isabel there. 'How the hell did you keep your diamonds free from all that red dust? Must have been a nightmare.'

'Well, I didn't take—' She paused…looked at him… shook her head again, eyes rolling. 'You're pulling my chain. Ha-bloody-ha. Well, let me tell you, it was *so-o-o* hard, the dust got everywhere, and I mean, everywhere. I had to polish my diamonds every night before I went to bed.'

'Yeah?'

'Nah.' But there was a smile there. It glittered, lit up her face. And for the first time since he'd been in this hemisphere it felt as if there was a breakthrough between them. Tiny, compared to what they'd had years ago—or at least what he'd thought they'd had—but it was something they could hang the next week on instead of all this anger-fuelled bile. She laughed then. 'Well, you still know how to wind me up, I'll give you that.'

'Too easy, mate. Too easy.'

She had some more wine. 'Tell me about your gap year.'

How to capture the wealth of experiences in one conversation? 'It wasn't much different from a lot of people's to be honest. I took the year off between university and internship. Went to India to do some volunteer work at a community hospital—went for a month, stayed ten. Then took two months to see some of Europe.'

Her eyebrows rose. 'Must have been interesting, India?'

He laughed. 'Interesting is definitely one way to describe it. It was hard, harrowing, enlightening and liberating too. Maternal death rates are diabolical. Infant mortality's the same...all for the sake of a little bit of knowledge and some simple resources. Running water would be a good start.'

'You always were altruistically minded. You wanted to save the world. You wanted to achieve so much. And clearly you have. Do you remember when we—?'

'Anyway, when I was in Paris...' He cut her off, not wanting to do any of that Memory Lane stuff. He didn't want to remember that all-consuming passion they'd shared—for life, for their futures, for each other. The soft way she'd curled around him, the kisses. She might have let her guard down a little but he needed to make sure that his was firmly in place.

She'd already shattered his heart once—offered no explanation at the time and expected him to accept the new status quo, her rules: no questions asked. What were the chances she'd changed? Very little. And maybe she was right, maybe he didn't know her now, but he knew she was all but married to her job. He knew she could be single-minded when she wanted. And, if her actions at sixteen were anything to go by, she didn't allow anyone into that private part of herself. Not really.

So yes, while he could be convivial and keep the peace and put up a decent social front, he was better to be always on guard when it came to Isabel Delamere.

'Best thing about these conferences is the extra-curriculars, right?' Phil, the man sitting on her left, a portly GP from Hastings, nudged Isabel's side with a conspiratorial wink and clinked his glass against hers. All around the long wooden table people swirled and sipped and laughed and chatted in a dozen different languages trying to identify flavours that Isabel was sure shouldn't be in wine. *Petrol? Asparagus?*

'Yes. Well, I guess so. This is particularly fun. Any excuse for drink.' Although, she'd probably had quite enough on the train. Any more and she might lose her good-sense filter. Thankfully they'd had check-in at the hotel and registration for the conference before coming out on this delegates' do, so she hoped the lunchtime wine had cleared her system. The only downside to the trip so far—apart from Sean's presence—had been finding out that his room was next door to hers, so any downtime activities he'd be having in the City of Love had better not take place in their hotel. She did not want to hear that through the walls.

'Ah…' The man next to her laughed. 'I detect a funny accent. Aussie, are you? Or Kiwi? I can never tell the difference.'

She gave her new friend a smile. 'No one ever can outside of the southern hemisphere, apparently, but we are very proud of our differences. And our wines. I'm Australian.'

'It's a bit like the league of nations here—that guy over there, Manuel, he's from Spain and Natalie's from Belgium.'

'Nice to meet you.' It was lovely to be surrounded by such a diverse group of people. Phil seemed pleasant enough, but even though Sean thought she was the queen of small talk Isabel just didn't feel in the mood tonight, which kind of went against the whole conference spirit. Thank goodness Phil wasn't one of the people she needed to schmooze, because schmoozing was the furthest thing from tonight's wish list.

Before she got embroiled in any more conversation she looked down the table to the woman standing at the end leading the wine-tasting, and noticed things were getting started again. 'Oh, she's talking. All this swilling and sniffing… I'm never going to get the hang of this.' Isabel listened intently and tried to think about the taste of biscuits and did Madame really say pomegranate? Isabel wasn't sure she could taste anything other than, well…wine. But she wasn't going to admit that.

It was lovely. It was. The wine was delicious, pomegranate or not. The atmosphere in the ancient stone wine cellar—*le cave*—was cosy and lighthearted. She was in Paris! She'd had a glimpse of the Eiffel Tower, and the amazing old buildings and the Seine River and it all looked breathtakingly beautiful, like a film set. She should have felt on top of the world to be here. Drinking wine. Lots and lots of different kinds of wine, with clever, articulate people. But something was niggling her.

And he was sitting to her right.

All six feet one inch of dark and distracting niggle.

By some cruel twist of fate the organisers had placed him next to her. Which did not adhere to the *keep out of my way* game plan. The seating had been arranged so they were all squashed in along narrow benches that meant that she couldn't forget him. She could feel him. Couldn't keep out of his angry gaze. Couldn't ignore him chatting up the beautiful French midwife on his right.

Brunette. Stacked. Young. Hanging, open-mouthed, on his every word. The dashing, antipodean doctor with stories of daring deliveries in deepest Rajasthan. Damn him. It was hard not to listen, as Isabel, too, was mesmerised by a history she knew nothing of.

'"*Rabies!*" my colleague was shouting. "This camel has rabies, get me off, I want a different one!"' Sean was entertaining their half of the table now. His smile engaging, his drawl lilting and captivating. 'He was half sliding, half scrambling round this poor animal's neck in his hurry to get off it. I told him not to be such an idiot. It wasn't rabies—male camels foam at the mouth to attract mates. "He's not sick," I said. "He just fancies you, mate." You should have seen his face…'

I could have been there, Isabel thought to herself. They'd planned volunteer work abroad. They'd planned a future. And instead of listening to his adventures she would have been the one retelling them. Oh, damn…this wine was going to her head and making her maudlin.

Paris, she reminded herself. *I am a Parisian woman. I care not for ze ex.*

The very beautiful Frenchwoman at his side seemed to have forgotten her haughty Gallic woman-warrior roots and was flicking her long bouncy curls in a very flirty way as she tilted her head back and laughed at Sean's story.

'Very good. Very funny.' Isabel patted Sean's arm and gave the brunette a hard stare before flicking her own hair and snagging her fingers in it. 'Ouch. I...mean... Can you please pass the crackers?'

Flicking and flirting were way out of her comfort zone. She made a mental note to practise in the comfort of her hotel bedroom.

'Of course.' Sean turned around and gave her a weird look as she dragged her fingers through a knot and grimaced, before he flashed her a lovely wide smile. And she was the only one in the room who knew it didn't have an ounce of authenticity to it. 'What do you think of the wine, Isabel? As good as back home?'

'Oh, I don't know...' She looked at her surroundings, breathing in the age-old aroma of fermenting grapes and oak barrels, and sighed. 'There's something about Paris... Sacrilege, I know, but everything seems better here.'

'Even me?' This time his grin was real. And her gut tightened in response. He was joking with her, and she was aware that she'd drunk more than her fair share of wine, so yes...he did seem a teensy bit better. Not that she was about to admit to that.

The newly adopted Frenchwoman in her wanted to throw him a disdainful shrug as if he were but crumbs on ze floor, but the Aussie in her came out fighting. 'Ah, Seany Boy, I don't want to burst your bubble, but there's only so much that grog goggles can enhance.' And so that had been a little over-loud and rather more matey than she intended.

His voice again, close to her ear. Too close. Was it hot

in here? 'Are you okay, Isabel? It's been a long day. You look a bit flushed. You sound a little…tense.'

Hardly surprising under the circumstances. 'I'm fine, thank you for asking.' The wine-tasting woman was handing out small glasses of something that looked like cough syrup. That made how many glasses they'd each consumed? Isabel didn't dare to think. 'Too much of this, I guess. I'd better be careful.'

'Spoilsport. We're in France—you need to chill a little.' He swirled the stem of his glass before he looked at her again. 'Vivienne and a few of the others are thinking of going to a club after this…'

'Vivienne?'

His confused frown deepened as he flicked his thumb to the woman on his right. 'Yes, Vivienne. She's from Aix-en-Provence.'

'Lucky her. She's very pretty.'

He shrugged. 'Yes, she is.'

A pang of something Isabel didn't want to acknowledge, but knew damned well was jealousy, arrowed through her tummy. He wasn't hers to pine after. She'd made sure of that years ago, and to hammer that message home she'd spilled her secret to him and watched any kind of hope shrivel. 'Well, have fun. At the club. With Vivienne.'

He grinned, eyes darting to the long dark tresses, the flicking. 'I intend to.'

I bet you do. Irritation rising from her stomach in a tight, hard ball of acid, Isabel tried to wriggle her feet out from under the table, which was easier said than done. 'Really? You can't wait until I've gone?'

'What the hell…' he growled, his voice hard and low, '…has it got to do with you?'

'Because…' *It hurts. Because*—she realised with a sharp sting in her chest—*I want you to look at me like that, as if you're anticipating a delicious treat.*

Definitely too much wine.

The best idea would be to leave him to it. Really, the best idea would have been not to allow him to come in the first place. No, the best idea… She sighed. Why was it that the best ideas always happened after the event? She finally managed to get her feet out from the bench and tried to stand up, wobbling a little, then losing her balance in her new high-heeled suede boots. 'Oops.'

Quick as a flash he caught her by the arm and steadied her. 'Are you okay?'

'Oh, for goodness' sake, I just wobbled. I'm fine.' But she wasn't, not now. At the touch of his hand on her bare skin, desire fired through her. It had been so long since she'd felt it, so alien to her, it was a shock. All at once her body craved more touching. More touching him. More everything.

Oh, God. She looked at his broad chest covered in a crisp white collared shirt. At the model-worthy jawline. At that smiling mouth that seemed to mock and tease and was still so damned kissable. At those dark eyes boring into her. But most of all she felt his heat against hers. And she realised, with even more disbelief, that she wanted Sean Anderson in her bed.

Which was…well, it was surprising. Ever since she'd lost the baby her sexual experience had been marred by a deep-seated fear of getting pregnant; she'd been uptight and never really enjoyed herself. And she'd always felt, strangely, as if she was betraying Sean. So she hadn't really explored that side of herself.

Of all the idiotic things. Of all the pointless want-

ing… She could not want him. After all, he'd made it
very clear that he didn't want her at all. And who could
blame him?

But it was happening. And not only that, his breath
was whispering across her neck sending more and more
shivers across her body. 'Do you need a hand getting
home, Izzy?'

She edged away from the heat. 'Not at all. I'm a big
girl now. Besides, don't you have *la belle* Vivienne from
Aix-en-Provence to consider? I don't want to cramp your
style.'

He blew out an irritated breath. 'Really?'

'Yes. Really.' She could hear her voice rising and
struggled to keep it low and steady so the others couldn't
hear, particularly the hair-flicking lady. 'I'm just saying
what I see. It's clear as day that you have plans for later.
And we all love extra-curriculars, right?'

Sean's hand dropped from Isabel's arm and she could
sense the rage rippling through him. His eyes darkened
beyond black. His voice was hushed but angry. 'You
made it very clear a long time ago that there was nothing you wanted from me. What the hell do you expect
me to do? Keep hanging on? Because I will not do that,
Isabel, I have my own life to live. I won't wait around
for you to decide what you want.'

'I'm not asking you to.'

'Funny, because that's not how it seems to me. You
don't want me to go with Vivienne? You don't want me
to have fun, that's for sure.'

'Never in your wildest dreams, Sean Anderson,
would I ever want anything from you. It's too late for
that, way too late.'

'And whose fault is that?'

As if she didn't know already.

His words were like daggers in her heart. And he was so close, too close. His mouth in kissing distance— which was such an inappropriate thought right now, but there it was. Her heart thumped in a traitorous dance.

'Whatever. Go, do what you like. I'm leaving now anyway.' Biting back her anger as much as she could, Isabel looked from Sean to Vivienne to the rest of the table, who were grinning in the candlelight and had no idea of the shared history and the huge amount of balls it was taking just to be here with him at all.

She needed to get away from him. To put their past life far behind her. To put this new attraction back where it couldn't hurt her. Who'd have thought it, but after seventeen years of fighting she needed to get over Sean Anderson all over again. And fast.

CHAPTER FOUR

TWENTY MINUTES AND a decent dose of fresh cold Parisian air later, Isabel was feeling much more in control. The walk—or rather, the angry stamp—back to the hotel allowed a good view of the Eiffel Tower down the Champs de Mars, and oh, what a spectacular light show as it changed colours; red and green like a Christmas tree, then the tricolour and then so many different colours it was enchanting…or it probably was to anyone else, but everything was tainted with their stupid argument and the feelings of jealousy and hopelessness raging through her.

Added to the glorious sight of the Eiffel Tower there were strings and strings of twinkling Christmas lights draped along the street lampposts and trees, giving the whole place a really magical atmosphere. She'd never been anywhere cold at Christmas so this year was going to be a first. It was already breathtaking—or might have been if she hadn't been struggling for a calming breath anyway. If she wasn't mistaken there was a hint of snow, too, in the cool breeze that whipped around her cheeks and blasted Sean from her skin.

Just about.

She decided not to think about him any more. She

was in France to enjoy herself, so that was what she would do.

Except…she couldn't get him out of her head. Annoying man! Annoying hormones that made her want him and want to run from him at the same time.

The claw-foot bathtub in her en-suite was just about overflowing with lavender-scented bubbles, a small nightcap of red wine was sitting on the window ledge, and if she craned her neck to the left she could see the street Christmas lights from the bathroom window.

A quick bath. A peruse of her presentation, then bed. If she could sleep at all with her emotions still coating everything she did. She slipped the white fluffy bathrobe off and stepped one foot into the warm water, stiffening quickly at the sharp rap on her door.

Probably housekeeping. Or room service—not that she'd asked for anything. But who else would it have been at this time of night?

Sean?

And there was a mind meld of thought process. Unlikely—Sean was out with a beautiful woman.

Another knock.

Ignoring the mysterious tachycardia and excitement roaring through her, she told herself not to be so stupid; it was probably someone knocking on the wrong door. She wrapped the bathrobe around herself again, and pattered one dry, one wet foot to the door. Through the little eyeglass she could see a man. *Sean.*

No. Not when she'd managed to flush him to the darkest corner of her brain. Not when she was pretty much naked. Not when she'd realised that these lurching feelings about him were a heady combination of guilt and lust. Which had to be the worst kind of concoction of

hormones, surely? Especially when the lust was not re-
ciprocated and the guilt just made him glare at her with
anger in his eyes. What did he want now? To gloat?
What to do?

Pretend she was asleep? Yes. Good idea. She turned
her back to the door and held her breath. He would go
away. She would sleep. She would be fine tomorrow.

'Izzy?' The knocking recommenced. 'Isabel, for
God's sake, woman, open the door.'

Starting to feel a bit light-headed from holding her
breath, she very slowly let the air from her lungs and
said nothing.

'Isabel… You are the worst liar in the world.'

'What?' Man, he really did know how to wind her
up. Irritation now skittering down her spine, she threw
open the door. 'What the hell are you talking about?'

'You. You were pretending not to be here.'

'I was not. And please be quiet, you'll wake the neighbours.'

'I am the neighbours.' Shaking his head, he gave her
a sort of smirk that made her heart patter and her breath
hitch. 'You were standing at the door, you saw who it
was and you pretended not to be here. Don't deny it. I
saw the shadows changing under the door frame.'

Busted. 'So, why are you here? Seeing as you hate
the air I breathe.'

'You know why. You don't get to talk to me like that.
To make me think…' He scuffed a hand through his hair
and shook his head. Exasperated.

'What?'

'That there's unfinished business here.'

She swallowed through a dry throat. 'What do you
mean? Unfinished business?'

'For God's sake, Isabel, you know exactly what I mean. We have to deal with this.'

She shook her head. She was so confused, her head muddled with the unending ache and so many conflicting thoughts. 'I remember that we agreed to stay out of each other's way. I remember you were going to go and have fun. Why aren't you out at a club? Vivienne seemed very interested in going, and particularly with you, if all that hair flicking was anything to go by.'

'I don't care about Vivienne.' Without seeming to give any thought to how this looked, or what she thought about it, he stepped into the room, his presence filling the space. *God,* he looked amazing, all wrapped up in a scarf and heavy coat, his cheeks flushed with cold and his hair peaky. Eyes glittering with emotions, ones that she couldn't quite read but she was pretty sure were rage. And desire. Oh, yes, she could see that. Maybe he was still thinking about Vivienne?

'She'll be very upset.'

'I doubt that very much.' He looked at her, his impassioned gaze running from her hair—all shoved up into a messy clip on top of her head—to her throat, then to her white bathrobe, and lower.

Heat prickled all over her like a rash. How could a man make her feel so…so turned on with just a look? He reached for the top of her robe and ran his fingertips across the fabric, touching, ever so minutely, her skin. Pulled the robe tighter across her body.

Standing here, almost naked but for one very precarious item of clothing, she felt set alight. Swallowing was hard. Speaking, finding words, even harder. He was so close and all she could smell was him and the lavender and Paris. He was so close she could have…might have…kissed him, invited him into her bath. To her bed. Her heart. Then she remembered.

Stepping away she snarled, because it was the only thing she could manage, 'You're drunk.'

'Don't be ridiculous.' And, truth be told, he looked about as sober as she'd ever seen him. He pulled the robe tighter across her chest, covering up her exposed skin. 'Do you think I'd only come here if I was drunk?'

'I can't see any reason why you'd come here at all. You hate me, Sean, you've made that very clear.'

He frowned, stalked to the console, poured a glass of red wine and sank half of it in one gulp. 'I don't hate you, Isabel. I just hate what happened—there's a big difference.'

'You said you couldn't bear to look at me.' She hauled in a breath, two; every moment she spent with him had her fired up one way or another. 'As far as you're concerned I lied to you, betrayed you, and that is unforgivable, no matter what I went through.'

He slammed the glass down. 'You think betrayal is excusable?'

'Yes, given the circumstances.'

'The circumstances were that I loved you, Isabel. You meant everything to me. And you said the same to me, over and over. *We* created that baby.' His jaw set. 'I guess that counted for nothing? You just cast me aside.'

She felt his dismissal keenly in her chest, ricocheting over her heart, remorseless. She'd known he loved her; that knowledge had carried her for a long time. It had allowed her to excuse what she'd done in the name of protection, of love. It had allowed her to function. To grieve, and to heal. 'Your love was everything to me and, God knows, I loved you too, Sean. More than you could imagine.'

'So, that's why you kept the truth from me? Why you refused to even speak to me?'

'Yes, actually it was.' She stepped closer to him, her hand on his chest. Because she wanted to touch him one last time, because she knew there was no coming back from this. How could there be? There was too much looming between them. Too much past, too much hurt. Too much for them ever to surmount. Too much lost love. 'What was the point in ruining two lives?'

'Knowing what you were going through, what we'd lost, wouldn't have ruined my life—don't you get it? It could have made us stronger. You just didn't give us a chance. You didn't give me a chance. You shut down, hibernated your life, ran away from any contact.'

'I was protecting myself.'

'That was my job,' he growled. The rest of the wine went down his throat. 'For the first time in your life you did exactly what your parents taught you to do, Isabel, you put on a mask and pretended all the pain had gone, that you were just fine. And by doing that you closed yourself off from anyone who might help you.' He moved away from her hand as if it were a dagger, a threat. 'What a waste. What a bloody shame.'

'Yes. Yes, it is. Because you're right, what we had was special and I regret not letting you in, more than anything. Happy now?'

'You think hearing that makes me happy?'

She waved towards the door, trying not to show how much his rejection hurt on the back of so much need. She just ached to feel his arms around her, to taste him again, to make everything right between them. And it would never happen. Not now. 'There isn't any more to say. Go. Please. Just leave me alone.'

'Fine.' He stalked to the door. As he pressed down the handle he rested his forehead against the wood, took a minute to regulate his breathing. Then he turned dark eyes on her. He held her gaze for longer than anyone had ever looked at her. She saw flashes of gold in there, anger. Pain. Desire. A struggle with all three. 'What did you mean, earlier, when you asked me to wait until you'd left before I went to the club?'

Her heart hammered against her breastbone in a panicked beat. 'Nothing. I didn't mean anything by it. I'd had too much wine.' But he knew exactly what she'd meant. That she still had feelings for him. That she wanted to be the woman he took home tonight, not Vivienne.

'And now?'

'Now what?' Dangerous. Heat skittered through her abdomen. Lower.

He stepped closer and grabbed her wrist, pulling her to him, his eyes wild now, his breath quick, his growing hardness apparent. Despite everything, he wanted her.

Her ragged breathing stalled. All the tension and emotion bundled into her fists and she grabbed his coat lapels, her mouth inches from his.

For God's sake, leave.

It made no sense to Sean that he wanted to hate Isabel Delamere, but couldn't. She peered up at him with questions in her eyes. And he didn't know the answers. Couldn't tell her any more than that he was crazy with the seesawing of his head, the push-pull of attraction.

As she reached for his coat her robe fell open a little and he looked away, not willing to glimpse something so intimate. He did not want to be intimate with her; he knew what price that came with. And it was way too high for him—long, long years of getting over her. But too late, he'd caught sight of creamy skin, a tight nipple bud. And a riot of fresh male hormones arrowed to his groin.

He needed to get out.

That was about as far as his thoughts went as he lowered his mouth. She gasped once she realised what he was offering. Then her lips were on his and his brain shut down.

The kiss was slow at first, testing. A guttural mewl as his tongue pressed against her closed mouth. But when she opened to him the groan was very definitely his. The push of her tongue against his caused a rush of blood and heat away from his brain and very fast headed south. She tasted divine. She tasted of wine and sophistication. Of anger and heat. She did not taste like he remembered, a sixteen-year-old girl fresh from school. She was different, hot, hungry, and very definitely all grown woman. And he wanted to feast on her.

'Oh, God, Isabel…' Dragging his mouth from hers, he kissed a trail down to the nape of her neck, his fingers grazed the edge of the robe and he slid his hand onto the bare skin of her waist and drew her closer. She softened against him with a moan and everything finally made sense. This was what he needed. *She* was what he needed. The chaos swirling in his chest cemented into a stark hunger as he slid fingers over silken skin.

She pulled back with a smile. 'Wait a minute… I'm here wearing relatively nothing, and you're dressed for an igloo. Too. Many. Clothes.' She unwound his scarf and threw it to the floor, pushed his coat from his shoulders and let it fall. Her hands stalled at his shoulders; she stroked the thick fabric of his shirt, down his arms to his hands, which she clasped into hers. 'I can't believe…after all this time…is it what you want? Am I, what you want?'

'Do you even need to ask?' He pulled her back to him, felt her melt against his body as he plundered her sweet mouth. The smell of her drove him wild, but the taste of her pushed him close to a place he'd never been before. God, yes, he wanted her, wanted to be inside her, to hear her moan his name, to feel her around him.

She wound her hands around his neck and pulled him closer, grinding her hips against his. He had no doubt that she wanted him as much as he wanted her, and that stoked even more heat in his belly.

Unable to resist any longer, he dragged the bathrobe from her shoulders and lay her down on the bed as she fumbled with his shirt, dragging it over his head. He kicked off shoes and socks, dragged down his jeans and then they were naked. Like all those years ago. But this was not the same. She was not the same. And he had so much more experience now—no clumsy fumblings, no teenage angst. He knew how to please a woman and he intended to please Isabel.

Taking a moment, he gazed at her face, at the kiss-swollen lips, and misted eyes. At the soft, sexy smile that spurred him on, that made him weak-kneed. Then he looked lower, wanting to feast his gaze on a body that he hadn't seen in seventeen years. And to learn about her. To relearn what she liked. To acquaint himself with the new dips and curves, with the smooth, silky feel of her skin. The perfect breasts, a tight belly that belied a miscarriage, that a baby had been inside her.

His baby.

At once he was filled with profound and gut-wrenching emotion—she'd been through too much on her own. He should have been there with her. He should have done something. He should have known—somewhere deep within himself he should have intuitively known that she was suffering, that a part of him was inside her and broken. That she'd carried that guilt around with her for all these years, too afraid to speak of it, too scarred to share it. Until he'd pushed her...that secret was theirs, only theirs.

The emotion had a name—he didn't want to think about it.

Pushing a curl of hair behind her ear, he gave her a gentle kiss on her mouth. 'Izzy, we can't do this.'

CHAPTER FIVE

'YOU'RE FREAKING KIDDING ME, right?' Isabel drew away from the best kiss of her entire life and took a deep breath. 'What do you mean? You just said you wanted to…'

'I do want to. I just don't think we should. It's late. We're probably drunk. We have to work tomorrow. And there's too much baggage and history that sits right here.' He pointed to the space between them. 'Getting in the way.'

Instead of feeling frustrated, she felt a rush of affection. God love him, he was trying to do right by her. And okay, well, she had to admit there was a teeny hint of frustration there. Wriggling closer to him, she smiled, relishing the touch of hot bare skin against hers. 'Oops, that baggage and history just got squashed under my gargantuan ar—'

'Whoa, Izzy.' His eyes lit up, the darkness she'd seen momentarily before now gone, replaced with humour and heat. 'I've never seen you like this before.'

'I've never felt like this before.' It was true. Suddenly so hot, so alive and fired up, Isabel stroked down his naked chest. Abs that she'd never seen before, honed to perfection. Arms so muscled and strong that she felt featherlight and ethereal in his embrace. A sun-kissed chest she wanted to shelter against, to kiss, to lick… She'd never wanted a man so much in her whole life. Truth was, she'd never stopped wanting him.

He was right. What a waste of all those years. Of running and hiding and trying to cover up real deep-down feelings. Of being so, so frightened of falling in love and risking her heart all over again. 'Don't stop. We *can* do this. We can do what we want. Don't wrap me up in cotton wool, Sean. Don't treat me any differently to any of your other—'

'There are no others.'

'Liar.' She knew he was attractive to every damned woman he gave five minutes' attention to and knew, too, through the MMU grapevine, that he had a history of breaking hearts. Couldn't commit. Never gave a reason why.

'No. Not any more.' He frowned but his hand stroked the underside of her breast, sending shivers of desire rippling through her. How could she have lived her whole life never having him again? How could she have survived? Being in his gaze felt as if she'd come home to a warm cocoon after being out in a freezing wilderness. Sure, there were things to work out. A lot of things. But right now, in this room at this moment, it felt so right to be with him.

'And Vivienne?'

'For goodness' sake. She is nothing to me.'

'In that case…' she pressed a kiss onto his creased forehead '…forget the past.'

Then, she pressed a finger to his mouth to prevent him from speaking as she kissed each of his eyelids. 'You don't know me. Not really. You don't know who I am, what I want, what I need.' Her finger ran along the top of his lip; she laughed as he tried to nip it with his teeth. 'Or what I like, Sean.'

'Izzy…' There was a warning in his voice.

'This. Is. New. Everything starts from now.' A kiss onto the tip of his nose. 'Hi, my name is Isabel. *Isabel*, not Izzy. I am an obstetrician and I live in Cambridge, England. I'm here in Paris at a conference and I want to have some extracurricular fun.'

Then she licked across his lips, hungry, greedy for his mouth. 'I'm very, very pleased to meet you.' Her hand stroked down his stomach towards a very-pleased-to-see-her erection. She touched the tip and enjoyed the sound his throat made as he growled her name in warning.

'Isabel, you want to watch what you do with that. It's got a mind of its own.'

'How very convenient.' She bent and licked the tip, then took him full into her mouth ignoring his protestations, and pushing him back against the duvet. She could feel he was holding back a thrust so she sucked down his length again and again, his throaty groans spurring her on. She loved the taste of him, the hard length. She loved that she could make him feel so good.

'Izzy.' His hand grasped her hair and she stopped. 'Isabel. You'd better stop.'

As she paused he shifted position, edging away from her grasp and sucking a nipple into his mouth. Heat shimmied through her. She arched her back, greedy for more, for his mouth on her body, on every part. Hot and wet. His fingers now on her thigh, higher, deeper, sinking into her core. And she was kissing him again, exploring this new taste that was laced with an old memory.

His smell that was different yet familiar. His touch...
my God, his touch was expert now. He knew just how
to take her to the edge and tease. His erection was dangerously, enticingly close, nudging against her opening.

'You still like this?' He pressed a fingertip into her
rib and she screamed.

'Stop that! No tickling. Kiss me.' She didn't want to
relive anything; she wanted to create new experiences,
to build fresh memories. She didn't want to look backwards. She wanted...she wanted him inside her. For a
second she was serious, the most serious she'd been in
a long time. Made sure she looked deep into his eyes
and told him the truth. There had been too many lies
between them. 'I want you, Sean. I want you so much.'

'Back at ya, kiddo.' This new kiss was slow and hard,
Sean taking his time as he stoked a fire that had smoul-
dered over the last year, burst into roaring flames over
the last week and was now burning out of control. She
moved against him, feeling the pressure of him, hot and
hard, against her thigh.

'Condom?' he groaned, his forehead against hers.
Eyes gazing down at her, startling in their honesty.

'Yes.' She held his gaze. The last time they'd done
this had ended in such heartbreak. Was it so stupid to be
doing it again? To risk everything once more?

He touched her cheek as if he could read her thoughts,
his smile genuine, so loving and tender it almost cracked
her heart. When had he become so thoughtful? So sexy
and so within reach? When had he become so expert at
knowing what a woman needed? When had he changed?
Her throat filled because she knew the answer: in those
wilderness years, without her.

His voice was soft yet filled with affection that went

deeper than sex. 'It's okay, Isabel, it won't happen again. I won't let it happen again.'

Neither would she. 'Of course.' And if a baby did happen again she would tell him, she wouldn't hide anything from him. This time she'd be honest. 'In my...in my bag.'

'In my wallet.' He reached down, took out a foil, and slipped on the condom. Then he was pushing into her, slow and gentle, and she felt him fill her. So perfect. So complete. She wrapped her legs around his backside to feel him deeper. Harder.

'Oh, my God, Isabel. You are so perfect. So beautiful.' He began slow thrusts, his fists holding her wrists above her head, snatching greedy, playful bites at her nipples and her breasts. She felt captured, captivated, possessed by him. This man. This wondrous man whom she had broken as much as she was broken. And yet he put her back together again with this act.

The moves changed and the air charged. He stopped the playfulness as he kissed her hot and hard and wet. Sensation after sensation pulsed through her. She was hanging on by a thin thread. His body tensed; she could feel pressure rising as she met him thrust for thrust, joining the rhythm as he picked up pace.

His eyes didn't leave hers. His hands didn't release hers. And as they both shuddered to climax—releasing the tension coiled so deep between them for so long— she wished, *God* how she wished, she had never let him go.

'Well, wow.' Sean shifted to Isabel's side and stroked her cheek. It was the first time he'd seen her looking so bone-deep relaxed. 'I wasn't expecting that.'

'Me neither.' She shuffled into the crook of his arm,

blonde hair splayed out over the pillow. 'That was very lovely, thank you.'

'Your manners are impeccable. Daddy would be proud. You sound very English all of a sudden.' He pretended to look under the duvet. 'Where's my Aussie girl gone?'

'I'm still here.' She stroked fingertips gently down his chest, her voice a whisper. 'I'm here.'

'So you are.' Something he'd never believed possible had been possible. He tipped her chin and kissed her again. She returned the kiss eagerly. It had been amazing and surprising that intensity went so deep. A dream. Something he'd imagined for years. Making love into the night, no reason to leave. Hours and hours stretched ahead of them. Days, years. A lifetime. He'd never had the chance to do this before. Time together had been so limited, snatched moments that had ended in disaster.

He felt frustration begin to roll through him. But tried to push it back.

He wondered when he'd be able to stop thinking about the baby. The lie. He wondered if he'd ever be able to truly move on now that he knew, and he realised that moving on was something Isabel had been trying to do when she'd moved to Cambridge. It wasn't to get away from him; it was to restart her life.

So lying in bed with him probably wasn't what she'd had planned. Or him, either. In fact, this whole sex thing had pushed them across a line now and made things even less clear than they were before. And even though he'd lain awake in many other women's beds over the years trying to work out just how to leave, he'd never felt so conflicted about his next step.

Everything he'd said was true. She was perfect. She

was beautiful. She was so much more than he'd imagined. And he'd wanted her so badly, for so long. All those years of wondering, of dating other women, of trying to put her behind him. But it had been pointless because the attraction was still there. The need. The visceral tug towards her—even though there was danger with every step.

He wanted to think there could be a future, but he couldn't get past the fact that she'd treated his heart with so little respect before—would she do the same again? Did he even want to give her the chance? Had it, in the end, just been sex for old times' sake?

Like he was even going to ask that dumb question. He didn't want to contemplate what her answer might be.

'What are you thinking?' Her voice brought him back to the now.

'That you, missy, have a very important presentation in a few hours and you need to get rested up before it.' He started to pull the sheet back ready to make his leave. They both needed time to get their heads around this whole new complication. Well, he did, that was for sure. What did he actually want now? Other than a rerun of ten minutes ago.

But before he could stand up her fingers slowly tiptoed across his thigh. She spoke, her words punctuated by soft kisses down his chest. 'For some reason…I'm just not…sleepy.' Her fingers connected with his now growing erection. Because he was, after all, just a red-blooded man with the most beautiful woman in the entire universe lying naked next to him. Oh, and a whole host of emotions swimming across his chest. Yeah, his body still wanted her, regardless of the past. It was his head that was causing trouble.

Her voice was a warm breeze over his skin, tender yet filled with a promise. 'Don't know about you, Seany Boy, but exercise always makes me sleep so much better. And short of going downstairs to the hotel gym, I can only think of one kind of exercise we could do at this time of night. You?'

'Isabel—' He turned, then, with gargantuan effort, to tell her. To put some distance between his feelings and his needs. But the trill of her mobile phone jolted her upright.

'Oh. Who could that be at this time?' Wrapping a sheet round her, she grabbed her bag from the floor next to the bed and pulled out her phone. 'It's Isla. What would she—? Oh? The baby? D'you think?' Throwing Sean an apologetic look, she pointed to the phone. 'I'm so sorry...but I've just got to get this. I won't be long.'

And so he was surplus to requirement. It was a decent enough excuse to regroup and rethink. To get the hell out, and work out what to do next.

Isabel watched the door close behind Sean and blew out a deep breath. Getting her head around whatever the hell had just happened would have to be banked until after she'd spoken to Isla. But she got the feeling he hadn't been able to get away quickly enough. Maybe he was having second thoughts, too? 'Isla? Isla, are you okay?'

'Isabel. Oh, my God, Isabel.' The line was crackly but she could still hear her sister's voice filled with wonder. 'He's beautiful. Perfect. I can't believe. Oh...'

'You've had the baby?' Isabel's heart swelled and she fought back tears. Her sister was a mother. She hadn't been there for her. Her mouth crumpled as she forced words out. 'Oh, sweetie. How was it? Are you okay? Is he okay? A name? What happened—aren't you early? Was Alessi there?'

Clearly having a better handle on things than Isabel, her sister drew a sharp intake of breath and began, 'Okay, I can't remember which question was first. You have a nephew. A gorgeous, gorgeous nephew, all fingers and toes accounted for and lots of dark hair like his daddy. Born three hours ago.'

'Oh, wow. Three hours? You were going to phone me when you went into labour.' Isabel stopped short. Three hours ago she was busy. With Sean. Speaking to her sister wouldn't have been the best thing to happen. But maybe if they had been interrupted she wouldn't now have these weird mixed emotions whirling through her chest. What they'd done had made things more complicated, not less. 'Oh, wow, I'm so happy for you. Mega congratulations, little sis.'

'It was all so quick, and I couldn't remember the time difference with my scrambled mummy brain—and the labour drugs—and your last email said you were going to Paris? So I wasn't sure—'

'Yes. I am. *Je suis ici*—in Paris.' *Having sex with my ex. And now I want to talk about it, but I can't.* Bad timing. All round. 'So, what was your labour like? Textbook? Knowing you it was probably textbook.'

'Quit schmoozing. It was okay. No, actually it hurt like hell…' There was a pause. 'Iz, are you okay with me talking to you about this? I mean…you know…because of before?'

Because of her own baby boy? Because he'd been too frail, too tiny to live, because she hadn't been able to protect him the way other mothers could. Hadn't been able to grow him to his full potential the way Isla had.

An arrow of pain seared her heart. He would have been a teenager now, getting ready to fly the nest. She would have had all those memories, sleepless nights, first days at school...so many firsts; long hot summers, a house full of primary-coloured plastic and arguments over too loud music. Instead she had heartache and an extremely unwise choice of sexual partner. She couldn't even blame that on mummy brain.

She had to let it all go. She had to move on. Her baby was gone. Gone, but in her heart for ever. *Do not spoil your sister's day.* 'Of course, I'm fine, Isla. Talk away. I want to hear about everything...absolutely everything. I'm so happy for you. I'm just sorry I couldn't be there to hold your hand. I'm sending hugs, heaps and heaps of hugs.'

'Oh, you know I'd have liked you to be here, Iz. I would have, but you need to be away from here... I totally get it. I love you.'

Emotion constricted Isabel's throat; she had to force words out. 'I love you too.' Ever since Isla had waved Isabel off onto the flight to London she had been nothing but supportive of Isabel's need to get away from Melbourne, to put her life there behind her. To forget Sean. Yeah, that plan had worked really well. 'So come on, a name? What did you go with in the end?'

'Geo, after Alessi's brother, the triplet who died. I told you about him, didn't I?'

'Yes, yes. The baby who didn't make it...' Another one. *Breathe. Breathe.* 'That's a lovely gesture, Isla. Alessi must be so proud.' Isabel had chosen a name for her boy too but had never properly given it to him. She hadn't been able to think straight after she'd given birth, after they took his little body away. There'd been no burial. Nothing to remember him by. But she did have a name for him.

'Alessi? Proud?' Her sister laughed down the line and it was so good to hear her so happy. 'Oh, yes, and then some. He's acting like he's the only man who's ever fathered a child. Still, if it means he continues to treat me like a princess then I'm happy. I'm not allowed to move a single muscle without him making sure I'm okay.'

'Lucky you, enjoy it while you can. Give baby Geo lots of kisses from his very happy auntie and email me some photos, now! Oh…who delivered you? Don't tell me it was Alessi?'

There was a kerfuffle in the background, familiar hospital noises—bleeps, voices. The sweet, soft snuffle of a contented newborn. 'No, he was too busy up the top end dealing with me, trying to keep me calm. Darcie was the attending, she was amazing. Very patient, all things considered. I think I may have been a bit rude to everyone, but at least it made them give me more pain relief. Talking of Darcie, did I tell you…? It's all hearts and roses over here. You'll never guess who she's dating. True love and everything.'

Sometimes Isabel really missed the gossip of her home town. The familiar. 'No? Who? Spill.'

'Only Lucas bloody Elliot!'

The heartthrob of the MMU. 'Mr Playboy himself? No way! I thought you said they hated the sight of each other.' But Isabel knew that there was a thin line between love and hate—that passion came in many forms and was fuelled by many different emotions.

Isla sighed. 'It's really cute to watch actually. There were fireworks all along the way—neither of them wanted to admit they were falling in love. Little Cora's thrilled too. Now she has an auntie as well as an uncle to watch her. Quite a unit, they are.'

Hearing all the news she'd missed out on made Isabel realise just how far away from them she was. Darcie had only been in Melbourne less than a year herself, having been part of the same exchange as Isabel. In fact, Darcie would be scheduled to return to Isabel's job in a few weeks, when the year's exchange was over. 'Well, that'll cause Darcie a few sleepless nights if she's fallen for Lucas, because he's firmly committed to staying in Melbourne with his brother and niece.'

'I know. He's been such a rock for them both since his sister-in-law died. There's no way he'd leave all that behind. But I hope it won't mean you're not coming home? Your job will still be open if she decides to stay here, right?'

Isabel had a brief image of her and Sean arriving off the same flight hand in hand stepping onto Aussie soil. Then she shook away such a fantasy. But whatever happened, she was definitely going home. And soon. 'Absolutely. Try and stop me. Oh, I do miss you all.'

'We miss you too. They all say hi.' It seemed the labour drugs were still in Isla's system as she chatted on oblivious to the fact it was five o'clock in the morning for her. 'Come home soon. I want you to meet Geo. Oh… and talking of babies…more goss hot off the press. Oliver and Emily are looking to adopt another baby. So sweet. Toby's growing into such a lovely boy and they want to add to their family.'

Another MMU romance—seemed there had been quite a few recently. Something in the water. Obstetrician Oliver and midwife Emily had been having marriage problems back when Isabel had been there; it was good to hear that they'd managed to put their rough past behind them. It was good to hear that at least some re-kindled relationships could work.

She'd bet that Oliver hadn't hot-footed out of the bed-room at the first opportunity. 'I'm glad things worked out for them in the end. Their marriage was put under so much pressure struggling with IVF. It was hard for them to see beyond that. Time makes such a difference.' Geez, she could have been talking about her and Sean. But there wouldn't be any happy endings for them. Not with the way he'd looked as he'd left. She couldn't help the yearning in her voice. 'But now everyone sounds so settled and happy.'

'They all want to know what you've been up to. Have you met anyone?' There was a pause, then Isla cleared her throat. 'How's Sean?'

What to say? *Hot sex is epic. It's the aftermath that's the problem. How to move on from here?* 'He's…he's okay. Actually, he's here in Paris with me.'

'What the hell? What do you mean? Here's me rab-biting on… Have you told him?' For a woman who'd recently given birth, Isla was very animated. Those pregnancy hormones were amazing. Isabel had seen some women act as if nothing earth-shattering had hap-pened—popped out a baby and gone straight back to normal life, thank you very much. 'Are you…? You know…?'

We just did. 'It's just a conference.'

'Nothing's *just* a conference if Sean's there. You're away with him? Isabel? In Paris?' A loud squawking zinged down the phone line. Voices. A lot of loud gar-bled language. Greek? Cries, a loud hullabaloo. Then Isla was back. 'Sorry, hon. I've got to go. Geo's hungry,

I think. Alessi's parents have just arrived. It's chaos. I'll call you. Call me. Talk soon. I love you.'

And she was gone. Isabel's head was spinning. There was never enough time to chat properly and the long-distance hum always interfered. She wanted to sit down and talk to her sister, to hold her precious nephew. She wanted to go home. A few more weeks and she would… only a few more weeks until the end of this contract. And then what?

She scrunched up the Egyptian cotton sheet in her hand and looked down at where Sean had been lying a few moments ago. Remembered how good he had made her feel. And how easily he'd slipped away. So instead of *then what*, it was, *now* what? Now how to face the elusive Dr Anderson?

Isabel had absolutely no idea.

CHAPTER SIX

ISABEL NEEDN'T HAVE WORRIED. There was no time for chatting at breakfast with Mr Incubator doing all the talking. No chance to catch up over lunch as she'd been cordially invited to the speaker's special VIP luncheon. Then after her presentation she'd been whisked away on a tour of the Sacré-Coeur followed by dinner and a show in Montmartre, which, it appeared, Sean, or rather Jacob when he'd registered, hadn't signed up for. And after all that French flavour she was good and ready for bed. To sleep on her own.

And no late-night visits. She didn't know whether to be relieved or disappointed.

Turned out there was rather more of the latter than she expected.

The next day flew by with more meetings—one a real success with the promise of a hefty discount on some new high-tech monitors—and interesting talks all round. She only had one more day to dodge Sean's questioning eyes, then he'd be heading back home and she'd have a couple of free days to shop. The French baby clothes were so gorgeous and chic, she just knew Isla would adore them; Isabel had no problem hanging on to spend time perusing and indulging her new nephew.

Right now, though, she was spruced up ready for the gala dinner and surveying the majestic ballroom for someone to hide behind. And yup, no Sean as yet. Thank goodness. She still had no idea what to say to him. But if she zipped towards the medical-rep crowd she might be able to get stuck in a conversation before he arrive—

'Wow, Isabel. You look amazing.'

Too late. His hand was on her waist as he drew in close and pecked French *un-deux-trois* kisses on her cheeks. She closed her eyes briefly at the sensation of his touch on her cheek, his aftershave mingling with his sunshine and sex scent. Goddamn, the man was irresistible.

But she was measured in her response. He couldn't hike out of her room after sex without an explanation. She needed to know what was going on in his head.

Hers was a lost cause.

'Oh, this old thing? Just something I threw on at the last minute.' She looked down at the midnight-blue silk shift dress that had cost the best part of a week's salary but, hell, it had been too beautiful to resist with its teeny shimmery jewels round the halter neckline and the cutaway back. She eyed her favourite sparkly silver sandals, then her gaze strayed onto him and she almost lost her balance. The man was drop-dead hot in a black tuxedo.

Worse, she knew how hot he was out of it too. And so that wasn't helping her equilibrium, not at all.

'Well, you're just too damned beautiful. Drink? Because I need one if I'm going to spend all evening looking at you, not allowed to touch you.' He took her elbow and steered her towards the bar. 'And I get the feeling you're avoiding me because every time I turn around you've disappeared.'

She drew her arm away. 'Oh, trust me, I know that feeling. Wham, bam and suddenly you're gone.'

'What are you talking about?' He leaned over the bar and gave the barman his order, then turned back to Isabel, his eyes widening as the penny dropped. 'Oh. You're cross because I left you to talk to your sister in private? Really? Or are you cross because I didn't come to your room last night?'

'Shh…people will hear.' Not that there were many people in earshot, but…well, really.

'I don't care who hears. *Did* you want me to come to you last night? Should I have?'

She looked down at the mahogany bar because that was safer than looking into those dark eyes and saying one thing but thinking the opposite. Yes, she'd wanted to sleep with him again. Had lain awake for hours imagining him naked in bed, the wall between them a barrier she hadn't been able to bring herself to cross.

Because she didn't want to want him so much, and put her world into free fall again. She didn't want to hand over that part of herself that she'd kept safe for so long, the memories and emotions locked away. She didn't want to feel anything. And right now she was feeling a lot of things. Mainly hot and bothered and very turned on. But more, complicated things she didn't want. 'Mmm.' That should do it. Nonchalant and undefined.

'Mmm? What the hell does that mean? Listen, Izzy, the truth is, I thought, seeing as we hadn't spent any time together talking, that it would be… I don't know, to use an old-fashioned word, unchivalrous to expect a booty call. But that was what you wanted? Yes? You wanted me to be unchivalrous?' His mouth tipped up, the grin widening as his hand smoothed round from her waist to the back of her neck, sending ripples of desire through her. His mouth was close to her throat. 'Go on, admit it. You wanted me.'

'No.' *Yes.* She couldn't help the smile. How had it gone from complicated to sex? From difficult to downright easy? Was it that straightforward? To stop thinking and start doing? She made sure she looked right at him. 'No.'

'Next time, say it and mean it. You wanted a booty call?' He nodded and smirked. 'Noted, naughty girl.' Then he handed her a glass of bubbles. French. Yummy. 'So, we're celebrating?'

'Sorry? Why?'

'Isla's baby? Boy? Girl? All's well?'

'Sorry. Yes, a boy. Called Geo, apparently...both doing fine. She's emailed me some photos and he's desperately cute.' She took out her phone and flicked through the photos, trying to stop tearing up, because Geo was so, so gorgeous and Isla looked as deliciously happy as she deserved to be. Alessi, indeed, so proud. And far from feeling jealous, Isabel just felt her heart filled with happiness for them.

Sean tilted her chin and looked at her. 'You miss them.'

She looked away because he saw the truth inside her as if he knew her too well. 'Yes. Of course. They're my family. It's my home. My place. Coming here was only ever temporary.'

He took a drink of the champagne. 'You're not enjoying it?'

'Oh, yes. The people are really friendly, I've had some fabulous work opportunities, like this conference. Job satisfaction is high.'

He smiled. 'The sex is pretty good too.'

'Exceptional, yes.' Her cheeks bloomed hot. She was still so new to this, she didn't know the art of flirting, but Sean made it easy today. Maybe she'd misunderstood his frown the other night or the reason he'd left. Maybe he had just been giving her space. Maybe he'd forgiven her?

Forgiving was one thing, but forgetting? She imagined that would take him a whole lot longer. It would always be there between them. Wouldn't it? God, if only she could thrash this out with Isla, the only person who knew everything.

Apart from Sean now, of course.

They walked towards a table, so beautifully decorated with silver tableware on a crisp white linen cloth and a small silver and white Christmas tree centrepiece. He nodded to the other guests sitting there, pulled out an empty chair and indicated for her to sit. 'So tell me, Isabel, why did you really come to the other side of the world? All this way away from your family?'

She sat. 'To develop my skills and knowledge. To take part in an international study and hopefully open a new Australian strand of it when I go back to MMU.' That was what she'd told them over the video interview anyway. There'd been no mention of running away from her ex because his questions made her uncomfortable. Made her remember things she'd prefer to keep under lock and key.

'So you'll be going back when your exchange has finished?'

'If my job's still there—I get the feeling that Darcie might want to stay in Melbourne. Apparently she's hooked up with Lucas.'

He grinned. 'Really? Now that's something I'd never

have predicted. They'll keep your job open for you too, though, surely?'

Isabel sighed. 'Yes, I hope so. That was one of the conditions of the exchange. I'm ready to go back, to be honest. I've had my year of living dangerously.'

'Not nearly dangerously enough.' His eyebrows peaked and his smile was as dirty as could be mustered at a dinner shared with two hundred delegates. 'There are a few things I have in mind that you could do. Only takes a bedroom. Well…not even that really. A willing mind.'

Her body was willing, it was her closed-off mind that she was having trouble with. To stop herself from slapping a kiss on that smirking mouth she desperately tried to keep the conversation on a civil track. 'And you? Will you stay here or move on somewhere?'

He shrugged. 'I haven't decided yet. My contract runs for a couple more months…then I'll make some decisions. I'm registered with a locum agency in London, so I may just stay in the UK for a while, perhaps see what Edinburgh's like. I'm happy moving around for now but I guess at some point that'll grow old. I like the challenge of new places, meeting new people. I like not having to commit to one place. There's a lot more to the world than Melbourne.'

Her heart began to hammer a little uncomfortably. 'You'll want to settle down at some point, surely? Family?'

And she didn't even know why she was asking him such a question…it wasn't as if that kind of life was anything she'd been working towards. She was happy being on her own, making her own decisions, living the single life. Wasn't she? At least she had been. A bit lonely, perhaps, but nothing serious.

Maybe that tiny ache in her gut that she'd tried to ignore was a reaction to Isla having a baby. Yes, that was it. Isabel decided she was a little unsettled by that, that was all.

The food arrived, and even though it might have seemed a little rude to ignore the other diners Isabel just wanted to sit and listen to Sean; his voice was lyrical and smooth. 'My parents have hinted about grandchildren. No, make that, my parents ask about potential wives and babies every time I phone or email. It's like something out of the eighteenth century. Neither of my brothers look like they're settling down either, so I'm in the firing line.'

'Your parents are lovely. How are they these days?'

'Same as ever, working hard on the business. Dad's still in accounting and Mum's still doing his paperwork, but she craves grandkids and won't leave me alone.'

Isabel laughed, remembering the not so subtle hints her father had been dropping about continuing the Delamere line. 'Mine too. So hopefully they'll be appeased by Isla's bub and leave me alone now.'

Sean looked surprised. 'You don't want that for yourself?'

And risk the chance of losing everything again? 'No.'

He paused to eat some of the amazing chicken pâté and bread, then continued with a frown, 'But you always used to talk about having kids—a whole mess of them, I think you said. You wanted to be a different parent from yours, you were looking forward to chaos.'

'You remember things I don't remember saying. And anyway, people can change, can't they?'

He put his knife down and turned kind eyes towards her. 'Not that much, Izzy. You can't give up on a dream because of one knockback. You help women achieve that dream every day—you can't tell me that things have changed so irrevocably for you?'

The food was tasteless now, a lump in her throat. 'A knockback? Is that what you call it?'

'No. That's not what I meant.' His voice grew darker. 'I could call it a lot of things. And I'm trying to deal with it…but damn it—'

'I'm sorry, Sean.'

'I know you are and so am I.' He shook his head, his fists tightening around his crystal wineglass stem. 'I promised I wouldn't hark back to it because just thinking about it makes me angry.'

He probably would never get over it—she hadn't, not really. But he had to deal with her lies as well as the loss. 'I've given you my reasons.'

'I'm trying hard not to be angry with you. I understand why you kept it from me. I'm angry about the whole sad scenario, Izzy. But you can't let it scar you for ever.'

'I've told you, I'm not Izzy, not any more.'

'And I don't know who you're trying to kid, but I'm not buying it. Older, yes. Wiser, definitely. More confident in lots of ways…apart from intimacy, which is a shame. Because that would be cool—you deserve to have that in your life. I'm betting that inside you're still the same girl who desperately wanted a family. A husband. The things everyone wants. And I bet that it's worse now that Isla has it. You're Izzy the girl, in here where it matters.' Touching just above her heart, he seemed to resettle himself, shake the demons away, and she envied him that. Or maybe he was just better at sorting his head out? 'Don't think for one moment that I'm belittling anything. I'm not. I know what you went through. I can't imagine what it was like to have it happen so young…so alone.' His hand covered hers now and the feel of him there… just there…made everything seem so much better. 'You said yourself, it happens. You have to look forward.'

She didn't want to be that frightened girl any more; she'd worked hard to be someone else. But yes, he was right about the intimacy—she didn't know how to let herself go, not on many levels. She hadn't dared. As far as she was concerned intimacy led to heartbreak. She knew it because she'd lived it. 'As it happens, I am trying to move forward and let go…that's the real deep-down reason I came to England in the first place. I needed to get out and breathe a little. Get away from you.' She nudged him playfully. 'But then you keep turning up like a bad penny and bringing me right back to the beginning.' Creating the same wild feelings she'd had when she was a teenager. Only this time they were more intense, more enduring. More potentially painful.

'You think? A beginning?' He frowned. 'Is that what you want to do? Start again?'

She rubbed her fingers across strong, skilled hands that had brought so much life into the world. 'I have no idea. I haven't dared want anything. It's too painful to risk going through all that again.' But he almost made her feel as if she could take a chance. She looked up into eyes that seemed so understanding and she felt as if she could pour her heart out to him. But that would surely send him running to the hills. So she deflected. 'What do you want?'

She didn't know what she wanted him to answer.

She just hoped it was somehow in sync with what her heart was telling her. That maybe, just maybe, she could work things out with Sean. Start afresh. If they both had enough courage. At least for a little while, they could have some fun and then she'd be gone and so would he.

He laughed. 'Hell, Isabel, it's messed up. I'll be honest with you and say I've gone round in circles. I've worked back and forth across the world, travelling thousands of miles just to get you out of my head and each time I end up back with you. I can't tell you straight up that I'm one hundred per cent okay with any of this. But I do know what I want right now, right this second. That's the best I can do.'

'Oh, yes? What do you want?' But she had a feeling she knew already. Just one look at the gleam in his eyes...

He paused as a gentleman stepped up to the stage and said something in French. The room hushed. There was applause while another man walked up to the microphone, all big smiles and wide arms as if giving the room a warm hug. She looked across to the woman opposite her and laughed when she laughed. Hopefully at some point there'd be a translation. But all Isabel was aware of was Sean next to her. The heat. And her unanswered question.

There was a break in proceedings as the microphone screeched, a brief technical hitch, and an embarrassed smile from the compère. Suddenly Sean's voice was in her ear, warm and deep. 'I want to peel that dress off you...very slowly. I want you and me naked.'

'Huh?' She swallowed, with difficulty. Her mouth was suddenly very dry. If she turned her head she'd be mouth-to-mouth with him and the temptation to kiss him was overwhelming. Where Sean was concerned there were no half measures, no light feelings; it was intense and deep and raw.

'I want to be inside you again. I want you, Isabel Delamere, with every ounce of my being. I want to kiss every inch of your stunning body.' He withdrew his hand from hers and placed it on her thigh. The heat and tingles arrowed in waves straight to her belly as he circled his fingertips towards her core. 'I don't understand what that bloke's talking about on stage. I don't understand much of the stuff that's in my head because it's like a washing machine all churned up. But I do know that I want you. Now. And I don't think that feeling's going to go anywhere for a while.'

She turned and whispered back, barely able to form words. 'It's bad, isn't it?'

Suddenly her heart began to thump in anticipation. Adrenalin surged through her veins and fired her nerves. Two people. That was what they were, just two people taking what they needed. No one was going to get hurt. She'd built that protective barrier around her heart over the last years; it was strong and sturdy; she knew what she was doing just fine. He was thinking of going travelling, she was thinking of going home. It was just two people taking what they wanted while they had the chance. They'd missed out on so much already. She dared to reach out and put her hand on his thigh too and felt the contraction of muscle at her touch. Heard his sharp intake of breath.

He growled. 'It's very, very bad. And yet somehow we keep ending up here. Maybe it's time to stop pretending and accept reality. This isn't stopping any time soon. There's nothing either of us can do.' He wrapped her hand in his and pushed it further up to his groin. Her fingers made contact with his growing erection. 'Hell, Izzy, it's bigger than both of us.'

'Good lord, it's very big indeed.' She knew he was fooling around, but she didn't want this to end. It was like a dream, a fantasy. 'Maybe when you go back to Cambridge and I stay here for a few days things will get back to normal again.'

'What exactly is normal? At each other's throats? Not speaking? Shouting? Not seeing you for too many years? Not sure I want to go back to any of that. I do, however, want to go back to bed, with you. Or, not bed... I have an idea.' He leaned in close and whispered, 'How about now? A night together. Then, what say we play hooky tomorrow? Have some fun in Paris?'

'We're supposed to be working.' Okay, so she said it out loud just for the record, but she didn't mean it. The last thing she wanted was to be sitting in a stuffy conference room when she could be playing with Sean.

'Who will know? You always were such a goody-two-shoes.'

He slid his hand up inside her dress, stepped fingers towards the inside of her thigh. Here in the middle of a gala. What the hell? Daddy would freak. 'And you always were such a tearaway.'

'No wonder your father didn't like me. Miss Delamere, this is not how you behave at dinner.'

'I was thinking the exact same thing.' He was hot and hard for her. 'Besides, I don't care what he thinks.'

'I wish you'd said that seventeen years ago.'

'Okay... I'm not apologising any more for stuff that happened a long time ago. Let's plan forward.' Her raging heart was thumping so hard she wasn't sure she could breathe properly. Or make much sense past *take me now*. But for the benefit of others on the table—if they could hear—she tried to sound normal. 'I'd really like to go on the field trip to the homeless perinatal clinic in the morning…but then? Maybe we could duck out after?'

He nodded. 'I'd like to take you on a boat ride down the Seine—we could have lunch. Then visit the Louvre… Dinner in the ninth arrondissement, I know a place…' As her hand wrapped around him he tensed, eyes fluttering closed. 'Okay. I can't take any more. Let's duck.'

'Now?' His hand was still over hers as she stroked him.

He looked as if he was in pain, or at great pains not to show any reaction at all. 'You want to spend the next two hours listening to a man droning on about maternal care in Limoges, that's fine. But I'd like to get some hot sex. *S'il vous plaît.*'

She almost choked on her champagne. '*Mais oui.* Since you asked so nicely.'

'Okay, so stay close, no one needs to see this.' He pulled her up and held her in front of him as they sneaked out the back way, then half walked, half ran to the lift. As he hit the down arrow he turned to her. His hand was on her thigh, warm through the thin layer of silk as he dragged the old-fashioned outer metal lift door to a close. Then the inner one. It jerked, then started to descend. 'You have any preference in venue?'

'None whatsoever.' She threw her head back and laughed, feeling the rasp of his stubbled jaw on her neck. The lift smelt of old leather and Paris. Of daring and adventure. Of the exotic and sophistication. 'How about here?' So she wanted to get dirty with him in the lift. That was new.

'Great minds think alike.' He jabbed the lower-floor-car-park button then pushed her against the mirrored glass, kissing her deep and hard. She pressed against him, feeling his hardness between her thighs. His hands skimmed her body, palming her breasts, thumbs flicking gently against her nipples. Next thing, he'd untied her dress at the neck, it fell to her sides and his mouth took over from his hands, slanting over her hardened nipples.

When they hit the empty dark cavern he reached out and grabbed the metal car park sign and jammed it in between the lift doors so they wouldn't shut. The lift wasn't going anywhere. Neither were they. Pulling him towards her by his now unravelled black tie, she breathed, 'Smooth move, Dr Anderson. Very smooth indeed.'

'I like to think so.'

Then, feeling the most turned on she'd ever been in her life, she wrapped a leg round his waist. 'So, come put that clever mouth to good use.'

CHAPTER SEVEN

'THIS WASN'T QUITE what I had in mind as a date,' Sean whispered to Isabel as he handed over the steaming plate of beef bourguignon to the eighteenth homeless man of the morning. But working side by side with her gave him a punch to his gut that was filled with warmth as thick as the heated cabin they were in. After the tour of the homeless shelter and perinatal outreach clinic she'd accepted the request to help out at the soup kitchen with grace and humility. Every day she surprised him just a little bit more. Not least last night with the lift escapade. He couldn't help grin at the thought. 'Still, this stuff smells delicious, if there's any left…'

'It's for them, not us.' She kicked him gently but smiled at the dark-haired, olive-skinned young woman in front of her, wrapped in layers and layers of tatty grey cloth and a dark red headscarf. She had a full round belly and was breathing heavily. Pre-eclampsia, probably, Sean surmised—*needs assessment*. A small boy dressed in clothes more suitable for summer perched on her hip, grubby, pale and with a drippy nose. *'Pour vous, madame. Merci.'* Isabel turned. 'Actually, no, wait…oh, never mind. I want to ask about the boy, I wish I could speak the language a bit better.'

'Don't worry, the smile says it all. She understands.'

'And I want to take the tray over to the table for her, but she won't let go of it. I think she's so glad to get some food she won't take a chance on losing it.'

'Then let her manage if that's what she needs to do.' The kid looked feverish. 'He's not looking too great. When they're done I'm taking them both over to the clinic.'

Isabel let the tray go. 'It's zero degrees out there and look at the poor state of them both. It's Christmas in a week or so—what's the bet he's not going to have the best day?'

The boy coughed. Wheezed. And as he breathed out he made a short grunting sound. He didn't smile. Or cry. Thick black rings circled sunken brown eyes. Mum didn't look much better. Pregnant. Homeless. Sean pointed to the boy and made a sad face. Mum shook her head and jabbered in a language that didn't sound French. Then she handed the child towards him.

Sean took him, noted his flaring nostrils as he struggled to breathe, and felt his forehead. 'He's burning up. He needs a good look over. I'll take him through to the clinic now.' He gesticulated to the mum to follow him, but she clearly didn't understand. He tried again. Made another dramatic sad face and pointed to the boy. Mum shook her head again and tried to grab the tray of food and her son back.

'Okay, okay.' Sean held his palms up in surrender and let her take the boy. She clearly wasn't going to let the kid out of her sight, regardless of where she was and the minimised risk. And she was determined to get that hot food in both their bellies before they went anywhere.

Not such a bad idea, all things considered. But the child needed help and soon. 'Eat first.'

She squeezed into a chair at a small melamine table and in between greedy gulps tried to feed the boy some of the meaty gravy, but he slumped down and shook his head. She tried again, jabbering in a smoky voice, cajoling him. Pleading with him. And still the boy didn't open his mouth.

Eat. Sean felt an ache gnawing in his gut. *Eat, kid. For God's sake, eat something.* He watched fat tears slide down the mum's cheeks and wondered just how awful it would feel not to be able to provide for your child. To not be able to make him better. To not be able to feed him. That ache in his gut intensified. How helpless must Isabel have felt to not be able to grow her baby, to lose their son? And he hadn't been there for either of them.

Sean had never been helpless and he wasn't about to start now. He was three steps towards them before mum looked up and shook her head.

He turned to Isabel. 'His breathing's laboured. Bluish lips. Exhausted. Won't eat. He's going next door, now.'

'I'll come with you.' Obviously seeing the danger too, Isabel nodded, handed the plates over to some of the other volunteers from conference and between them they managed to get mum to follow them into the outreach clinic. As they tried to lay the boy onto a trolley he had a severe coughing fit, then went limp.

'Quick. Oxygen. Come on, kiddo. Don't give up on us.' Sean checked the boy's airway and grabbed a mask and Ambu bag, wishing, like Isabel, that he could speak the mum's language. Or even the language of the healthcare workers. But luckily they all spoke the language of emergency and in a flurry of activity anticipated what he needed, drew up blood, cleared secretions, put in an IV line—eventually. The boy was so dehydrated that finding a vein was almost impossible. 'Come on, buddy. Come on, breathe for me.'

As he watched the kid's chest rise and fall Sean blew out a huff of relief.

He caught Isabel's eye as she stood waiting with an intubation tube. 'I think we're good. He's settling a little. Pulse rate down from two twenty to one sixty. But we need blood gases and a blue light to the nearest hospital. Probably a bolus of antibiotics to be on the safe side. Who knows what the French is for that?'

Dr Henry, whom Sean and Isabel had met earlier on the clinic tour, appeared from the kitchen and explained in his very decent English that the paramedics had been called. The boy would be given the best care available at the public hospital and he thanked them very much for the help.

Mum, meanwhile, was another issue. As she stood and watched them working on her son a keening cry came from deep in her throat as if he were being ripped from her body. She refused to let go of the boy's hand, getting in the way of the staff. They tried to encourage her to take a step back. She pushed forward. In her confusion and distress she became more and more distressed. In her world, control was key. One wrong foot and you lost what precious little you had.

'It's going to be okay. It's going to be okay. Come with me, love. Let's sit down, shall we?' Isabel took her hand and gently pulled her away, wrapping an arm round her dirty clothes and walking her to a quiet corner of the room. The clinic was a prefabricated building with curtains delineating cubicles—the little fella's crisis had stopped any other consultations from happening and all eyes were on the emergency. A perinatal care centre they might have been, but an emergency care facility they definitely weren't. 'They're doing good. He's sick, but he'll be okay.'

Mum clung to Isabel and jabbed a finger towards the trolley. 'Teo. Teo.'

'The boy?' Izzy smiled and pointed towards the child. Her calm demeanour seemed to have an effect on the woman as she stopped gesticulating quite so frantically. 'His name is Teo? He's beautiful. And he's going to be okay. He's with Sean, and Sean won't let anything bad happen.'

Now that belief in him was another hard punch to his gut. She believed in him? She believed in him.

'*Oui*. Teo.' This was getting surreal. The woman was speaking French now to Isabel.

Isabel nodded, smiling, and pointed to the woman's belly. 'Another baby there?'

Mum rubbed her stomach and sighed, dejectedly. '*Copil mic.*'

Taking her hand, Isabel monitored the lady's pulse. 'Hey, Sean, hand me that sphyg, will you? I'll take her blood pressure while I'm here. I have no idea where she's from. Are there any translators?'

'I'll grab Dr Henry when he's finished. Oh, wait… he's just there.' They waited until the doctor sauntered over.

Isabel took it from there. 'I'm a bit worried about her, blood pressure's skyrocketing—I think she's pre-eclampsic; swollen feet… I need a urine sample but I don't know how to ask. Kid's sick and she's scared for him—it's not helping. And I have no idea where she's from. What do you do about language barriers?'

The doctor shrugged. 'It happens all the time, we have a good network of translators. I'll call one in.' He turned to the mum. 'Romania?'

'*Oui.*'

'She's from Romania? Wow. That's a long way from home. Who's looking after you? Where do you live? Will she have to pay for her medical treatment? Because I don't think she'll be able to. I'm sorry, I have too many questions and none of them in French or Romanian. Pretty useless, really. I don't even know her name.'

Dr Henry gave her a big smile, because, really, who wouldn't? 'That's okay, Dr Delamere, you care, it is enough. We have about twelve thousand homeless people in Paris and many of them are immigrants. But we also have good medical facilities to look after them, if we can reach them. Many are illegal aliens and don't want to be caught, so they get lost. Or worse. She may have friends around outside—they often meet people from their home country and hang out with them. Or she may have no one. I didn't see her come in with anyone. You?'

Isabel shook her head. 'No. She was on her own, and, in this state, that's a very scary place to be.'

Sean looked over at the kid and thought about Isabel all those years ago, on her own, dealing with the worst thing possible. That would be how this mum felt right now—even worse, she didn't understand what was happening and couldn't communicate. But she'd quietened down since Isabel had befriended her, so he wasn't going anywhere. 'So we'll stay with them until we get her and the boy into a stable state.'

'Are you sure? You don't mind?' Isabel was still hold-

ing the woman's hand, which she stroked as mum gave
a small sheepish smile. 'We'll stay with you. It's okay.
It's okay.' Then she turned to Sean. 'Thank you. I know
you had things planned.'

Nah. Other than give her the best doctor award? The
boat cruise would have to wait. 'I'm not going anywhere apart from to check on Teo. I'll be right here
with you.' His heart swelled just watching her compassion. So much for guarding his heart; where Isabel was
concerned it seemed she was determined to blast it wide
open.

Two hours later as they stepped out of the maternal
and paediatric hospital onto the Rue de Sèvres, Isabel
inhaled deeply and tried to stop the hurt in her heart.
'Wow, that was an eye-opener. But thank you for staying. I don't know how I'd have felt if we'd just left them
all alone. By the sounds of it Marina lost contact with
her friends when she got evicted.' Thank God for Sean,
too, because his quick thinking had stopped that boy
deteriorating. 'I'm going to go back to the hospital tomorrow to see how they're doing.'

'You know, you don't have to. They're quite safe now.
In good hands, as we always roll out to our patients. And
they are, so cheer up.' He slipped his hand into hers, and
she still didn't know how to deal with this rapid turn
of events. She was holding Sean Anderson's hand, discussing patients, looking forward to spending a date…
in Paris. She felt a surge in her heart that quickly evap-
orated. They'd done good, but she felt… She couldn't
put her finger on it. He must have sensed it because suddenly he asked, 'You okay?'

'No. No, I'm not okay. I mean, I should be, I know

this stuff happens. But it's still distressing to see. That poor woman, what kind of a future does she have? She lives on the streets of a city where she doesn't even know the language. She's going to be the mother of two kids under four. She has no easy access to medical care... Aaargh, it's so unfair.'

His warm hand squeezed hers. 'You can't make everyone better.'

'I know. But I can help this one. I can make one difference today and that's enough for me. But it still makes me so cross.' Not least because there were so many little lives out there that needed saving.

He bent and pressed his lips to hers, pulling up her collar around her ears to protect her from the icy wind. 'There she is. That's my girl. She's back.'

'What do you mean?'

He ran a thumb down her cheek, making her shudder with warm fuzzies. Didn't seem to matter what scenario they were in, he made her shiver with desire. No, more than that. She liked watching him work, liked his cool calmness and the way he put others first. Not many did that in the precious little downtime they had. Not many offered to spend a few hours in a soup kitchen instead of sitting in a plush hotel eating dainty finger food from silver platters. 'There's the old Izzy...the spunky girl who wants to save the world. She's here. Don't tell me that you've changed, that all your dreams are different, because they're not.'

Isabel didn't want to admit anything, because right now she didn't know what she wanted—from him. From this. From anything. 'She was on her own and frightened. I've been there and I don't recommend it. One thing I promised myself back then was that if I ever saw someone else going through a hard time I'd try to help.' She looked up and down the busy street. 'Er… where are we?'

He shrugged. 'Damned if I know. I was thinking we could go to the Louvre, but I fancy some fresh air after that little adventure. You? Fancy a walk down by the river? We can grab a taxi—look, there's one.' He stuck his hand out, told the driver where to head to then bundled her inside the warm car. The journey through the Parisian streets was halted a little by congestion. Snow had started to fall and the roads became chaotic.

'Look! It's snowing. My goodness, just look.'

'Isabel Delamere, you've seen snow before.'

'I know, plenty of times. But it's just so perfect to be snowing while we're here. It makes everything seem like a fairy tale.' But then she thought about Teo and his flimsy cotton shirt and sandals and decided that whatever else she did in Paris she'd find him something decent to wear. A Christmas present. Because he wasn't exactly living any kind of fairy tale at all.

She looked out of the window and dragged a huge breath in. There was one thing she'd never confessed to anyone, one reason why she'd always hated and loved Christmas at the same time. Why she wanted to keep busy, why she'd offered to work, why she always tried to surround herself with people at this festive time and not dwell on what-might-have-beens and what-ifs.

She brushed a threatening tear away from the corner of her eye and hoped Sean hadn't noticed. She was getting too soft in her old age. Maybe it was seeing the little that Teo had and the fight in his mother. Or maybe it was being with Sean and feeling all these new emotions rattle through her that made her a little off balance.

They were let out by Notre Dame cathedral. Isabel looked up at the grand façade of the famous building. 'Amazing. I always wanted to come here. I've seen so many pictures of it, brochures in the hotel, I feel like I'm looking at something so familiar, it's almost like I've been here before. Look—' She pointed up at the huge rose window and the majestic arches. 'It's breathtaking.'

'Do you want to go inside?'

'No. Well...' There was a small part of her that wanted, for some reason, to make a special commemoration of their newfound friendship. And of the child they'd both lost. Perhaps a candle? But she didn't want to add something so solemn to the day. Didn't want to dwell on how she felt about Sean, given that things were so uncertain between them. Another day, maybe, when they were on a more even footing. She gave him a bright smile. 'No, let's walk. I want to tramp along the riverside in the snow, and, if you're not careful, hit you in the face with a snowball.'

'I'd like to see you try.'

She reached out and caught the falling snow in her hand, watched the snow melt on contact. 'It's not snowball kind of snow.'

'Never mind—I'm sure we can find something else for you to play with.' Then he picked her up and twirled her round, pressing cold lips against hers. 'You want to go straight back to the hotel? I know a good way we can get warm...'

Oh, it was tempting. 'Yes...but I'd like to spend some time out here. It's like a wonderland. Look at that cathedral, all lit up. It's amazing.'

'In that case...' He put his hand into one of her deep

coat pockets. Didn't find what he was looking for. So shoved his hand into the other one.

'What are you doing?'

'Gloves.' He pulled out her woolly gloves and shrugged them onto her hands. 'Now you're appropriately dressed, which, I might add, is a shame. I liked you a lot better with your dress round your waist.' He gave her a wink that started an ache down low in her belly and spread to a tingle across her breasts. 'But I wouldn't encourage that here—you'll get frostbite. Later…definitely.'

'Is that a promise?' Suddenly she found herself looking forward to later.

As they trudged across the square in snow that had started to stick the street lights flickered into life. Looking up, Isabel watched the swirl of the flakes as they danced around her. Sean wrapped an arm round her shoulder and she hugged into him as if it was the most natural thing in the world to do. They walked in silence for a few minutes, crossed through the souvenir stalls, round the side of the cathedral to a garden. 'If you want we can walk through the Latin Quarter…the Left Bank. We can cross over there.' Sean pointed to the left, past a large fountain and through the gardens. 'Or over there.' To the right.

'It's prettier through the gardens.' And it was; snow tickled the tree branches, coating each leaf like ice frosting.

As they walked Sean began to talk, his voice surprisingly serious. 'Isabel, is it hard for you to do your job after what you went through?'

'It's hard when I see a young frightened kid having a baby, hard when I see a difficult birth, but it's made me

more resolved to help, to strive for a happier outcome.'
It was actually quite a relief that they were side by side
as they talked, so he couldn't see the pain she knew was
in her face. Couldn't see the need for him to hold her.
And yes, it hurts like hell when things don't work. She
still shed a tear for the young mums; she felt the righ-
teous anger when a baby didn't make it. She still felt the
kind of pain that Marina had voiced earlier. Would it be
different if she'd never been pregnant, never had that
chance? She didn't know. 'Why do you ask?'

'I'll be honest with you—I had a different feeling in
there with Teo and Marina. Watching her trying to feed
him and failing gave me a gut ache like I've never had
before. I felt her pain. Viscerally. I needed him to eat.
I was willing the kid on. Sure, I'm driven to help them
all, but this was different.'

'Empathy? You've always had empathy, Sean.'

'It was more than that. This was like a weird force in
me.' He turned to her. 'You know I'd have done anything
to help you, don't you? I'd have fought for that baby with
everything I had.'

'I know.'

He was speaking so quietly now she had to strain to
hear him. 'I wish I'd been there.'

'I know. Me too.' Her heart twisted. She tiptoed up
and kissed him, hoping that whatever he felt could somehow be kissed away. She doubted it, but he pressed his
lips to hers and held her close, his eyes closed, rever-
ent. And he pulled her closer, wrapping his arms tightly
around her as if she were a lifeline. An intense kiss that
shook her to her soul, had her falling, tumbling into
warmth. And even when there was no breath left they
stood and held each other, listened to the distant traf-

fic, to people laughing. People living their lives. People sharing, kissing, loving—taking a chance. When she eventually stepped away she felt as if a small part of her heart had been pieced back together again.

And shaken a little by the ferocity of it all.

It comforted her to have him close, but it scared her too. It was happening so quickly—they'd fallen so fast. She could lose herself in him, she thought, in *us*. She could let herself go. But what would that be like, in the end? Would it last? Or would she have to piece herself back together all over again?

That was something she couldn't contemplate. But, for now, he was here and she wanted him to know how she felt. 'I'm sorry, Sean, for the way I treated you. You're a decent, smart and sexy guy. I did bad by you, I should have been honest instead of selfishly hiding myself away.'

'You did what you had to do to cope. I understand.' They walked a little further through the tree-lined park leaving footprints in the snow, large and small behind them. Then, 'His name?'

'Sorry?' Her heart thumped.

Sean looked at her. 'I'm sorry, I have to know. What was his name? Did you ever think about giving him one?'

'Yes.'

'And did you give it to him? Did you tell him what his name was? Did he hear it?'

'Yes. I told him his name. I told him I loved him. I told him I was sorry.' *I cried it out to the skies and whispered it to the silence.* 'But then they took him away… and…I never got to hold him again.'

His lips a thin line, Sean dragged her to him. 'I'm so sorry. I'm sorry. I'm sorry.'

'It was a long time ago.' Her throat was thick with hurt, words were hard to find, even more difficult to speak. And her chest felt blown wide open.

Wrapped in his arms, she stood for a moment looking up at Sean, at his earnest face. The smooth line of strong jaw, the turmoil in his eyes. She hadn't wanted to put it there. Her gaze was drawn skywards to the fading light and the dance of snowflakes as they fluttered around them shrouding the cathedral in a magical white blanket.

The sound of bells ringing made her jump. She pulled away from him and started to walk again. As the light began to fade Isabel thought it was possibly the most beautiful place she'd ever visited. So serene through the gardens, the crisp crunch of snow the only real sound around them. Most of the tourists and hawkers had headed away, but a few stragglers remained. As they approached the stone bridge a man peeked out from behind a stall laden with postcards, mini Notre Dame cathedrals and paraphernalia.

'*Pour vous? Une serrure?* A lock? You buy?' His croaky voice made little sense.

'Keep walking. I don't know what he's talking about.' Isabel kept hold of Sean's arm as they stepped onto the bridge. The last dying rays of sun bathing the cathedral in an eerie light. 'Oh, my goodness. Look at that… What are they…? Are they locks?' Thousands and thousands of locks of all shapes and sizes covered the metal railings all along the bridge. She peered closer. 'They all have names on.'

'They're love locks, Izzy. Surely you've heard of them? People bring them here, write their names on the locks, attach them to the railings and toss the key into the Seine. Apparently if the key can't be found, the love can never be broken…or something like that.'

'"A 4 M…" "Marry Me…" "Love You Always…" "Ever Mine…" Oh, so sweet. But so many. There must be thousands.'

'And more. Look, there's another one just going on.' Sean pointed to the far end of the bridge where a bride and groom were having their wedding photographs taken, the sunset-captured cathedral in the background. The groom kissed something in his hand and then pressed it against his wife's lips and together they threw it into the gurgling water below.

'Wait here.' Sean left her side. She watched him jog back to the stallholder, who had almost finished packing up. From inside one of his bags he passed Sean something. Isabel's heart began thumping. Surely not. Surely Sean wasn't going to do something…something like… Looking over towards the bride and groom, she held her breath.

What the hell was he doing?

CHAPTER EIGHT

IF HE LET them go, Sean reasoned as he walked back to Isabel, if he pretended these keys held the past and hurled all the lies and the history and the hurt into the river, then that would be the end of it, right? He would let it all sink to the silted bottom, drowned in everyone's shared promises of everlasting love. Surely some of that would rub off onto him? Surely he'd be able to let her in? Surely he'd be able to stop thinking about it. Draw a line.

Maybe it was that easy. Maybe having her was as easy as that.

'Here.' He handed her a marker pen the guy had sold him for way more than it was worth. But how much was the price of casting off these emotions and facing her renewed? 'I want you to write our son's name on this lock.'

'What?' Her eyes widened, although there was some relief there too—he couldn't fathom why. 'Okay, I just thought…oh, never mind.'

'Write his name.'

Her hands were trembling as she tried to take the top off the pen. He took it from her, pulled it off with his teeth and handed it back. She wrote wobbly letters across the bronze lock.

Joshua.

'I hope you like it.' She was heaving great breaths while her whole body, his beautiful brave Isabel, shook.

'Yeah. Yes, I do. It's solid. Strong. It's a good name for a fine boy.' He'd had a son, and he'd been called Joshua. Sean's chest felt as if it were being squeezed in a vice. Above and to the left of the boy's name he wrote his own, to the right he wrote Isabel.

Damn it, if his own hand wasn't shaking too. Maybe it was the freezing weather.

'He was due at Christmas, right?' He'd done the maths. They'd only had sex a couple of times so by his reckoning their baby had probably been due around December.

'Yes.' She looked away, her eyes glittering. She gripped the top of the railings, for a moment he thought she might faint or tumble or scream, but she held her ground, staring into the distance along the river. Snow fell onto her shoulders, into her hair like tiny pearls. When she turned back her eyes were dry. 'He would have been a Christmas baby. He would have been seventeen this year. All games consoles and mobile phones. Maybe a girlfriend. Definitely smart and handsome.'

'And that's why you offered to work?'

She nodded. Her mouth about to crumple. 'Yep. I always work this time of year.'

'Oh, God, Isabel.' He pulled her close again, trying to protect her from something he couldn't stop. 'You spend every Christmas thinking about him? You must hate it.'

She let go of the railing and curled into his arms, her head shaking against his chest. 'No. Because it means I can think about him more. But…well, yes. I hate it.'

His chest constricted. She'd carried this for too long on her own. 'Okay. Let's do this.'

She nodded. Hauled in another breath; this one was stuttered as if her lungs were blocked. 'Okay. I'm ready.'

He lifted his fist to attach the lock to the tiny speck of space they'd found amongst the other locks bearing the love of thousands of people from around the world. All that love right here in this one place, all those promises, all that uplifting belief—he didn't know if he had it in him, but he'd damned well try.

But her hand closed over his, making him stop. 'Wait, Sean, look, there's a sign there saying the people of Paris don't want us to do this. It's damaging the bridge and the water, apparently. There's a picture of the railings collapsing under too much weight, of fish being poisoned by the toxins from the metal.'

Below them a pleasure boat chugged along, splaying dark water from either side, a commentary in French coming from speakers. When it had gone and the water smoothed out a little Sean peered as close as he could. There were no signs of any keys. No sign of damage. But he knew that you couldn't always see the damage. That nature had a habit of keeping that kind of thing locked deep, the harm seeping out slowly and steadily over the years, poisoning everything. Like his life. Like hers.

Not any more.

Rapidly blinking, she gave him a brave smile. 'I don't want to add to any more destruction. Can we do something else?'

He gazed down at the lock, at the names written there, and the sharp pain in his chest intensified. 'It's just a symbol, that's all.'

'Exactly. So… I suppose we should…just go.' She seemed deflated.

'Okay. I have an idea. Stay here.' He dashed back to

the gap-toothed man and bought another lock—a different one with a different set of keys. Then he walked back to where she was shivering. After writing the names in the same configuration he gave her the keys to his lock. 'Take these. Now, give me the keys to your lock.'

He wrapped her fist tight around his keys. 'You have the keys to my lock—I can never open it without you. Keep them safe. These are a symbol of what we had. *Who* we had. What we lost. All that love, Isabel. It was there, it was ours. We can't deny it or forget it, but we can honour it. And him. I want to honour him. Joshua.'

Still no tears, but her bottom lip quivered. How she held it all in was beyond him—not once had he seen her truly cry. As if it was some kind of weakness, he presumed, she wouldn't let herself break down. She took the keys and put them on a chain round her neck. 'Here. Take these keys, Sean. These are the keys to my lock. These are a symbol of what we shared. Of Joshua. Take them and keep them safe.'

'Always.' He fixed them to his key ring and put them in his inside top coat pocket.

'Next to your heart.' She pressed her palm against the pocket and he took the moment to shield her tight from the wind. From the snow that had continued to fall. From the past.

Now he had the keys to her lock, and, despite what he'd promised himself over the years, she had the keys to his heart again.

But then, the simple shocking truth was she'd always had them, hadn't she?

'Okay. No more of this. We have to get moving before we freeze our socks off.' He straightened up and gave her the first smile she'd seen from him in hours. It was gentle and honest and trusting. And with such intention Isabel watched Sean cast away the pain and the fear and the past. It was the right thing to do and yet somehow she couldn't quite let it all go. Almost all…but there was still a part of her, a tiny corner of her heart that clung to that long-ago night as if determined not to forget.

She took another huge breath and blew it out. Like cigarette smoke it plumed in the air, then was gone. The lump in her throat still lodged there though, but with every smile of Sean's it lessened just a little bit more.

'Okay.' He was right; it was time to move on. She took his hand and walked the length of the bridge, and onto the other side of the river, the lights from the old sandstone buildings reflected in the dark water. *Paris*. 'Yes. No more of this…we're in Paris for some fun and extracurriculars. Can I say, I particularly like the extracurriculars.'

His eyes glittered. 'Me too. Phil from Hastings does have a point. As did Jacob—this *entente cordiale* is good for the soul.' The hurt had gone; now all she could see as she looked at him was light and fun and teasing. His hand crept close to her bottom. 'I intend to fully indulge myself in *beaucoup d'entente cordiale*.'

'I am fully aware of your intentions, Dr Anderson. That poor lift. Those poor people waiting on the ground floor.' She grinned, remembering exactly why the lift had been halted. Dangerous. Exciting. Sex. 'So where to now, maestro?'

'The Latin Quarter,' Sean told her, filled with resolve. 'Full of quirky shops, decent cafés. There's a second-hand English bookshop along here you might like, too.

Or we could stop and get your portrait done. There will be lots of opportunity between here and the Louvre.'

Never. 'My God, you're going full-out tourist.'

'I thought you might like a memento of your visit.'

She didn't need one. She had every memory of this day engraved on her heart, and it was wide open for more. 'Not if it means staring at my ugly mug for ever more.'

At her frown he grinned. 'Okay, okay, no portrait. So it takes us about half an hour to walk to the Louvre. Of course, that depends on how many *chocolats chauds* you have between here and there. Or there's always cognac to chase away the chill. Chocolate and cognac, how's that for a combination?'

'Now you're talking.'

The afternoon was, indeed, filled with chocolate and cognac and a little red wine and a lot of kissing and many, many shops. By the time they took another taxi and did the rounds of the sparkling Christmas village at the Champs-Élysées Isabel's cheeks were pink, her legs tired and her arms filled with Christmas gifts, decorations and festive food. What a day, filled with extremes, some heart-wrenching lows and adrenalin-pumping highs. Some very, very highs.

'Okay, smile.' Sean snapped a selfie of them with nothing but dark sky and stars around them. It wasn't hard to smile; they were sitting at the top of a huge Ferris wheel—the central cog lit up like a shining Christmas star, or snowflake, Isabel hadn't quite decided—bright white in an inky-black night. Below them the streets of Paris stretched out in all directions, long straight roads of lights, a thin layer of snow on the rooftops as if someone had dusted the city with icing sugar. The tinny sound of a mechanical organ played the tune of 'O' Come All Ye Faithful' somewhere below them. And even though Isabel knew her nose was probably running she couldn't feel it because she was so very, very cold, and she didn't rightly care. She was high above the most beautiful city she'd ever visited, with a gorgeous sexy man at her side. For the first time in a long time she felt light and free and she had a sudden urge to scream out her joy, to release all the emotion knotted in her chest.

But she didn't, of course.

'That down there is the Tuileries Garden.' Sean pointed to the left, his voice raised because the breeze up here was quite strong…like being jabbed with tiny icicles down underneath her collar, on the tips of her ears, onto her cheeks. 'When I was here before we brought a picnic of baguette and cheese and some pretty rough red wine and ate down there. We had a packet of playing cards and spent hours playing blackjack and watching the world go by. Pretty cool. Mind you, it was July, so the temperature was a little different.'

She realised, then, that he hadn't talked much about those long intervening years. The focus of their conversations recently had been so much on their dark shared past and the now, but not on his life. The wheel jerked downwards and she was able to breathe a bit more evenly as the wind dipped. 'Where did you stay when you were here?'

'In a pretty scuddy backpackers' hostel in the fifth *arrondissement*. We couldn't afford much else. We did the cut-down tour of Paris, actually of Europe—mainly exploring cities on foot and on a very strict budget—so we never managed to go *in* to any of the tourist attractions, we just looked at them from the outside. Basic doesn't describe it. We spent a lot of time sleeping rough at train stations and during train journeys, to save money... which we spent, mostly, on beer.'

'I bet it was fun, though.' Intriguing. Carefree. A stab of envy ripped through her gut. 'Daddy always insisted on luxury travel so I've never done anything like that.' This trip had been safeguarded by a job—but now she felt as if she wanted to spread her wings a little, to live a little bit more, to move away from that very safe comfort zone she'd erected alongside the emotional walls. She wanted to breathe deeply, to fill her lungs with exotic air.

And then there was the question that had been forming on her lips for the last couple of minutes. 'We?'

He shrugged. 'Yeah. I travelled around with a friend.'

'Girl?'

His eyebrows rose. 'Yes.'

'Er...romantic friend?'

'Yes.'

It was silly to be jealous, and she wasn't really; after all she'd had her share of liaisons. None of them serious, she'd made sure of it...but she'd dabbled. And she couldn't help wanting to learn a little more about Sean's past. How much dabbling had he done? 'What happened to her?' *To your relationship. Your heart.*

'She went back to Brisbane. She's a GP now up on the Sunshine Coast.'

'Was it serious?'

He turned to look fully at her. 'Whoa, so many questions, Isabel. We broke up, a long time ago. So no, clearly it wasn't serious.'

'What happened?'

He looked away then, out over Paris, and she wanted so much to ask him again. *What happened to her? To you?* But then he turned back. 'Apparently I don't trust enough. Or commit...or something.'

'Because of me, what I did to you?' She waved that thought away. Too self-absorbed to think she'd be the reason his relationship had broken up. 'No, forget I said that, way too silly. I didn't mean it.'

'You really want to know?' His eyes blazed. 'Okay. Stacey—my ex—reckoned there was a part of me that was always looking backwards, comparing everyone to you. All that first love angst...yada-yada...'

'Oh. Wow. Really?'

His hand was on her arm now, which he squeezed, almost playfully. 'Of course, that's a whole lot of crock, so don't get any ideas of grandeur. Things just didn't work out. Now, after the day we've had, after what we've just done on the bridge, on a night like this—with the snow and the lights and the laughter everywhere—we are not going to talk about my old doomed relationships.' He shook his head and laughed, but Isabel got the feeling that there was a lot of truth in what he'd said and he was making light of it. That he had been affected by what had happened. Had she really ruined him for any other woman? 'Unless you want me to ask about your past lovers too? A pity fest?'

He had a point. Even though he was making a joke, what they'd shared all those years ago had been very real and raw and if she was honest she had been searching for that connectedness and never found it since. 'No, you really do not need to hear about my shabby love life.'

'Good.' The Ferris-wheel attendant opened the gate and let them out. Once on terra firma Sean shivered and stamped his feet. 'Okay, I'm hungry. You want to find something to eat?'

Isabel indicated the food in her brown paper sacks. 'We could have a picnic?'

He laughed. 'It's probably just about hit zero degrees Celsius. There's no way I'm having a picnic out here. The food will likely freeze, if we don't first.'

'I wasn't talking about outside, you idiot. I was talking about in my room. It's warm and dry and there's wine in the cupboard, Cognac in my bag.'

He took hold of the bags in one hand and wrapped his other round her waist. 'I like your thinking. Mine has a view of the Eiffel Tower. From the main room. Straight across.'

'Yours it is, then. But, Sean…' She rose on her tiptoes.

'Yes?'

'Don't think for a minute that I'm going to pretend that all those years haven't gone by. I want to know what you did. I want to know what you like. I want to know who you are now and what shaped you. I want to know everything.' Instead of creating a reality in her head that clearly wasn't true.

'Everything?'

'Everything.'

His grip on her waist tightened as he crushed her against him. She could feel his heat and his strength and she wanted to feel more of it. Preferably naked. His voice was rough with desire. 'I can tell you what I like if that helps? Actually…I can show you.'

If he meant what she thought he meant, they needed a taxi, and quick. 'That works for me.'

Within half an hour they were in Sean's room. The view was indeed breathtaking, but she'd come to realise that every view of Paris took her breath away—it was that kind of place: stunning buildings, amazing artworks, sophisticated people. Was any of it rubbing off on her? Was she becoming that nonchalant French-woman she'd tried to be? She sorely doubted it. But at least some of who she'd been had been stripped away a little. She was starting to feel new, different.

He'd found plates and knives in a drawer, opened a bottle of Bordeaux and sat in the middle of the bed with food on a blanket and two glasses in his hand. And with far too many clothes on.

Just the wall lights were lit and the way they high-lighted the dark curls of his hair and the ridges and shadows of his face made her want to lean in and kiss him. To run her fingers over his face, to explore the new terrain of his features. Breath left her lungs when he raised his head and his dark gaze locked with hers, his intentions very clear now. There was stark hunger in his eyes; desire, thick and tangible, filled the heavy air around them. The strength of her need shocked her. It took all of her resolve not to undress him right there. But this was a day she wanted to remember as much for the loving as the letting go—she wanted to take her time getting to know him properly.

'What are you waiting for, Isabel? You know, I still can't get used to calling you that. You'll be my Izzy for ever.'

Those words gave her a shiver of delight because, more than anything, she wanted to be his Izzy today.

As he lifted his glass to his lips she saw a bare patch of skin on his forearm, a linear scar about three inches long. 'Come sit down. I have wine.'

'You have a scar there. What's that about?'

'This?' He looked down at the place she was pointing to. 'Geez, I can't even remember. Maybe a sports thing? Surfing, maybe? Yeah, probably surfing. I took a bad dunking down at Portsea, which ripped a layer of skin off. Years ago now.'

'You used to love surfing. Sometimes I thought there was no contest—you'd choose that board over me any day.'

'Nah…it was just a teenage obsession. I haven't done it for a while. Not since…' He ran his hand through his hair as he stared at the scar. 'Well, probably not since I did this.'

'Oh, well, I'll kiss it better anyway, seeing as I missed my chance when it happened.' When her lips made contact with his skin she tasted soap and imagined the salt and sunshine taste of the beach. She imagined him wet and bedraggled. Hot and languid from exercise. At the touch of her tongue on such a tender place he groaned. She smiled and pulled his thick sweater over his head, revealing a navy-blue body-hugging T-shirt. Her fingers trailed down to his hand, where she slid her fingers in between his. 'Any more injuries that need some care and attention from a very dedicated doctor?'

'Hmm… I like where you're going with his.' He levered himself up against the headboard. 'When I was nineteen I was playing Aussie rules footie and broke my wrist.'

'Poor you.' She picked up his left arm and kissed his wrist.

'It was the other one.'

'Oops.'

'Aha.' He slid his hand to the back of her head and pulled her in for a kiss; he tasted of wine and promise, and hot lust coiled through her gut. Her heart was beating hard and fast and the shaking had melded into confidence and daring. His eyes still didn't leave hers. 'When I was twenty-two I broke two left ribs in a motorbike crash.'

'Someone else's bike? No?' She guessed she must have looked pretty prim, with her mouth wide open at his admission, so she tried to look as if his having a death wish was the most acceptable thing in the world. 'You had a motorbike?'

'When I lived in Sydney, it was a lot cheaper to get around. I loved that motorbike.' His hands pressed under her top, around her waist—bare skin on skin making her shiver with more need—pulling her closer. 'Still do.'

'You have it here? No, surely not.' She crawled across him to straddle his lap; the warmth of his skin stoked her soul, spanning out from her core to her legs, arms, fingers. 'In Cambridge? How do I not know this?'

'Clearly I have a different one in Cambridge, but my old Triumph is waiting for me in Melbourne, at my parents' house.' He cupped her bottom and positioned her over his hardness. 'And why would you know? This is the first time we've really talked about anything in between the last end and the new beginning.'

Getting to know him all over again was very illuminating. Was there nothing about him that didn't excite her? 'Very dangerous. Very edgy…although most people have bicycles in Cambridge. I'd like to see you ride it. In fact, I'd very much like to see you in leathers.'

'I'd like to see you strip them off.' Pulling her top over her head, he palmed her bra, unclipped it, let it fall. 'About those ribs…'

'Oh, yes. Well, clearly this needs to go too.' Naked. She wanted him naked. Without wasting any more time she dragged the T-shirt over his head, exposing his broad, solid chest. She ran her fingers across to his back, skimming over muscles and sinews. Kissed her way from his spine forward to his solar plexus, her tongue taking a detour to his nipples where she sucked one in, making him groan all over again. 'Better?'

'Almost…' His voice raspy and deep. 'When I was twenty-four I had acute appendicitis…'

Giggling, she looked down at his perfect, unblemished abdomen, then back at him. 'You don't have a scar.'

He gave her a wry smile. 'No, it was just a stomach ache in the end, but I think you'd better kiss it better just in case. Just to avoid a flare-up.'

As she licked a trail from nipple to belly button her nipples grazed his jeans. The rough fabric against such sensitive skin made her pause. She was nose to…well, nose to bulge. 'Well, hello, hello… We seem to have a flare-up happening. You…you haven't had any injuries down here?'

'No. All in full working order, ma'am. As I'm sure you remember.'

'I most certainly do.' Thank the good Lord for that. She flicked the button and dragged his jeans off. Took a sharp intake of breath as she looked at him. So supremely sexy. Hard and hot.

'Anything else you want to know? Blood group?'

She knew enough, that he was rhesus negative, because she'd had a Rhesus immunoglobulin injection when she'd had Joshua. But he didn't need to know that. This wasn't the time or the place. 'I want to know…when are you going to kiss me again?'

Then his hands were under her arms, pulling her to face him, his mouth slanting over hers, whispering her name over and over, then fingers plunging into her hair as he kissed her throat, her neck. 'Isabel… *God*, Isabel, the way you make me feel…'

'I know.' Knew what he needed. Another kiss. Touch. The soft silk of skin against skin. The press of heat. Another kiss.

And another. It was in his eyes, in his words, in his voice, in a look. In the beat of his heart against hers. 'Isabel, no more questions… I *know* you now, here.'

'And I *know* you.' She had no care for thinking, for analysing the past, of worrying for the future. She knew him this moment and that was enough.

His teeth grazed her nipples and her head dropped back, her fists in his hair as he feasted. Then his hands moved over her body in a slow teasing study, as if in reverence, down her shoulders, over her breasts, down her belly, slipping to the inside of her thigh.

Oh, God. Yes. She kissed him again full and hard, clutching him closer, and closer still, erasing any space, any past.

'Wait.' He grasped for his jeans and took out a foil, turned onto his side a moment—too long…she couldn't wait. The ferocity of need stripped her lungs until she gasped for more air, more kisses, more him. He kissed her again and more, and more kisses, wet and greedy, mouths slipping, tongues dancing.

'Sean. I need you.'

'I know, baby. I need you too. So much. So much.' He laid her down and covered her with his body, his hardness so tantalisingly close, his fingers exploring her folds. His thumb skimmed her hard nub and she moaned, opening for him.

'Now, Sean. I need you inside me.'

He slid into her, stretching, filling her so completely

it was as if he were made for her. And she gasped again, fitting herself to his rhythm. Her orgasm rising, swelling with each thrust.

'Sean… I…' The rise of emotions thick and full in her chest, she couldn't put them into words.

'I know. I know, Izzy. I know.' This time his kisses were frenzied, hard, rough. And she loved it. Loved his taste and his touch and his scent. Loved the knot of muscles under her fist moving with every thrust. Loved this moment.

Her orgasm shook through her, unbearable and beautiful in equal measure. His thrusts became faster, deeper, as he too shook as his climax spiralled through him; he was calling her name and clutching her close as if he couldn't bear to ever let her go.

CHAPTER NINE

SEAN WOKE TO bright light filtering through the curtains. Down in the street below there was a siren, voices, the beep of a horn. Paris was awake and, apparently, it thought he should be too. Facing him, curled over onto her side, slept Isabel, blonde hair splayed over the pillow, sheets pulled tightly around her. She looked so peaceful, so rested, so damned perfect that his heart tightened as the questions that had stampeded through his head at midnight played over and over like a stuck record.

Did he want her?

Yes.

Were they rushing things?

Yes.

What did the future hold?

Damned if he knew.

She was everything he'd ever wanted in a woman—back at school and now—the ideal woman every male wanted to be with. Compassionate. Kind. Beautiful. Sexy. Fun. He'd never been able to believe his luck when she'd chosen him above all the other sixth formers. He could barely believe she was here right now.

Whatever it was that was developing between them was huge. Intense. But she'd broken him once and he'd spent so many years erasing her from his heart, so letting her fully in was causing some trouble. He wanted to. Man, he wanted to, but there was a part of him that just wouldn't let go. Even after yesterday. Such a symbolic and profound moment on the bridge—but that had been about Joshua, not about them. He knew she was scared too and, knowing Isabel, she was a definite flight risk. He couldn't even think about committing to someone who would always be looking over her shoulder and planning when to leave.

Like him, right now.

She reached a hand to his thigh, her voice groggy with sleep. 'Hey there, good morning. Don't even think of going anywhere. I have plans.'

'Me too.' He stroked the underside of her breast. She was so gut-wrenchingly beautiful. 'You wanted to go to see Marina and Teo, and I need to pack if I'm going to get that two o'clock train. Work waits for no man, so I'm told.'

'Do we have five minutes before we start to rush around? Yes, I'd like to see Marina and the boy, but can we just wait a few more moments? I'd like five. Just five.' She curled into his waiting arms and lay there, her breathing calm and steady, oblivious to the turmoil in his head. 'Thank you, Sean, for such a wonderful day yesterday.'

'My pleasure.' And it certainly had been. Just watching her smile had been worth every second. But he wanted more and more and more—and that wanting scared the hell out of him. 'It was a good day all in all.'

'I wish you didn't have to go back. I wish we could stay here like this, warm and cosy and…' she wiggled towards him, her fingers straying upwards along his thigh '…content.'

Content? With a juggernaut of questions steamrollering through his brain? 'How about you ring down for some room-service breakfast? We can have a quick shower, eat and then go?' And maybe with fresh air he'd get some more perspective.

'We can have a shower? Great idea.' Shoving the covers back, she bounded out of bed, then she stopped and looked back at him. 'Come on, what are you waiting for?'

'Just taking in the view…'

'Oh, and you like what you see?' She wiggled her backside at him. Naked. Pretty as a picture. Her long limbs stretching with ease, there were still the vestiges of her last Australian summer there in the fading freckles. Her breasts bobbed slightly as she moved and he remembered how they'd felt under his tongue, how she'd felt astride him.

Apparently perspective was difficult to come by when he was already hard for her again.

What sane man would walk away from this?

'Isabel, I have to leave today.'

The smile fell. 'I know.'

'So we have to talk—'

She came back to him, sat on the duvet and stroked a hand across his bicep. 'No, we don't.'

'Yes.' He anchored her to the bed, hands on her shoulders. 'Stop and listen—'

'No,' she interrupted him, her mouth on his lips now. 'I get it, you know. I totally know that when we leave this room, things will be different. When we go back to work things will be different. So don't go raining on my parade just yet, got it? Give me five damned minutes, that's all I'm asking…give me some of the fairy tale.'

'But—'

Now she'd climbed onto him, straddling his legs—her favourite position, it seemed—pressing herself over his erection. Her lips on his throat. Her glorious heat and wetness on him. Puckered pink nipples pressing against his chest. 'Please, Sean. Don't break the spell…not yet.'

Yes, that was how it felt—as if she'd bewitched him. She kissed him again and his resolve wavered. He cupped her bare cheeks and pulled her closer. The woman wanted five minutes.

Five lifetimes and he'd never have enough of her.

And, what the hell, he was all for a little magic every now and then…

And so she'd taken more than five minutes to savour Sean all over again. *So sue me.* But she'd had to do something to wipe that look from his face—the one that said *I'm sorry, but…*

She hadn't wanted to hear how much he regretted spending these past few days with her or that it had to end because they were going back to work. Or anything other than *let's do it all again.* Because she knew he'd wanted her as much as she'd wanted him—at least, his body had; his brain seemed to be working overtime trying to find problems. And she'd just had to kiss him one more time before the inevitable happened. But the kissing had led to so much more…and now she was in deeper than she'd ever intended.

As they walked up the paediatric ward corridor towards Teo's bed she saw Marina waving at her. She'd showered; her hair was in a neat plait down her back.

She was dressed in a hospital gown…and, wait? 'Sean,' Isabel almost screamed as she gripped his arm. 'She's had the baby. Oh, my God, she's had the baby.'

How the heck would Marina cope now?

Isabel dropped her bags, rushed forward and wrapped her new friend into a hug, tussled the grinning boy's hair and then stood back as mum unwrapped the bundle she held tightly in her arms.

'Izzbel…' Marina held the baby out to her, smiling. 'Lucia. Lucia.' And then she garbled something that Isabel didn't understand but she took the sleeping baby from Marina's outstretched hands and held it close. The distinct smell of newborns hit her and her heart melted at once at the tiny snub nose and the dark watchful eyes that seemed to know so much already. She thought about Isla and little Geo and felt a mixture of homesickness and pride. All these babies were true miracles. 'Boy?' She pointed at Sean because the white gown the baby wore gave no hint as to gender. 'Or girl?' She pressed a finger to her own chest, which was thick with joy at this little life, and fear for its future.

Marina pointed at Isabel. '*Fată*… Lucia.'

'Lucia? Her name is Lucia? It must be a girl. Oh, Sean, come and look.' He was sitting down and building bricks with Teo. Just watching him play so gently with the boy made her heart sing. He'd have made a wonderful father, she had no doubt.

She really had to stop berating herself about events of seventeen years ago and start to live for now. She'd promised herself that. She'd even kissed Sean's doubts away long enough to make love with him again, but she couldn't help having a few herself. And being with him brought all those memories to the forefront.

Could they survive the past?

'Sean, come look at this gorgeous girl.'

'Hey there, little one.' He stood and gave Marina a kiss on the cheeks and offered her a very proud smile, but, as with Isabel, there was a question there. What would Marina do now?

Just then, she noticed another woman hovering close by, in a smart straight black skirt and buttoned-up black jacket, dark hair pulled tightly back into a bun. 'Hi. I'm Isabel. I met Marina yesterday at the shelter—we brought her here.'

She didn't smile back. 'Yes, you are Izzbel. Good to meet you. I am Ana, translator.'

'Pleased to meet you. I'm so glad you're here to help.' Isabel nodded, cradling baby Lucia in one arm while she gingerly reached for her bag and brought out the nappies and babygros she'd purchased yesterday. 'Can you please tell Marina I'd like her to have these? And here's some toiletries for her too. Hospital ones are so basic, it's nice to have some luxury.'

Ana did as she was asked. 'Marina says, thank you very much.'

'How is Teo?'

Sean cut in, 'I've just checked through the notes—looks like his fever's settling. Still a bit high, but it's coming down and that's the main thing. He seems chirpier today.'

Isabel brought out the toy fire engine she'd bought for him, leaving the outfits she hadn't been able to resist in the bag. She'd just leave it all here for him rather than have him overwhelmed all at once. 'Here you go, buddy. Here's something for you to play with.'

He took it shyly from her hands and grasped it close

to his chest. Marina's eyes pricked with tears as she grabbed Isabel's sleeve and muttered something.

Ana translated in that mechanical voice. 'Again, she says thank you.'

Isabel knew she should probably not ask this question, it was none of her business, but she just couldn't help it. 'Can you tell me, what's the plan for her? Where are they going to be discharged to?'

Ana looked over at Marina, then took Isabel to one side. 'They want to check her for a few days. She has… high blood pressure from the birth—'

'I thought so—pre-eclampsia? They induced her too? That should resolve easily enough, but she has nowhere to live and two small children. It's freezing—'

Ana nodded. 'There is caseworker assigned now. She go to hotel and then to lodging in Éragny when available.'

The baby started to stir and Isabel felt the usual pull she felt when a baby cried, the ache in her breasts. Her milk had come in after a couple of days and she hadn't known what to do, how to deal with leaks…for the record, tissue stuffed down a bra just made everyone at school think you were trying to impress. She offered Lucia back to her mum. 'I think she might want you.'

Garbling again, Marina shook her head and pushed the baby back to Isabel.

'What's she saying?'

Ana shook her head and looked at the floor. 'She says you can have the girl.' Ana spoke to Marina in the lyrical language, her voice raised. '"Take her," she's saying. "You and your husband can give her better than I can."'

'Husband?' If she wasn't mistaken the look Sean threw her was one of abject horror at the suggestion.

Now a different beat began to play in her chest. He didn't want her? Was that it? She wasn't wife material? Did she want to be? She'd never thought about it before…images flashed through her head of a wedding, and smiling Sean and kids….all so inappropriate and yet, so wonderful.

But he didn't want it. And Marina wanted her to be a mother, and Isabel didn't know if she could do that either. Not that she'd ever accept a baby like this, but, well… She walked to Marina and tried to place the baby into her arms. 'No, Marina, take her, please.' It was all becoming just a little too intense. The baby was sniffling now and no doubt preparing to wail for her lunch. And yes, Isabel had material wealth and stability and probably looked like a damned fine bet in Marina's eyes, but she wasn't this baby's mother. And that was what Lucia needed more than anything—her mother's love. Isabel tried to reason with her, lowered her voice and got her eye contact. 'Take your baby, Marina. You're a good mum. Take her.'

Marina shook her head and turned her back as if the deal had been settled.

'Marina, take your baby, please.' Sean's voice had a ring of authority, but was laced with gentleness. He took the infant from Isabel's shaking hands. 'Marina, take your baby. Lucia. Needs. You.'

He handed the baby back to Marina and she took her with tears streaking her face. She said something very quietly and then turned away again, sat down and started to breastfeed Lucia.

Ana explained, 'She said she had to try. She loves her baby too much to keep her.'

Isabel fought tears of her own. She would not cry. She would subsume this emotion and pretend it didn't exist.

But, oh, it was one thing to have your baby cruelly ripped away because you just couldn't nurture him, another altogether to be willing to hand your child over to strangers in the hope of a happier life. Isabel's heart just about broke into pieces. She sat down next to Marina and stroked her back. 'You'll be okay. You have so much strength and determination. Look at Teo, he's a happy boy chatting away to Sean, he's bonny and—oh, you poor, poor thing. You love her, and that's the most important thing. I'll help you. Somehow.'

Sean was by her side as she looked up; he gave her a soft smile. 'Does this happen a lot? People offering you their babies?'

'No, it's usually a one-way street. I hand the baby over at delivery—no one's ever offered it back to me.'

'Are you okay?' He ran a thumb down her cheek.

She curled into his touch as his fingers reached her neck. 'I think so.'

'Good.' He pressed a hand to her arm and urged her to stand. 'I think it's best if we leave now. Marina's probably feeling distraught and guilty and...well, I think we've done our best here.'

Isabel shook her head; she wasn't finished. 'I'd like to help her further. Maybe there's a charity I can contact? There must be.'

Ana nodded and gave her a business card. 'We have charities that can help with baby, with childcare and getting Marina job when she is ready. I have network of Romanian people who will help too. Contact me and I give you details.'

'Thank you. So much. I will.' Isabel decided that the formidable Ana would probably not want a hug, so she gave two to Marina instead. Then she kissed little

Lucia and knuckled Teo's cheeks gently. If there was one Delamere gene she was proud of it was the determination to help and to make things work out. She would do that for Marina. 'I'll come back soon, I promise. Tomorrow, hopefully.'

Once outside Isabel sucked in a deep breath. 'This was supposed to be just a conference and then some holiday time. I feel wrung out by it all. I think I'm going to need a holiday when I get back to Cambridge.'

Sean's arm was round her shoulder as they walked down the steps and towards the Metro station. 'You take everything to heart, and you shouldn't. She's not your responsibility. Are you like this with all your patients?'

Isabel laughed. 'As if! I'd never get through the day. I manage to keep a perfectly good professional distance but I do care. It's my job to care. But Marina's not my patient. She's…well, she needs a friend, everyone needs that.'

'You don't know anything about her.'

'I know that she loves her kids and that she'd do anything for them. I know that she's desperate and I've been there too.' And he was right, she shouldn't have got involved. But how could she not? Somehow the emotion of the week had got to her.

He'd got to her. Spending time with him had cracked open that barrier she'd so carefully built around her heart and now it seemed she was prey to every emotion out there. That had to stop. And right now.

They'd arrived at the Metro and her heart began its funny little thumping and her tummy began to whirl.

Sean looked at his watch then shrugged a shoulder. 'I'm going to have to go and get that train, but I want to make sure you're all right.'

And now he was going to leave and the moment she'd been dreading reared its ugly head. 'Of course, I'm fine. There are thousands of people like Marina all over the world and I can't help them all. I do understand.'

He pulled her collar around her ears and gave her a look she couldn't read. 'I didn't mean Marina. I meant us. This.'

Us. The thought of it made her hopeful...but then the doubt fairies started to circle again. 'Of course, I'm fine. After I've waved you off with my white handkerchief I'm going to do more shopping...'

He grinned. 'Oh, yes, of course. The deep and meaningful way of dealing with goodbyes.'

'The only way of dealing with anything, surely?' Part of her wanted to cling to his arm and refuse to let him go into the station, to drag him back to bed and replay last night, to never go back to Cambridge or Melbourne and stay here, in Paris, and just be *us*. Her throat was clogged with words she couldn't say to him out loud— the poor guy would run a mile.

But he wasn't going to let it go. 'That's not what I was asking, Isabel.'

Oh, she knew what he was asking, all right, she just didn't know how to answer. 'I mean, it's been really great, Sean, but...geez, husband? I had to chuckle to myself when she said that...'

He frowned. 'That stupid an idea, is it?'

She'd thought he'd have seen the joke too. Thought that the notion of them being married would have made him smile and raise his eyebrows in disbelief. 'What? No. I mean...well...'

His shoulders dropped a little. 'Things will change when we go back to work.'

She infused her voice with fake joy. 'No bed picnics and lie-ins for us…not when we're playing stork and delivering much-wanted babies. Busy on-call rosters. And, besides, in a couple of weeks I'll be heading back to Aussie. You'll be in Cambridge, then who knows where…?'

He nodded. 'You sound as if you're trying to convince yourself that it's not worth the effort.'

'No. That's not it at all.'

He tucked a lock of her hair behind her ear, then his hands skimmed her arms and locked her in place. 'I know you're scared. I understand—it's freaking me out too. So it's probably a good thing that we have this time to take stock. There's a lot to work through.'

'Yes. Of course, so much to think about.'

She thought he was going to walk away but he stepped closer, cupped her face in his hands and brought his mouth close to hers. 'I was angry about what happened, I admit that. I said some stupid things and I apologise. I was a jerk on the train and an idiot at the wine-tasting. It's taken some time for me to get used to the idea of what I missed out on—and it hasn't been easy. Isabel, I'm not a heart-on-my-sleeve kind of bloke, but…it could work, you know. If we wanted it to. We just have to believe. Can you do that?'

The kiss he gave her was lingering and warm. It told her without any doubt that he was willing to do anything to make this work, that he wanted her, that he wanted this.

Did she? *Yes.* Her heart was cheering. Yes.

And still the questions buzzed in her head along with the one true belief she'd kept all those years: *you'll get hurt.*

Plain and simple.

'Can you do that, Izzy? Can you believe?'

Izzy. Oh, yes, in his arms she was Izzy again, she couldn't deny it—he had her down pat. He was the only guy who ever had. But was it enough? She'd done wrong by him and they would never get away from that, from that one night that changed everything. It happened; she couldn't pretend it hadn't. 'I don't know, Sean. I'm sorry.'

He pulled away. 'You need to stop apologising for everything and start to believe in us again.'

She grasped the keys on the chain round her neck. 'I'm going to try. I promise. I'll try.'

'Good. Me too. When are you back in Cambridge?'

'Twenty-third, late...then I'm on call Christmas Eve, dinner at Bonnie's in the evening if I can get away...' She watched him try to keep up and it sounded like a load of excuses, but it was her life—just her life. This was how it was going to be if anything became of *us*—two busy professionals trying to fit each other in—none of the all-consuming togetherness they'd shared here. None of what they'd had all those years ago when life was theirs for the taking. 'I'm at work Christmas Day.'

He pecked a kiss onto her nose and tilted her face up to his. 'I'll see you on Christmas Day then, at work—maybe we can do something after our shifts? I don't want you to be on your own.'

'Thank you, that would be wonderful. I don't want to be alone, either. Dinner, maybe?'

'Yes, dinner. And the rest...everything.' At her smile he found one too. 'Believe, Izzy. Take a chance.' Then he let her go and turned away, his duffle bag high on his back, taking long, long strides into the busy tube station. And taking, along with him, her heart.

CHAPTER TEN

'OOH, LOVELY, MORE CHOCOLATES!' Isabel reached across the labour suite nurses' station desk and grabbed a chewy toffee from the box before they all disappeared. 'From another grateful client?'

'Hmm, yes.' Bonnie looked up from her seat in front of the computer screen, popped a chocolate into her mouth and sucked; she had a pair of red velvet reindeer ears on a band over her lovely russet-coloured hair. 'It's the best bit about working at Christmas—all the patients get nostalgic about gifts and babies and mangers and we get the benefit. Although there only ever seems to be strawberry creams left when I get to choose.'

'Aww, that's because, as labour suite sister, you make sacrifices for your staff. It's very noble of you.'

Bonnie laughed. 'It's because I'm too busy to stop and eat, more like.'

She did indeed have a busy life, what with a little daughter and now Jacob in her life, plus this unit to run. But, if anyone could make it work, Bonnie could. Isabel felt a wee pang of jealousy—it looked like Sister Bonnie had managed to get it all: family, a man who adored her and a job she loved. Some people really could put their past behind them and believe things could work out. 'Don't worry, sweetie, I'll bring a box of yummy French choccies tonight just for you, specifically with no strawberry creams.'

'Oh, good, are you still coming over for dinner? Freya's so excited to see you—but be warned... Father Christmas is on his way so she'll be hyped-up beyond belief.'

After her now ex-husband's tawdry affair with her best friend, Bonnie had made a fresh start in Cambridge, bringing her daughter away from everything familiar. She had worked hard to make her happy here and to provide everything the girl needed. Isabel had to admit to having fallen just a little bit in love with the little tyke... hyped or not. 'Okay...no worries at all, I'm looking forward to it. Christmas Eve is so special when you're five. How's Jacob bearing up with it all? Must be strange for him to be sharing his house with a ready-made family?'

Bonnie sighed. 'Don't tell him I said so, but he loves it. Underneath that brooding exterior is a sucker for candy canes and Santa sacks. Between you and me he's about as hyped-up as Freya.'

Isabel laughed, imagining their straight-as-a-die, oh-so-professional boss in a Santa outfit. Somehow the image just didn't fit. 'There's a side to him we don't get to see, obviously. I got Freya some gorgeous dresses in Paris...you'll just die when you see them!'

'Oh, that's so sweet, but you know you didn't have to buy her anything, really. Anyway, never mind my terrible twosome, tell me about Dr Dreamcakes. I'm all ears and green with envy. A vacation with him in Paris...' Bonnie put the back of her hand to her forehead and pretended to swoon. 'Naughty Jacob for setting you two up like that. I swear he had an ulterior motive, but he denies all agendas other than a work one. And I'm sorry he couldn't go to Paris with you—that may have been my fault. I wanted to make the build-up to Christmas a special one for Freya, and I put some pressure on Jacob not to go. Still, up close and very personal *à la* France, with a hunk like Sean, what's not to like? How was it?'

Bless her, all loved-up and finally with the full fairy tale, Bonnie hadn't got a clue about the state of Isabel's mind. Her history with Sean had been a well-kept secret from day one and, truth was, Isabel didn't know how it was.

The few extra days in Paris had been filled with thinking and shopping and worrying. And helping Marina, Teo and Lucia move into temporary accommodation. And then there had been a lot more thinking and wishing and panicking about how she really felt. Which was…confused. She'd spent the last few hours at work grateful that Sean had the day off today and that she wouldn't have to face him until tomorrow, because no doubt he'd want some kind of an answer. One more sleepless night to try to sort out her head. 'Oh, you know…it was…Paris.'

'Hey, you're back!' Hope Sanders, one of the other unit midwives, walked out of a side room and wrapped Isabel into a big hug. 'How're you doing? Have you seen the crazy amount of stuff we've got for the first Christmas baby?'

'I know, lucky winner! How on earth they'll get that lot home I don't know. They're going to need to call in Santa and his sleigh.' A huge mountain of gifts now swamped a shopping trolley; the generosity of the unit staff, clients and relatives had been amazing. 'We could halve it and give a prize for the first baby of the new year too.'

'What an excellent idea, Isabel. We could do that and share the love.'

For a moment Isabel thought that her trip might well have been forgotten. Prayed so. Alas no... Hope squeezed a drop of sanitiser onto her hands, rubbed them vigorously and grinned. 'So, come on, how was it? How was Dr Sex-On-Legs? How was Paris? Oh... Wait... Hang on, I've just got to go to the ladies'. Don't say a single word until I get back.'

'Don't worry, I won't...' *Won't say anything at all, if I can help it.* Isabel smiled at her friends. Gosh, she was going to miss this lot when she went home. There was nothing quite like a group of warm and welcoming women to bridge that homesickness gap. They'd all made her very welcome despite their own troubles, and, God knew, they'd all had their fair share over the last year. Bonnie had moved from Scotland and moved in with Jacob before she even knew him; Hope had met and fallen for Aaron, the totally gorgeous American infertility specialist; and rumour had it that midwife Jess Black was also loved up with sexy SCBU doc Dean Edwards, if their spectacular kiss at the Christmas party was anything to go by; but not without a few road bumps along the way for all of them. Somehow they'd survived, the better and happier for it. Apart from Isabel, of course. She was just muddled.

Bonnie smiled as she watched Hope walk down the corridor towards the bathrooms. 'Not that I'm counting, but that's the third time Hope's been to the loo this morning. I hope she's okay. None of my business, of course.'

'No, none whatsoever.' Isabel raised her eyebrows in question, which was girl code for *tell me what you're thinking*.

Bonnie's eyebrows rose in response. 'She seems very happy. Glowing, I'd say.'

'What? D'you think…? No, not Hope…and Aaron? And…pitter-patter?'

'I have no idea…but peeing a lot is one of the first telltale signs…'

Really, nothing was terribly secret on this unit. They all worked long hours and much of their social time was spent together too; they were like family. Everyone knew how gooey Hope went over the newborns, how much she desperately wanted one of her own…and the heat between her and Aaron had been off the scale every time those two had laid eyes on each other. She'd had IVF planned to become a single mum and no one had dared ask her how it had gone; they thought she'd tell them when she had news. Maybe Hope had finally got her dream too?

After a few minutes Isabel watched Hope sauntering back onto the ward, smiling to herself, her hand gently rubbing her abdomen. 'I think if she had anything to tell us she would. It's not for us to speculate.'

Bonnie shrugged and winked. 'All I was saying was that she's spent a lot of time on the loo this morning. And she seems quite happy about it. Nothing gossipy about that, it's all just facts.'

Hope reached them. 'Sorry about that. Now, Isabel, tell me about Paris. Was it wonderful?'

'We had a very interesting conference, thank you.'

'*Interesting?* What exactly does that mean?' Bonnie

checked her watch, stood and walked across to Isabel. 'Come on, you can dish the dirt on the way.'

'To lunch? Aww, no, sorry, ladies, much as I'd love to come with you I have so much paperwork to catch up on, emails and stuff, I don't have time today.'

Bonnie's arm looped through Isabel's. 'I thought you'd say that. As it happens we need some extra personnel downstairs...so you're coming with us. We won't keep you too long. I said we'd meet Jess down there.'

'Jess?' Isabel sensed mischief. 'Down where? The cafeteria? I said I can't do lunch. Are we doing lunch?'

'Not so much.' As they strolled towards the hospital main exit Jess walked towards them, arms full of Santa hats.

'Oh, great, you made it.' Jess gave them all a big grin. Another one in the unit to have had a difficult year, but for whom things were very definitely looking up. 'Thank you so much. I have some extra people coming down from SCBU too, a backing track and some collection boxes. We should make quite a bit, fingers crossed.'

Oh-oh. Isabel felt as if she'd been duped into something she might not enjoy. 'Make what? Doing what?'

'Carol singing.'

'Really? At lunchtime? Why?' *Me? Sing?* 'It's not my thing, really. I have work to do.'

'Oh, come on, sweetheart. You're a long way from home and we thought you might enjoy it.' Bonnie draped some glittery red tinsel over Isabel's shoulder while Jess stuck a red hat on her head. 'Because this is what we do at Christmas. Here's some tinsel—wrap it round your stethoscope. You are going to have a taste of our lovely British traditions. No beach and prawns on the barby...'

She put on a terrible Australian accent. 'It's all mince pies, roast chestnuts and lots and lots of singing.'

'We sing. I just don't like doing it all that much.' It was too much of a reminder, all that little baby Jesus stuff. Away in a manger. Lay down his sweet head.

'You'll love it, honestly, and it's for a good cause.' Jess grinned. 'I've even managed to coerce Dean to help out, and that's got to be a first.'

Isabel had had a few professional dealings with Dean Edwards over preemies in SCBU; he was a damned fine doctor and a pretty decent colleague. A bit of a heart-throb too, if she was honest. But no one ever seemed to match up to Sean, no matter how much she looked. And she'd look a heck of a party-pooper if she didn't join in now. Better to get it over with and then leave. 'Dean Edwards, singing? Well, if he's in then I guess I am. I have got to see this.'

'Oh, there he is.' Jess walked towards him as if she were floating on air. She gave him a shy smile and he gave her one in return, oblivious to anyone else in the room. Jess handed him a hat. More *facts* in the department: Jess and Dean were now dating... 'Thank you for coming down.'

Hope stopped mid-tinsel-wrapping. 'Oh...hang on. I just need...wait. I just need to pee. I'll be right back.'

Bonnie threw Isabel a look as if to say *I told you so*, then back at Hope. 'You just went.'

Looking a little sheepish, Hope stuck out her tongue, but the smile stuck. 'Who are you, my mother?'

'Sometimes it feels like I'm everyone's mother here—it comes with the job description.' Bonnie looked at her seriously. 'Hope, are you okay?'

'Yes... Yes, I'm fine. Oh...come here all of you. I

need to tell you something.' Hope steered the three of them, Isabel, Jess and Bonnie, across to a quiet corner, took their hands. 'Listen, ladies, this has so got to be a secret, but I can't think straight unless I tell you... I'm pregnant! Sorry, *we're* pregnant, me and Aaron...'

Isabel pretended to look blown away with surprise. 'Wow! That's so fabulous, honey. Well done you. The IVF worked?'

Hope looked as if she was going to burst with excitement. 'No...no, that's just it... I never thought it would happen like this... I went for the implantation and I didn't need it. I was already pregnant. I'm so excited.'

Jess gave her a cuddle and squealed a little. 'Wow, that's just so brilliant. What a Christmas present. You look amazing—feeling okay? No nausea?'·

'Not yet. Apart from needing the loo a lot, I'm fine.'

'Okay, yummy mummy, you nip off to the ladies' while we set up. Now, gather round, or we're going to run out of time. I have to get back in twenty minutes.' Jess got them all together into a semicircle by the main doors, in front of a beautiful scented floor-to-ceiling pine Christmas tree, and flicked on the sound system. Handing out sheets of lyrics, she joined them and started to sing 'Away In A Manger'.

Just peachy. As she read through the words Isabel wondered about little Lucia and how she was doing in the new crib that she'd found for her in a Paris baby shop. For some reason the thought of that little scrap of life made her feel a bit heartsore. Or it could have been the excitement of Hope's pregnancy. Or, it could have been, as Sean had suggested, that perhaps she still had that small part inside her that wanted a baby of her own. That perhaps that dream hadn't died along with Joshua after all. Maybe she could open her heart to thinking about that, some time, in the future. She decided as she stood there surrounded by all this love that maybe she would.

As they moved into the second chorus people stopped rushing about and started to listen, and they were smiling and joining in. Beyond the doors the sky was thick and heavy as more snow threatened. Isabel knew that by three-thirty it would be dark outside and that every child in the country would be counting down the hours until that very special jolly man paid them a visit. And so it wouldn't be a swim, then champagne and a barbecue, it wouldn't be sunbathing and lounging around with her family. She'd be here, with this new family of hers, having a very different time, delivering babies and making some people's Christmas a very happy one indeed.

And, as the saying went, a change was as good as a rest.

She watched Hope wipe her eyes as the carol came to an end. The audience had grown quite large and people were generously donating into the buckets at their feet.

Then, at the back of the crowd, she saw a face that sent her heart into overdrive.

He wasn't supposed to be here.

His gaze caught hers and he watched her sing, a small smile on those sensual lips. The world seemed to shrink a little and she felt herself singing the words just to him, and she felt the heat in his gaze. From this distance he probably looked, to everyone else, just like any other guy. But she knew differently.

She knew he was capable of great things, the greatest things anyone could ever do; he was capable of forgiving, of trying to let go, of believing in something that not everyone had the chance to experience in their lives; he was capable of believing in love. With her. He was offering her a chance to have what Hope had, what Jess and Bonnie had, what Isla had, and what everyone deserved: a rich, fulfilling future.

And no, nothing had changed in those last few days, damn it, nothing had changed in those last seventeen years, she still felt gloriously attracted to him; she still craved his touch. Her heart still swelled at the sight of him. She wanted to lean into those shoulders and feel his arms around her; she wanted to lie next to him and talk about the day. She wanted to grow old by his side and somehow make up for the lost years without him. She just had to pluck up the courage to say yes. That was the problem.

After two more songs he gave her a slow wink and walked away.

'What the hell was that about?' Bonnie whispered out of the corner of her mouth as she too watched Sean's back disappear up the corridor. 'What just happened between you two?'

'Shut up and sing.' Isabel smiled through gritted teeth.

And she did. And nothing more was said as they went through another five carols and raised a couple of hundred pounds for the SCBU.

But later, when just the two of them were walking back to the labour suite, Bonnie stopped and looked straight at Isabel. 'I know it's none of my business—'

'No, it's not.' But she knew her friend had the very best intentions.

'So here are the facts as I see them.' Bonnie smiled gently as heat hit Isabel's cheeks. 'Every time you and Sean are in the same room there are sparks. Tensions soar so high we all feel a need to switch on the fans and get ice. Fact number two: you were heard arguing about your past, about a relationship you had. About lies you told, apparently. And he said he didn't want to see you again. But you went to Paris together. And it was *interesting.*' Another girl-code stare. 'Fact three: the way he looked at you out there just about set the hospital alight. I was torn between decking the halls with boughs of holly and phoning the fire brigade. The man clearly wants you and yet, here you are, looking glum and worried. You want to talk? Because I can listen, very well.'

It would help, Isabel knew, just to say the words out loud. 'Maybe later?'

'Later it'll be Freya and Father Christmas and Jacob and chaos. Trust me, we won't get a chance. I have time now. My office?'

'You hate your office.' Everyone knew that Bonnie never went in there unless she could help it.

'I know, which means no one will find us, so we won't be disturbed.'

Thirty minutes and two cups of strong black coffee later Isabel felt as if she'd bled all over Bonnie's desk. 'So now I have to decide what to do. Take a chance on him, or walk away. I have a plane ticket to Melbourne on New Year's Eve, so essentially I have a week to decide the rest of my life.'

'When are you seeing him again?'

'Tomorrow.'

'So, in reality, you have twenty-four hours.'

'Geez, girlfriend, you are not helping.'

Bonnie shook her head and with a formidable glint in her eye she leaned forward. Isabel could see why she was a very good match for Jacob—Bonnie would fight for what she wanted, tooth and nail. 'Do you think that if you had a hundred more years to decide it would help? If you love the man you have to take a chance. Do you love him?'

Well, wow, that was a question. She'd tried to put him behind her, she'd tried to erase those feelings, ignored them, subsumed them, but in the end the real question was: had she ever stopped loving him? 'But, Bonnie, how could you dare to let go after what you went through?'

Bonnie's shoulders rose then fell. 'Sometimes you've got to take a risk, and, believe me, I didn't do that lightly. I had Freya to think of. But, well, once I realised I loved him and he loved me I wasn't prepared to let that chance slip through my fingers.' She covered Isabel's hand with her own, and it was almost as if Isla were here talking sense to her. They'd get on well, she thought, her sister and this woman who was fast becoming like one. One day she'd get them to meet, somehow. What a party that would be. 'Come on, Isabel, I understand what you've been through, but that's all in the past. You have a lot of living to do. What have you got to lose?'

Isabel nodded, fighting the lump in her throat. Bonnie was right, of course—what did she have to lose by loving Sean Anderson? 'Everything. That's the problem.'

'And if he's worth that much to you, you'll take that risk.'

CHAPTER ELEVEN

'ANY ROOM AT the inn?' Johnny, one of the paramedics, breezed into the labour suite, stomping snow from his boots while pushing a young woman on a trolley. For five o'clock in the morning, Christmas Day, the man looked remarkably chipper. The girl, not so.

'Yeah, yeah, very funny. I've never heard that one before. Happy Christmas to you, too.' Sean shook his head and laughed, giving an extra-special smile to the girl on the gurney. She looked so young, pale and frightened. And on her own. Who the hell wanted to be here instead of unwrapping presents? Which was where she should have been right now, with her family looking after her—she barely looked old enough to be out on her own. 'Hello there. Who do we have here?'

The girl gave him a grimace and curled up around her distended belly. Tears streaked her face as she sucked on portable gas and air. Sean took her in—straggly hair, clothes that were scruffy, long thin bones, skin stretched tight over her cheekbones. Man, she was way too thin.

Johnny handed over a copy of his observation chart. 'This is Phoenix Harding. She's eighteen years old and, we think, about thirty-two weeks pregnant. She's had lower abdominal pain for the past week increasing over time. Lower back pain too. Using gas and air to good effect. Contractions started at around midnight, getting closer together and stronger, every two to three minutes.'

'Okay, thanks, Johnny. We'll take it from here. Hi there, Phoenix, my name's Sean and I'm one of the doctors here. Can you manage to tell me what's been happening?'

She shook her head. Terrified.

'Are you okay if I do some prodding and poking around? I need to have a listen to baby—that will help us work out what to do next.'

She nodded, but hid her face in her hands.

Sean began his assessment, had Hope attach the heart monitor across Phoenix's belly, and heard a strong quick heartbeat. 'That's sounding good. Baby seems to be quite happy.' But the girl doubled up in pain. He tried to get her to look at him. 'Phoenix, he's not as cooked as we'd like, so we'd prefer to keep him in a little longer. But it looks like he's keen to meet you.'

Phoenix shook her head. Still no words. She looked so young. So frightened. And, as he watched Hope leave the cubicle with an apologetic raise of her eyebrows, in need of a friend and a chaperone.

'Have you got anyone we can call to come and be with you? Friends? Family? Baby's dad?'

Again she shook her head. It was going to be difficult if he had to conduct the assessment by telepathy. 'Hey, missy, just a quick question: can you recall whether your waters broke? It'd have been like a gush of water…an unexpected trickle?'

There was a knock on the door. Isabel stepped into the cubicle and Sean's heart felt as if it were tumbling, mixed with a sharp sense of relief. He never could get used to seeing her without having some kind of reaction. 'Hope's just had to pop out—she thought you'd need a chaperone, everyone else is busy so she asked me to come in.'

After he brought her up to speed with Phoenix's case he added, 'But Phoenix isn't feeling like talking at the moment, so we're taking things slow.'

Isabel nodded, as if she understood exactly what he meant. Thirty-two weeks meant a risk to baby—it was too immature to be born yet. But if it was, they'd need extra care—usually a stint in the SCBU to monitor progress and for special feeding; babies that young often didn't quite get the hang of sucking at a nipple or a teat. Never mind the dangers of immature lungs trying to suck in hospital air.

Isabel smiled at the girl. 'Oh, that's okay, we can take all the time you like, Phoenix.' She paused and stroked the girl's back as she curled into another contraction. 'Although we can't do anything to help if we don't know what's happening. That baby is a bit young to be born yet—so we need to try to keep it in there a bit longer. Phoenix, do you mind if I examine you?' Time was running out if they wanted to stall the labour; obviously Isabel was fully aware of this.

The girl shook her head and turned onto her back. She looked grateful to have Isabel there at least and when Isabel had done her examination she breathed out a big breath. 'Eight centimetres—wow, you're doing well. And your waters must have broken some time? You don't remember? Can you try to think?'

'No.' Finally a voice.

'Never mind, honey. The main thing is, your cervix is dilating quickly, your baby's on the way. We'll have to give you an injection of steroids to make his lungs good and strong for when he's born. He's going to be a bit small as yet, so we have to give him all the help we can. Is that okay? And I'd like to work out why this is happening now… Have you had any problems or anything over the last few days? Taken any different medicines, drugs? Alcohol? Any accidents, bumps? Done anything really strenuous?'

'No.' As if grabbing onto a life raft Phoenix took hold of the hand Isabel offered to her. 'I've been going to the toilet more. I thought it was just the pregnancy— I read somewhere that you pee more often. But looking back it was twice as many times for half as much wee.'

'In which case we'll need to test your urine as soon as we can. Any fever? Lower back pain?' Isabel reached for a thermometer to continue her assessment.

'Pain, yes.' She pointed to her lumbar region. 'And when I pee.'

'It sounds as if you might have a kidney infection. We'll set up some intravenous antibiotics to help you and to prevent baby getting an infection too.' Isabel inhaled sharply as she helped Phoenix to sit, revealing her skeletal frame under her nightie. 'Have you eaten recently?'

The girl clung to Isabel's arm. 'No, not really. I'm so stupid. I'm so stupid.'

'No, you're not.'

'I should have been more careful. I should have looked after him instead of pretending it wasn't happening.' Then she began to cry thick tears. Isabel held Phoenix as her chest racked with deep sobs for a few minutes. When she'd finished the girl managed to force a few more words out. 'I'm sorry. I'm sorry. I didn't know what to do. I was scared so I didn't tell anyone and I haven't been doing the right things. Have I killed him? Hurt him? Will he be okay?'

'Hey…hush now. We'll sort you out. Don't worry.' Sean watched for Isabel's reaction. It must have been like a rerun of her own life. Which she steadfastly would not allow to interfere here, that much he knew.

She pressed her lips together, took a long deep breath. 'I understand. I do. I know you were scared and that you're scared now. But it will be fine. It will. The main thing is that baby has been growing—clearly. Maybe you'd like a little walk around? Sometimes it's easier if you move.'

Make yourself useful, Sean was telling himself. *Find someone to help her.* 'It's okay. Really, we're here to help. Are you sure you don't want me to phone anyone?'

The girl shook her head vehemently. 'There isn't anyone.'

'There must be someone, surely, sweetheart?'

She was gripping onto Isabel's hand now as pain ripped through her. 'No.'

Damn. Whether there was or wasn't anyone in her life to help her was clearly not up for discussion. 'What are you doing in Cambridge? On your own? Working? Student?'

Phoenix took a deep breath. 'It was supposed to be a fresh start for me and my ex—things hadn't been going well between us in Manchester—he got a job down here so we came. But as soon as he found out about the baby he ran a mile. Or a hundred miles. I have no idea where he is.' She cradled her belly as another contraction rippled through her. When she got through it she asked, her voice weak with fear, 'Have I done something bad to him? Why is he coming so early? I'm not due until March. I can't have him now. I can't.'

Sitting down in the chair next to her, Isabel stroked the girl's arm. 'Sometimes infections can bring on an early labour. All sorts of things can—not eating properly…'

'I was trying to lose weight to hide the bump when I went for job interviews.' Looking defeated, Phoenix slumped forward. 'It didn't work—I never got any job, I'm starving, he's coming now and I've made a mess of everything.'

'Look, sweetheart, sometimes babies come early. We'll do everything we can to make sure he's okay. But what about you? Have you got any friends to come and help you?'

Their patient shook her head. 'You don't make many friends when you don't go out.'

'What about your midwife? Who did you register with?'

'I didn't. I didn't think. I just wanted it all to go away.' She blinked up at them both with frightened eyes. 'Will you stay with me? And him.'

'Of course we will. Whatever you need, Phoenix.' After giving her the injections Sean stepped forward and took the girl's other hand as another, stronger contraction ripped through her. They were coming thick and fast. No woman should have to face this on her own. 'We'll stay with you, and Hope—the midwife—she'll be back soon and we'll all help you get through this. You'll see.'

Isabel looked across the bed and he felt the punch to his heart as she gave him a weak smile; gratitude shone from her eyes. It gave him some hope for their next conversation. Although there was that nagging sensation again, the one that said she would run as fast as she could, far away from him, all over again. And even though he knew that, the familiar warmth curled through his gut. What was it about her that held him captivated?

He dragged his eyes away from that mass of blonde hair that he loved to run his hands through and turned to listen to Phoenix. Her voice was starting to sound panicked. 'What if I can't do it? What if I'm not strong enough? I'm scared.'

'Don't worry, really. You'll manage. You're young...' He was going to say *and fit and healthy*...but she'd neglected herself a little too much. He had only to hope that the little one had got what it needed from her.

Her body began to tense and she screwed her face up. 'Owwww. I feel like it's pressing down, like I need to push it out. But I don't want to. He's too little. It's too soon. What if it's...what if he...?'

Isabel gave her a warm smile. 'You're fully dilated now, sweetheart. Your body will work whether you think it's the right time or not, honey. Whatever happens we'll deal with it. You can do this. You can do this.'

But there was a catch in her throat that made Sean lift his head and look at her. She blinked and turned away, shaking her head. Then she turned back, in full control again. 'It's okay, Phoenix. You have me and Sean. We can do this together. Okay? So I need you to breathe like this.'

Isabel began to pant and count.

When Phoenix screamed and bore down, squeezing against Isabel, Sean took over. 'Okay, so breathe with me, Phoenix. Breathe with me. That's a good girl. Lift your legs a little. Well done. I can see the head. Not long to go now.

The girl began to cry. 'Owwww. I don't want to push.'

'You have to push when I say so. Okay? Okay? Okay, Phoenix…you need to push now.' Cradling the head with one hand, he caught the body as it slithered out. He laid it on Phoenix's chest, but she turned away as he cut the cord. Closed her eyes tight shut as tears trickled anyway down her cheeks.

'A girl, you have a daughter, Phoenix.' But the little one wasn't happy to be out in the big wide world. He rubbed her chest with a towel. And again. *Come on. Come on. Breathe for me. Breathe, damn it.*

His gut twisted as he carried her to the Resuscitaire, worked on her until she took a short breath and squawked. A river of relief ran through him. He would not have been able to look at Isabel if this little one hadn't made it. God knew what she was feeling. Dealing with a young desperate teenager and a preemie baby. Although not as preemie as Joshua…

Isabel seemed to have overridden any emotion and was handling the situation with warmth and professionalism; she'd delivered the placenta and was clearing up with a sunny smile. But he could see the stretch in her shoulders, the clench of her jaw. It was costing her a lot to be here, he knew. She'd done that ever since he'd been back in her life again: borne every emotional insult with fastidious grace. She might have called it coping. He called it denial. She refused to be broken. No, she refused to allow anything to reach her emotionally.

'She's beautiful, Phoenix. Do you want to hold her just for a few moments?' He carried the little one over. 'Just hold her against your chest, skin to skin. They love that.'

'No. I don't know what to do. I don't know what to

do.' The girl was shaking. 'She's so small. Her skin's too big. She looks…she looks so tiny.'

'Look, she'll love being against your skin.'

She turned away. 'No. I don't… I can't. I'm too scared.'

'It's okay to be scared, sweetheart. But you have the strength to do this. She needs you. She needs her mum.' Isabel cast a worried flicker of her eyes to Sean. This teenager was experiencing the most traumatic experience possibly of her young life—having a premature baby with no emotional support. She needed someone she knew and loved to be with her. 'Hey, are you sure you don't have a friend, your mum, someone who you can at least talk to on the phone? You need someone here for you, Phoenix. You and…your daughter. Have you chosen a name yet?'

'No. I don't know… I thought it was going to be a boy… I thought she was going to die. I thought—'

'Look, she's doing okay. Your daughter is perfect.'

Clearly Phoenix was struggling and needed time to get to grips with all this. And baby needed to be looked after properly—she needed a full assessment, warmth and care. Sean bent to speak to her. 'Okay, so she's managing to breathe fine on her own, she's a trooper, but she's quite little and may not be able to feed properly as yet. I'd like to get her along to the Special Care Baby Unit as soon as we can—get her checked out and warm and looked after. How about I run her along there now and you come with Isabel or Hope when you're a bit more settled?'

Phoenix looked up at Isabel, saw the quick nod of her head. 'Okay. Yes. Okay. Thank you.'

'I'll stay here with Phoenix.' Isabel caught his gaze.

She looked as shaken as he felt. He didn't miss the irony—that Isabel had been almost in the same situation, with no one experienced to help her. She'd been through months of worry and anxiety. She hadn't told a soul about her pregnancy. And yet here she was dealing with this.

Her face was fixed in a mask, her emotions hidden so deep that it made his chest ache. Was this how she'd been? Had she shaken like this? Cried? Or had she internalised it all? Damn, he didn't want to think about any of that. Like her, he didn't want to meet those emotions head-on.

But they were there, glittering brightly within him. He wanted to comfort her. He wanted to stroke her worries away. Goddamn, he wanted her, body and soul, more than anything he'd wanted in his whole life.

So, yeah, he loved her. Which was hardly a surprise given that he'd probably been in love with her for most of his life.

Which was a dumb move on his part, because he knew that loving Isabel Delamere was the single most destructive thing he could do. Because she wouldn't allow herself to love him back.

But still, all he wanted to do was take her in his arms and hold her, soothe her pain away. To make her believe how much she meant to him. But he couldn't. He had a professional responsibility to Phoenix and the little scrap of new life in his hands. He also had a responsibility to himself. 'Excellent, I'll see you up there in a little while.' And that would give him a few precious minutes to get his act together too.

CHAPTER TWELVE

HOLD IT IN, Isabel reprimanded herself as she walked to the SCBU. Hopefully he'd have gone by the time she got there. Hopefully she wouldn't see the love in his eyes and feel the need to walk straight into his arms and cry like a baby over things that had happened too long ago. To be held in arms that she still longed to be wrapped inside. To let herself go and love him right back.

No such luck. He was lifting the tiny baby from the incubator; she looked so frail in his strong hands. 'Hi, Isabel. Where's Phoenix?'

'She's having some food and going to have a shower. She's exhausted, poor thing, and overwhelmed.'

'She doesn't want to come?'

Avoiding eye contact, she walked to the baby and gave her a wee stroke on her head. Someone, one of the nurses, she assumed, had popped a little knitted red Santa hat on her head. It just about broke her heart. 'I think she will. She needs some TLC herself. She's just getting her head around everything. I managed to get a bit of history from her. Basically she has no one. Her mum died a couple of years ago and her dad's been pretty absent for most of her life. There are no siblings. She needs a lot of support. I've warned her about the bells and whistles up here, and the feeding tube and the oxygen. But she's terrified, poor thing.' Then she remembered about the good news she had to tell him. 'But, after all that, she won the first baby of Christmas prize, so at least she's got a few things to tide her over.'

'You don't think she'll decide to put this little one out for adoption?'

'I don't know. She needs a little time to work it all out.'

Cradling the baby in the crook of his arm, he rocked side to side as he spoke. 'How are you?'

'Bearing up, thanks.' She would not break down. She would not let the pain in. And he had no right to look so damned beautiful standing there with a baby in his arms. Her heart thumped with desire, with emotion she did not want to recognise.

'You don't have to hide it from me, you know.' He leaned close enough that, if she'd wanted to, she could have touched him. She could smell his scent, the one that had clung to her body after he'd left her in Paris, and her heart thumped a little more.

She shivered. 'I'm not hiding anything. I'm at work, is all.'

'Isabel, it's been a very emotional morning. You're about at boiling point.'

Thankfully, Dean sauntered over. There was safety in numbers. 'Hey, Happy Christmas!'

'Thanks, you too.'

Dean tickled the baby girl under her chin. 'Is mum coming soon? This little one needs some cuddles.'

'No. She's having a rest.' Grateful for the chance to speak and not to feel Sean's insistent, concerned gaze on her, she filled Dean in on Phoenix's history. 'She's scared stiff and feeling guilty all round, so we need to be gentle with her. I think she'll come round. I'll pop down in an hour or so and see if she wants to come up then.'

'And in the meantime this one needs a cuddle. You want to hold her, Isabel?' He took the baby from Sean and gave her a quick check over. 'Kangaroo care. She really needs some love—especially on Christmas Day. Who doesn't?'

Whoa. Skin-to-skin contact? No. No way was she cradling this baby against her bare skin. That would be the worst thing she could ever do. That would bring back so many memories—she shook her head vehemently. 'No—oh, no, I couldn't.' The little thing was wiggling and her bottom lip had started to shake and Isabel's instinct was to reach out and comfort her, but she couldn't, wouldn't…but, oh, suddenly Dean was helping her to sit and lowering the baby into her arms, onto her chest, which—as bad luck would have it—was covered with a blouse that easily stretched open. She felt the tiny little shudder and curl into her breast, felt the warmth and smelt the just-born fresh scent. For a moment she held her there skin to skin, feeling the life force in this tiny thing, the beating heart where she'd felt none with her own child. And suddenly everything was swimming and blurred from tears she'd steadfastly refused to shed. Ever. It was all too much for her to deal with. The baby. Her memories. Sean. All on Christmas Day. 'I—I just can't.'

And then Sean was there taking the baby and in his eyes he was telling her it was okay, that everything would be okay. He was telling her all the things she'd said to Phoenix. That she was strong enough to deal with it, that she'd be okay.

But she wasn't. She wasn't okay at all. None of this was okay.

'I'm sorry, I think I might… I just… I need to go.' And she hurried out of SCBU, down the stairs and out into the falling snow, trying to force cold air into her lungs.

'Isabel! Izzy, wait. Stop.' It was Sean behind her, his footsteps muffled by the deadening snow. Where it had been beautiful and magical in Paris, now it just felt grey. Ice. The thick air suffocating. 'Isabel.'

She turned. 'I'm going for a walk.'

Warm hands skimmed her arms. 'You have no coat. You're shivering. You shouldn't be out here.'

'Please, Sean, just leave me alone.'

'I can't. I won't.' He caught her up again and pulled her round to face him. 'I know you enough that I feel the pain inside you, Isabel. Talk to me. Let it out.'

If she did she might crumble. She started to walk again, with no idea where she was headed. But the words just tumbled out; she couldn't stop them. 'I used to think it was something I'd done, you know. I thought it was my fault he didn't make it. That I could have saved him if I'd only done…this…or that. But I know he wasn't ever going to make it, Sean. Not like that little one in there. So tiny, so precious and perfect.'

'I understand.'

She came to a halt, whipped round to rail at him. 'Do you? Did you fight against your own body, trying to keep him inside you? To protect him? When you failed at that, did you hold him against your bare chest and sing to him? Did you whisper his name over and over? Did you pray for someone to hold you too? And did you have no one who was capable to take care of you? Oh, yes, Isla was brilliant and so was Evie…but in the end it was me. Just me, and this little lifeless thing that I loved with all my heart. And that broke it into tiny pieces that will never ever mend. And just when I had survived and was getting on with my life, just when I was okay, this is reminding me all over again.'

'You will mend and grow again, Isabel. Look at everything you've achieved with your life so far—what an amazing and compassionate doctor you've become. What a beautiful, sensational woman. Just think of what a tour de force we'll be together.' That was a promise from him for the future. He believed in them, that this could work. His arms were round her now and he'd found a bench in the white-coated garden and she was sitting on it and hadn't even noticed. He was warm and safe and for a moment she let him hold her, let him soothe her memories away with a kiss against her throat. He was here, he was making his claim, his stand, his promise and she felt so close to letting go, to believing him. To feeling that everything would turn out fine.

That realisation was enough to jolt her away from him.

She stood. Closed down every emotion, just as she always had, because it was safer that way. Because she had never felt as if her heart had been wrenched from her chest until today—and that surely must mean that she'd allowed herself to get lulled into feeling too much again.

She'd seen him hold a baby, seen the look of contentment on his face, the joy. And she knew she would be unable to commit herself to give him that or anything like it. Ever. Because it couldn't be fine, because she would always be thinking about the worst things that could happen, never giving herself totally to protect herself from breaking into pieces again, and he deserved more than that. So much more.

She'd been too close to the edge just now and she did not want to fall from it. She was too scared, too darned terrified because it would be too hard, so very, very hard to pull herself up from it again. Life had been fine before she'd met Sean again. Empty, but fine. Monochrome, but liveable. She could survive without colour and a full heart and making love, without Paris and without Sean. Without memories and pain and the risk that she could feel so lost again without him. Some time. Once had been enough for any lifetime.

She did not want to bleed for him again. 'I'm so sorry, Sean. I can't do this. *Us*. I'm sorry. There isn't a future and I don't want to let you think there could be.'

'What?' He stood to face her. 'After everything we've been through? You're saying you don't want to try?'

She took a deep breath of the cold, cold air, filled her insides with ice, let it infuse her veins, her blood, because that way she would be able to say these things. 'Yes, that's exactly what I'm saying. It's over, whatever it was, in Paris—whatever I let you believe, I'm sorry.'

But instead of giving the understanding, thoughtful gentle response she expected, he frowned. His voice was laced with anger. 'No, you're not sorry at all. You just want to protect yourself. You want to live a half-life. You want to hide. That's not living, Isabel.'

'Please don't make this harder than it is. It's what I want.'

'And what about what I want? Ever think about that?' When she looked away he huffed out an irritated breath. 'No. I didn't think so.'

'It's not you—' Then she shut up, because all that *it's*

not you, it's me gumpf was just a sweetener, and nothing about this was sweet. He had so much to offer, so much promise, so much capability to love—he deserved far more than what she could give him. It made her stomach hurt. It made everything inside her twist and contort and knot. He was right: she hadn't given much thought to how he would be after all this. It had all been about her.

How selfish. How typically Delamere girl. But there it was... She had to do what was right for her; there was no point letting him believe in something that she just couldn't do.

He glared at her. 'Really? You were going to trot out some well-worn phrase? Don't we deserve more than that?' And even though she'd made him cross he was still devastating to look at. His dark eyes still entranced her. There was still that magnetic pull to him that was so hard to resist. She'd been resisting it for too long already. Snow whirled around him like a vortex sticking to his scrubs. He didn't seem to notice. 'You really mean it, don't you? You don't want any of it.'

'No. I don't.'

'You're a coward, Isabel Delamere. You have closed off your life, shut down, checked out. You don't have to bury yourself along with Joshua, you know. You deserve to live.'

'I do live.'

'Hardly. I mean, sure, you get involved with your patients, because that's safe, you know where the line is and you never cross it. You allow yourself to feel their pain, like some sort of proxy for actually feeling things inside you, and then you try to fix them—because you couldn't do that for yourself. But with someone who really cares for you, with me, you totally shut down. You're afraid. I get that, but you have to let people in some time or you'll end up sad and lonely and, well...dead inside.' He pulled her towards him, anger and desire mingling in his eyes. 'I love you. I just think you should know that before I go.'

'Don't—' She put her hand out to his lips, trying to erase his words. 'Don't say that.'

He shrugged her hand away. 'I love you. And I know you love me. I saw it in Paris. I saw it in the way you looked at me. I saw it when we made love. For God's sake, Isabel, don't run away from it this time.'

'No—' She couldn't love him; she'd tried so hard not to. She'd fought and fought to stop him affecting her, to stop him reaching inside her soul and meeting her there, raw and pure. But here she was, out in the snow, having almost lost the plot with him and a preemie and a young girl on Christmas Day. In Paris she'd almost felt that things could be perfect; she'd let them be. She'd almost believed him.

She remembered that feeling at the top of the Ferris wheel—the freedom, the joy of being with him. The way her whole body craved him, and still did now, even more than ever.

And she was struggling to let him go, because she wanted him so much to stay. She did...she did love him.

She closed her eyes against the bitter reality. She loved him totally, utterly...needed him in her life. It was the single worst thing she could do. She hated that she needed him, that she wanted him so much. She hated that they'd become *us* and she couldn't allow herself to be part of that. She'd fallen further under his spell, with his total faith in things working out okay. She needed to go home, to be with Isla—the only person in the world who understood. She needed to put herself back together again.

When she opened her eyes he was closer, his gaze smoky with intent despite the layer of snowflakes in his hair, on his cheeks, on his shoulders. Despite the freezing gale both outside and in her gut. 'Tell me you don't love me and I'll walk away. Tell me, Isabel, that Paris meant nothing to you and I won't stay here another moment.'

'I... What does it matter? I don't want to love you. I can't love you. There it is. Now go, please.'

He stood for a moment, not moving, just looking at her as if willing her to change her mind.

She didn't.

Then he shrugged his shoulders and took one last step towards her. She'd never seen him like this—so coiled and taut, so angry and explosive. And, damn her hormones, she wanted him even more for it. This Sean loved her. This formidable man had been there for her years ago and she hadn't taken him then, this man who had come to find her, who had loved her once, loved her again. It was a second chance.

But he wasn't taking it any more than she could. 'You know what? I'm done chasing you, Isabel. All those years ago you thrashed my heart to pieces because you didn't trust that I would look after you, you couldn't trust me with your secret or your love. All those wasted years we could have been together, exploring the world. Living. Being. Together. That was all I ever wanted from the moment I first saw you in that classroom. And even now, when I've told you again that I love you, you throw it back in my face. Well, that's me done. If you're not willing to take a risk and let me in then I'm gone.' His fingers ran across her throat to the chain that held the keys to his lock. He looked at them, then shook his head. 'I'm finished trying to fight for you, Isabel. I'm finished loving you.'

No. Don't go. She wanted to call to him, to cling to him. To make him stay. He had been her constant. He loved her, still. After everything, he still wanted her. All she had to do was take a step. But she was scared, terrified, so deep-down frozen that she stood there and looked at him. And said nothing.

Don't go. In her head, a tiny voice. *Don't go.* That got louder until it was all she could hear, all she could feel. She clasped the keys on her chain into her fist and tried to swallow through the thick wedge of sadness. *I love you with every beat of my heart.*

But then he swivelled in the snow, stomping long wide footprints back to the hospital entrance, to the happy smiling relatives, to the big sparkling Christmas tree and the jingle-jangle music of Christmas songs. Leaving, in his wake, her frozen body and broken heart.

And only then, when she knew she'd truly lost him, when there was no scrap of hope left, did she crumble to the bench and let the tears fall.

CHAPTER THIRTEEN

HAPPY BLOODY CHRISTMAS?

Yeah, right. Happy bloody life. The growing pressure in Sean's chest almost stopped his breath. He had to get away from her.

It was like Groundhog Day. It was as if he'd gone right back to being seventeen again, only worse because, hell—he'd been forewarned and forearmed, he'd known exactly what she was like and yet he'd loved her anyway.

Fists clenched tight against his sides, Sean walked back into the warmth of the hospital, kept on going past the cafeteria, past the labour suite, past the wards and the cleaners' department, past the delivery bay and out to the street at the other side. Then he ran. Along deserted roads covered in a thickening layer of snow. Past closed shops, further past magnificent colleges and the cathedral and onwards to the river.

Along the footpath he ran past laughing families out throwing snowballs, screeching kids on their new bikes struggling with too-big wheels and too-high seats. He ran past hedges of brambles asleep until spring. Past punts, empty of passengers until summer sun hit the city. Past riverside pubs that murmured with laughter and cheer that he did not feel in any cell in his body, past trees and parks and fields. He ran and then he ran some more.

And eventually, when he no longer had the energy to put one foot in front of the other, he came to a stop.

Goddamnit, he had no clue where he was. 'Isabel.' He shouted her name to the sky, to the empty field, as if she might hear him and look for him. Louder, like a lunatic, like a desperate man. 'Isabel!'

But he wasn't desperate; he'd just made a fatal error in falling in love with someone who didn't know how to do the same. He'd tried, he'd laid his heart on the line and she'd stomped on it again. He'd been so close—they'd been so close—to having it all. And she just didn't want it.

Then he realised he had no breath left and he was doubled over trying to fill his lungs, but all he got were icy vocal cords and a searing hacking cough. He was supposed to be on call. He was supposed to be at the hospital doing his job. Not running to get Isabel out of his system—because she was there, indelibly printed on his heart and it was all pointless. He loved her, for God's sake—how bloody stupid. He loved her, needed her, wanted her more than ever and she couldn't see what a wonderful gift the two of them could be together. And even though he'd known this going in, he'd fooled himself into believing it wouldn't happen. Well, no more. He straightened up, looked at the clear blue sky, emptied of its white load, a thin weak sun. But sun nevertheless. He would go onwards, travel some more. See the world. He would put her behind him, forget Paris and Cambridge and the hope and the love. He would recover from the hurt.

Somehow.

He stamped his feet and began to walk back to work.

'How's she doing?' Five hours and a couple of less straightforward Christmas deliveries later and Isabel had managed to find some time to visit SCBU again. Better that than to wallow in her own troubles. He was gone from her life—she had a week to endure working on side with him, loving him. Then she'd be home in Melbourne and she could put today behind her.

She would get through this, start her life again. In the meantime she just had to make sure she didn't come face to face with him. The crying had eventually stopped—although she had never known that a person could sob so hard for so long. And after she'd splashed her face with water and drunk two cups of fortifying coffee she'd filled her voice with Christmas cheer and come back to her world. She couldn't leave the hospital, but she could certainly fill her day with people so she wasn't free to face him again alone. She could do this. She could. 'Baby Harding? Is she okay?'

'Absolutely fine.' Dean jerked his thumb towards the incubator and gave a wry smile. 'Mum seems to be taking her time, but she's getting there.'

Dressed in some over-large clothes that Isabel guessed were from the goodwill cupboard, Phoenix was sitting on a chair staring at the cot while her baby gurgled in her incubator kicking her waif-like legs in the air. Poor mite. Both of them. They needed each other and neither of them knew how to go about it. Hoping she could perhaps set them on a path, Isabel crossed the unit and bent down next to Phoenix. 'Hey, there. You made it.'

Phoenix shrugged. 'I couldn't leave her here, not on her own.'

'You did good. Now you can watch over her.' And hopefully feel a mother's need to hold her, some time soon. 'How are you feeling?'

'A bit better.'

Isabel nodded and gave her what she hoped was a re-assuring smile. 'That's good, isn't it?'

'Yes. I think so. Hope said she'd speak to a social worker and get me some help.' Phoenix looked at her hands. 'I need it. I'm not sure I can do this on my own. It's a big responsibility—a life. Someone else's.'

'You'll be okay. There are people who can support you. I'll make sure of it.'

But Isabel felt guilt settle on her shoulders. Phoenix had no one. No family, no partner, no one to care for her. She'd thought that she'd been in a similar situation, once, but there had been people there for her if she'd asked. Isla, of course. Her parents, if she'd taken a chance. Sean.

Not any more. The sharp stab in her stomach was startling.

Baby Harding started to stir; her body went rigid as she prepared to bawl. 'I think she needs some company.' Isabel gestured towards Dean, asking if she could pick her up. He nodded and winked.

'Phoenix, is it okay if I pick her up?'

'Sure.'

Isabel bent into the crib and scooped up the little one. This time she would keep her feelings out of it. This time there would be no skin to skin—at least not hers. 'Come here, sweetie. You want a cuddle?' She cradled the baby in her arm, trying to soothe her. Singing a soft lullaby as Phoenix watched from behind her fringe.

'You see this tube?' Isabel pointed to the nasogastric tube, managing to keep it together. But, oh, how she wished she didn't keep having that image of Sean in her head—the one where he'd looked at her so angrily and walked away. Where he'd finally, totally, given up on her. 'This is to help with her feeds. She hasn't mastered the art of sucking yet, so she needs a bit of help. If you get a chance, hold her close to your breast so she can smell your milk, try popping the tip of your little finger into her mouth and see if she tries to suck. Oh, and that tube in the crib is just for oxygen, if she needs it. But, as you can hear, her lungs are in pretty good condition.'

As bub wailed Isabel continued to chat, inching closer and closer to Phoenix… 'She's got your hair colouring. Look at all that dark fluff. She's gorgeous.'

Tears filled Phoenix's eyes. 'Why won't she stop crying?'

'I think she needs her mum. Maybe?' Dragging a chair next to Phoenix, she sat, still cradling the baby, grateful to have a distraction from Sean—and a little bit of interest from Phoenix if the flicker in her eyes was anything to go by. 'Have you chosen a name for her yet?'

'I was thinking of Sarah. After my mum.'

'It's a pretty name. For a pretty girl.'

Isabel could see Phoenix's fingers twitching. Then the young mum sat on her hands. Maybe she did want to hold her baby, but didn't know how to ask. Didn't dare. Some people were like that; some people had to be guided and were slow to build their confidence, whereas others dived right in. *Like me,* Isabel thought; no confidence whatsoever when it came to relationships. And then she tried again to rid her mind of all thoughts of Sean.

But it wasn't working. She couldn't not think of him. Her heart swelled at the memory of his face, of his promises. Then it broke all over again.

Noticing all the staff were busy, Isabel tried her strategy to help Phoenix. 'I don't suppose... No. It's okay. I'll ask someone else...'

'What?' Phoenix sat up straight.

'I need to go to the loo. I don't suppose you'd want to take Sarah for a moment. Just for a moment, mind you. I wouldn't ask...only everyone seems busy with feeds and those poor babies needing extra care...'

Biting her lip, Phoenix gave a little smile. 'I...well, I suppose I could. Try.'

'Oh, thank you. You'd be doing me a huge favour.' Very slowly she handed the baby over. 'I thought I'd be useless at holding them when I first started doing this job, but babies are very easy... Look, just support her head here, and keep that hand under her little tush. Good. That's great. You're a natural, Phoenix.'

The baby began to turn her head towards Phoenix's breast and nuzzled in.

'Oh, she knows you're her mum, all right.' Isabel glanced up at Phoenix's face, trying not to place too much emphasis on this because she didn't want to frighten her, or put pressure on her. Gentle was the way to go. But Phoenix's eyes were glittering with tears again. 'She's so small.'

'But you watch, she'll soon put on weight. Now, just sit tight and I'll be back in a mo.'

As Isabel stood she caught a glimpse of Sean's reflection in the entrance-door glass.

Oh. She sucked in a breath. Wow. It was a physical pain in her heart.

She did not want to see him. Did not. 'I…er… I think I'll stay a minute.'

She could do this. She sat back down.

Phoenix watched her. 'Dr Delamere, are you hiding from Dr Anderson?'

'No. I'm just…well, I'm just trying to…'

'I know it when I see it. I've been doing it for the last seven months. Trouble is, it catches up with you in the end.' The girl grinned and lifted Sarah as evidence. 'There are some things you just can't deny any more.'

'Don't be so clever.' Isabel didn't know if he'd seen her, but he hadn't come into the room.

And Phoenix just wouldn't let it drop. 'So, he's a nice guy. Helpful. Good with his hands…'

She would not discuss her personal life with a patient—that would be absolutely stepping over the line. 'Yes, well, I think you need to focus on Sarah.'

'She's asleep.' Phoenix craned her neck to watch the door.

'Ah, yes…anyway…'

Phoenix turned back and grinned again. 'It's okay, he's going now.'

Relief flooding through her, Isabel breathed out and started to relax. 'Good. Thank you.'

'But if I were you I wouldn't run too far away from him. Sexy guy like that.'

'And none of your business.'

Phoenix raised an eyebrow. 'Just saying…if I had a guy look at me the way he looks at you I'd be walking towards him not hiding in a wing-backed chair. You're lucky to have someone like him looking out for you. You're lucky to have someone, full stop.'

So it turned out that young Phoenix was wise beyond her years—and so very alone. And in stark contrast Isabel could have had everything. He'd been there offering her a future regardless of their past but she'd pushed him away. Again.

How lucky was she to have someone like him in her life, someone to share everything—good times and bad—to walk with her through whatever life threw their way? How very selfish to wallow in the past and not take a chance on loving someone, and having them love you right back. Just because she was scared. Scared of feeling something…but wasn't she feeling things right now? Despair, mainly. Loss. Broken. As if she'd ripped her own heart out of her chest, because it had all been her doing after all.

Isabel turned and watched him disappear down the corridor. Was he avoiding her too? Did he really not want to see her again?

And it hit her with force that she couldn't bear the thought of not having him in her life. Of not loving him for ever. Because she had, it dawned on her now; she'd loved him her whole life. And it was painful and beautiful and every colourful emotion in between. The joy of it all was that he loved her too.

Isabel glanced at Phoenix, who was now pressing her lips against the baby's chest and murmuring the words to a Christmas song that was playing through the speakers. This girl had been so frightened to love her daughter and now it seemed she had decided to. Just like that. She was going to do it alone and it was going to be hard, but she was taking her first steps along that road. She was brave and strong and everything Isabel could be too—if she let it all in. If she let Sean in. Miracles could happen if you let them. Isabel brushed the rogue tears from her cheeks. Maybe it was her turn for one.

But she couldn't find him. She'd tried the labour suite, the cafeteria, the postnatal ward. She'd popped into Theatre and he wasn't there. Which was probably a good thing because she had no idea what she was going to say to him when she caught up with him.

She wandered along the second-floor corridor with her heart beating too fast, panic setting in, looking in every room—stopping short of calling his name. And then, there, he was calmly ambling along towards her, deep in thought, hands in pockets.

She stopped by the chapel and waited for him to see her, watching his reaction as he slowly came to a halt in front of her. She tried to read his face—but it was a mask. It seemed she wasn't the only one who could hide their feelings. 'Isabel. Hello.'

'Sean.' She didn't know how to begin. What to say.

But he spoke first. 'Phoenix seems to be doing okay.'

So he was keeping it professional. 'Yes. Yes, she's getting there. As am I.'

His forehead crinkled as he frowned. 'Sorry, I don't understand.'

'I wanted to tell you that I do love you. That being with you in Paris was the happiest I've ever been in my life.'

He gave a sharp nod. 'Good to know. Now, I need to go—'

'Wait. Please. Don't go, Sean.'

'Is there any point to this?'

'Yes. Yes, Sean…' Pressing her palms against his chest, she made him stand still—because this was her only chance to say how she felt. Out loud to him. This was the only chance and she was going to grab it—and him and their love, whatever it took. 'I was so scared, so very scared to love you—but it happened anyway. In fact, I don't think I ever stopped loving you all these years. But I didn't know how to let you in. I've spent so long pushing people away, not letting myself feel anything, in case I got hurt... I'm sorry. It's taken some time for me to realise, but I know now that I don't want to live my life without you.'

He shook his head and confirmed all hope was gone. He took her hands in his and she thought he was going to drop them, but he spoke, his voice weary. 'I'm tired, Isabel.'

'It's Izzy.' She squeezed her eyes closed to press back the tears, but this time she just couldn't hold them back. Because she was his Izzy. 'To you.'

'I'm tired, Izzy.'

She opened her eyes, because he'd used her pet name. A flicker of hope bloomed bright in her chest. 'Of me?'

'Of having to fight for you, of having to believe for two people. I'm tired of trying to be that person, the one you trust, the one you choose. And then you not choosing me anyway. I'm over that. I need a life for me. I can't do this any more.'

Her hands stilled against his heart. It was there, solid and strong. He'd been so strong for them both. 'I trust you.'

'Do you, really? Because I haven't seen any sign of that.' He looked as if he didn't believe her, didn't want to. 'Since when?'

'Since for ever.'

'But I need to see it, you needed to show me instead

of bottling everything up inside. I love you, but I won't go through that again. I don't want to.'

So she'd pushed him to the edge and he'd stepped right over. 'I see. So there's no chance…?'

There's a small chance, she thought, because he was still holding her hands.

She gripped his tightly and peered up into his dark eyes that shone with light. 'I know I've been a Delamere disaster to live with, but you've got to understand, I love you with all my heart—and I always will. You, me and Joshua—we were a family, even if just for such a short time, and somewhere along the line I stuffed that up. Big time. I lost you and I don't ever want to lose you again, because that would be too much to bear. You remember those dreams we used to have when we were younger? Those happy, silly dreams that we had a lifetime ahead of us, all the things we could do together? Conquer the world and have fun in the process? I know I lost that— it's taken me all these years to find that again—and you've reawakened it. I know we can do great things, we can be great together. Look at how we helped Teo and Marina…'

'That's charity, Izzy. You can do that on your own.'

'Like hell I can. You give me the confidence to do that. You believe I can do that. You make every day worthwhile—waking up with you is the best gift I've ever had.' She wrapped her fist around the keys on the chain at her throat. 'I want to spend the rest of my life with you. I want to wake up with you every day. So, please, Sean—I love you. I want you in my life. I choose you. Please…don't make me beg.'

His eyes widened. 'Why the hell not?'

She swallowed. 'Really? You want me to beg? Is that

how it's going to be?' God knew, she'd really, really stuffed up. 'Okay—if that's what it's going to take—'

'Not on your life. I'm joking.' Sean let his hands slip out of hers and made a decision. It was one he'd been toying with in Paris. One he'd made years ago and one he hoped he'd never have to make again. He could hardly believe what she was saying—but he had to. He had to take the chance. She loved him and wanted him.

And he knew it was early days, that she had a long way to go—but he believed she wanted to walk that journey with him. He reached into his pocket and pulled out the box he'd been carrying with him ever since he'd arrived in Cambridge.

'In that case, Isabel Delamere...' Then he took one of her hands and knelt onto one knee. The look on her face was one of love and joy—and he knew he'd seen that before, in Paris, and he would never tire of seeing it. She loved him. He knew it, he felt it.

'Oh, my God, Sean?'

At that moment the chapel doors opened and out streamed a congregation of smiling people who came to a standstill at what they were witnessing. Great. Now he had an audience.

'Izzy, I know this is soon for you—but I want you to know that I will be here for you, I will walk this road with you. I want nothing more than to be part of your family. I will give you all the time in the world for you to choose whether you want more children to add to it, or if you want our family to be just the two of us. But whatever you decide, I will be by your side. I love you, Izzy. Will you marry me?'

He offered her the ring and his solemn promise.

Her soft green eyes were brimming with tears. 'Is that…is that the ring you gave me when I was sixteen?'

'The very same.'

'You kept it?'

A collective *awww* had him turning his head towards the grins and smiles—everyone seemed to be silently cheering him on.

He was starting to get stage fright. 'I guess I always hoped…one day we'd get to use it.' He took her hand again. 'The wait is killing me… And everyone else?'

A murmur of *yes* rippled around the space.

She laughed, her mouth crumpling. 'Oh, Sean, I couldn't imagine a life more wonderful than being with you.' Then she was pulling him up and in his arms and the congregation gave a cheer and a round of applause. As she pressed her lips to his all the other people melted away and he was alone again with her. Just her. The thought that had come back to him time and again over too many wasted years. Just her. His Izzy.

Something akin to the joy he'd seen on her face roared through him. 'I guess that's a yes?'

'Yes. Yes. Yes! When?' Her arms were round his neck.

'Whoa…someone's keen.'

'I want to start now… I want to be with you from now until for ever.'

'Let's start with today, then. Merry Christmas, Izzy.'

'Oh, yes. A very happy Christmas to you, Sean.' Then she gave him a long lingering kiss that left him in no doubt that this would be the happiest Christmas ever.

EPILOGUE

'I CAN'T BELIEVE it's happening...' Isabel looked out of her old bedroom window at her parents' house down to the manicured garden below. If they weren't quick the flowers would droop in the lovely summer heat. She turned to Isla, who looked so exquisitely beautiful in her long pale lilac silk dress, her hair woven with white flowers, eyes glistening with tears, it made Isabel's heart ache. In fact, her heart hadn't stopped aching—in a good way—for the last three hundred and sixty-four days. 'It's like a fairy tale down there.'

'It's your fairy tale—and we need to get on with it. I love you. I'm so proud of you.' Her sister squeezed her hand; her voice was tender and calm and so not the way Isabel was feeling inside. Calm had left her somewhere around the rehearsal dinner last night when nerves and excitement had taken over. Then sleep had evaded her, not because she was scared—those days were long gone—but because she was just counting down the hours until she could see him again and become Mrs Anderson.

'Okay, let's do this.' Isabel swallowed, inhaled deeply and then walked to the door. Would it be too unbridely to just run down there and jump into his arms? She guessed it probably would.

As she took her father's arm and began to walk up the makeshift petal-strewn aisle behind cute-as-a-button flower girl Cora Elliot, Isabel kept her focus on Sean up ahead waiting for her.

He smiled at her.

He had no idea.

She smiled back, hugging to herself the new secret she'd kept from him for the last two days. And she kept that smile as she nodded to the guests who sighed as she walked by. To Darcie, who had become a firm friend and job-share partner over the last year. The part-time role giving her lots of opportunity to volunteer at the homeless clinic and to raise money for those charities that supported pregnant teenage girls.

And she smiled at Lucas, the dashing man by Darcie's side, who was grinning proudly at his little niece, Cora. Then on to Alessi, who was trying—and failing—to wrestle a wriggling Geo into some sort of quiet. Her gorgeous nephew had taken his first steps recently and was causing every kind of mayhem in their household.

The only piece missing from their day was the staff from Cambridge Royal Maternity Unit, who had been such a huge part of their lives, but they'd had a long email from Bonnie this morning wishing them all the luck in the world; news that Hope's baby had been born, a lovely boy for her and Aaron, and that Jess and Dean were just back from honeymoon with very big smiles. Bonnie and Jacob had some good news of their own—a wedding and adoption plans approved.

Gosh, she missed them all. One day…one day, somehow they'd all be together again, but if not in person they talked regularly over the Internet and their friendships were solid and lasting.

But it was so lovely to be here, sharing this day with these special people she loved, at home in Melbourne—and since opening her heart out to Sean she had truly never felt so loved in her life.

And then she was there, facing him, in front of the celebrant and surrounded by so much love.

As she said her *I wills* and *I dos* she kept her secret tight inside her.

As her husband kissed her she didn't say a word.

But as the speeches were made and she had to raise a glass she just couldn't hold it in any more. 'Hey, husband of mine, this has been the best day of my life.'

'Mine too. Now chink my glass and drink…they're waiting.' He gave her a kiss and a very sexy wink that had her looking forward to her wedding night at the plush vineyard hideaway they'd booked for a honeymoon.

'I…er… I don't think I should do that.' She leaned in closer, careful not to mess up his dark charcoal suit that made him look very definitely the most handsome man in the world. 'Not for the next nine months or so anyway.'

He looked at her, dark eyes shining. 'What? Really?'

'Yes,' she whispered. 'I'm pregnant. And I have a clean bill of health, all going exactly to plan. Perfect? Yes?'

'Yes, you are, my darling.' Then he kissed her again as if he would never have enough.

When he put her down she clinked his glass and the crowd cheered all over again. But still they didn't share their news…because, well, because some things just needed to be enjoyed in private for a while.

The marquee provided decent shade from the searing

summer sunshine, but there was a barbecue and music and later a plan for a trip to the beach. Sean surveyed the mayhem as their friends and family began the informal part of the proceedings. 'A little bit different from last Christmas?'

'And next year will be different again, with a little one.' She patted her tummy, which was as flat as it ever was, but she *knew*...she just knew that everything was going to be fine.

Sean ran his thumb down her cheek and she honestly didn't think it could be possible to be any more happy. But she was, a little more every day, by his side, and now as his wife.

'A baby would be totally perfect, but, Izzy, I don't care where we are or what we do or who we're with, just as long as you and I spend the rest of our lives together.'

'Oh, yes, I promise with all my heart.' She picked up her glass and, one last time, clinked it against his. 'Together. For ever.'

* * * * *

LET'S TALK
Romance

For exclusive extracts, competitions
and special offers, find us online:

facebook.com/millsandboon

@MillsandBoon

@MillsandBoonUK

Get in touch on 01413 063232

For all the latest titles coming soon, visit
millsandboon.co.uk/nextmonth